SOMETHING LOST

ALSO BY PAT DUFFY HUTCHEON

A SOCIOLOGY OF CANADIAN EDUCATION
LEAVING THE CAVE
BUILDING CHARACTER AND CULTURE
THE ROAD TO REASON

SOMETHING LOST

Pat Duffy Hutcheon

Pat Duffy Hutcheon

Copyright © 2004 by Pat Duffy Hutcheon.

Library of Congress Number: 2003099086
ISBN : Hardcover 1-4134-4074-6
Softcover 1-4134-4073-8

All rights reserved. No part of this book may be reproduced or transmitted in any form or by any means, electronic or mechanical, including photocopying, recording, or by any information storage and retrieval system, without permission in writing from the copyright owner.

This is entirely a work of fiction. Although inspired by experience—both direct and vicarious—the characters, setting and narrative have sprung entirely from the imagination of the author. Any apparent relationship to real events, or to people (either living or dead) is entirely coincidental.

This book was printed in the United States of America.

To order additional copies of this book, contact:
Xlibris Corporation
1-888-795-4274
www.Xlibris.com
Orders@Xlibris.com

ACKNOWLEDGMENTS

I would like to express my appreciation for all those who read and commented on this story during the process of its evolution. Pamela Humphreys and Mike Buckley did a highly commendable job of editing. Blanche Howard provided many extremely helpful suggestions as well, as did Cornelia Fuykschot, Khushi Ram, Ross Woodward, Diane Schmolka, Dr. Joseph Malikail and Fran Cluett. I am also grateful for having had the opportunity to benefit from some of the unique knowledge of Dr. David Ambrose of the National University of Lesoto. Finally, my heartfelt thanks are extended to Graham Humphreys, who created the picture for the cover, and to Glenn Baglo, whose photograph of me is on the back cover. Copyright permission for use of the picture has been granted by the Pacific Newspaper Group of Vancouver, British Columbia, Canada.

CHAPTER 1

JUNE 2004

It was a voice from the past, strangely familiar yet somehow foreign to Evelyn's North American ear. In spite of the soft, well-modulated tones in which it was uttered, the question cut like a knife through the festive air surrounding this, her crowning moment. "Professor Ashton-Brent," she heard. "What really happened to Cynthia Montague all those years ago?"

Until that instant the day had felt joyful indeed. For this ceremony marked the apex of the career of Dr. Evelyn Ashton-Brent: her grand finale preceding a prestigious retirement as Professor Emeritus of Women's Studies at the University of South Ontario. It was the reward for which she now realized she had always secretly hungered: a country-wide recognition of her role as one of the chief pioneers of the new discipline which, but for her steadfast commitment, might not have found its place and prospered in universities throughout the English-speaking world. Just a few months previously Evelyn had received The Order of Canada for her contribution to the goal of equality of educational opportunity for women. Now, in the midst of a crowd of well-wishers, she was approaching the entrance of a downtown dinner theater for a celebration in honor of her retirement.

It can't get much better than this, she had told herself that very morning. All those years of effort and compromise and sacrifice had paid off after all. It *had* been a successful career. She truly *had* made a difference. The experience of so many people voicing heartfelt appreciation of her efforts was like manna to her sense of self. It was a confirmation from those who truly mattered, that her life and work had been worthwhile.

All day Evelyn had been feeling that, for the first time in her life, she understood fully the meaning of that well-worn phrase, 'on cloud nine'. The sensation of skipping along from one soft, fluffy cloud to another had been with her since morning. But now, at one sudden, cruel stroke, she found herself no longer immersed in that mystical 'lightness of being'. For a brief moment it was as if an avalanche had struck, and she was trapped in the heavy deadness of surrounding ice. The persistent voice had shattered the noisy, congratulatory atmosphere, creating a stillness in its wake as the questioner materialized at her shoulder. With an almost physical effort, Evelyn forced herself to face the young woman who now stood before her.

"I hate to interrupt," came the voice from the past. "But I am the niece of a student whom I believe you taught almost thirty years ago. Her name was Cynthia Montague. I happen to be a reporter for the *London Daily News* over here on assignment. We're doing a story about mysteries surrounding the disappearance of British female students in North America, and I thought it might be a good chance to do some investigating of Aunt Cynthia's unsolved murder as well."

Evelyn sensed again the sudden silence in the group surrounding her. "Murder," she heard someone repeating the appalling word in a frozen monotone. Then, realizing that it had been she who had spoken, she cleared her throat. "Murder?" she asked, her voice rising to an undignified squeak. "But I don't understand. Cynthia Montague's death was officially declared to have been an accident. I remember the case very well."

"I was told that you would," came the response. "And that, given your longtime professional commitment to women's concerns, you would be more than willing to help me. I hope you won't mind my taking up some of your time during the next few days, as there are a number of questions that I would really like to ask. And some recent progress on the case that I want to tell you about."

The drift of the crowd moving into the dining room pushed the two even closer, and the full-face view of her questioner was like a second hammer blow to Evelyn, propelling her back more than a quarter century in the space of a few seconds.

"Why you look and sound exactly like Cynthia!" she said. This was what had really shaken her. For one breathless moment it had seemed that the person who symbolized one of the darkest experiences of her past had suddenly reappeared to cast a shadow over what was, until that moment, a gratifying and joyful present. But no sooner had the thought come than she brushed it aside. Why should the memory of Cynthia make her feel personally guilty? She had done all she possibly could for that peculiarly wayward young person, both before and after the accident. If accident it was. Or suicide. But *murder*? What on earth could this stranger mean?

Like the long-dead Cynthia, the woman accosting her was beautiful—almost Marilyn Monroe-like in her soft, blond femininity. Strangely, the style of her clothing resembled what Cynthia had worn as well. She was dressed in a stylish black, with a long, clinging skirt and a simple, close-fitting, low-necked top and hip-length jacket. Even the sapphire necklace and earrings seemed to speak of Cynthia. But the voice, with its refined English accent, conveyed an assertiveness that had been absent in the movie idol and in the former student as well.

"I hope . . .," her questioner began again. But, at that moment, the awkward encounter was interrupted by a familiar voice, and Evelyn turned to see a colleague from her days at North Pacific University pushing his way through the little group surrounding her.

"Evelyn, my dear, congratulations!" came the enthusiastic greeting as the still-handsome face brushed hers and the muscular arms enveloped her, and the still-trim body pressed against her. The warmth and reassurance of that embrace kindled within her a long-familiar surge of pleasure. How many times, she thought, had she been gathered up by those arms in precisely that way during the past quarter-century? The man greeting her was clearly one of the fortunate people who seem to age well. Now in his mid-sixties, he was a platinum-haired facsimile of what he had been in his prime, with the cheeks that were once a bit too full, now firm and fully bearded. The always-powerful body was merely somewhat broader and more stately.

Harvey Garfinkle's career had in many ways parallelled her own. They had been propelled into the same scholarly community time and time again in their movement eastward and upward across the Canadian academic landscape. All those decades ago, as Head of the Foundations of Education Department in which she was a mere Assistant Professor, Harvey had been very much Evelyn's superior. But the explosive growth and popularity of Women's Studies in the interim had changed all that. For the past twenty-seven years their relationship had been on a very different footing. Now Harvey was turning to the young journalist, his blue eyes twinkling appreciatively in a practiced survey of the attractive youthfulness coolly posed before him. Then, the twinkle turned to steel and his face froze.

"Don't . . . don't I know you from somewhere?" he faltered.

"This is a British journalist from the *London Daily News*," Evelyn explained quickly. "But you've probably noticed her resemblance to her aunt, our former student, Cynthia Montague." Harvey was uncharacteristically silent, his body motionless. Turning now to the young woman Evelyn said, "I'm sorry, but you haven't given me your name."

"I'm Anthea Montague. Cynthia was my father's younger sister." She directed her gaze toward Harvey. "Do I understand correctly that you were also one of Aunt Cynthia's professors at North Pacific University?"

"Not really," Harvey seemed to have recovered his customary aplomb. "I was merely an administrator there, but of course the tragedy brought all of us into the picture. I hope that Professor Ashton-Brent has told you how shaken the entire Faculty was by what happened. Such a young life, and so much promise, snuffed out in an unnecessary, meaningless accident. We all felt guilty afterwards for not having been more vigilant. Guilty and thoroughly devastated!"

"Why you must be Dr. Harvey Garfinkle!" Anthea exclaimed excitedly. "Please, I realize I'm interrupting things here, but I'd like to arrange interviews with you both as soon as possible. Could you set aside some time for me within the next few days?"

Evelyn felt trapped, but tried not to betray it as she agreed to a time and place of meeting. Harvey hedged somewhat, taking the journalist's cell-phone number and promising to contact her before the following week was over. Then, almost as if a tide had come in without her noticing, Evelyn felt herself being swept along toward the banquet area where the dinner in her honor was about to begin.

A few minutes later, securely settled at the head table, she consciously willed herself to relax and enjoy the rest of the evening. Her shining hour had arrived, and no event from the long-ago past was going to be allowed to spoil it. She looked around the room and was immediately captivated by the surroundings. Clearly, this was no ordinary conference hall. She was seated on what was apparently the stage, and from her vantage point in its exact center she had an unimpeded view of the entire area. The tables were arranged in a widening arc, with those furthest from the stage on slightly raised platforms, so that none blocked the view of those behind. The pale-lime, windowless walls were decorated with softly falling leaf-colored drapery hanging at intervals. This—along with the concealed lighting system cleverly designed to allow the entire area to radiate an unshaded morning-like glow—somehow contributed to the impression of spaciousness combined with warmth. The variegated clusters of flowers on the yellow linen tablecloths added to the garden-like atmosphere. The tables were now filling up fast, and Evelyn began to recognize and wave to acquaintances and friends from the past, as well as those familiar to her in recent years. For the first time, she noticed that Harvey was seated immediately to her left. The empty chair on her right was now being taken as well, by a long-time colleague, currently the Head of a new Cultural Studies program at a neighboring university.

"Hello, Evelyn," Dr. Ursula Whitaker's warm greeting was accompanied by an awkward adjustment of legs and flowing folds of skirt as her ample hips settled into the chair. "How are you bearing up? Is all this adulation getting to you?"

"I think I'm going to make it as long as I don't lose my voice at a critical moment," Evelyn laughed. "But I've been known to do exactly that."

"I'm going to need my voice too. I'm one of the after-dinner speakers. I've been asked to talk a bit about your recent contributions to scholarship in the field of Cultural Studies. I understand that Dr. Garfinkle will discuss your educational and early teaching background and your pioneering work in the women's movement. And the Head of Gender Studies at Harvard is slated to speak as well."

Evelyn had no fear that Ursula would have trouble expressing herself easily and at considerable length. In many ways her fellow national feminist leader and close friend was everything she, herself, had sought to become. Ursula was a large, capable woman with a heavy head of dark-blond hair streaked with grey, swept up and tied attractively at the back of her head. Now, as always, she was exuding self-assurance and competence. Her all-too-familiar, colorfully patterned dress, designed in a rather garish style usually avoided by stocky women, was typical of her taste in clothing. Evelyn had always associated this distinctive manner of dressing with Ursula's desire to assert her independence, not only from men but from the consumerism and fashions of the day. Invariably, it made her feel somewhat guilty for what she considered her own good taste in clothes, and her love of shopping. Tonight, for instance, she had decided to wear a new silk gown with long, shapely skirt, complete with matching jacket. The outfit was of a dark burnished gold color that complemented her artistically streaked brown hair. At the moment, she couldn't help but register how well her dress blended with the surroundings. And how the outfit's beautifully simple lines flattered her figure—still thin and wiry after all these years.

"And I'm to share some memories of you as one of my first Education professors and later as a longtime friend." Further down the table another familiar figure had called out. Meredith Walker who, like Evelyn and Harvey, had moved to Eastern Canada from the Lower Mainland area of British Columbia, was her usual spirited, engaging self as she approached for a hug. "I've been wondering just how discreet I should be."

As she responded in similar joking vein Evelyn thought of her early encounters with Meredith, who was only a little less overwhelming and even more beautiful in those far-off days when, jet-black hair flowing in loose waves, dark-blue eyes flashing and voice trilling authoritatively, she had become the natural leader of the fledgling women's organization at North Pacific University. It was among the first of such groups in the country and it had helped to shape the strategies and goals of the national movement for years to come. Evelyn recalled how, without quite knowing exactly why or how it happened, she had gradually begun to feel at home among these young revolutionaries—in spite of the fact that, in her own student days, feminism had been very far from her thoughts.

On her left, Harvey cleared his throat. "I need to check a few details with you, Evelyn," he said. "I was going to do it on our way in, but we were so rudely interrupted."

In the rush of conversation, and the serving of food that followed, the time flew by all too rapidly. In recognition of Evelyn's early life on both the Atlantic and Pacific coasts, fresh wild salmon was served as the main course, followed by her favorite dessert: a delicious and distinctively Canadian lemon meringue pie. Evelyn had not seen Meredith recently, and there was considerable catching up to do with others at the table as well. Almost before she realized it was happening, people were relinquishing empty coffee cups, movements back and forth to the kitchen had ceased, and a lull had settled on the room. Harvey was rustling his papers and looking expectant. Two places to her right, she saw the president of her university rising from his chair. His introductory comments were perfunctory and concise, and before many minutes passed he had introduced Harvey and lowered himself to his chair in the midst of polite applause.

"When I first met the woman seated this evening on my right," Harvey began in his usual practiced style, "I knew at once that right there, in our little Foundations of Education Department in the boondocks of 'Lotus Land', was someone with a great future ahead of her. To begin with, her credentials were mind-boggling. A graduate in anthropology from Barnard, she was one of the first females to be accepted into the doctoral program in sociology at that most Ivy League of all the top American colleges, New Oxford University in Connecticut. We considered ourselves fortunate that she came to us in the summer of 1969, with her brand new PhD. I had recognized the need for effective female leadership, and did my best to help her along until she found her stride."

At that point Evelyn's mind began to wander, but she was aware of the jovial voice going on and on. *And to think that I used to consider him a self-serving character!* she mused, almost startling herself with the memory of the blatant disloyalty of that earlier judgment concerning someone who had now proven himself a true supporter and friend for more than a quarter century. Not since the days when she had been influenced by the general attitude of irreverence and skepticism of her colleague, Millie Eisenstadt, had Evelyn found any reason to entertain a negative thought about Harvey Garfinkle. However, with hindsight, she did allow herself the ironic reminder that, if his opinion of her had been so positive right from the start, he had certainly done a good job of hiding it. For the first time in decades she experienced the old familiar flash of resentment about having been kept at the level of Assistant Professor for eight long years, while every male who had come on board during that time was promoted over her. It even occurred to her that, if it hadn't been for the growing power of the women's movement and their political action on campus, she might be sitting there without tenure to this very day!

Harvey's voice intruded, then subsided once again. Something he had said aroused another poignant memory of that irreverent colleague from their British Columbia days. For a moment the voice of Millie, her old friend from all those years ago, was more real to Evelyn than Harvey's good-natured drone beside her—as was the memory of the large body with its head of roughly cropped red hair and expressive hazel eyes.

"Those lucky buggers!" Millie used to say of their male colleagues, especially of Harvey with his loyal, homemaking wife. "With a slave at home to bring their slippers and wait on them the moment they get off work, and to support them in all their projects. While you and I have to spend our weekends housecleaning and cooking so that we're free to attend to our professional work on weekdays. At least, that is, until we rush home to make dinner. And they congratulate themselves on supposedly deigning to give us an even break!"

Suddenly refocusing on her surroundings, Evelyn noticed that Meredith Walker was being introduced and was now moving smoothly to the podium. Her opening remarks were so effusive, however, that Evelyn soon felt vaguely embarrassed, whether for herself or the speaker she wasn't sure. Now Meredith was retracing her experience at North Pacific University, her discourse accompanied by numerous dramatic pauses in mid-sentence to allow for graceful posturing, along with exaggerated emphasis on relatively insignificant words. When was it, wondered Evelyn, that the young women who assumed leadership positions in the eighties and nineties began to speak in that strangely affected way? Then, as quickly as the question had formed in her mind, came the realization that, to be honest, she would have to admit to some responsibility herself. The roots of the phenomenon no doubt lay in the very different mannerisms of the female graduates of previous decades. She was aware that her own generation had somehow acquired the habit of expressing every comment as a timid question. (Almost as if they were implying "I realize my opinion isn't worth much, but . . . ?") Evelyn herself had been accused of this by Millie too often not to suspect that it was true.

Lately, however, and possibly as a reaction to this earlier expressed timidity, a strange and apparently gender-related tendency had emerged: one that was now beginning to assume a new form and a more general public pervasiveness. Evelyn had been noting the affliction in females (and lately, even a few males as well) in the world of television journalism. It seemed that, in some misguided reach for assertiveness, these people had been told to emphasize at least one word in every sentence, as well as to make generous use of 'the dramatic pause'. Speakers in university and public life were now obeying the rule in a random fashion that had no apparent relation to the meaning of their utterances. Along with this was the tendency to overuse and even mis-use certain phrases, such as "this will *impact* us . . .", "*in no small way*", "she has *issues* concerning that", etc., etc. Had they all studied under the same communication-destroying voice teacher, Evelyn wondered, or is it that people no longer relate words to context in their reading and speaking? Could it possibly be her own favored 'deconstructionism' in action?"

"We had to discard *a lot* of chaff!" she now heard. "This included . . . [long pause] traditional religious dogma such as the notion that the *Supreme* Being was necessarily of the male *gender*. With the advice and help of Professor Ashton-Brent we returned to ancient beliefs *concerning* harmony with nature, including Wiccan practices honoring the *Earth* Mother. To the Goddess religions *and* mystery cults that had been *driven* underground first by the horse-*taming* male ancestors of Homeric Greece and later by the patriarchal *culture* of the Christians!"

Evelyn found herself thinking anew of the courage it had taken to mount that kind of challenge to traditional religion and conservative politics in the mid-to-late 1970's. For a while she relived a few of the most exciting of her good-humored clashes with a certain Mormon colleague at North Pacific University. Then, with an effort, she tried to attend once more to Meredith. It was some time later that her thought processes, exhausted from laboring in the search for connections among the beautifully articulated and randomly accented words, suddenly snapped to attention as she recognized a change in topic.

"You are no *doubt* assuming that . . . *our* major enemies were the men on campus", she now heard. "But I assure *you* that was not the case. Many of the female faculty were against us *and* . . . *some* women students opposed our stand as well. I recall a particularly painful situation involving a female *professor*, one who herself had been successful in the world of male rationalism and scientism that was so rampant in universities *at the time*. She expected all her female students *to* do . . . the very same. She taught in a special new teacher-*training* program for those of us who *had come* to the Faculty of Education with prior degrees. She made no allowances for gender. Nor would she update *her* material or alter her teaching *approach* to incorporate the new female perspective. As one of our first revolutionary actions we took it *upon* ourselves to do what had to be done to sensitize her to our problems . . . *and* needs. But it was no easy task, let *me* assure you. Some of the male professors *were* much easier to reach. But, of course, through all our early travails, Professor Evelyn Ashton-Brent was the real champion without whom we *could* never . . . have persevered!"

So, 'sensitizing' was how they had viewed it! Evelyn realized that the reference was to none other than her old friend Millie Eisenstadt. Sensitizing her had been quite a challenge, she thought, at first with amusement and then with some discomfort as she recalled what all this had indeed meant for Millie. *But I don't know what more I could have done at the time*, she agonized, once again losing track of Meredith's message as the meaning-destroying, overly expressive patter went on and on. Eventually she realized with some relief that the speech was being applauded and Meredith was in the process of seating herself. The chairman now motioned to a young female student from one of Evelyn's recent classes who had apparently signaled from the student table. Her obviously spontaneous comments were spoken from a seated position. Although clearly from the heart, the rush of words came so fast as to be almost indecipherable.

"I've been sitting here listening to all this," the speaker's voice, high-pitched and almost inaudible throughout her brief spiel, now rose as she approached the closing exclamation. "And I'm going like 'I'm like so lucky to have had Dr. Ashton-Brent for a professor!' Someday when I have grandchildren I'll go 'I was in like one of the last classes this great feminist pioneer ever taught!'" This concluding torrent of words served not only to amuse Evelyn but to remind her that yet another language fad was now competing with the quirks of Meredith's generation, and of her own before that.

At this point Professor Whitaker was introduced, and Evelyn settled back to enjoy what was to come. However, after a few appreciative comments about the accomplishments of her colleague, it began to appear that Ursula was launching into one of her scholarly treatises on the necessity for 'perspectivism' and 'deconstructionism' in university scholarship. Obviously she saw the occasion as an opportunity to push her favorite academic hobby horses, but Evelyn couldn't help but think that she should at least have defined these two key terms—if only for the many in the audience who were not in her particular field. Again, she imagined Millie's likely comment on this.

"Why all the gobblygook?" she might well have exclaimed. "If those deliberately abstruse formulations mean anything, it must be the vacuous notion that there's no such thing as relatively reliable knowledge, and that universally meaningful utterance and thought are impossible. And that there's not even a reality external to the human mind. That, instead, each person's particular 'perspective' on reality, as momentarily experienced, is all we can ever have, coupled with the artificial, self-contradictory language system acquired from birth onward. Thus the need to 'deconstruct' anything said or written. So why doesn't she just say so? Could it possibly be that the nonsensical quality of the whole thing would then be all-too-obvious?"

But, apparently, Professor Whitaker saw no need for explanation of the complex concepts so central to her world view. Enthusiastically and pitilessly she pursued her aim of expounding that view, with the reason for the gathering apparently forgotten as her favorite subject took center stage. Evelyn's old familiar symptoms of stress began to manifest themselves and she struggled to relax and control the stabbing pains now flashing down her spine.

By now, another uncomfortable memory was intruding, forcing Ursula's voice into the background. This time it was her old Mormon adversary at NPU. His name was Sam Barnes, and the critically sardonic persona which he had always cultivated seemed almost to be there beside her, along with Millie. She could imagine Sam taunting her about her own all-too-predictable subservience to this latest academic 'band wagon'. Again, it required a conscious act of will to clear her mind once more and force herself back to the present moment.

Why couldn't she just sit back and enjoy all this? Why was her mind so occupied with absent friends when all these people, grouped in this entrancing room, were here to honor her? What was the matter with her? After all, who was she to judge that the audience was less than entranced with Ursula's academic jargon in her recounting of the details of the struggle for the liberation of women's thought-processes? For these were indeed important historical events that were now being described by one of the major participants. But was this really the place and time for such a profusion of esoteric language and seemingly infinite detail? However, to be fair, she reminded herself, Ursula's enthusiasm was one that she had shared for many years as well, along with the majority of those in the Women's Studies movement. And not only the women. Abdul, too, had supported this position. Abdul! Why on earth was she thinking of him at this, of all moments?

"We used to wonder why women were not succeeding in the sciences." Finally there were signs that Ursula was building up to a finale. "Male instructors were always expressing puzzlement at the fact that their female students had trouble grasping what were to them relatively simple mathematical and scientific concepts. But we now recognize that these concepts were merely constructs of male conceptualization throughout history. Of a cold, left-brain-oriented type of rigid linear logic. The creative, lateral, right-brain thinking of the female was derided and relegated to an inferior position. Not because it failed to lead to understanding, mind you, but because it was the male who, alone, had the political and economic power to impose his brand of science on all of the rest of humanity. And specifically, the imperialistic, white-skinned Western-European male! Emotional intelligence was downplayed or ignored. Only the rationalistic version was recognized. But no more! Females are now rapidly becoming the most revolutionary force the world has ever seen. And, I promise you, we will no longer allow only the peculiarly male version of intelligence, or of science or any other subject, to monopolize our universities."

At this point, Evelyn couldn't help but notice a slight whispering and shuffling among some of the men in the room, who were beginning to look distinctly uncomfortable. Only partially covering this was the scattering of applause, possibly from a number who assumed Ursula's previous sentence had signaled the end of the address. However, Ursula ignored the hint, if hint it was, and plowed ahead.

"During earlier decades," she saw fit to remind her listeners, "women fought to achieve equality of opportunity with their brothers, to vote and to attend institutions of higher learning. We now know that particular battle was merely the initial skirmish. And, increasingly, the numbers are on our side. Today we realize that, as long as the ideas of 'dead white males' continue to dominate modern civilization, women will not assume their rightful place in the world. Nor will all the other exploited peoples everywhere. The aggressiveness of American policy ever since the tragedy of September 11, 2001 indicates clearly that male-dominated Western Imperialism and its accompanying worship of science and technology remains all-too-alive and well. The obvious fact that we have learned nothing from the message that was intended to be conveyed by the event does not bode well for the future of the world's victimized peoples." Again the signs of a less-than-enthusiastic reaction from some members of the audience. This was followed by a wave of hopeful hand-clapping which, although acknowledged by Ursula, failed to throw her off stride as she raced toward her conclusion.

Evelyn began to feel, once more, a vague sense of unease, although she could not locate the specific cause of it in anything that Ursula had said. Unless it was the idea of the perpetrators of the bombing of the World Trade Center in New York being coupled with North American women, as 'victims'. Ursula's definition of 'victim-hood' here did not entirely jibe with her own analysis of the '9/11' attack.

As a transplanted American, Evelyn had recently found

herself experiencing vague feelings of discomfort with the responses of her feminist students and friends to the horrifying occurrence, and to the role of the United States in the course of following events. It was almost as if there had emerged from some place deep within her, a wellspring of forgotten patriotism: a flash of recognition and appreciation for the basic decencies undergirding the guiding principles of her too-often-resented homeland. Once again, Millie Eisenstadt had come alive in her memory, as she imagined what her old friend would have said about certain speeches made recently by some of the leading feminists in North America.

"What these radicals can't seem to comprehend," the remembered voice seemed to be saying, "is that the festering hatred of the United States now fueling world terrorism is not the result merely of the persistence of poverty in the third world. Hell, most of the terrorist leaders happen to be the offspring of the wealthy oligarchs in oil-rich Islamic nations. It's time we recognized that the resentment of the United States and other developed countries on the part of people within these nations stems from something else entirely. It's caused by the fact that, *in spite of their wealth*, theocracies inevitably throttle the growth of science, thereby denying their citizens the technological advantages of a thriving urban community. In fact, such theocracies, *by definition*, abhor and criminalize doubt. Just as they fear and hate all manifestations of modernism, such as democracy, the rule of law, and (ironically) feminism. But, in the eyes of these tribal fundamentalists, *something and someone*, beyond their own leaders, must be blamed for the helplessness of the average individual and the backwardness of the state. And, when all this is confounded by a religion-dominated culture endlessly communicating that every problem can be laid at the feet of the Infidel, the entire system is bound to operate just as Christianity did in the days of the Crusades. By that I mean it will conveniently and happily justify the murder of innocents."

Could it really be Millie's spirit intruding, even here and now, in her old brash, impulsive and ironic way? Or that of Sam, with his simple, skeptical honesty? Or had she, herself, actually begun to consider her fellow radical feminists from this detached, critical perspective? And was she merely using the imagined opinions of Millie and Sam as a way of avoiding any personal responsibility for her change of heart? Could it be, she wondered, feeling a stab of pain at the thought, that what was really bothering her was the resurrected memory of Cynthia Montague and her own failure to ensure, for that young female, even the chance to live?

Mercifully, Evelyn was suddenly pulled back into the room as the voice beside her rose. The pace of Ursula's speech had slowed, and each word was now being emphasized.

"Professor Evelyn Ashton-Brent has devoted her entire academic career to improving the lot of one particular group among the world's under-classes," she was declaring. "This is a woman who willingly grasped the challenging task of presenting the female perspective in Western society and, in the process, challenging the power structure within our universities. It's my privilege to assure her that she can now safely retire in the knowledge that there are countless numbers of her sisters ready to dedicate themselves to the cause she so bravely helped to pioneer."

Ursula then sat down, to a rush of obviously relieved applause. The remaining speeches took up the story from where Harvey, Meredith and Ursula had left off, charting Evelyn's rise to national prominence within the women's movement throughout North America, her successful academic career in Eastern Canada during the 1980's and 1990's and, finally, the honors showered upon her recently. Many of her former and current colleagues grasped the opportunity to entertain the audience with amusing stories from her past. Although at times embarrassed, she gradually began to feel happily gratified by what she was hearing, and decided to do her best to express those feelings in her own comments at the conclusion of the festivities. She was aware that this might not be easy as, in anticipation of the audience having had a surfeit of 'speechifying' (and possibly wine) by the time her turn came, she had made a special arrangement the day before. Her talk was to take the form of an interview conducted by some students from her final semester's classes. These young people were seated at the special student table just below and to the left of her, and she noted that a microphone was set up in front of them.

The first question had been planned to serve as a broad opener. It was to come from a youth who had impressed her all term with his speaking ability. He now rose and spoke.

"I wonder if you would like to tell us how this entire celebration makes you feel, Dr. Ashton-Brent."

"This has been the best night of my life," she began, and immediately experienced a rush of dismay to realize that the sentiment was probably true. And, what was worse, that this was probably the best there was ever going to be! She found herself faltering, her rehearsed response momentarily forgotten. "I . . . I'm afraid I just can't express to you how much it has touched me." She paused, and again the thought of Cynthia engulfed her.

"Would you tell us something of what your life experience has meant to you, in a personal sense?" the student prodded helpfully. "For instance, what was it that started you on the road leading to where you have arrived this evening?"

"Oh yes, of course. That's a very good question." Evelyn had recovered, and now began to speak easily and naturally. "Well, it seems that many who are here tonight have shared in the charting of my experience along that road in one important sense. That is, my professional progress in the world of academia. I thought that perhaps I might take a moment to tell you a bit about my parallel voyage. The voyage of the mind during these same years. But don't worry, I intend to keep it short! I was born into an upper-middle class Unitarian family in Boston, Massachusetts. I never really questioned my inherited privilege until I attended university. In fact, I traveled in Europe for a year after high school without even realizing that not every young person had the opportunities that my parents' economic position had provided for me as a matter of course.

Fortunately, at Barnard I was exposed to all sorts of mind-opening ideas and systems of thought. Among these was, of course, the cultural relativism of my great intellectual heroes Franz Boas, Ruth Benedict and Margaret Mead. I always believed that this perspective, which celebrated the inherent worth of *every* culture, melded beautifully with the emphasis of Karl Marx on the all-determining effect of environment. It was also consistent with the theories of Carl Jung about the 'collective unconscious', within which humans are joined at a level beyond the merely material. For I was immersed in the works of these latter two great pioneering scholars during the course of my studies, as well. Cultural relativism, Marxism and Jungian psychology! The essential compatibility of all three great belief systems that were destined to shape the entire twentieth century was no accident, in my opinion. All were rooted in the philosophy of nineteenth-century Germany. Looking back now, I can't help but think that anyone with even a tiny bit of compassion, who was living and studying in the early sixties, had to be a socialist. And anyone who was aware of the complexity of the human condition had to be a Jungian. Just as anyone with respect for our First Nations and for historically marginalized groups everywhere had to be a cultural relativist."

"What about after you earned your Bachelor degree?" One of the female students had now taken over the questioning. "Did you go right on to graduate school? Or did you have to go job-hunting?"

"Following graduation I was active in the Civil Rights Movement. Then, after working in my father's Senate office for some time, I applied to New Oxford and was among the first females to be accepted in 1965 into their PhD program in sociology. I moved into the brand-new women's residence and later joined a group of young women who were supporters of George McGovern. In those exciting years I was finally able to live my philosophy. That was one of the happiest periods of my life."

"What sorts of things did they teach in graduate-school sociology in those days?" Another questioner was now taking her turn at the mike. The audience seemed to be listening closely, appreciating the change of pace.

"I recall that the New Oxford sociology faculty were divided into two opposing camps: the philosophical Marxists who, by then, considered themselves mainly 'sociologists of knowledge', and the 'structural-functionalists' who represented the mainstream in sociology. However, I felt much more at home with the Marxist group, and took most of my classes with them. I soon learned, though, that one had to be careful not to antagonize the other faction, who actually wielded most of the power. The 'in' thing for mainstream sociology at that time was an effort to emulate the 'hard' sciences by trying to make exact measurements of everything. However, most of the 'structural-functionalists' at New Oxford were also involved in the Sociology of Development, and many of their students did their doctoral theses on Southeast Asia. The Marxists suspected that what these people actually deduced from their model was the superiority of their own system, and thus the necessity for an American-style colonial development of the third world. To me it all felt more like a new version of the old Western Imperialism. Needless to say, I was careful never to say so. One valuable lesson that I had taken from the experience in my father's Senate office was the need to recognize the actual power structure in any organization and to be discrete in its presence."

"I was wondering if you would describe your own preferred sociological theory. Could you tell us something about how you arrived at it? And whether you felt free to teach it once you became a university instructor yourself?" The student who had chosen this question was one who had excelled in theory in Evelyn's last class.

"My first academic position was in Canada at North Pacific University in British Columbia. When I came there to teach I was overjoyed to discover a peculiarly Canadian freedom to express my political opinions in class and elsewhere. And, as time went on, my ideas gradually matured into a more sophisticated world view. I began to realize that the older Marxism had its faults, just as has every other ideology, *including* the ideology underlying the practice of Western science. What a freeing experience it was to discover that each perspective is a distinctive 'realm of meaning' containing within it a unique form of knowledge! And that, as individuals, we construct our own version of ultimate truth out of the fire of our personal life experience. And, above all, to be assured that every woman's intuitive version of that truth is as valid as the next person's. Even the next man's!"

"Now I'm sure we'd all like to hear about what you consider your greatest contribution to academic thought." This query came from a female student whom Evelyn had recognized as an ardent feminist. It had been planned as the launching pad for her summing-up statements on that very issue.

"As many of you will realize by now", she began, "I have just been expressing what was then the pioneering 'Sociology of Knowledge' perspective. It was thanks to this remarkable new theory that I was able to make some small contribution, I think. I was able, to some extent at least, to help my students recognize the female experience as different in kind from the male experience. But no less valid for all that.

The problem was that, for centuries, those who had the opportunity to write and think, and those with the power to decide what should be taught in higher education, were exclusively male. It merely remained for an enlightened and sufficiently privileged generation of women to come along, and I just happened to be fortunate enough to be one of these. We also had to be knowledgeable enough, and intimidating enough, to grasp the political power within the university system. I mean, the kind of power that was necessary for freeing up the curriculum from the strictures of an obsolete, male-oriented and Western-oriented 'sacred' canon. I like to think that I played some small part in the accomplishment of removing Plato and Socrates and Aristotle from their dominant positions in the university curriculum."

Another student, a stranger to her, was now waving his hand. As Evelyn paused, puzzled at this unexpected intrusion, she heard a voice that seemed laced with mischief.

"Now how about describing what you consider your greatest failure? Or, at least, your greatest disappointment where your goal of advancing female equality was concerned. Did you ever feel that something may have been lost in the climb to the top of your field?"

Something lost! But . . . but . . . this had not been part of the rehearsal! Evelyn was momentarily stunned at the brazenness of the question; and of the questioner. Could this be an accusation? Had he overheard her conversation with the journalist? Did he know about Cynthia? She tried her best to erase from her consciousness the appealing femininity and implicit accusation reflected in her mind's-eye-view of both young women. She found herself being forced to make a physical effort at pulling herself together for the planned finale.

"Of course there were many failures. Too many to count. And, at my age, certainly too many to recall." Evelyn decided to try for a laugh as she searched for the closing words.

"Nevertheless," she spoke strongly now, hitting her stride once more, "I *can* say there is one thing that I always tried to give my students in Women's Studies. It was a sense of pride in the previously neglected 'Great Women' of the past, and in the unique identity that comes from understanding all the deeper meanings associated with being female. Your generous comments tonight have given me the courage to hope that I might be remembered at least for that attempt."

She sat down to ringing applause, and with a sense of having managed a quick recovery and a reasonably coherent expression of what mattered most to her. The rest of the evening passed in a happy, congratulatory blur, concluding with a moving choral offering from a group of female singers called *The Sacred Circle*. Dressed in white and carrying candles, they moved slowly around the head table as they sang a song with the title of *Tell Me Your Name*, ending with a chant comprising Evelyn's complete name repeated over and over. This was possibly the crowning moment of the evening for her as, for once, she was able to give herself over completely to the mystical arousal and sense of belonging induced by the music and rhythmic chant.

All too soon, however, the evening's events were over. Evelyn found herself back in her own home, trying to settle down for the night, alone once more and feeling somehow vaguely dissatisfied. *I should be thoroughly happy*, she admonished herself. What more could any woman ever hope for than the kind of recognition she had received tonight? What was wrong with her, that she should feel, now of all times, this old familiar emptiness within? Was it because, now that the celebration and the adulation had died away, she found herself coming home to an empty house? For there was indeed no one to greet her; no one to share with her the chuckles and high points of the evening; no one to replay with her the congratulations and resurrected memories of both good times and bad. Was this loneliness the necessary price of success for a woman in her time and place? For a moment, Evelyn allowed herself to wonder if she could have made different choices at key junctures. Should she (like many of her acquaintances) have chosen a sustained live-in relationship with a close woman friend or colleague? But as always, when the experience of loneliness forced her to consider sharing her home with anyone, the thought of Abdul Issa intruded.

The memory of her overwhelming infatuation and insatiable sexual need for him could still cause her to writhe in embarrassment for the person that she had been in those far-off days at North Pacific University. *The love of my life,* she thought. *How could I have known that there would never be another?*

It came to her with the suddenness of a blow to both head and heart, that her entire life had amounted to nothing more than a succession of steps. At the time she selected it, each step had appeared to point to the best way toward eventual progress up the mountain of success. The top of that mountain had always beckoned and driven her on, sometimes at the expense of resting at a waterfall and taking time out to assess the possibilities in trails that appeared to lead in less rigorously upward directions. Had she taken a wrong turning somewhere along the trail? How was it possible to really know if the trail one had chosen was indeed leading to the top and not to the dead-end of a yawning chasm? And, an even more dismaying question: How could one be sure ahead of time that the beckoning heights did, in fact, offer the rewarding view they had promised?

Harvey's presence at the party had been unsettling, to say the least. Although Evelyn had shared with him much of her experience in academia in recent decades, for some reason the sight and sound of him on this particular night brought back memories of an earlier time, when their relationship had been on a very different footing. She was bombarded with thoughts of the two people to whom she had felt closest in those far-off, difficult days: Abdul and Millie. Unwanted, there came to her the image of two other favorite colleagues from that momentous time: both true iconoclasts. If only the term 'politically incorrect' had been invented then, both her Mormon friend Sam Barnes and a certain pipe-smoking former Untouchable from India, known to them simply as Muthu, would have been universally recognized as its epitomes. (Somewhat disconcertingly, the very instant she *thought* the historical name for the lowest Hindu caste, she chided herself for her own political insensitivity in using it, given her current awareness that this category of Hindus was now referred to officially as Dalit, or 'scheduled caste'). What, she now wondered, would those two have made of the celebration tonight?

But all these intruders were definitely going to have to go! A concerted effort to rid her mind of such memories would have to be made if sleep were to come tonight. With an almost physical effort she forced herself to focus once more on the happy events of the evening. How very far removed it all was from the prevailing attitude toward female students that she had encountered in higher education in her youth! The knowledge that she had played some small part in this change for the better, in this triumph of feminism, however incomplete, would be with her always. That, indeed, was her claim to success and, surely, it had been worth betting her life on. This was the mountain she had tackled. And making it to the top was no small thing!

But it was not only memories of once-treasured friends that disturbed her rest that night. Strive as she would during the ensuing hours, Evelyn could not get clear of the shadow cast over the evening by the encounter with the British journalist, the niece of Cynthia Montague. She attempted to relax with a stiff drink, knowing that sleep would elude her otherwise. But memories of the past kept crowding in, and they were not the congratulatory and amusing ones with which people had been entertained during the evening's speech-making. In spite of her self-admonition not to think any more about the tragedy of Cynthia which had propelled them all into such turmoil at the time, her mind toiled on and on in its relentless reliving of the months following their student's death, and the role of Abdul, Millie, and Sam in the affair. She realized now that those three had meant more to her than anyone who had been a part of her life in the years since. More than anyone present in that room tonight.

Why, she wondered, had the pursuit of closeness in love and friendship been so all-important for her, yet so singularly unsuccessful? Had she been wrong to have wanted it so badly? But surely it was necessary for everyone. Love was the principle by which she had tried to live her life. She had always maintained that loving relationships were essential both for the individual and the functioning of the social group. Love was the source of the energy needed for the climb to the top.

"Not love, you idiot!" she could almost hear Millie scoffing, "Affirmation of the self! Of one's identity. And recognition of ones accomplishments! That's what all social beings require from their fellows. Wanting to be loved can be self-defeating. People get turned off by too much emotional need in others. And you should take note, Evelyn, of your hero Freud's comment about what he considered the dangerous idea that human society should be ruled by love. It opens the way, he warned us, for those who would rule by hate!"

Was that what tonight had been about then? Not an outpouring of love from friends but merely a formal affirmation of her identity as a successful academic? According to Millie that should have been satisfying enough. But here she was at the end of the day when the celebration was over—alone and without the love she had always craved.

But she had craved something else as well. Professional success. And surely that success was now confirmed. She had succeeded in completing her climb. But, seeping slowly into her consciousness was the appalling suspicion that the price may have been too high. Relentlessly, each recurring cycle of memory ended by propelling Evelyn back once more into the concerns of the present moment; and to the immediate future. As the long hours wore on she found herself returning again and again to the ordeal of the day to come, and reciting over and over the explanations and justifications that might possibly be presented in the morning to the niece of Cynthia Montague.

CHAPTER 2

SEPTEMBER, 1976

It was at the beginning of the second week of September in 1976 when Evelyn heard the horrific news. Her first response was one of denial. "It can't be!" she gasped, fully aware, as she uttered them, that the words were nonsensical. "No one has ever been found dead on the campus of North Pacific University!" Mrs. Parker, the secretary in the outer office of the Head of the Foundations of Education Department, where Evelyn had come to pick up her mail, was clearly unimpressed with this display of logical thought on the part of a member of the faculty.

"There's hardly been time for that, has there? After all, we're only ten years old this month. Anyway, she wasn't exactly *on* campus. They found her Saturday morning in her car in the garage of that old house near the south edge of the university where she lived with a bunch of grad students. Slumped over the steering wheel with the motor still running. Dead. Carbon monoxide poisoning, they think."

Evelyn thought of Cynthia Montague as she had seen her the previous Friday night at the Dean's beginning-of-term party. Fragile, pale blond beauty. Eyes a clear, disconcerting dark blue. Pouting lips. Apparently drinking a lot as usual. The girl exuded sexuality; an impression somehow heightened by the upper-class English accent so foreign to the general student body of a university in the Lower Mainland of British Columbia. A graduate student of some promise, a number of her male colleagues had told her over the past couple of years. But Evelyn had never been quite sure. Thought that she promised more than she delivered, at least in *her* course. But dead? The wall seemed to sway, and she leaned into it. Mrs. Parker, plump face suddenly puckered with concern, left her desk and held out a muscular arm.

"On your way to class, aren't you, Dr. Ashton-Brent? Here, let me get you a quick cup of coffee."

Ten minutes later Evelyn, now running late, paused at the door of her classroom. It was the sound of her waiting class that brought her up short. Or, rather, the absence of sound and movement. Instead of the usual cluster of laughing, gesturing young women and men, she was aware of a large gathering on one side of the room. No one sitting at the desks, but no one quite standing either. Slumped and leaning haphazardly about, and strangely silent, it seemed to her. Waiting for their professor's reaction to the news that, in such a small Department, must have affected them all to some degree. *So this is what it's like when disaster strikes*, she thought. *A frozen immobility.*

She made an effort to orient and calm herself. The stabbing, almost rhythmic pains in her lower back were a warning of stress that must be controlled. Deep, steady breaths. If only she could remember those relaxation techniques people were always recommending. She tried picturing the mountains where she was hiking for the past two days. It failed to work. As always, any form of the meditation so popular among her friends seemed beyond her. Should she cancel the class? But the term had only just begun. She was still laying out the objectives and general outline of the course. She really couldn't afford to lose a precious forty-minute period.

She decided to attempt to control her whirling emotions by momentarily rendering herself the 'outsider' to this scene. In spite of the sexism entrenched in the term, she would become the sociological 'Marginal Man'. She would concentrate on the observable aspects of the group of young people before her. Certainly the range of styles in clothing was something strictly visual on which she could focus for the few moments required to get her bearings. The thought occurred to her that Western society seemed now to be in a transitional stage, where women's dress was concerned. Conformity within the group before her remained only in the slinky sleeveless tops and, possibly, in the calf-length sweater-coats and swinging capes that were rapidly gaining popularity. The straight-cut little mini-skirted dresses and booted legs and the ankle-length, clinging gowns from the late sixties appeared to be hanging in there. They were stubbornly competing in the scene before her with new mid-calf fussily frilled, wide skirts and business-like pant suits made feminine by subtly flared bottoms. As always, there was less variation in the garb of the male students. Sport shirts or pullovers hanging loosely above jeans seemed to be the norm, at least in this class.

"Look", she now began almost coaxingly. "I'm sure you've all heard about the unfortunate death of one of our graduate students, Cynthia Montague." When no questions came she realized that they probably knew more about it than she did herself. There had been a weekend for the news to spread.

"It's the kind of event that shocks everyone, and I sympathize with how you must be feeling, especially those among you who were her friends. But I'm sure that Cynthia would have wanted us to go on with our work regardless of our sorrow. So if we can just all sit down and try to gather ourselves together, we'll begin by taking a minute to review what we discussed on Friday."

With these words the strange tableau before her eyes broke, and in the normal shuffling of chairs and audible exchanges accompanying the settling-in process among thirty-six students, Evelyn had a chance to calm herself somewhat and check her notes for the morning's lecture. She had deliberately chosen to avoid either eliciting or offering details of Cynthia's accident, and it seemed her spur-of-the-moment decision had been the right one. Gradually, the class resumed an almost normal tone.

Evelyn left her last morning class as quickly as possible, as she was anxious to meet with some colleagues who might be able to enlighten her further on the tragedy in their midst. Upon reaching the unusually crowded faculty lounge just before lunchtime, she deliberately paused for a moment to relax, as she savored the warmth and general sociable atmosphere of the room. As always, she marveled at how there was something about it that seemed to generate good conversation. Its generous size and the arrangement of comfortable but easily movable chairs around the profusion of tiny tables no doubt had something to do with it. Or perhaps it was the way the wood-burning fireplace was centered in the far wall, not too far from the coffee-making cupboard. (Alongside this there was even a cocoa-making machine available, as well as one for dispensing soft drinks, thanks to the insistence of Sam Barnes, their resident Mormon.) Or possibly it was the colorfully draped windows on the wall to the right of the entrance that invariably promoted lively fellowship.

Whatever, she was once more reminded that this was indeed her favorite room in any of the buildings on these rather unprepossessing university grounds.

Suddenly, the unusually crowded nature of the lounge struck home. She found herself entering to a crescendo of exclamatory comment and regretful conjecture, but little more in the way of information. No one could seem to recall just when Cynthia had left the party on Friday night; or with whom. There *was* general agreement, however, on her condition as the evening wore down.

"That girl was drinking far too much, and I suspect she was high on something else as well." Helen Korensky, English Education. Thick black hair braided into a bun; sensible, navy-blue suit loosely fitted on the large, well-shaped body; sensible navy-blue oxfords. Evelyn, as always, made an effort to squelch the unreasoning feeling of antipathy roused in her by Helen's pronouncements. She was reminded of the old saying which summed up her first impression of the English professor; that she was one of those people who believed in speaking the truth, especially when it was unpleasant. But she could not deny the truth of what had just been said. Not for the first time she found herself wondering if it was just that Helen was so overwhelmingly puritanical or if, instead, her negative response to the woman was related to their radically different academic backgrounds and world views.

Helen Korensky was one of the old-timers who had been with the institution when it was merely a 'Normal School' for the training of teachers. She had a myriad of tales to tell of the early days of what was later to become North Pacific University. One that Evelyn had particularly enjoyed concerned its naming. It seemed that the 'powers that be' had preferred simply 'Pacific University', but were eventually persuaded that the acronym (PU) might affect the new institution's reputation somewhat unfavorably.

Evelyn had long been accustomed to associating the term 'Normal School' with relatively low status in the academic world. Therefore she was startled one day, soon after her arrival, to find herself being lectured on her uninformed bias. The person who launched the surprise attack was a member of the History of Education group. His name, she discovered, was Dr. Stanley Wheeler.

She was told, in no uncertain terms that, far from being derogatory, the term had been used throughout North America to denote the desired norm or standard of excellence required of all would-be teachers. Furthermore, it had a long and prestigious history, having originated in the early eighteenth century, with Austria's *normalschule* and the *Ecole Normale Superieure* of France.

All this obviously pleased Helen, justifying as it did her previous refusal of the opportunity offered by the new university to take a leave of absence in order to complete a doctorate. Of course she already had tenure, as well as the rank of Full Professor, as had all those who still remained of the teacher-training group established prior to 1965. And she did have a book to her credit: one which had become something of a standard text in English Education Departments across Canada.

The information concerning the origin and history of the Normal School evidently confirmed Helen in another of her strongly held opinions. She was particularly given to remarking on the superiority of teacher training in her own day. This, she would say pointedly, was before it was considered necessary to subject students to a lengthy theoretical program offered by professors who, themselves, had never seen the inside of a school classroom. She now returned to her favorite subject, to the obvious boredom and impatience of most of her listeners—including Evelyn.

For Evelyn had arrived in the summer of 1969 complete with a shining new PhD in sociology from New Oxford, one of the most prestigious of the American Ivy League universities. It still rankled somewhat that she had been forced to work so hard and wait so long before being rewarded with an Assistant Professorship a mere three years ago, in 1973. And she had still not been granted tenure. The Head's private explanation that this was simply because of the top-heavy situation within the entire faculty, 'rank-wise', due precisely to the assimilation of the old Normal School, did not really help matters. For she had noticed that this stricture appeared not to apply to some of her male colleagues.

"Helen," she now interrupted. "as you know, I left the party early. But I still feel terribly guilty about Cynthia. Why did no one assume the responsibility for seeing that the students at the party were not getting high on drugs and alcohol?"

"I did stay until quite late, trying to keep an eye on things. But what could *I* have done anyway?" came the answer. "It's not as if any of the younger faculty members ever listen to *me*. Most definitely not the male instructors who like to fool around with the female grad students."

"I listen to you, Helen. I have learned a great deal from you."

The voice now entering the conversation sounded just above her head. It was quiet compared to the English Ed. professor's friendly aggressiveness; deep and melodious with its careful, almost stilted diction and rounded, elongated, African-sounding vowels. Abdul Issa slid into the seat beside her. No more than the stirring of antagonism aroused by Helen Korensky's presence was the wash of pleasure now flowing through Evelyn's body subject to her control. She knew that most of the other women in the Faculty of Education were similarly charmed by Abdul, and attributed it chiefly to the animal beauty of the man. The creamy, chocolate-colored skin and perfect bone structure that seemed to represent the very ultimate in human beauty; the muscles rippling with movement; the tightly curling cap of jet-black hair and the white-toothed smile and distinctive black eyes—one moment sparkling like dark diamonds, then suddenly turning liquid and soulful: these alone would have loaded the competition for female attention in his favor. But Evelyn thought (when she thought about it at all) that Abdul's appeal for her had more to do with the sense of mystery and romance surrounding him. So many widely varying streams of genes must have combined to produce his marvelously distinctive physical qualities!

Abdul's appearance today was strikingly different from usual, however. His face looked drawn and his eyes blurred and slightly swollen. The long-fingered, dark-brown hands were shaking when he was not running them through his hair or twisting his tie around them. The distinctive accent which had always seemed to add to the sense of mystery surrounding him was more than usually apparent in the precise enunciation of the words that he now spoke.

"I am happy to see you functioning so well, Evelyn. I was afraid that you might allow this tragedy to worry you too much. I sometimes think that you and I are both by nature too compassionate."

"You surely don't consider it too compassionate to feel sorrow for a vibrant young life nipped in the bud in such gruesome circumstances!" Why did she feel that somehow there was some hidden meaning in his comment?

"Of course not. The loss of any young life is difficult to

accept, especially when it is the result of a needless accident. But we must remember that there was nothing any of us could have done to prevent this. Nothing!" He was so adamant in this that Evelyn wondered momentarily if he might be trying to persuade himself. For an instant she was silent, then gathered her courage and spoke hesitantly.

"Abdul," she searched for the right words, "Unlike you, I'm afraid that it might be *guilt* that I'm suffering from. Not just compassion. You see, the fact is I'm afraid that maybe I *could* have done something to prevent it. I was aware that Cynthia and some of the others (faculty as well as grad students) were, at the very least, smoking marijuana at the party Friday night. And I suspect that there was some LSD around as well. I was uncomfortable about it, but told myself it was none of my business and decided to resolve my dilemma by going home early. At any rate, I had promised to join the hiking group on that weekend trip to Mount Baker, and we were starting out at the crack of dawn Saturday morning. So I used that as an excuse. By the way, I noticed you didn't show up that morning."

"You know very well that Cynthia's problem was not drugs." Abdul's body had stiffened almost imperceptibly. He seemed not to have heard her last remark. "She was drinking far too much, that was obvious. I am not the only one to have noticed this."

"Maybe you're right. But, then, why didn't we stop her? It *was* a party sponsored by the faculty, and we were surely responsible for the students we had invited. And, anyway, there's worse than that." As she spoke, the stiffening spread to Abdul's face, replacing the tortured grimace with which he had approached her.

"What do you mean?" he asked softly, as he moved closer.

"I think she was romantically involved with a member of the faculty, and she may have been getting in over her head in some way. At the Banff conference on "Education and Society" this past summer, where both you and I presented papers, you may remember I shared a room with her. Well, I turned in at about 1:00 a.m. on the two nights, and in both cases she was still absent when I dozed off. On the second night I had trouble sleeping because my talk was coming up the following day. At 5:00 a.m. I noticed that she hadn't yet come in, although she *was* in her bed when my alarm went off at 7:30."

Now Abdul was attempting a smile, and creeping into his partly strangled voice was a semblance of the usual teasing quality.

"I doubt that staying out most of the night is particularly unpredictable or alarming behavior for graduate students. Surely even *you* must have done it at times."

"You're right, of course, Abdul. Even I did it once in a while, long ago." Helen Korensky obviously felt that she was being left out of this conversation. "But I agree with Evelyn. What she's describing is somewhat different, and may be cause for concern."

"She seemed upset," Evelyn worried on as if her two table companions hadn't spoken, "and said she wanted to talk to me about something that was troubling her. But I put her off. I was slated to speak that morning and I was annoyed that she had already destroyed my chance of being alert and focused. I kept thinking about the ghastly impression I'd probably make with my bleary eyes. So I can't say that I was very sympathetic."

"Why would you conclude that she was involved with one of our colleagues?" Abdul asked. "That was a broadly based conference, with people from numerous educational specializations and varying qualifications. And students from many universities. I remember that your other graduate students were there as well. I mean those two young would-be philosophers, Gerald Davis and Tony Kohut."

"I know. They had the room next to mine. I heard them come in together at about 2:30 a.m., and I knocked at their door and asked if they had seen her. They said they hadn't, but they exchanged rather knowing glances."

Evelyn found herself mentally visualizing the young men in question, as she had encountered them that night. From the first time she met him, Gerald Davis had struck her as a bit strange. He was a large, stolid person with eyes, magnified unnaturally by a pair of perfectly round lenses, that always appeared to be looking through her into some blank wall behind. For her, this had the result of making it inordinately difficult to engage him in meaningful conversation, so she tended to avoid him as much as possible. Even given her concerns that particular night, she had paused momentarily when she saw that it was he who opened the door. Her reluctance seldom deterred Gerald, however, and she often found herself the target of his ponderous pronouncements—never questions—on scholarly subjects. Once she had caught herself in an unwittingly imitative posture, gazing emptily across the short bristle of closely cut hair on his head into the distance while he wallowed in abstractions no doubt picked up in class that day.

Tony Kohut was a different kettle of fish entirely: a small, darting person with facial features camouflaged by a scraggly beard and mustache and long, unruly hair. He seemed to specialize in rapid repartee and studied irony. Always seen as a duo, the two had no doubt been thrown together initially by the fact that they were the only graduate students in Philosophy of Education. By now, however, their relationship seemed almost symbiotic. Evelyn was not comfortable with either of them. She sensed that they had little respect for her, although whether that was due to her gender, her subject area, or her relatively low position on the academic totem pole she wasn't sure. Their cynically amused responses on the night she had asked about Cynthia had only added to her discomfort.

"Whatever Cynthia was up to that night," she now concluded, "It certainly was not with one of them."

Suddenly a fourth cup joined those already on the coffee table, with an enthusiastic abandon that splashed contents into all three saucers. Evelyn looked up to see Millie Eisenstadt's massive body blocking the view. The usual cheery smile was missing from the round, freckled face; the hazel eyes seemed to be flashing with anger more than with grief; and the short cap of wiry auburn hair looked more windblown than ever.

"This is bloody gawd-awful!" the words echoed from wall to wall. "How could we have let it happen?"

Abdul's voice had become louder than usual and more uneven. "*We* did not *let it happen,* Millie. I have just been trying to convince Evelyn that we cannot hold ourselves responsible for the private lives of our graduate students. How could any of us have guessed that Cynthia would drive home alone in the condition that she was in on Friday night?"

"Well I, for one, sure as hell wouldn't have guessed that she'd drive home *alone*! Did no one see her start out? I left rather late, but the party was still in full swing, with Cynthia the center of attention as usual." Millie's voice dropped, and she looked at him searchingly. "This may not be the time to hassle you about this, Abdul, because I know you must be feeling rotten just now. But you guys really shouldn't have been leading Cynthia on the way you were doing. You and I know it doesn't mean anything, but students can get the wrong notion sometimes. Even graduate students."

"I couldn't agree more!" pronounced Helen, as Evelyn winced in embarrassment.

"Really, Millie!" she felt a twinge of exasperation. No one but her singularly outspoken friend would have thought of saying such a thing, and at such a time. "You know that was just a game the male professors all liked to play with Cynthia. I think she enjoyed it fully as much as they, and took it even less seriously."

Millie looked dubious, as did Helen, but they let the subject drop. *What other people might merely think, Millie blurts right out*, Evelyn thought. Perhaps that was why she seemed to be a lightning rod for trouble. Maybe it was this particular inclination, as much as her pride and inflexibility over what she considered principles, that had been at the root of the problems that time at New Oxford University, where they had both once been graduate students in sociology. They met soon after Millie arrived there from her home province of Alberta, fresh from a speaking tour in which she had been castigating American involvement in the Vietnam War. Her entire experience in the doctoral program in sociology might have been different if only she had known enough to keep her opinions on the subject to herself; or to restrict the voicing of them (as Evelyn very quickly learned to do) to the group of McGovern supporters on the campus at large and to the Marxist sociologists within the Department. But, of course, that was just not Millie's way. Her new acquaintance had struck Evelyn from the first as a strangely independent person, apparently never seeking the approval of others. The two had now been friends for almost nine years. In 1967, Millie (then at the age of thirty-six, a decidedly mature student) had arrived at New Oxford University, armed with a prestigious fellowship for the three-year post-graduate doctoral program in sociology. Evelyn, also somewhat older than most of her fellow students, had then been in the final two years of her studies, busily organizing and writing up the results of the research for her PhD dissertation. The period was an eventful one—in fact, at the time it had seemed tragic for Millie from a career standpoint—and there was much in Evelyn's memory about what had happened during those months that felt like unfinished business. And much that still had the power to make her writhe with discomfort. In the end, however, Millie had simply cut her losses and returned to her tenured position in Alberta. She had done extremely well in the meantime—earning an Associate Professorship before taking another leave of absence in 1973 to complete her PhD work at the University of Miami. Whereas Evelyn, the graduate of one of North America's highest-ranking universities, had all this time been slaving away in an unappreciative, male-dominated Department, without tenure.

The lounge door opened with a noisy flourish, spilling a group of newcomers into the room, and the tension of the moment broke.

"Oh, oh," breathed Millie, "Here's Baby Blue Eyes!"

"You're going to refer to the Head that way once too often," Evelyn murmured with a barely suppressed giggle. Abdul visibly relaxed, the strangely distant look in his eyes replaced momentarily by a flash of amusement.

Harvey Garfinkle was indeed handsome, and he knew it. A tall man of muscular build, his wavy blond hair gleamed as he moved easily among the seated faculty, greeting each in turn, his relaxed manner serving to neutralize the formality of the expensive dark suit. Now he was stopping at their table, smiling warmly, yet with a touch of barely concealed grief in his expressive face.

"I've canceled the afternoon classes." he said. "I should have done it this morning, but I was tied up with official business in connection with Cynthia Montague's fatal accident. And I wanted to tell each instructor in person that I blame none of you for that tragic event. I've given the police all the information available to me, and they have assured me that the matter will not be exploited by the media if they can help it."

"I hadn't even thought of the media. My God, what this could do to the reputation of our university!" Evelyn turned to see Sam Barnes, a professor of History of Education whose specialty involved changes in the structure and role of the family over the centuries. She was all-too familiar with his field of study, largely because the two of them shared a double set of offices separated only by a wall extending about six feet from the floor. This meant she could hear virtually every word spoken in the room beyond. She had always thought that Sam, a big bear of a man sporting a sand-colored brush-cut, would look more at home driving a truck than teaching university students. Now he was towering over them with rumpled tweed-jacketed arms grasping an unwieldy collection of papers and files, the usual cup of cocoa in hand, and the typical crooked grin including and engaging them all. Evelyn had to admit that she could not help but like Sam, in spite of his rough mannerisms and rigidly conservative opinions.

"Of course I've been considering that." Dr. Garfinkle's voice took on what appeared to Evelyn to be a decidedly forced optimism. "We'll just have to be extremely careful not to talk about this to any journalists who might possibly come prowling around the place. And let's all do our best to discourage rumor and gossip here on campus. I know I can depend on *you*, Sam. And the rest of you too."

"Yeah . . . for sure, you can count on me to be discreet, Harvey. You, especially, should know that my record is unblemished in that department."

It seemed to Evelyn that there was a flash of something left unsaid between the two men. Harvey looked disconcerted for an instant then, as if Sam had not spoken, he began to move on.

"We'll need the prayers of all of you, as well as those of every other God-fearing group in this city, if we're to get through this unscathed!" Then, speaking over his shoulder, as he turned to go, "I know I can count on you for that as well, Sam. Although I'm not so sure about any help from our skeptical Millie here in that regard."

"Mmm . . . yeah." Sam's eyes narrowed at the attempt at humor, and an ironic grin diffused his features as the door closed behind the Head and his entourage. Sam was that rare species in a Canadian university setting: a transplanted Mormon from Southern Alberta. He was accustomed to being teased about it. As was Millie, an outspoken freethinker from a Jewish family background.

"Wouldn't you know he'd find a way to bring religion in?" This was accompanied by Millie's loud laugh. "Ever the crowd-pleaser, our Harvey! The only thing he neglected was to blame Cynthia's death on capitalism."

Evelyn did not join in, for the levity seemed inappropriate, given the tragedy that had befallen their only female graduate student. And she suspected that the remark may have annoyed Abdul, with his strong Marxist sympathies. She had always considered herself to be a 'left-winger' as well, although she had to admit that to be leftist liberal in the United States was beginning to seem a far cry from the doctrinaire Leninism and Maoism she was encountering among the academic Left in Canada. But, she thought, Sam Barnes often did succeed in rubbing the majority in this rather radical Department the wrong way. He didn't quite fit in with the sociologists, philosophers and other historians in what was known as the Foundations of Education. They had a reputation for being the most academically elite group among the members of a Faculty commonly considered not quite up to the level of the Arts and Sciences at North Pacific University.

This relatively superior status of Foundations people was no doubt due to the fact that more than a few had, like Evelyn and Millie, earned their advanced degrees in fields other than education. Evelyn knew Sam to be merely a Doctor of Education, however, so in the eyes of some of her colleagues he didn't quite measure up. She was also aware that they all saw him as profoundly and consistently reactionary—not only theologically, but in an economic, political and social sense as well. As a self-defined socialist she disagreed with everything that he appeared to stand for. Yet she found his down-to-earth manner appealing, and realized (to her chagrin) that they often seemed to arrive at the same position on practical issues. And at times she even worried about the extent to which it had become a popular pastime among the students to vilify him for his conservatism.

Sam's comment seemed to have irritated the staid Helen Korensky as well. Helen was an active member of the United Church. As she had explained in great detail to Evelyn, this church was unique to Canada, having resulted from an amalgamation of the majority of Presbyterians and Methodists in 1925. Helen now launched into a sincere, albeit rather lengthy, discourse on why it was natural and even necessary, in times of tragedy, to turn to one's faith for comfort.

"I'm perfectly aware," she ended, "that religious faith is considered in many quarters within academia to be somehow naive and old-fashioned, and that it's okay to make fun of it. But, I think you'll find that most people, even sophisticated scoffers like some of you, will find yourselves turning back to it when the going really gets tough."

Evelyn mumbled agreement, as did most of the others in the group. Some even referred to their own current and intended future prayers for the soul of their deceased graduate student. In fact, Evelyn had already decided to attend the Unitarian church that coming Sunday, and to light a candle in Cynthia's memory. Millie held her peace, as she usually did in discussions in which universal belief in God was assumed. Sam hastened to explain that he had not intended to malign the Head's religious faith—whatever it happened to be at the moment. To Evelyn's relief, this rather uncomfortable diversion into a subject which she knew put both Abdul and Millie at a disadvantage was eventually interrupted by Gus Rasmussen, who had come in with Harvey but remained in the lounge when the Head left. He now sauntered over to join them.

One of the younger members of the Foundations Department, Gus wore his fair hair in a braid down his back and sported a thin goatee and a badly wrinkled T-shirt and jeans. Both literally and metaphorically, he had come of age during the early sixties. Evelyn sometimes had the feeling that he had frozen into the norms and dogmas of that exciting time, while she liked to think that she herself had grown somewhat in the interim. Her most vivid impression of him was formed during her first year at NPU when he had instituted 'barefoot study sessions' in which he and his students sat around the fish pool on the campus lawn with their feet in the water and their heads (or so it had appeared to her) somewhere off in space.

Today, Gus looked even more bedraggled than usual. His eyes were bleary and his face had the tired lines of someone who had not slept for days. Evelyn thought it better not to raise the issue of Cynthia's death with him, but she soon realized that such reluctance was unnecessary.

"I hear you've been trying to get the university administration interested in starting a Women's Studies program," he said now. "This awful business with Cynthia Montague might get the ball rolling on it, don't you think? At least it might drive home the fact that young girls, even the sophisticated ones, need someone to turn to if they're in trouble." Evelyn was anxious to discuss the subject and appreciated the opener.

"It's possible that it just might," she replied, "At least, Cynthia's needless accident does force us to recognize the vulnerability of young girls far from home. I believe that Women's Studies is the coming thing, and our university could be one of the first in Canada to establish it. Of course it has to be done at the general Council level, but the main thing is to get a group together in this Faculty to push the idea. Would you be willing to help us with it?"

"Yeah, you bet I would. Not only have you my full support, but I've been working with a group of female students, friends of mine, who are trying to organize around the idea of a politically active women's movement. Meredith Walker is the force behind the group. Maybe you know her? A number of the others have taken classes from me in the past, and I expect they're going to be putting a lot of pressure on the 'Old White Boys' Club' that's been running this place for so long."

Evelyn was not surprised at Rasmussen's enthusiasm for her cause, for she had learned long since that he was a militantly Maoist sociologist whose courses were wildly popular with the group of student radicals dedicated to achieving what they referred to as a more democratic sharing of power within the university.

"Is that the organization calling itself the Women's Cultural Revolution?" she asked. "I've been hearing something about them lately. I understand they hope to recruit members right across the campus. I've been asked to join, but I'm not sure it's appropriate for a member of faculty to align too closely with any one particular group of student activists."

"I'm a little surprised to hear that you're against the reigning 'White Boys', Gus." Sam Barnes spoke with scarcely veiled sarcasm, as he placed a bottle of ginger ale on the table beside the coffee cups. "I could have sworn you've been mighty close to our own crown prince ever since I've been on board here. Or doesn't our renowned Dr. Garfinkle qualify as a member of the establishment?"

Abdul intervened, obviously attempting to head off any possible altercation between the two practiced antagonists. "I gather, by the name, that the Women's Cultural Revolution is not open to men. At least I have not been asked to join. I wonder, Gus, if they have considered calling it the Cultural Revolutionaries? I think they might get more general support."

"Why don't *you* ask them?" this from Millie. "Meredith Walker is in one of your classes. You know, the 'Bachelor of Education After Degree' (or BEAD) group that I'm teaching as well. And she's not shy about expressing opinions. By the way, I'm of two minds, myself, about this Women's Studies business. While I agree that there's a serious problem of sexism throughout the university system, I'm not sure that's the way to solve it."

Evelyn was aware that Millie was not with her on this matter. They had discussed it often enough. "All my professional life I've been struggling like mad for a level playing field," Millie liked to say, "but you people seem to want to change the goal posts and the very rules of the game. Why is it better simply to turn the tables on the men than to have a situation of real equality for everyone?" Evelyn thought it was probably true that she, herself, had little use for the current rules and achievement criteria of academia. They didn't seem to be working for women. Clearly they were too male-oriented.

Millie's answer to that was that there were two sets of rules in academia: the bureaucratic ones and the standards or principles of scholarship. She liked to point out that the first set functions merely as the organizational means to provide an appropriate setting, and means for achieving, the second—and crucial one.

"Like any other tool," she once said, "a formal organization is inevitably a two-edged sword, available for either constructive or destructive and corrupting ends. It all depends on the rules actually employed for reinforcing performance, and the degree to which policies and programs are being constantly assessed as to effectiveness and efficiency. Too often the wrong behaviors are rewarded, and the most power-hungry people are encouraged to climb to the top in monopolistic organizations, whether private *or* public." At the present time, according to her, power brokers among the male professors were simply more accustomed than their female counterparts at using the bureaucracy for their own advancement. But Millie's conclusion was that usually neither set of rules was the real source of their problem.

"It's the manipulation of both by unscrupulous people for self-serving ends that we should be fighting," she maintained. "The fact that, so far, only men have possessed the power to do this manipulating is merely an accident of history, and not due to any essential gender difference or superiority on either side."

"So it *does* come down to the issue of power," was Evelyn's response. They had ended the discussion in agreement, for once.

"Speaking about revolutionary movements on campus," she now heard Sam saying, "how is the Rain Forest Federated Indian College coming along?" He was addressing Gus and Abdul, "I understand that you two have been involved in developing the curriculum in social studies for their students."

"Oh, it's just great," Gus burst out enthusiastically. "We got the idea that they should prepare a textbook on Canadian history in the form of a comic strip. It's only recently been published, by the way. Have you shown it to them yet, Abdul?"

"No, actually I haven't. For one thing, I am aware, Sam, of how opposed you historians in the Foundations Department have been to the entire idea of a separate college for the native Indian students, right up to the time it was opened last year."

"If you remember, Abdul, our problem with it wasn't only that the college is organized as a separate unit. Granted, we didn't like the idea of institutionalizing apartheid (which I'm surprised that you seem to favor in this instance, given your background). But what Muthu, Stan and I objected to, in particular, was the notion that the academic standards would be different (and inevitably lower) for the graduates of the new college than for those in the rest of the university. We felt that a far better approach for solving the problem of inequality over the long term was to provide catch-up classes aimed at compensating for the lack of background skills and knowledge on the part of the Indian students. We argued, and I will repeat our position for those who haven't heard it," (this with a wry grin) "that you couldn't do anything more insulting to people of aboriginal ancestry than to assume they will not to be able to meet the standards we expect of others!"

"So that's why I keep hearing the beating of drums every day from that building I pass on my way to the office!" Millie, never one to withhold her opinions, now joined the conversation. "I've been wanting to ask someone 'in the know' just how it is that a bunch of students have the time to spend on that kind of thing for hours on end, during class hours. Seriously, I'm really intrigued and puzzled by it."

"Millie, surely you've learned by now not to expect reason to rule in a university!" Sam teased. "The answer, of course, is that they've been brainwashed by the 'powers that be' to believe that they're enrolled here chiefly to learn about their tribal culture. Not about the culture of the society and world they're going to have to live in, and make a living in!"

"That's enough, Sam," Evelyn heard herself interjecting. "You're going to get a reputation as a racist if you're not careful!"

"Don't I know it! Especially after what was to me the high point of the entire Council discussion concerning the establishment of the new college. Remember," he asked Abdul, "when that colleague of yours in Social Studies Methods accused one of our historians of being a racist simply because he raised a number of reasoned arguments concerning the principles underlying the proposal? Imagine! Our good friend and colleague Professor Muthu . . . an Untouchable from an illiterate family in India who managed to get an education with all the cards stacked against him. Hey guys, if Muthu is a racist, with his background of the kind of systemic discrimination that even our badly maltreated Indian population couldn't even *imagine*, then I guess I'd be honored to be called one too!"

In the general laughter and ensuing silence, Evelyn considered entering the discussion in support of Abdul and Gus, with a rational explanation of why standards and curricula suitable for the general population of students might not be appropriate for those from Canada's tribal cultures. However, her well-intentioned musings on the subject were now interrupted by a sudden surge of surrounding movement and mumbled excuses and goodbyes. Sam ambled toward the door. Millie was packing up her books and lunch things and moving off as well, followed by Abdul. The pair were now engrossed in rapid and excited conversation on what must have seemed to them to be the safer issue of Women's Studies. Evelyn wondered, as she had often done during the past month, how two such different people could get along so well. And why Millie, with her bulk of excess pounds, was usually surrounded by interested (and interesting) males, and yet seemed so oblivious of the fact. As always, her warm feelings toward her friend were mixed with a degree of irritation.

For a moment she found herself toying with the notion that Abdul might possibly be attracted to Millie sexually. But no sooner had the idea formed than she dismissed it as utterly inconceivable. It was merely that the two had a number of interests in common. Both were social scientists, although Abdul's specialization was economics. He had been hired about the same time as Evelyn, as a Lecturer in Social Studies Education: an arm of the Teaching Methods Department. However, Evelyn was aware that Abdul's chief enthusiasm was actually the novel that he was writing. He had given her good reason to suspect that she might be featured in it. For it seemed that, in spite of what she had always considered her plainness, Abdul Issa found her attractive. A momentary glimpse in the wall mirror across the room made Evelyn wonder anew at this. There she was, angular rather than slim; straight, somewhat wispy brown hair parted on the side and falling almost to the shoulders; costly glasses that had disappointingly failed to enhance her attractiveness; lips a little too thin; nose projecting a little too sharply. (It was at moments like these that she wished that the stylish wigs of a few years before had not so quickly gone out of style.) Nevertheless, and perhaps to compensate for her mediocre looks, she dressed expensively and carefully. She was aware that good taste as well as money was apparent in the graceful lines and exquisite texture of her light-tan pantsuit and green silk blouse. But Abdul was such a beautiful man, and could surely have his choice of women far more attractive than she! Whenever they were in a room together, this sense of her own inadequacies made her want to reach out and proudly publicize her claim to him. However, she knew that Abdul would not like it.

Evelyn always humored him in this, assuming that his attitude may have stemmed from the fact that he was a refugee from the oppressive policy of the South-African government toward 'Coloreds', as he had put it. He had also told her that he had originally moved there from the little neighboring country of what was now called Lesotho (formerly Basutoland) to join Mandela's African National Congress. And that he had eventually been forced to flee from Southern Africa in order to avoid incarceration.

Evelyn remembered fondly her introduction to the details of Abdul's background. It was in the early fall of 1970, when one of his colleagues in the Methods Department had persuaded him to join the hiking group that had been an ongoing feature of the campus faculty for some years. The hike which drew them together happened to be a first for both. Evelyn had seen the handsome, dark-skinned man in the faculty lounge a number of times during her first year at NPU. She had felt curious about him, and attracted, as well. So it was with considerable pleasure that she noted his presence at the designated gathering place on the morning of her first attempt at hiking. She introduced herself at once and they ended up in the same car for the trip to Buntzen Lake, where a relatively easy hike had been planned. Although she tramped along with a number of different colleagues during the morning, she found herself in conversation with Abdul for much of the time following the lunch break, which they had enjoyed in a clearing on the far side of the lake. It happened that, by then, her body—tired and unaccustomed even to the relatively mild elevation gain of this particular trail—was beginning to rebel. She stumbled at one point and would have fallen if Abdul had not graciously helped her to regain her balance and then begun to measure his pace to hers.

"I'm new to all this," she explained with some embarrassment. "And I'm afraid I'm getting a bit over-tired. My home territory doesn't have mountains like these. So I can see it's going to take me a while to get into condition. I came here only last year from Boston, Massachusetts, and this is the first mountain hike I've tried. How about you?"

The ensuing conversation fascinated Evelyn. With a little gentle prodding on her part, and during the course of the afternoon of hiking, Abdul told her a great deal about his home country and his own family. He said that his father was an Indian scholar at the University of Botswana, Lesotho and Swaziland, and he referred vaguely to Basotho ancestry as well. In fact, once, in what Evelyn was later to realize was a moment of uncustomary frankness as he was helping to steady her for the third time, he opened up even more about his family background. This was no doubt part of his effort to relieve her of embarrassment by taking her mind off her poor physical condition, compared to his own obvious agility. Abdul allowed that the latter might be due to the genes of his mother: the African second wife of his Islamic father. This explained, for Evelyn, the interesting features and mannerisms that had, from her first sight of him, indicated an ethnic origin of considerable complexity.

Their sexual relationship did not begin until some time after. Evelyn suffered so severely in the following days from aching legs and back that she didn't dare return to hiking until after having spent a couple of weeks working out in the campus gym. On her first hike following this, Abdul had seemed pleased to see her, and their conversation took off almost from where it had ended on that first day. From that time on she had never ceased to admire his gentle ways and handsome features.

The relationship with Abdul had confirmed her in the wisdom of her decision to come to Canada, in spite of the obvious fact that it had been disappointing from a career standpoint. She was bound that she would stick it out in what was to her 'the wilds of the Canadian northwest' for at least one more promotion and the tenure which would inevitably accompany it. This would give her the necessary clout to allow for a successful application to a larger and more prestigious institution back in the United States. And, happily, the 'northern wilds' were proving much less forbidding than she had initially expected. The first year of culture shock was long behind her. In fact, she now quite enjoyed the relative quiet of this small urban center south of the city of Vancouver, and the more subdued and polite behavior of Canadians: all so different from the frenzied atmosphere in the American cities where she had spent her childhood and youth. Even her hometown of Boston had lost some of its appeal for her. On her rather-infrequent return visits she now noticed an unfamiliar loudness and nasal quality to the women's voices; and the pervasive bland assumption of national superiority, and universal ignorance of all things Canadian, increasingly made her squirm.

The flat flood plain of the Lower Mainland's Fraser River with its dikes, along with the proximity of the Pacific Ocean, were tranquil and typically Canadian reminders of the more robust and unpredictable Atlantic thundering off her own familiar Boston Bay. The hiking club to which she devoted most of her spare time had introduced her to a new experience: the still-relatively unspoiled nature in the nearby mountain countryside. Little in her earlier, predominantly urban, life had prepared Evelyn for the wonders of wilderness hiking. The sheer animal thrill of standing on a rocky peak and seeing the terrain descending in every direction was something that she could never have imagined. Nothing could match the triumph of realizing that one had arrived at this awe-inspiring place by nothing more involved than a companionable process of tramping and climbing along, step after pleasantly spongy step, interspersed with an occasional scramble over rocky ledges! Nor the awareness that, in mountain wilderness like this, one could still find traces of the story of life's long-ago beginnings. And, above all, there was the knowing that in the deepest recesses of one's being, this moment was encased forever, to be drawn upon for comfort when trouble intervened.

Such as now, she thought. Evelyn eased back in her chair in the now-silent lounge, closing her eyes and summoning an image of Garibaldi Lake, her favorite hiking destination nestled high in the mountains near Whistler. For a moment it seemed to work. But almost immediately the calm of the lake's turquoise surface appeared to shift, as a disturbance erupted, and in the mirror of the water's depths she saw a familiar slim, girlish body, slumped over a steering wheel.

An abrupt movement at the table next to them brought home to her the realization that the room's occupants had been dispersing for some time. With this came the awareness that she and Helen were now the only ones remaining. She knew she should return to her office, but felt almost immobilized by the wave of despair and guilt that the thought of Cynthia's death had once more aroused.

"I suppose you left the party early as well," she said, more in an attempt to compensate for her unwarranted negative feelings toward her colleague than because of any real curiosity.

"No, as a matter of fact, I didn't. I felt that someone who was clear in the head should hang around as a . . . well, sort of chaperone. Because of students being present, I mean." Helen paused, then her words came slowly and thoughtfully. "There weren't many still there when I went home. The Garfinkles were on the point of departure just then, so I left with them. Cynthia was the only remaining student. As the three of us walked down the hall I saw her in one of the side rooms with Abdul Issa. He seemed to have taken her in hand. She was clinging to him and hanging on his every word. You know the way she is . . . was . . . with men. And he was trying to get her to drink some coffee. I thought she'd be okay. Odd, that."

Walking home late that afternoon Evelyn found herself going over and over the day's events; except for Helen's remarks, which she pushed to the periphery of consciousness each time they intruded. They didn't fit, somehow, and they aroused a feeling of unease, as the English prof's comments often did. The walk was relatively short, since she lived in an apartment complex not too far from the southern edge of campus. Cynthia, never in any way close to her in life, was now a brooding presence. Even more so than the dike along which she was moving, and the quiet sea beyond. She was oblivious to the silken stretches of sandy beach within stone-throwing distance on her right, and to the gentle rise and fall of the waves of incoming tide. Oblivious, even, to the rare beauty and plaintive cacophony of the snow geese, early arrived from Siberia and drifting like a cloud of giant snowflakes along the surface of the water—except for the vague sense of sorrow their cries invariably aroused in her. Always, when she heard that distinctive sound, the words of a poem from her childhood came back. Why could she never remember who had written it?

The geese have gone over, the geese have gone by, the words came without conscious recall, as they always did. *Far and away I heard them flying. Their strange wild cry made me start and shiver, as at something lost and gone forever.* She tried to shrug off the surge of feeling of some impending loss. If it was Abdul's love, she thought wryly, had she ever really had it? What nonsense! Of course the loss was represented by the tragic death in their midst.

Again the image of the girlish body slumped in a darkened car had intruded without warning. *Something lost!* What had that young woman gotten herself into? What sort of a mess would make someone as ruthlessly egoistic as Cynthia come to the conclusion, even in a befuddled state, that the only way out was to kill herself? For Evelyn had been certain, from the moment she had heard the news, that the death could not have been accidental. Girls like Cynthia didn't have accidents; at least not accidents as stupid as this one would have to have been.

Not until after dinner, when Abdul arrived from his apartment two floors below, was Evelyn able to break out of the ceaseless circle of her mental chewing and re-chewing of the situation. Abdul was adamant. Let others solve the problem of their graduate student's death. It simply wasn't their responsibility. No more talking about it, he said. In fact, talking was not the remedy they both needed this evening. And in this, Evelyn soon found that he was right. There was nothing like Abdul's lovemaking for removing all her tensions and concerns. Absolutely nothing in her previous sexual experience had prepared her for the extremes of bliss which he was able to arouse in her. None of her past lovers had ever seemed to be so entirely focused on the desires and needs of his partner, rather than his own.

Afterwards, with Abdul prowling restlessly about the apartment while she relaxed on the bed by herself, she thought about the puzzle of the man. How his first visit had taken her by surprise. No date or anything. He had merely appeared at the door one night, with the news that they were neighbors. She had wished so many times since that night almost five years ago that she had not been so immediately accommodating; that she had not accepted him so hungrily; that she had insisted on at least the admission of a degree of commitment on his part. Now her need for him was like an addiction. He could arouse her to extremes of sexual passion she had only imagined before, seemingly without losing himself in her as she did in him. And invariably, after one of these encounters, he pulled away, and she was left to descend from the heights with no clear assurance that it had been the same for him. Always, in these moments, she sensed a strange kind of impenetrable elusiveness in him. Tonight, as so many times before, she felt frustrated and powerless, in spite of satiated desire, by the mere fact of his unfailing self-control.

Even their conversation had begun to feel unsatisfying. In his serious moments with her he became the dedicated teacher who required nothing so much as a willing listener—a role she was beginning to suspect that she had fallen into all-too-readily. But not tonight, she thought. I'm going to insist on something more from him tonight.

"Abdul," she aimed a conversation opener toward his back as he paused, strangely tense, at the window with its remarkable ocean view. "Did you manage to convince Millie to support our feminist cause at NPU?"

That was clearly a mistake. Abdul breathed in slowly, then turned, eyes focused not on her but on some source of illumination beyond her. Was it the flame of 'true belief', she wondered, and had she unwittingly supplied the spark with her question?

"Oh, I will. I will. We are really not so far apart. Millie's instincts for justice are very sound, but she has never bothered to acquire the specific type of philosophical background that could have provided her with an appropriate frame of reference. In fact, I sometimes think she has trouble thinking theoretically at all. Rather than merely pragmatically, I mean. Too much the empiricist, I expect. And then, of course, she herself has had no problem in succeeding in a man's field, so she has difficulty feeling the pain of those who are prevented from a fair chance in life because of their gender or class or the color of their skin. But she will come around, I think. She would be a great asset to the movement. Perhaps you could persuade her of that."

"Which movement? Feminism or Communism?" Abdul's face closed over, and she continued hurriedly. "The truth is, I never try to propagandize Millie. She'll join us once she decides that we're moving in the right direction, and not a moment before. And, anyway, I have trouble countering her arguments. Every time she brings up Hungary and Czechoslovakia I have to agree that Marxism in practice leaves a lot to be desired. And that makes me wonder about aligning feminism too closely with it."

"Stalin distorted Leninism from the very outset, and Lenin himself had made serious errors of interpretation in the writings of Karl Marx. One must not associate true Marxist theory with these failed experiments, as I have explained to you before. For one thing, the historical conditions in Russia in the early 1900's were not ripe for revolution. Because of that, more than mere midwifery was required. The same holds for Mao's China. But, then," he spoke teasingly now, "you are so hopelessly Bourgeois, Evelyn. How can we expect to educate you members of the Bourgeois class unless we begin when you are very young? I should have known you when you were a student."

Evelyn liked Abdul somewhat better when he dropped the pedantic tone and resumed the teasing manner that seemed to be his only other way of relating to her on an intellectual plane. But not a whole lot better, she realized.

This loving while not quite liking and not really knowing one's partner was something she had always had difficulty in coming to terms with, and tonight it seemed, suddenly, not to be borne. Tonight she needed the closeness of a committed lover and friend—not the pedantic teacher or the romantic tease. But he was on the prowl again, moving with the grace of a panther, through the bedroom door.

"Abdul," she ventured, raising her voice so she could be heard. "Let's talk. Let's *really* talk. I need you to help me sort through this Cynthia Montague thing." The answer came from down the hall, almost muffled by the opening door. Abdul, who only a few minutes before had held her so close, was now suddenly his old elusive self.

"Sorry, love. Not tonight. I've got to go now. Time and tide, you know. The novel to work on and papers to mark. Try to sleep well, dear one. Remember that it will not help to worry at things one can do nothing about. I will see you in the lounge at lunchtime tomorrow."

The door closed, and something seemed to close in Evelyn as well, collapsing into itself all the budding softness she had felt within. She swung her legs off the bed, determined not to sink into depression, and glimpsed herself in the mirror. The face looked drawn and lined, the eyes dark-rimmed. *No wonder he left*, she thought, *I look at least a decade older than my thirty-eight years. And Abdul's so young—surely not much more than thirty!* Again she wondered what he had seen in her. And how long it could possibly last.

CHAPTER 3

OCTOBER, 1976

Often, during the following weeks, Evelyn found herself wondering at the way in which a traumatic event can so rapidly become submerged in the sheer immediacy and urgency of the daily demands of teaching. In fact, it was not until mid-October that she found herself once more openly discussing the subject of Cynthia's appalling end. No officials had questioned them about the incident, and the press coverage had been restrained and confined to a back page. There was a funeral service but, for Evelyn at least, that had involved no more than a brief appearance at St. John's Cathedral in Vancouver in the midst of a busy weekend. On the whole, the tragic death of their graduate student had apparently become, for most of the faculty, something best forgotten.

It was Millie who re-introduced the subject. Harvey had finally announced a formal meeting of the Foundations of Education Department and, when the day came, the two women decided to enjoy a leisurely lunch together first. They drove to a pleasant restaurant in downtown Richmond and ordered the meal. Their food had just arrived when Millie spoke thoughtfully, twisting her fork in the air and gazing at it as if it might hold some secret.

"By the way, Evelyn," she said, "there's been something bothering me. I have this strong hunch that what happened to Cynthia Montague wasn't accidental. She always struck me as someone who was used to drinking, and I know for a fact that she could hold her liquor with the best of them. I'd say she was far more experienced in that sense than our average North American student. In the first place, I just can't see her planning on driving home alone that particular night with all those panting men about. And, if she did choose to leave the party on her own, she was smart enough not to have driven her car if she'd been on the verge of passing out. It just doesn't seem to fit the opinion I had formed of Cynthia. But I admit that, as a newcomer, I didn't know her as well as the rest of you did."

"You mean you think she may have killed herself?" It was a thought that Evelyn had no wish to hear expressed by someone else. It brought back all the guilt feelings concerning the girl that she had been trying to submerge.

"She wouldn't be the first grad student to have got herself into a mess that she thought was hopeless. I can't help wondering about her. She had all that surface sophistication and sort of brittle superiority but, from what little I saw of her, I'd begun to suspect she might be just a scared little girl inside. Maybe I'm merely projecting my own weaknesses on to her. I remember all too well how I felt so alone and far from home, even as a very 'mature' graduate student, when I found myself in that strange 'looking-glass world' of the Sociology Department in our old alma mater in New England."

"Well, whichever it was, accident or suicide, it won't help now for us to lose sleep over it. I'm trying my best to forget all about Cynthia Montague, and I advise you to do the same."

"I don't see it quite that way. It intrigues me . . . piques my curiosity. The poor girl doesn't haunt me, nor even worry me particularly. The whole affair is more like a puzzle with a missing piece." Millie dived energetically into the all-too-apparent delights of her king-size special.

Evelyn, profoundly upset by the conversation, picked at her shrimp salad. She thought about how different they were, of their enduring friendship in spite of all the disagreements, and how they had managed to remain in touch since parting in early 1969. It had been due to Evelyn's urging that Millie had written to North Pacific from the University of Miami where she was completing a PhD dissertation in sociology. The fact that Millie had not remained at New Oxford to finish her program, along with the series of events leading up to her abrupt departure, had never ceased to weigh on Evelyn's mind during the intervening years. She found herself wondering if she should have spoken up at the time. But, she immediately reassured herself, it was just not in her nature to attract attention to herself in that way. Now, with the friend who had for so long burdened her conscience ensconced—in all her bulk and effervescence—across the table from her, she began to wonder aloud.

"Somehow, Millie, I feel that if we had only approached the matter differently, that time in graduate school, we could have prevented all those wasted years for you."

"I really don't consider them *wasted* years, Evelyn." Millie's eyes revealed a mixture of amusement and wry regret. "But do I see how they might appear that way to others. I produced three quite significant articles after aborting my doctoral program in 1969, as well as a number of less major ones. They were actually papers that I had done for classes, and on which I had worked tremendously hard. Remember how I spent almost all my time in the library? (And, gawd, what a magnificent library that was!)

All three of the most significant papers were published in top international journals. And don't forget that I had the position at my old university to go back to. In fact, I was promoted to Associate Professor soon after returning from the States. The five years of teaching after that debacle amounted to a great learning period for me. I was able to pull all my thinking together and really integrate my world view. I could never have accomplished what I did for my dissertation at the University of Miami these past two years if I hadn't had that time to consolidate all the results of my reading and thinking and teaching experience."

"And, of course, you published your book as well." Evelyn realized with a flash of discomfort that she had momentarily forgotten the textbook on social theory which had been widely acknowledged and was now being used throughout the country and abroad. In fact it had been largely due to that book that the Dean of Education at NPU had pricked up his ears at her remark at a general faculty meeting about Millie's impending availability.

"Things have been so hectic ever since you arrived here," she continued, "that I've never got around to asking you about your contract. I hope you insisted that they recognize your rank as Associate Professor."

"That's one of the reasons I wanted to talk to you, Evelyn. I'm afraid I just assumed that everything would go according to what Dr. Garfinkle implied when he phoned me in Florida. He told me the Foundations of Education Department here would have a senior tenure-track position (at my present rank) available for me next year but that, in the interim, I would just have to be taken on in a visiting capacity. I wasn't the least concerned at the time. After all, he said my book is being used in several classes here. I'm afraid I just assumed that the Department was anxious to have me as a colleague. I've never been one to haggle about a promotion or things like that."

"Now Millie. Don't try to tell me that your rank isn't important to you. I know I'd give my eye teeth right now to be promoted to Associate Professor with tenure."

"Of course it's important. It represents the acknowledgment in my profession of my contributions to the fields of education and sociology. I'd sure as hell resist being *demoted*. But I guess I've always believed that if I did good work it would lead to recognition by my colleagues. I mean I didn't want to be in the position of begging for something that was sure to come in due time. As it did. But I admit that I wasn't about to give it up easily. That's one of the reasons I didn't accept the offer of a position with temporary Assistant Prof. status from the University of Miami."

"My rank, or at least the one I seem to be stuck in." Evelyn grinned ruefully, although even as she spoke, she was fully aware that she would move heaven and earth this term to get that promotion. She knew, just as surely, that Millie seemed to lack the instinct for climbing—perhaps even for surviving—in a bureaucratic organization of the type that prevailed here. The Alberta situation must have been unique in modern academia. Maybe the generally rural setting of the neighboring province, which her British Columbia colleagues associated with a typical rural 'redneck' lack of sophistication, had something to do with it. She herself had decided some time ago that a certain amount of ruthless self-interest was an imperative for success in a university community. Millie's New Oxford graduate-school experience had taught her that, if nothing else. How strange that Millie herself had not learned the lesson, for the consequences of naivety in that instance had been paid for dearly in terms of her own career prospects, with Evelyn merely a troubled onlooker. To be deprived of the chance for a doctorate from a prestigious Ivy League university for purely political and personal reasons—after having been awarded a coveted three-year Fellowship for study there—was something that should surely have resulted in the loss of innocence. Even for someone as stubbornly unworldly as Millie. *Some people are hard to help*, Evelyn thought, regretfully.

"I've been waiting anxiously for a Departmental meeting, thinking that my status would be cleared up then. I'm counting on something being said about it today. Surely Baby Blue Eyes will introduce me formally and indicate at that time what my official position is to be next year. The guy's not much for calling us all together, though, is he? I've never before worked in an organization where there weren't official meetings at least once a month."

"Harvey doesn't believe in formality. He always says that we're just one close-knit family here, and we don't have to get caught up in all that bureaucratic garbage of formal motions and votes and so on. He believes in rule by consensus, and claims he achieves that by getting together with people on a one-on-one basis. It's probably why he made all the arrangements with you by phone, rather than by letter. But, I have to say, I'm a little worried about that, Millie."

Evelyn was indeed worried, but she did not want to communicate the extent of her alarm. For she was aware of something that Millie had obviously heard nothing about. The permanent position, concerning which she had contacted her friend in Florida the previous March, had already been assigned to the Department and budgeted for. That was why the Dean of Education had responded so enthusiastically to Millie's written query, and why he had taken a step seldom resorted to by a senior administrator. He had, in fact, put some pressure on the Foundations people to reconsider their decision to angle for a certain American male Marxist scholar favored by Harvey and Gus and one or two of the others.

"Here we have a well-known Canadian educational sociologist. And a woman at that!" Dean Scott had exclaimed, in Evelyn's hearing. "Why do we have to look outside the country? And, fortunately for us, she happens to be available just now when we have a senior position open. I'm not talking here about *favoring* females. But how about giving them an even break?"

It had seemed in the bag. Nevertheless, she should have warned Millie not to leave Florida without a firm offer in writing. She should have known that Harvey and his clique weren't likely to give up so easily. But it was too late now to say anything. Recriminations wouldn't solve what was beginning to emerge as a sticky problem for her friend.

"What about the University of Alberta?" she asked. "You still have tenure there, haven't you?"

"No, I don't." Millie replied. "I didn't think it was fair to keep them dangling and holding my position for possibly as long as two years. (Remember, they had already done it for me once before, when I went to New Oxford on my Fellowship, but that time I had no intention of looking for a position elsewhere.) In fact, I'd been sounding off for ages about faculty who did that very thing. They'd go off for lengthy periods seeking greener passages while tying the hands of the university and denying younger people a chance at advancement. So I submitted my resignation when I left to complete my doctorate. It seemed the only honest thing to do. Anyway, after I had finished my work at the University of Miami, the Dean at my old university did, in fact, offer me a Full Professorship if I would return. But I felt that I simply couldn't take any more ice and snow. With my weight I always had a hard time navigating those Edmonton streets in the long winters. In fact, I had a bad fall the last year I was there."

"At the time, I guess you were considering staying in Florida."

"I certainly was. And, as it turned out, there were plenty of opportunities. Did I tell you that I had the chance to be Head of a Department in a small college there? Also, there was that offer of a position at the University of Miami. And I was the runner-up for a good job at a place in Georgia. All in all, my career prospects were excellent down there, and I had fully intended to remain. Then your letter arrived, and I got thinking of returning home. I realized that my friends are all here in Canada. In fact, my mother (who is slipping into senility, sad to say) has now moved to Vancouver as well, just to be with me. And, as you know, I've recently sunk all my savings into the down-payment on a house here in Richmond."

Millie had been looking increasingly concerned as she spoke. "I'm beginning to wonder if I may have made a bad mistake. Surely there isn't actually a problem?" she asked, her eyes alert. "I simply refuse to believe that Harvey would encourage me to come all this way and buy property and everything if the Department didn't actually *want* me. And to bring me under false pretenses at that!"

"I shouldn't think so." Evelyn chose her words carefully. "You're fairly widely known and respected in this country. I noticed, to my own discomfort, I must say, that you're the only sociologist here at NPU who's mentioned in that new book on Canadian Sociology. And everyone knows you're a great teacher, what with your background in the public school system and the Master Teacher Award that you were given that time. There aren't many professors who could remotely claim to be 'master teachers.'"

"Or experienced researchers. I don't know if I ever told you, Evelyn, but in my former life I was a research chemist with Canada's Department of National Defence."

"Good Lord, Millie! How is it that you've never mentioned that before? And tell me why in the world did you decide to make such a drastic career change?"

"It was simple. We were located at Suffield in Southern Alberta. I discovered that our entire enterprise was about one thing only. Producing and testing the products for chemical warfare. So I decided to start all over again in the Education Faculty at the University of Calgary, ultimately adding another degree to my repertoire. And then I taught in high school for a couple of years. After saving up a bit, and winning that teaching award which paid for a year of university, I went for a Master's degree in sociology and anthropology."

"I still don't quite understand. You mean you had a doctorate in chemistry and gave it all up and started over just because of the principle of the thing?"

"What do you find so remarkable about that? You're part of the sixties generation. Wouldn't your crowd be even more likely to have done the same?"

"Was that why you were so adamantly opposed to the Vietnam War?" Evelyn was rapidly readjusting her picture of Millie.

"I wouldn't put it quite that way. Both my active opposition to the American role in that war and my refusal to be part of a particularly obscene aspect of the war machine in this country stemmed from the same set of values. What's there to understand, especially for a left-winger like you?"

Evelyn was still puzzled. "But neither action seems to jibe with your lack of support for our Women's Cultural Revolution here right now. Or with your reluctance to throw in your lot with the Marxist group among the professors at New Oxford nine years ago. They would have stood by you, as I've told you before. As it was, you were left all alone, blowing in the wind."

"I'm not saying that my choices have always been prudent. Knowing what I now know about the consequences, I'm not at all sure whether or not I would be brave enough (or reckless enough) to make the same choices again. In the earlier case, you might say that I threw away my chance to be a research scientist with a promising future. But at least I can sleep at night. And, in New Oxford with you that time, maybe I could have somewhat compromised my principles concerning the domination of the social sciences by reigning ideologies, and joined the Marxist faction. And maybe I shouldn't have taken issue with the total lack of counseling for the fellows who were being called up for active service in Vietnam. Do you remember Nat Penner, by the way, that gentle young man?"

"Yes I do, but only after-the-fact as the person whose case you made such a fuss about. You and your friend from Jamaica, and that black Kentucky girl, used to hang around with quite a crew of young fellows there that I didn't get to know at all."

"I guess it was because they accepted us, and your crowd didn't seem to. Except for you, of course, at least in my own case, after we found ourselves inhabiting neighboring rooms. Anyway, I tried to persuade Nat to come home to Canada with me at Christmas time that year, and simply remain here. He told me that his father was an important figure in the Pentagon, so he had no choice but to 'answer the call of his country', misbegotten though he thought it was. 'But I'll never kill anyone,' he said. What a sitting duck he must have been! I'll never forget that awful day, barely three months later, when we heard that he'd been reported killed in action."

"But if criticizing the general call-up of students for the war was the cause of your problems with the Head, you'd think he would have been even more upset with those of us who were avowed Marxists, and were fighting it in an organized way. However, if I remember correctly, you weren't comfortable with our position either."

"Maybe I *could* have been less critical of Marxism in certain classes and less critical of 'structural functionalism' in others. But the problem for me in academia has always been that, growing up in rural Canadian prairie country, as I did, is a pretty surefire way to develop a nose for bullshit. As you say, if only I'd learned to keep my big mouth shut, I might have had some faculty support when I had to stand up to Horny Dick. But, given my values and my need to be upfront with my opinions, and the way I read the situation at the time, there was simply no other route that I could have taken. I guess, in the end, we all do what we have to do."

"The very idea that you could even think of the Head of one of the most prestigious Sociology Departments in the United States as 'Horny Dick' makes me despair of your prospects for success in any academic establishment." In spite of her words, Evelyn found herself laughing delightedly at the Millie's all-too-apt epithet. "And you never have told me exactly what it was the guy did . . . or tried to do. If he just made a pass, why that was nothing. He came on to all of us, as did a good number of the professors. We soon learned to cope, or else to keep out of his way. You notice that I didn't take his class on social theory until my very last year, when I wanted to expand my knowledge in the area for my thesis, but didn't need it for credit."

"I wish someone had warned me. You see, Evelyn, when Dr. Hall left for a two-year sabbatical, I inherited Horny Dick as my thesis adviser. There was no way I could avoid him, especially since I was concentrating on his own field of social theory. And, of course, he insisted that I take his course that term. Actually it was some of the male students who told me about him, but that was after I'd already tangled with him in class a few times. They said he was having a hard time adjusting to females in those heretofore strictly male halls of learning, and particularly to females who presumed to discuss ideas. Like all his kind, he saw only one role for women, in university or anywhere else. I'd already begun to suspect that because of the way that you and Jane Bascome were playing it. Remember, he flirted outrageously with you in class and you responded in kind. And you never . . . but never . . . entered the serious discussions, let alone challenged his ideas. I should have realized much sooner what that was all about."

"Well, I did warn you once about being a bit more circumspect where your opinion of his much-vaunted research was concerned." Evelyn was chuckling now, as a particular memory surfaced. "I'll never forget the time he was describing the study in demography that he had done in the days before he began to specialize in social theory. The details of all his measurements were unutterably boring, but finally he arrived at his chief finding. It was a major breakthrough, he claimed. You looked puzzled, then began to question him."

"Oh yes, now I remember. I merely wanted to be sure that I'd got it straight, because his research results seemed so inconceivably trite. So I tried to force him to express them in simple English. Was this great new breakthrough, I asked, simply the conclusion that the population density of urban areas tends to decrease the further one goes from the city's core? That's all I said, but it seemed to offend him."

"The fact that the entire class erupted in a wave of laughter may have had something to do with his reaction. Can't you see, Millie, this was typical of your irreverent attitude. All the rest of us knew better than to challenge any of his research, much less make fun of it."

"Damn it all! How could I have been so bloody stupid? I realized as soon as I spoke that I'd made a mistake. And, looking back on it all now, I see that I really should have been more aware of his general approach to females."

"Would you have behaved any differently if you'd known?" Evelyn had been wanting to pose this question for a long time. Why hadn't she warned Millie? Was it because, unconsciously, she had assumed that no man, even a notorious wolf like Richard Horne, the esteemed Head of the Sociology Department of New Oxford University, would ever feel inclined to make a pass at someone so appallingly obese? So obviously lacking in sex appeal? The thought was an uncomfortable one.

"I would've moved heaven and earth to keep away from him. Whatever you may think of my recklessness, I'm not suicidal, Evelyn."

"Then he *did* come on to you. It wasn't just that you had made an enemy of him over the Nat Penner affair and by insisting on entering the discussions in class?"

"I . . . guess you could call it that . . . coming on to me, I mean." Now Millie was forming her words slowly and hesitatingly, sounding most unlike her usual forthright self. "It was so strange and so inconceivable that I've never told a soul about it since leaving New Oxford. I felt no one would ever believe the story. I scarcely believe it myself, and yet it happened *to me*. I've wished ever since that I had gone in to his office that day armed with a tape recorder. But how could I have possibly predicted what would happen? And afterwards, I felt that there was simply no way that I could ever survive as a student in that Department. He had all the power and credibility on his side. I had nothing. I *was* nothing."

"What *did* happen? Please, Millie, I've been wondering about it for years."

"I went to see him at his instigation, just after my final exams. He asked me to come to his office to discuss the topic for my dissertation. We had no more than settled down comfortably when he said, quite suddenly, that he'd always had a yen for fat women. They turned him on, he told me."

"What did you say?"

"What *could* I say? I was flabbergasted. I think I mumbled something like: 'I beg your pardon?' And then he smirked and reached for my breast. I wish I could tell you that I responded with a good right to the chin, or at least some clever verbal put-down, but I think now that I was totally immobilized by surprise and horror. It must have shown on my face for he said, quite sneeringly: 'Don't look so holier than thou! You can't tell me that, with your deficient, rural academic background, you managed to get this far, and with the marks you've got, without sleeping with a hell of a lot of professors!'.

The thing is, you know, it had never happened to me before. No instructor in Canada, in all my years of university study, whether in the sciences, education, or sociology, had ever even hinted at such a thing. It could be that it *was* happening all around me. On the other hand, maybe it wasn't merely the four-legged species of rat that Alberta was free of in those days. Or maybe it was merely my weight and general lack of sex appeal that had protected me. I simply don't know. But I find that hard to believe."

"What did you say to him after that? I can't imagine *you* at a loss for words!"

"I only wish I could remember. I must have said something that angered him, for I have this vision of him, eyes like cold steel, suddenly switching to my 'intransigence' in class (as if that were what we had been discussing all along) and telling me that he had the power to ensure that I had no future in sociology. 'You'd better learn to play the game,' he said, 'or else I can see that you never get anything published. Not ever! Not in any sociology journal in North America.' By that time I was totally confused about just which *game* he meant that I must learn to play. Then he told me to go home and think it over, and we'd talk about my doctoral dissertation another day, when I was in a more obliging mood. As you know, I *did* think it over and realized that, regardless of whether there was to be any future for me in sociology, there was definitely none for me in that Department of that university as long as *he* was in control. So I packed up and left. I think I was in shock for months, actually. If it hadn't been for the fact that I had my job to go back to, I don't know what would've happened to me."

"God, Millie! I wish you had discussed it with some of us before you acted so precipitously. We might have been able to marshal some help from the Marxist faculty group. At least we activist students might have made a collective stand."

"I did hint about it to Jane Bascome, by the way. She merely laughed and said that there were ways to handle such a situation if one weren't too fussy or prudish. She seemed surprised that I was so unsophisticated in these matters. I felt that there would be no help from that source. Then I discussed it more openly with the bunch of the fellows that I mooched around with. To a person they said that they wanted to boycott his classes in my support, and to make the reason public, but they didn't dare jeopardize their careers at that critical juncture. A doctorate from that institution was just too precious, they all said, and no one could take the chance of losing it. I agreed with them. I told them that I wanted only one thing of them, in the name of friendship. I asked them to think of others like me when they became part of the academic establishment, as they no doubt would in a few years time, given their launching so near the top of the ladder. They said they would.

'Only this once,' each of them promised, in so many words, 'will I ever look the other way when something like this happens. But I have no power to help you now. When I make it I'll work to change the system.' I guess I'll always wonder if they really *have* tried to change things, or if not speaking up just got easier and easier for them."

"I feel so ashamed. For all of us. We all knew that something rotten was happening to you. But you left so quickly, before we had time to really think about it." However, Evelyn knew, even as she spoke, that she would not . . . *could* not, have acted on Millie's behalf. She had been putting the final touches on her own doctoral dissertation at that time. Even more than in the case of those male students, she had sacrificed and compromised too much, with too many professors in too many classes, to get to where she had climbed by then. And nothing could have persuaded her that Millie was too pure to do a little compromising too.

"Enough crying over spilt milk," Millie pronounced as she adjusted her bulk in the restaurant chair. "None of this solves my current problem right now with Harvey."

"Right. And I wouldn't trust Harvey any more than I trusted Richard Horne. However, he couldn't get away with anything really underhanded in a Faculty the size of this. Not with someone of your reputation, and with the Dean in your corner. Still, it might be a good idea to raise the subject with both of them soon and try to get your status more clearly spelled out."

"I'm not much good at that sort of thing." Millie laughed, her never-failing good humor resurfacing. "I just can't see myself groveling in front of Harvey or any others of his ilk. And I shouldn't have to. After all, I expect university professors to behave at least as honorably as the students they teach. Why is it, I wonder, that so many male administrators still think they can treat women with less respect than men?"

"Perhaps because we let them?" Evelyn thought uncomfortably of the compromises—moral and otherwise—that she had been forced to make during her progress through the system: compromises with which she knew her male colleagues had never been faced.

"You know, I never even had to ask for the two promotions I got at the University of Alberta. Could be I was spoiled. But I always felt confident of my abilities and performance, and I'm not going to let Harvey, or any other relocated American militant, change that. (Sorry, Evelyn, I don't really include you in that category.)"

"Point taken, Millie. I guess I *am* as much of a Marxist sympathizer as Harvey Garfinkle is, but I could scarcely be considered a militant. To get back to your future here, certainly most of our colleagues consider you a fixture already, even if you *are* a female who presumes to deal with subjects involving abstract ideas. They seem, in fact, to be accepting you more than they do an American like me. I'm sure everything will sort itself out as the term progresses."

"I'm actually more concerned right now about this 'B. Ed. After Degree' thing that I seem to have been landed with."

"You mean Harvey's special project? The program that's new this year? You'd better not let him hear you criticize *that*! It's actually now a Faculty-wide affair, isn't it? Isn't Abdul involved in it as well? And Ken Mueller from English Ed.?"

"That's right. There's a teaching team from a number of the disciplines apparently deemed most essential to a degree in Secondary Education." Millie was now speaking between bites of chocolate cake.

Evelyn was all-too-aware of the new experimental program. She had hoped to be included—partly because Abdul was in it, as a representative of Social Studies Methods. And she had wondered at the assignment of a newcomer to this sort of team project.

"Is there a problem?" she asked.

"I'm not sure." Millie paused for a moment, gazing into the distance. "I'm beginning to feel distinctly uncomfortable about the whole thing, but I don't quite know what to do about it. Something strange seems to be happening with the class, at least when *I'm* teaching them. I think it began just after that weekend in the third week of September when they all went somewhere up north of Gibson's Landing for a retreat of some kind, along with most of the members of the teaching team. I realize now that I should have been part of it. But that was the Saturday of the service for Cynthia, and I felt that the retreat should have been postponed. Abdul agreed with me, but at the last moment he decided to go along anyway. The arrangement had been virtually set in stone, he told me, and couldn't be changed at such a late date."

"Does it really matter that much?"

"Ordinarily it shouldn't. But, look, Evelyn. We're both sociologists. We know something about small-group dynamics. I think now that a lot of bonding went on that weekend, and I wasn't part of it. Harvey was there as designated program coordinator, and his pal Gus Rasmussen apparently went along to take my place.

Both had a chance to present their type of introduction to the Sociology of Education—you know, that Marxist-Existentialist-relativistic interpretation of theirs (sorry, I guess it may be yours as well). But I'm sure you're aware that it's quite at odds with my essentially Deweyan-Mead evolutionary-systems approach. Then I come along the following Monday and present the class with a decidedly different slant on things. Not nearly so simple . . . nor so romantic. The villains not so readily discernible. (Sorry again, Evelyn, I realize we don't agree on this.) And remember, this is not your typical class of Education students, gathered as a group for one course only, and then scattered all about the Faculty for their other courses. This bunch is relatively small in number . . . only twenty-four. And they move as an entity from prof to prof. And they're totally segregated from the rest of our student body."

Evelyn thought that she could understand what was happening. She had already heard rumors—from Helen Korensky, to be exact—about this pioneering B. Ed. After Degree class in Secondary Education. They didn't mix with their fellows in the Faculty of Education, with neither the rank and file of undergraduates nor the graduate students. They had even shunned Cynthia Montague.

"They think they're superior because they're Arts or Science graduates, rather than from Education," Helen had complained.

"Maybe they *are* superior!" Evelyn had suggested, with a laugh. "I'm not so sure that some of our Methods courses are all that scholarly. Or even that practical."

"Nonsense!" Helen bristled at the suggestion. "Aside from a few capable nuns who have been sent here for special teacher training, those BEAD students are nothing but a bunch of cocky youngsters who failed to get into law or medicine, or whatever, after graduating in the Arts or Sciences. Education is merely a last resort for most of them. One with reasonably good pay and lengthy summer holidays. How dare they look down on those who are entering the teaching profession for all of the *right* reasons?"

Evelyn had noticed the emerging in-group nature of the class and begun to be thankful that she had not, after all, been selected to represent Foundations of Education on the teaching team. Bad luck for Millie, she thought. Again! Now her lunch partner had resumed speaking, somewhat reluctantly, and Evelyn focused on her once more.

"The other instructors on the team seem to have developed a sort of close, joking camaraderie with them. I don't usually have the slightest problem relating to students, but this bunch seems to have deliberately cut me out. I swear they've decided to play some sort of game with me. They waste time in class by asking me to repeat directions several times, and they pretend not to know simple procedures like how to do library research. And I suspect that some of the girls have been making fun of my appearance. One mentioned 'shopping for tents' in my presence when I came in wearing a new dress the other day, and they all doubled up with laughter. Except for the nuns, who looked uncomfortable. I guess I'm an easy target. But that sort of thing hasn't happened to me since high school."

"It doesn't ordinarily happen because people don't think of you in terms of your weight, Millie. It's just never represented a problem of any kind. You're so confident and happy with yourself. And so obviously in control. I've often envied you for that." Even as she spoke, however, Evelyn was uncomfortably aware that she wasn't being strictly truthful. Millie's massive girth *did* matter. It was what everyone had mentioned to her when her friend arrived. It was startling, and more than skin color or gender or any other observable attribute, it was fair game for snide comment and humor, even in the 'socially sensitive seventies'. And Millie's wardrobe *did* in fact resemble nothing so much as a procession of tent coverings, all apparently sewn from the same box-like pattern.

"Yes . . . well . . .," Millie was saying, "It doesn't make any sense, really, but when I overhear these scornful comments about my appearance, from the very students we're relying on to be good moral models for all those children they'll be teaching in the future, it hits me harder than any of the other things they seem bent on doing to me. How can we expect to get rid of bullying in our schools if we graduate teachers who are, themselves, bullies? And there's something else. I know this will sound crazy, but I'm beginning to wonder just who's really in control of that class! It doesn't seem to be me. I swear I even go so far as to fantasize at times about who *is* actually pulling their strings. The responses and insubordinations of the students seem so *well coordinated*. And that kind of student-induced paranoia is a new experience for an old veteran of the high-school battlefields like me."

It was time to leave if they weren't going to be late for the Departmental meeting. On the drive back to campus the car, in Millie's capable hands, hummed along the tree-lined roadway. Evelyn's thoughts wandered and she found herself mentally reliving that momentous year in the Sociology Department of her old alma mater. Her last year there and Millie's second. The two wouldn't ordinarily have been thrown together, for Millie definitely did not belong to the 'in' group among the young women on campus to which her own socioeconomic and educational background had guaranteed membership. Evelyn thought again about how Millie had become a member of that threesome of what were sometimes referred to cruelly as 'the losers': the group which included the black female student from Jamaica and the other from Kentucky. And of the accidental nature of their own acquaintance. Of how it was only the fact that she and Millie happened to be living in the women's residence, in neighboring rooms, that had brought the latter into her orbit.

All this reminded her, suddenly, of the difference between the housing provided for her cohort of pioneering female students at New Oxford and that of their male counterparts. On visits to the abodes of some of her men friends, she had been utterly overcome by their old ivy-covered residences. Each student apartment had its fireplace-equipped lounge and separate study and sleeping area. What a contrast to the tiny single rooms with their basic amenities that were assigned to the women in their newly constructed building!

Evelyn recalled that she and her close female friends—most of whom had been McGovern supporters during that exciting period leading up to the 1968 election—occupied an entirely different world from the three outsiders with whom they shared the minimal women's residence. It happened, however, that Evelyn decided to pick up that course in social theory from Professor Richard Horne because she had been advised that it was directly relevant to her thesis. So she encountered Millie in that context, and immediately recognized her as a next-door neighbor.

Now, as she thought further about it all, she realized there was much more to discuss about her friend's disastrous experience later in the year. For instance, why hadn't Millie come to *her* for help, rather than Jane? But clearly this was not the time for, even now, they were in sight of the sprawling university campus, with its seemingly unplanned scattering of mediocre-appearing buildings. Soon Millie was pulling into the parking space close to the three-story affair that housed a major part of the Faculty of Education.

With only minutes to spare, the two women entered the now-crowded little meeting room. It was actually one of the two office spaces attached to the Head's large entrance area, in which his secretary had her desk, and just barely allowed room for the discussion table and the blackboard behind it. Millie's first Departmental meeting. The members of the entire Foundations of Education Department would be gathered here, supposedly to plan their programming for the year. Not that there were that many—only ten in all—comprising the four sociologists, three historians and three philosophers. Evelyn realized she was tense with hoping that her friend would make a good impression. After all, she *had* recommended her highly, so her own reputation was on the line. And, given the Head's propensities, this might well be the only meeting of the year.

"Great gawd almighty!" Her companion's exclamation

came on the heels of Evelyn's thought, shattering any hopes of a suitably dignified entrance. "Are you characters trying to asphyxiate yourselves?" Millie dashed to the only window in the crowded, smoke-filled room—as usual, with surprising speed and grace for one of her considerable bulk. The window slammed open, the conversation stilled, and a scattering among the seated men butted out their cigarettes. Sam Barnes, nursing a half-empty bottle of pop, grinned with observable relief.

The gathering was entirely male except for the two newcomers. The three historians (Sam Barnes, Stanley Wheeler and Muthu) were grouped along one side of the table, with the three philosophers facing them. In general appearance, Muthu presented an interesting contrast to his two colleagues. He was small, dark and wiry whereas they were both rather burly men with tanned, closely shaved faces and nondescript, light-brown hair.

The youngest member of the philosophy group was Edward (or Ned) Smith. Ned, with his brown suit, tan-colored shirt and dark-brown tie, his neat black mustache and slicked-back hair and boyish features, looked like nothing so much as a successful businessman impatient to get the show on the road. Seated next to him was Willard Grange, a slim, soft-spoken, rather prissy, scholarly type wearing glasses and informal attire, whose features gave the distinct impression of being shaped into a peak by the pointed nose and receding chin. Evelyn had always thought that Willard's bird-like quality was increased even more by the way he wore his hair. It began at the back of his bald dome, then was fastened with an elastic band before flowing uncertainly about a foot downward along his back. And, finally, there was Leslie Brittan—also informally dressed—with an unruly head of grey-streaked hair and a heavy, tousled beard. His broad, flat face, dominated as it was by a pair of knowing eyes, had seemed to Evelyn to be forever communicating ironic scorn. She now noted, with some amusement, that the philosophers had responded to her friend's outburst in a predictable fashion. One by one, they were studiously relighting fresh cigarettes from the old, and beginning to puff vigorously in Millie's direction.

Occupying two of the four remaining seats were the other sociologists. Harvey, in a patterned sports shirt open at the neck, matched with casual pants, now rose from the seat at the far end and called the meeting to order simply by beginning to address the table at large. Gus Rasmussen was seated in the chair beside him. Millie and Evelyn quickly pushed their way into two empty chairs at the opposite end of the table.

"As most of you know," Harvey opened, with the usual warm smile that somehow managed to appear to be aimed personally at each one of them, "we don't hold with formality here. We all like to consider ourselves the members of one happy little family. Most of us have been together for some time, and we're familiar with how each person operates and what to expect from one another. So I don't need to remind you that I won't be wasting your valuable time with meetings and with the production of a lot of meaningless bureaucratic paperwork. Not like some of the Education Departments I could mention!"

After a pause for the expected and duly provided laugh, Harvey continued. "As you're all aware, my style of leadership is collegial. And I believe in an egalitarian, or lateral, organizational structure. I like to discuss problems as they arise, on an informal basis, with the people concerned. And I know that you folks favor that as well."

"Why are we here today, then, Dr. Garfinkle?" This from

Muthu, spoken with scarcely veiled amusement. Millie grinned across the table at the pipe-sucking history professor. Evelyn thought of him only in terms of his 'first' name, as this was invariably the way he introduced himself. He had always been a favorite of hers. He told her that he had emigrated from Kerala in India in the early sixties. Obviously he took to Canada like a duck to water, and the ready acceptance was mutual. The fact that there had been a Christian community in Kerala from late Roman times had no doubt been a major factor in the easy adjustment to his adopted country with its similar strong Judeo-Christian roots. Muthu was not Christian himself—nor was he an adherent of any other religion. A self-defined agnostic, he claimed that, in his growing up as a member of the 'Untouchable' caste in India (or Harijan', to use Gandhi's kinder expression) he had directly experienced the fruits of too many religions to believe in any of them. He liked to say that he had `cleansed` himself of religious ideas and rituals in the process of maturing. And that it was this broad early experience of a variety of world views which had motivated him to become a historian, specializing in the historical development of ideas. All in all, Muthu came across as an intensely and authentically scholarly man, yet with none of the tendency to obfuscation so often observed in academics. In fact, Evelyn had noticed that he delighted in puncturing pretensions whenever he sniffed them out among his colleagues, and did so at every opportunity.

"Patience, Professor Muthu." Harvey smiled benignly, not rising to the bait. "The Dean has called my attention to a few matters that we have to settle. The first is this business of the BEAD program in Secondary Education. You are all probably aware that I am coordinating it for this initial year. So far we've been asked to provide only one member of the actual teaching team. Our new member of the Department, Millie Eisenstadt, whom I'm sure you all know by now, agreed to take that on as part of her regular class load. I thought that you might want to discuss how we should handle it for another year. I mean, whether we should alternate among the sociology, philosophy and history of our discipline, or whether we should work out an offering that would amount to a combination of all three."

"I've been wondering how it was decided that our one and only contribution to this initial year of the program should be restricted to the Sociology of Education." Muthu was speaking again. "Of course I wouldn't think of suggesting that it had anything to do with the fact that you are yourself a sociologist."

"It all developed rather fast." Harvey joined in the general laughter. "It was during the summer, and to tell the truth, we hadn't given the program much thought until then. Nobody that I spoke to seemed to want to take it on at the last moment. But I'm giving you fair warning now. We're expected to come up with some kind of coordinated approach to our contribution by next year. Meanwhile, Ms. Eisenstadt has been good enough to fill in for us, even if she *has* had to fly by the seat of her pants."

This evoked more laughter, even from Millie, who obviously noted the covert glances now aimed at her overly ample rear end, overlapping—as needs it must—the rather inadequate seat of the chair beneath her.

"I move that we postpone this discussion until later in the term, seeing that Dr. Eisenstadt no doubt has the course well in hand by now, but won't yet be in a position to evaluate the enterprise. How does that suit you, Millie?" Sam Barnes was obviously attempting to bridge the awkward moment and acknowledge Millie's contribution at the same time. She smiled at him as she answered.

"Why yes. I think by the end of this first year I should have a good idea of what works and what doesn't with a group at that level. At least I'll be able to share my experience with the Department so that we can firm up plans for a more permanent offering. I'm not at all sure that *I'll* want to continue with it, however, as I'd like to concentrate next year on courses more directly related to my own recent work, if that's likely to be possible."

Harvey referred to his notes and cleared his throat to speak, but Muthu interrupted.

"I'd like to hear what ideas you might have for new courses, Dr. Eisenstadt. After all, it's not every year that we get someone fresh from PhD studies in another country, and a well-published author at that. We need some new input here."

Millie barely hesitated. It was obvious, to Evelyn at least, that she had been thinking of this for some time.

"For one thing, I'd like to offer something for our grad students on the nature of knowledge, exploring both the strengths and weaknesses of recent developments in the Sociology of Knowledge and in the Philosophy of Science."

"And just what does knowledge have to do with Education?" asked Harvey, with a chuckle. "This is not the Philosophy Department in the Faculty of Arts, as you must surely be aware by now."

"Granted," Millie responded, a noticeable flush engulfing her face. "But it does seem to me that a Faculty of Education might be expected to consider, in a disciplined way, the nature, justification and historical sources of those beliefs which our society has specifically designated us to pass on to the upcoming generations. Not to mention the possibility that a better understanding of the nature of knowledge and of the knowledge-building process might help teachers produce students more adequately equipped to be producers as well as transmitters of culture."

"Well then, culture! That's scarcely the same thing as knowledge, dear girl." This came from Dr. Willard Grange, his precise diction and rather high voice tending to emphasize the supercilious manner now directed toward Millie. "I think our Department can safely leave matters concerning the nature of knowledge to those qualified for the task, Harvey. And we'll let the sociologists and anthropologists in the Faculty of Social Science handle culture and social norms and whatever it is they do. Much better people than you and I have been puzzling over the nature of knowledge for a good many centuries, Ms. Eisenstadt. I advise you not to worry your head about it."

The amused glance accompanying Dr. Grange's comment took in the assembled group, and there was a ripple of answering laughter from some members while others—particularly the historians—looked uncomfortable. Millie was silent.

Once again Harvey referred to his notes. Evelyn asked if a seconder to Sam's motion was in order. Harvey Garfinkle, in simulated horror, reiterated his refrain about the advantages of informality. The meeting went on for what seemed to her to be an unnecessarily long time, leaping from subject to subject as many of the participants seized the opportunity to express to the Department as a whole their pet peeves about the lack of preparation of the students in their classes, and the 'Mickey Mouse' nature of many of the courses offered by the Teaching Methods Department. Evelyn had long since concluded that it was safer not to put herself forward by speaking too much or too assertively—either at these gatherings or at the more regular and comprehensive Faculty meetings. Except for Millie and a couple of educational psychologists who had recently joined the Faculty of Education, all of her female colleagues taught Methods courses. Like Helen Korensky, they were, for the most part, hard-working and competent in their chosen fields, but felt no need to participate in larger concerns within the university. Once, as a newcomer, Evelyn had engaged in an argument at a general Faculty meeting on a policy issue only to discover that her contribution was met with stony silence from the men and not-a-few embarrassed sidelong glances from the women in attendance. Always alert to nuances in the social climate, she had resolved never again to risk her chances of promotion by placing herself in that position.

Now, as the wayward discussion waxed and waned about her, she was suddenly alerted by Millie pounding her fist on the table in her usual exuberant manner, and wished that she had warned her not to challenge her male colleagues. In fact Millie shouldn't have needed reminding, seeing that she had suggested to Evelyn just the other day that Harvey's surface congeniality and informality might well be a mask for an overruling need to control. A few moments earlier he had mentioned a request from the Dean for input from their Department into the student-teaching component of the program for the following year. Millie was now enthusiastically endorsing this move and offering to participate. Evelyn noticed that her friend was being studied in a calculating way by Gus Rasmussen as she presented her views on the subject. Today, in his sloppy sweater and jeans, Gus could easily have been taken for one of his students. He seemed vaguely amused by Millie's stout advocacy of active student-teaching responsibility for the Foundations people—something they had apparently always steadfastly refused to assume at NPU—and, as she elaborated on the reasons, he exchanged meaningful looks with Harvey.

Evelyn knew that both Willard Grange and Ned Smith—the two philosophers who were now volubly disagreeing with Millie—were proponents of 'linguistic analysis', as were most who taught Philosophy of Education in these decades. This particular philosophical perspective was based on the idea that most (if not all) of the issues debated by philosophers could, if appropriately analyzed, be reduced to merely differing interpretations of the terminology involved. Only Leslie Brittan, the third member of the philosophy contingent, had somehow resisted the popular analytic approach. In fact, he liked to tease his colleagues by labeling their model as amusingly oxymoronic, in that, although the movement claimed to advocate the need for clarity of language and thought, its practitioners were noted for their inability to provide a clear explanation of what their theory was all about. Les was, instead, deeply entrenched in the radical revolution-based theories of Jean Paul Sartre, Herbert Marcuse and Franz Fanon. Stanley Wheeler, colleague of Muthu and Sam in the History of Education group, was interested primarily in what was becoming known as Comparative Education. Evelyn now noticed that he had plunged into the discussion in support of the increasingly beleaguered Millie.

"Perhaps a little time in the school classroom every term would help to keep us focused on our real task . . . preparing people who can actually teach and who understand what should be taught and how to motivate children to learn it," he suggested.

"We only wish it were as simple as that, Stan." Harvey's

voice was loaded with the weight of the burden of esoteric knowledge clearly not available to mere practitioners. "At any rate, I'm sure we don't want to rush into anything at this time. I'll discuss this in depth later with any of you who might be interested. And now, there's the little matter of the Philosophy of Education Conference at the University of Oregon in late November. I understand that Professor Brittan is presenting a critique of a controversial new book, and Professors Granger and Smith have submitted proposals for papers as well. I have requested funds for all three to attend the conference. I'm sure you will be in agreement on that. We'll just leave it to the people concerned to arrange for transportation and accommodation."

"Why yes!" Millie exclaimed. "I believe that must be the conference where I've been invited to present a paper on my doctoral thesis."

"I hardly think so." Dr. Brittan shot a glance at his two colleagues. "It happens to be a *philosophy* conference, Ms. Eisenstadt. I very much doubt that they would have asked *you*." His condescension was only slightly veiled, and Evelyn could see Millie's eyebrows shoot up. She searched desperately for a bland comment, hoping to ward off an explosion that could only harm her friend's prospects. But when Millie finally responded it was with surprising restraint.

"I don't rightly know why I was invited. It could be because my specialization is social theory. I expect you'll find that I encroach on your field somewhat. When they contacted me, they specifically mentioned my book, which actually deals quite a bit with philosophy."

"Maybe we'll be able to persuade one of our local philosophers to review *your* book, Millie." Stan Wheeler laughed delightedly.

Evelyn was relieved that Harvey chose that point to

return to his agenda. She was aware, as Millie did not seem to be, that their new colleague's impressive publishing record was a sore spot with some of the members of the Department. One more item, they were now told. It seemed that the Women's Cultural Revolution had decided to focus on the Faculty of Education for this year. Cynthia Montague had not been a member, but her death had now provided the movement with a needed catalyst. Harvey was all sympathy with the feminist cause, but he could not quite see what Cynthia's accident had to do with sexism. Could any of them help him out? Had not Cynthia always been well treated by the Department—favored even, over their two male graduates? He'd leave the matter with them. Maybe they could, as individuals, persuade the women's movement that, although there might indeed be rampant discrimination within the larger tradition-bound Education Faculty, the situation was totally different in their own admittedly maverick and, yes, even 'revolutionary' area.

"Let us all welcome them into our classes", he said, as he closed the meeting. "Let them learn first hand that we in the Foundations of Education Department are at the forefront of the feminist revolution."

CHAPTER 4

NOVEMBER, 1976

There were times when Evelyn felt that the autumn weather in the rain forest of the northwest coastal area was simply not to be borne—not by humans, at any rate. Day after sunless, dreary day, she trudged through the 'low cloud' to her classes, passing other unrecognizable rain-coated creatures bent, like herself, into the moisture-laden off-sea breeze. The only change came on the days when an all-enveloping smog descended suddenly and those in the building who commuted by car—students and professors alike—began to look out the windows with such obvious unease that teaching became almost impossible. Even more unsettling to the class, it seemed, was the appearance of snowflakes on the windows. Evelyn soon discovered that there was good reason for this. Indeed, a fall of snow, an event rather uncommon in that part of Canada, tended to leave roadside carnage in its wake. Evelyn's first experience of a British Columbia Lower Mainland snowfall had been one of unmitigated surprise and puzzlement, as she watched the members of her class silently pick up their books and melt away in mid-lecture. Although she usually walked the two miles to work, she had brought her car that day with the intention of driving up to Vancouver after classes. Only when she had left the flatness of the delta behind and found herself being forced into a weird version of stunt driving in order to avoid the cars zigzagging backwards down the slopes toward her, did she appreciate the wisdom of her students' decision.

Today something other than the winter climate was adding to her sense of general malaise. Recently, she had found the atmosphere inside the Education building fully as dreary as the weather outside—and only slightly more enlightening. Friction, utterly unacknowledged by the leadership, was festering just below the surface.

As usual, Millie was at the center of it, but seemingly unaware of what was happening. At least she had not revealed any further personal problems or worries, although Evelyn noticed that her old friend was unnaturally quiet and becoming daily more distant. No further Departmental meetings had been called, so there had been no opportunity for Millie to repeat, in a formal setting, her queries about financial support and transportation to the coming conference in Eugene, Oregon. Lunch and coffee breaks in the general faculty lounge were the only opportunity for the Foundations people to gather for any in-depth conversation.

However, around mid-November, faculty concerns of every hue suddenly faded into the background. The subject of daily gatherings became the surprise election of René Lévesque, leader of the French-speaking separatist party in Quebec. There was a widely shared concern about what the implications might be for the country as a whole if the new Premier were to be successful in making that province a separate nation. However, most of those entering the spirited conversation appeared to feel there was a possibility that the election, though cataclysmic, might benefit Canada in the long run.

"If it helps to lift Trudeau's Liberals out of their current malaise, by making them face up to the real possibility of the country's break-up, it might be worth it." Stan Wheeler mused in the lounge one day.

"Take it from me. Absolutely nothing is going to revitalize the Liberal Party." This from Sam Barnes who, Evelyn had noticed, was the only one of their group who remained stubbornly in support of Joe Clark: the awkwardly honest young Conservative leader and would-be Prime Minister.

"He's the best hope," Sam now claimed, "against the new threat to Canada's future clearly posed by that charismatic rascal, Lévesque. Of course, I realize there's no way I can convince you guys of that, what with your ongoing infatuation with the New Democrats."

Evelyn disagreed with Sam on this, as on most issues. She, like the majority of her colleagues, had great respect for the federal New Democrats, Canada's official party of the Left. And especially for its earnest leader, Ed Broadbent, who had assumed leadership two years before.

"I know why you're so fond of Joe Clark," she decided to tease Sam a bit. "I've just realized that he's very much like you."

"Would that *any* politicians were as straightforward as our Sam!" Stan Wheeler interposed. "But I do have to admit that Clark may be the best of the current bunch in that regard."

"Who would *you* select for the honor, Evelyn?" asked Sam.

"What about Dave Barrett?'" she responded readily. Barrett, the current leader of the provincial arm of the New Democratic Party, was Premier of British Columbia from 1972 until being voted out of office only last year. Evelyn had followed that election closely, and was fascinated to learn at the time that what was now known as the NDP had originated, not in British Columbia as she first thought, but in the province of Saskatchewan. She was told by the historians that its roots had been planted by the Regina Manifesto, drafted back in 1933 by two professors: Frank Underhill of the University of Toronto and F. R. Scott of McGill. And that it had originally been called the Cooperative Commonwealth Federation. They said that the party changed its name in 1961. And then, the new Saskatchewan NDP (inspired by a lawyer named Emmett Hall and the Premier of the time, Tommy Douglas) had pioneered what eventually became a country-wide universal Medicare scheme. All this only added to the impression Evelyn had formed, by then, of a distinctive (even un-American) quality about the country. She had to admit that, ever since her arrival in 1969, she had found Canadian politics surprisingly intriguing. And no wonder, she now thought, given the interesting history that her colleagues were always ready to recount for her benefit. And the perennially exciting present! And the variety of controversial leaders!

"Evelyn, your commitment to the New Democrats is admirable, but I seem to recall that you were once similarly staunch in your support of Pierre Elliott Trudeau." The mischievous comment came from Muthu, who had been listening quietly throughout the exchange. "Whatever happened to your enthusiasm for the Liberal Party?"

Evelyn felt a surge of embarrassment at being reminded of the time, soon after settling into her university position, when she had found herself falling head over heels in love with the engaging Prime Minister Trudeau. Of course, Millie had previously told her about this remarkable man. As

Evelyn became immersed in the national news soon after her arrival in the country, she was surprised that she could agree with her friend on this subject at least. However, in late 1970, Trudeau did something that caused her to see him as an enemy forever after, and restored Millie and herself to their usual status as friendly political antagonists.

Evelyn remembered how, in early October of that year, they had witnessed the explosion of the notorious crisis concerning the *Front de Liberation du Quebec* (FLQ). Whenever she thought about it, she found herself experiencing anew the rush of emotion aroused by the stress and excitement of that time. None of her colleagues could predict what the daily news would bring, and what it would mean to the security and even survival of the country. It all began with the kidnapping of James Cross, the British Trade Commissioner, by a group of anarchists claiming to be fighting in the cause of freeing Quebec from the domination of English Canada. Two days later, the faculty members gathered around the radio in the lounge and listened wordlessly to the broadcast of the Anarchist Manifesto. They applauded when Prime Minister Trudeau steadfastly refused to deal with the terrorists, and were united in their scorn for Robert Bourassa, the Quebec Premier, as he appeared to vacillate. Until, that is, the fateful day of October tenth, when Evelyn arrived at work to hear that Pierre Laporte, the Quebec Deputy Premier, had been kidnapped. This time she and her colleagues exchanged relieved and approving comments when Bourassa, with his provincial police showing signs of exhaustion, requested the help of the Canadian army. Obviously he had also become alarmed by the fact that Montreal's university students were rallying in the cause of the anarchists; and the province's elites were beginning to succumb publicly to pressure to negotiate with the FLQ. However, Evelyn later recalled experiencing a strong feeling of discomfort when, in immediate response to Bourassa's request, Trudeau asked Parliament to pass the War Measures Act.

Soon after that, Pierre Laporte was found murdered by his captors, and subsequently several hundred innocent Quebec citizens were rounded up and arrested. Although, at the time, Sam was quick to point out that it was the provincial authorities who were responsible for the extremity of this response, Evelyn couldn't buy it. It was at this moment that she had suddenly emerged from what she was later to refer to as her 'Trudeaumania' phase. Predictably, however, she discovered during several phone calls that Millie disagreed vehemently with her change of heart. Evelyn was informed that Trudeau's stand was the only one possible.

"Wait and see," Millie said. "There will be no more terrorism in Quebec! And," she added, "Trudeau's move may well take the wind out of the sails of all those 'mindlessly marching Maoists' who are threatening the lives of the political leaders out there in your 'Lotus Land' as well." *How typical of Millie's exaggerations*, Evelyn had thought at the time.

"How can you possibly support such authoritarian measures?" she asked. "How can a man as intelligent as Trudeau not understand that he's propelling the country down a dangerously slippery slope?" Now totally disillusioned with him, it seemed to her that Trudeau had revealed himself as a slimy, unprincipled liberal pragmatist of the worst order. Millie's response was, again, all too typical.

"Pierre Trudeau is very far from being unprincipled," came her spirited reply. "He just doesn't cut the world up into two neat boxes of absolutes. What you view as the holy white one of socialism (on this issue bedded down, somewhat contradictorily, with libertarianism) and the evil black one of right-wing conservative authoritarianism. It seems to me," she continued, assuming what Evelyn had once labeled her 'holier-than-thou philosophical mantle', "that all the really difficult moral issues actually *do* inhabit a grey area of . . . yes, 'slippery slopes' if you will, going every which way as far as the eye can see, with the precise effects of every choice impossible to predict. I think Trudeau's job as leader right now is to hold fast to basic principles. In other words, he has to keep his eyes on the horizon defined by the concepts of democracy and the rule of law. And at the same time, he has to try to figure which path (slippery or otherwise) will ultimately lead toward that horizon."

When Evelyn interrupted to ask what in the world she was getting at, Millie continued unabashed.

"I mean which course, among the choices available to him, is most likely to have the best long-term consequences for Canadian society as a whole. Sure, maybe at times this calls for a temporary curtailment of a few individual freedoms for the greater freedom of the entire social group over the long term. But I fully agree with what Trudeau cited as his guiding principle on the matter. He said that *'so long as an illegitimate power exists which actively seeks to replace the power of elected representatives in a democratic state, then that power must be stopped in its tracks'*. Like him, I would say it's only 'bleeding hearts' who don't understand what's at stake. And I'm betting that history will prove him right. On this, at least."

Evelyn had been rendered temporarily speechless by Millie's diatribe. As so often happened in their friendship (and considering that they were speaking on the phone, and long distance at that) the two finally had to agree to disagree. But she had been surprised to discover that Muthu, when she told him about the conversation, supported Millie.

"I can think of a number of historical situations where personal liberties in democracies have had to be limited, temporarily, for the greater good," he said. "For example, there were the British people in those agonizing days in the spring of 1940, when all their European Allies were falling before the onslaught of Hitler. Mussolini was joining forces with him and Stalin appeared willing to do the same; and you Americans were continuing to stand aloof. Almost to a person, the Brits gladly accepted limits to individual freedom, with no whining. They knew only too well what was at stake. For that brief, critical period in the war, Britain stood virtually alone. With the support, of course, of the Canadians and other former colonies. And, because Winston Churchill had the courage and farsightedness to take the difficult stand that the situation demanded, the world was saved from the Nazis. But it could not have been done had not the British people remained together behind Churchill, ready to sacrifice much more for freedom from totalitarianism than a mere temporary suspension of personal liberties."

"By the way," he added with a trace of his habitual wry chuckle, "when I say the Canadians were supportive perhaps I should not include the province of Quebec. I understand there was some reluctance expressed there."

Evelyn had been taken aback by the fervor of Muthu's response. It was quite unlike his usual detached, sardonic self. She realized she must have touched a nerve. She was forced to recognize anew that there was much about recent history that she had not been taught in her American schools. Certainly, she had no previous awareness of any critical time in World War II when the United States was not assuming the major role. And to think that Canada was totally committed at that early stage! Except for the notoriously independent-minded Quebec? And now, once more, Quebec's struggle for separation from Canada—or for 'Sovereignty'—was in the news. And in the conversation of her colleagues. *Never a dull moment in Canadian politics*, Evelyn thought as the opinions ebbed and flowed around her in the lounge, bringing welcome surges of emotional stimulation to these dark November days.

It was only after the excitement from this seminal national event had declined somewhat that Millie was able to resume her increasingly desperate attempts to elicit information about whatever plans may have been put in place for the trip to the conference. But Evelyn couldn't help notice that she was drawing a total blank in terms of helpful response.

"I really would like to know who's intending to drive down to Oregon next week," she heard Millie blurt out rather desperately during lunch in the faculty lounge one day. "I'd gladly use my car if it's needed, or I'll help buy the gas for anyone else who prefers to drive. Will we be taking three vehicles or two?"

This was addressed in a general way to the philosophers whom Millie had approached as they were busily engaged in a conversation among themselves in a corner of the room. The talk stopped abruptly, and for a moment there was an uncomfortable silence during which Ned Smith and Willard Grange exchanged meaningful glances.

"I understand that the Departmental office has a list of participants and others looking for rides." Les Brittan's hesitant response, when it finally came, was accompanied by an uncomfortable clearing of the throat and nervous stroking of his beard. "Just confirm that your name is there and I'm sure the matter will be attended to by the staff", he finished lamely.

"And now", he continued his interrupted discussion with Ned Smith, "back to the question of whether or not Jean Paul Sartre is an 'essentialist'. I would argue that, indeed, he is not. In fact, he is the extreme opposite. He was a rebel against the reigning 'essentialism' of the time. Anyone who has perused his Existentialism thoroughly should be aware of that."

"That misogynous bull-shitter!" Millie's uninvited opinion echoed across the room. "Sartre's so full of contradictions that he assumes the very premise that his theory denies. Consider, for a minute, his conclusion about there being no such thing as human nature because there is no God to have created it! Sartre begins by taking for granted the old Aristotelian gospel of everything having been divinely created with its 'essential nature' intact and unalterable. Of course that axiom, when combined with his denial of the existence of a creative divinity, forces him to reject the possibility of a human nature of any kind. Even a social or a biological one. All the stupid bastard has to do is to recognize what any biologists or social scientists worth their salt could have told him. Human nature is not something fixed by God, or by Aristotle and Augustine as his spokespersons, but is evolving all the time within the species, and continuously developing with experience in the case of individuals."

These remarks, delivered in the full fire of Millie's boundless enthusiasm for ideas, appeared to strike the three philosophers as particularly pernicious heresy put forth by a know-nothing upstart blatantly ignorant of the finer rules of philosophical discourse and terminology. Obviously they considered both the approach and the comments unworthy of response. Propelled from their seats almost as one 'essential nature', they headed for the exit. Evelyn couldn't help but think that they made an interesting procession: tall and willowy Willard Granger, like a bird in flight, neck projected forward and an almost shocked expression on the narrow face as he took the lead in a rush to the exit; the youthful Ned Smith in his business suit and neat mustache following in angry silence; and the grey-haired, bearded Les Brittan snorting in either scorn or amusement, as he ambled along in their wake. Millie was left staring after them with a wondering, somewhat lost look, while the remaining faculty gradually resumed their various conversations, some with obvious discomfort but more than a few with barely concealed glee.

Evelyn rose at once to join Millie, and noticed both Abdul Issa and Stan Wheeler approaching as well. A warm, concerned expression was registered on the historian's craggy features, and he drew the fingers of one hand through his head of wayward hair as he appeared to search for a comforting comment. Abdul rushed in to fill the void.

"You are not to worry about getting to the conference," he said. "It is not at all necessary for you to join those inflated egos for the drive to Oregon. Think of the boredom! I am quite sure that you would prefer to travel alone. But I have a better idea. I am proposing to accompany you, Millie. I have not crossed the border since arriving in Canada and have been awaiting a good opportunity to do so." Evelyn's offer followed quickly on the heels of Abdul's.

"I've been looking for an excuse to get back to the States for a few days," she exclaimed. "Let's the three of us make a party of it!"

"I was going to suggest that my wife and I go along as well, just to hear your presentation, Millie," Stan chuckled. "But it looks as if you've already got a carload."

Millie smiled gratefully at the other three and they moved as a group to join the ongoing conversation in another corner of the room. Helen Korensky, leaning animatedly toward Muthu, was describing the latest moves by the Women's Cultural Revolution.

"Have you heard that they're digging up the Cynthia Montague affair, calling it 'unfinished business' and implying that the faculty have been involved in some kind of a 'cover up'?", she asked the group as they approached. Evelyn was skeptical.

"I haven't heard anything remotely like that," she assured them. "And I've been seeing something of the women who are doing the organizing and actually leading the movement. In fact," she laughed, "I'm seriously considering throwing my weight as an instructor behind them, to give them a little more credibility in the university as a whole. It *is* true that they referred to Cynthia at the only meeting I attended, but the discussion chiefly concerned a proposal to do something to respect her memory as a fellow female who had come to harm a long way from home. I rather like the idea myself. I have to admit that I've never felt comfortable about that incident, and with the way we all seem bent on pretending that it never happened."

"Bully for them!" Millie exclaimed. "I'm still puzzled about it all as well, and I think that someone should at least be discussing it, if only to learn from Cynthia's mistakes. If her own mistakes actually were the cause of her death."

"That's just it!" Helen Korensky was not one to back off once she had introduced a subject. "They're saying right out that it *was not* an accident. That there's something sinister about the whole thing. And they're pointing the finger at certain men in this faculty. They may well have a point," she added thoughtfully. "For instance, I've always wondered just what went on after most of us had left that party. Abdul, you stayed behind, as I recall. Did you notice anything wrong with Cynthia when she left? And did she really go home alone?"

"I . . . I am not exactly sure about that." Abdul spoke hesitantly. "I can only tell you the facts as I presented them at the coroner's inquest into her death. I offered to accompany her because I was somewhat concerned about her condition, but she said she had a friend waiting outside, someone she could depend on to do the driving. At the time I assumed that it was a girlfriend who had either gone out ahead to get her car, or had arranged to come by and pick her up. Since then I have wondered if the person she expected had really seen her safely to her door, and wished many times that I had at least made sure that she was not alone when she actually left. Especially when she was found in her own vehicle . . . and no one has ever admitted to having driven her home."

In the ensuing silence it seemed that everyone was engrossed in digesting Abdul's revelation. Strangely enough, he had never before mentioned it to them.

"It'll be ironic if our Women's Cultural Revolution *does* take up Cynthia's cause," Sam finally spoke. When Helen asked what he meant, he wondered aloud how someone representing everything the feminists were rebelling against could conceivably be made into a heroine of the women's movement.

"Now you can't just stop there, Sam," Millie said. "Remember, some of us weren't around here before this term. Explain yourself."

"Well . . ." Sam appeared to be choosing his words carefully. "It's my understanding that modern feminists are opposed to all this business of girls resorting to feminine wiles to further their careers. Of course, I'd be the first to admit that it's the fault of the men who exploit them, and thereby put themselves into the position where they can be used by their victims in turn. It's also the fault of a system that maintains such men in positions of power over women, and provides their victims with no recourse. I agree with all that, and up to that point I suppose I'm a feminist. But in no way was Cynthia rebelling against the system. She was happily using it, and very cleverly too, to get what she wanted. I know one shouldn't speak ill of the dead, but I had some problems with Cynthia in the class she took from me a couple of years ago. She didn't appear to be doing any of the required reading, and her work wasn't nearly up to par. Her performance in my class just didn't jibe with her record, either here or in England. The thing is, she was continually coming into my office, not for help with her work but merely to chat, and if I weren't such an old, unattractive, married stick-in-the-mud, I would have thought that she was trying to flirt with me. And when she discovered that she wasn't going to get marks out of me by those means, she turned all tearful, accusing me of having led her on. My wife Mary could have told her that crying doesn't work with me. I ended up ordering her not to come back to my office ever again, and gave her failing marks for the course. Thank goodness, I heard no more from her."

Here was a revelation that seemed to render Abdul's previous information insignificant. For once even Helen Korensky was momentarily immobilized. Then she began to murmur, haltingly. "But it does, you know. Jibe with her record I mean. I looked up her official transcript after the tragedy and discovered her marks were strangely erratic. Very high or else extremely low."

"This term...", began Muthu, then cleared his throat. "This term Cynthia had signed up for my graduate-level class on Twentieth Century Educational Thought. I suppose she was attempting once more to pick up her required course in the History of Education. Of course I did not yet know much about her work, but I had gained the distinct impression that she may have been in over her head where advanced study was concerned. She appeared rather lost whenever the lectures and discussions involved abstract ideas. But I must admit that, for the brief time that I knew her, she managed to resist the fascination of my masculine prowess."

Although this induced a restrained chuckle from most of the others, as was typical with Muthu's droll, self-deprecating remarks, Abdul merely frowned down at his coffee cup for a few minutes. Ignoring Muthu's contribution, he began to speak slowly.

"That is a very ugly story you have just told us, Sam, especially since Cynthia is no longer here to speak for herself. And what does it say about her other male professors here? For example, I gave her a passing grade last year in my advanced class on Social Studies Methods. Does that mean that she earned it in some way other than by scholarship? Assignations, rather than assignments ... is that what you intend to imply?"

"So what if it is, Abdul?" This from Gus, who had been, as usual, listening in from the outer edge of the group. "Why does that make *you* so hot under the collar all of a sudden?"

Abdul turned as if to reply to Gus, but at the same moment Sam, looking distinctly uncomfortable, gathered up his books and stood up, with the result that his bulk was between the other two.

"Sorry you choose to view it in that light," he said. "You can see why I hesitated to mention it before. But the fact remains that it happened, and it may even be important for us, as a faculty, to consider it carefully in light of what occurred in September."

Later that afternoon, in the quiet of her office, Evelyn thought again about Sam's revelation. She found herself overwhelmed by a mixture of emotions. Unlike some of the others, she had no doubt whatsoever that his claims were true. It was because of the semi-detached position of her office and that of Sam; the fact that they were separated from one another only by a partial wall. Furthermore, anyone going to see him had to pass her (usually open) door, as they were located in a row of offices off a hallway ending with a fire door used only for emergencies. Last term she had seen Cynthia going to and from Sam's office too many times to count. In fact, for several years, the sound of Sam's loud voice in discussions with students had been a nuisance when she was attempting to concentrate on her own side of the shared cell. She was thus already all-too-aware of his problems with Cynthia, and of the nature of the final denouement.

At the moment, however, Sam's story—and what it had indeed implied about at least some of his fellow male faculty members—was pushing her backward in time. She thought of her own years as an undergraduate, then again of her experience at New Oxford. Of her innocent susceptibility, her overriding, family-instilled ambition. Had she, like Cynthia, been too ready to allow herself to be used by some of her male professors—those exalted beings whose fond attentions, when she first realized that they were being directed to her in a special way, had flattered and thrilled her so, with the implicit promise of an unlimited future of mutual high-status collegiality?

She recalled the first time, her first real experience of sex with a man. It had been in her second semester of university. The occasion was a party at the apartment of a young male teaching assistant in anthropology. They had been sampling LSD during the evening. She was relatively new to the drug, and in her fuzzy state had been easily persuaded to remain behind. Nothing promised on either side, but had she really been so naive as not to be aware that it would harm her prospects if she turned him down? After that it became progressively easier to acquiesce whenever and with whomever a similar occasion arose. Now, looking back from her current situation as Abdul's lover, she realized that those sordid early experiences had never been even remotely fulfilling for her, either sexually or emotionally. But it was what they had done to her sense of self worth that she regretted most. They were undoubtedly the source of the need for reassurance from Abdul that never seemed to be satisfied; of her continuing concerns that, yet again, she was allowing herself to be used by a male, in a partnership marked by inequality of commitment.

In her graduate-student days she had persuaded herself to count a few casual sexual encounters as merely part of the cost of getting where she wanted to go, in a social climate where that sort of compromise was expected from the relatively few females who made it to the top. But now, for the first time, she forced herself to face an appalling fact that any call girl could have told her—she had sold herself too cheaply. A wave of long-submerged anger rushed over her. What it all came down to in the end was that she had allowed herself to be used by sophisticated charmers in positions of power who hadn't really viewed her as anything more than a convenient receptacle for their semen. It didn't make the realization any more pleasant to recall that some of these men had been prestigious scholars, for this memory forced her to face once again the humiliating fact that they had been careful not to risk their reputations by ever being seen with her in public. Was that why she had covertly resented Millie's stubborn intransigence at New Oxford? Was it what her 'holier than thou' attitude had implied about the rest of them who had long since learned to 'play the game'? Was it because Millie had inadvertently forced her to take fresh measure of her own actions? And what about her years in academia since? Why hadn't she, Evelyn Ashton-Brent, like the young members of today's Women's Cultural Revolution, taken a stand against a system that allowed this sort of thing to happen to inexperienced young girls? Well, perhaps it was not too late. Here, before her, was an instrument that she could help hone for just such a purpose. She would devote herself from now on to the battle for equal rights for women in university. Cynthia Montague would be the last victim—at least on the campus of North Pacific University! Deliberately without giving herself time to reconsider, she walked over to the phone, picked it up and called Meredith Walker.

The morning of the trip to the conference dawned dark and windy, with a steady downpour of driving rain. The night before, Evelyn had discovered with a flash of disappointment that Abdul's plans had altered at the last moment; that he was to meet with Harvey Garfinkle this very day, over some pressing Faculty matter. She was mildly curious as to what it could possibly be. Abdul, in his temporary position as a Lecturer in Teaching Methods and one whose position came up for renewal each year, would not ordinarily be involved in administrative concerns, and especially not with those beyond his own Department

So the two women set out alone. At least, thought Evelyn, this avoids any momentary embarrassment about hotel rooms. Only a couple of these had been available near the university at this late date, and she had expected Abdul to agree with her suggestion that the two of them share. It would have been a great opportunity to break the news of their relationship to Millie. But it seemed that this was not to be. Obviously, privacy as to sexual encounters was to remain, for Abdul, the preferred order of existence.

Evelyn decided to seize the opportunity of the enforced companionship of the long ride to quiz Millie a bit further on her employment status.

"I haven't been able to nail Harvey down on anything," was the answer. "He keeps telling me that it's out of his hands. He says that the Dean's office won't be firming up the permanent Associate Professor position until late spring. But I'd feel better if he at least promised that it would be mine when it *is* available, as he did most effusively on the phone before I burned my bridges and settled in here. Gawd, but he's a wily bastard! I don't feel that I can trust him, but I'm trapped now and he knows it. If I leave after only one year here it will look as if there's something terribly wrong with me. It will be the same whether I depart voluntarily or with a push. I certainly won't be able to count on any honest evaluation or recommendations from Harvey or Gus, as fellow sociologists, and there's bound to be gossip about what actually happened here. And now it's beginning to look as if the philosophers have it in for me as well."

"Well at least you know the historians in the Department aren't gunning for you. Sam, Stan and Muthu all seem to admire you and enjoy our discussions. And I happen to know that you're well respected by the Ed. Psych. and Methods people. Also, you can be sure that *I'll* give you a good recommendation to anyone who asks."

"But what I want to know is, just what's going on with

the others? I've never had any trouble getting along with my colleagues before. At worst, I've been tolerated for my big mouth and subjected to a degree of good-natured teasing. Why the big freeze here from almost the first day?"

Evelyn had to struggle to come up with an honest but palatable answer for that. How could she tell Millie that much of the problem stemmed from her own personality, combined with an almost aggressive confidence and obvious competence not only in sociology but in related areas as well?

"Could it be that your publishing record is somewhat better than that of most of the members of this faculty?" she suggested. "There's a lot of jealousy in these places, especially when it's a woman who is excelling in what has always been considered a 'man's field'. That would definitely apply where the philosophy of science is concerned." She had scarcely finished the comment when she was struck with an idea.

"Why don't you join me in sponsoring the Women's Cultural Revolution?" she asked. "Then you'd have a ready-made support system. I suspect that Harvey's a bit frightened of them. It's the only reason I can think of to explain his apparently boundless enthusiasm whenever the subject comes up. All of a sudden he's a fervent feminist. Of course he's always claimed to be a left-wing radical, so perhaps I'm misjudging him. Maybe he *is* sincere. Certainly Gus is, as a committed Maoist. It would be a chance for you to get on better terms with both of them. And I believe Abdul is already quite involved in the movement as well."

"I'll think about it. Right now I have a lot of reservations about the line that group is taking. And they haven't really been pounding at my door, you know."

That was as much as Millie seemed willing to divulge about her problems and worries and, for the remainder of the drive down the rugged Oregon coast to the city of Eugene, the conversation focused on the coming conference. It was to begin in the late afternoon with an introductory session and refreshments and, as it turned out, there was little time for the two of them to freshen up after their arrival and registration in the hotel where most of the people attending the conference were housed. The evening was spent happily renewing old acquaintances at the welcoming ceremonies in the large conference hall of the university. By bedtime, Evelyn was pleased to notice that Millie had regained her bounce and in general was looking and acting much more like her old self. They returned to their rooms late and said goodnight immediately, as Millie's paper was slated for first thing in the morning.

It happened that Evelyn slept in and discovered her friend long gone when she went down to breakfast. After eating hurriedly and rushing over to the university she slipped into a back seat in the lecture theater where the presentation had already begun. She had been aware of the general thesis of Millie's doctoral dissertation, and had even scanned a few chapters of her book, but not until she listened for some time to the concise argument being laid before the audience did she realize just how inflammatory the content actually was. The usual time constraints of conference schedules were now forcing Millie to approach the conclusion of her talk, and she was summing up her main points in her typical forthright manner.

"Perhaps this all-too-brief summary will help you to understand how my attempt to analyze and explain the lack of any real progress during the first seven decades of this century in the social sciences (and, consequently, the formal study of education) has led me to identify a number of key obstacles that are, sooner or later, going to have to be cleared away. And what are they?" Millie began counting these off on her fingers.

"Well, in the first place, for decades we've had an uncritical acceptance by the opinion leaders within anthropology of a thoroughgoing cultural relativism. This position was rooted in the Romantic Idealism inherited from Hegel and others, and spread throughout Europe and into North America by Franz Boas. Second, we've been burdened for far too long by a similarly uncritical acceptance, by sociologists, of Marxism and its modern derivative, Karl Mannheim's 'Sociology of Knowledge'. And third, we've experienced, within the social sciences as a whole, a general downplaying (if not outright ignoring and denying) of the role of biology in human behavior. And of the complex interplay of genetic and environmental factors in the evolution of our species. Fourth, and similarly unfortunately, there has been an overwhelming acceptance by leaders in the field of psychology of the major premises and implications of Freudian and Jungian psychoanalysis. I grant that many of these psychoanalytic beliefs were originally presented in the context of a crude sort of evolutionary model. But they have since been shown to be narrowly culture-bound rather than of the universal significance that their founders claimed.

Fifth, we've witnessed a corresponding refusal to take into account the work of social behaviorists such as Pavlov and Skinner, and child developmentalists such as John Dewey and Jean Piaget. Their findings appear to indicate numerous critical *cross-cultural similarities* in behavior and cognitive development within the human species (and between our species and other animals) which we sociologists should have been noting. All this has resulted in what I think we can all agree as an additional failing: a general confusion on the part of educators concerning the major concepts and principles of the very knowledge on which their discipline must depend for its validity and reliability. Not surprisingly, this has been accompanied by an inability to agree even on a common language."

Evelyn recognized the dead hush following the applause after Millie's speech as a hint of what was to follow. The first comment came in a steely voice from Ned Smith of NPU. "If I understand what you are saying, Ms. Eisenstadt, all of us poor ignorant social scientists and educators in this room, other than yourself, have been wasting our lives."

"I'm sorry to see you taking this so personally, Professor Smith," Millie replied with a pleasant smile. "But I can't agree that it's too late for you and all the rest of us to learn something new. You appear to me to be young enough to benefit from the opportunity to take out your prejudices now and then, and at least give them a bit of an airing in an open discussion such as this."

But what she's recommending is not new, Evelyn thought. Millie seemed to want to resurrect everything the new wave of social scientists had rebelled against. Surely she was merely spouting the old organic biologism of people like Herbert Spencer and William Graham Sumner, which had culminated in the notorious eugenics of the 1930's! Her unspoken rebuttal was interrupted by the wave of laughter instigated by Millie's response, in the midst of which came the familiar, precisely articulated words of Willard Grange from the other side of the room.

"I am sure that you are quite well aware of the previous speaker's meaning, Ms. Eisenstadt," he said. "You paint with far too broad and far too shallow a brush, if you don't mind my saying so. One cannot help but wonder whatever gave you the impression that educators are universally confused. The entire project of modern analytic philosophy as applied to education has been to clarify the thinking of theorists and practitioners in our discipline. It is obvious that you are totally unaware of this development."

"I've read your work on the subject," came Millie's terse reply. Then, after an uncomfortable pause she continued. "I have to concede that, if your book is an example of analytic philosophy in action, you and your colleagues do indeed succeed in descending into mighty deep waters on behalf of all of us. The only problem is that, at times, you seem to come up more than a bit muddy! But, of course, I recognize that the problem may well lie with me as a reader."

Almost drowned out in the surge of laughter from the audience, the amused voice of Professor Leslie Brittan erupted condescendingly from yet another corner of the room.

"My dear girl . . . er . . . Ms. Eisenstadt. Clearly you do not to understand the very ideas you are presuming to criticize with such abandon. You imply that the well-known Jungian archetypes were necessarily viewed by their creator as being of organic origin within the human species, and therefore represent a crude and internally inconsistent jumble of evolutionary biology and cultural relativism. But that is simply not the case. Modern Jungians consider archetypes to be perfectly consistent with both evolution and cultural relativism, simply because they are *of a different order altogether from biology*. They are, instead, a reflection within the individual psyche of the super-organic realm of culture, as defined by modern anthropology. Both are aspects of a supersensual 'collective unconscious', somewhat related to Freud's 'super ego': a construct of which you do not appear to be aware. Furthermore, all this can be understood in terms of Hegel's *Realms of Pure Being* as expanded upon by Martin Heidegger. But naturally, with your rather outmoded positivistic and rationalistic background, you were not to know all this. Your confusion on this all-important point does, however, considerably weaken the presentation we have just heard. Not to mention your dissertation and the book on social theory which I must admit I have not yet read."

"*Pure Being*. Yes of course. A state of existence above and beyond (and unrelated to) the *merely* physical or material. Now that certainly clarifies everything for all us lesser organic creatures here today. And what a sound foundation it is for a scientific theory from which reliable knowledge of education can be derived for the practice of teaching! I can see lots of testable propositions being generated from *that* model. Yes indeed."

Evelyn was becoming increasingly uneasy, and not only with the ironic nature of Millie's responses which were, admittedly, continuously eliciting appreciative laughter from several quarters. The fact that the concerted attack on Millie was being led by her own colleagues was obvious to Evelyn, if not to the rest of the gathering who were bound to be misled by the fact that the NPU people were—deliberately, it now appeared—widely dispersed around the lecture theater. The disloyalty and pre-planning evidenced by this was what had initially bothered Evelyn. However, as the discussion progressed and her friend continued to fight back with spirited confidence and every appearance of competence, she began to experience another sensation as well. It was a distinct feeling of resentment toward Millie herself. Having not read Millie's work with any thoroughness, she had previously been quite ignorant of the devastating nature of the latter's critique. What on earth could have possessed her friend to attack everything that her own discipline stood for? How could she possibly justify the things she was saying about Franz Boas, and about Margaret Mead's book on *Coming of Age in Samoa*, for instance? And the sophisticated new Marxist-oriented field of 'Sociology of Knowledge' which demonstrated so compellingly the culturally determined nature of even science itself? All this was sacrilege to Evelyn and it placed her in a quandary about how to handle the matter where her colleagues were concerned. She certainly did not want them to think that she agreed with Millie!

Numerous people unknown to Evelyn had now seized a chance to enter the fray, many of whom were (surprisingly, to her) in support of the speaker. Then, one after the other, again from different locations in the room, the two graduate students from the Foundations Department at NPU spoke up. Evelyn was aware that both, unlike Cynthia who had been in her own sociology area, were majoring in the Philosophy of Education. Gerald Davis was the first to rise to his feet.

"I thought we had long since left Social Darwinism behind, at least after we witnessed its culmination in Nazism," he intoned. "But, unfortunately it has entered the academic world once more with that disgusting new book by the Harvard biologist, Edward O. Wilson. *Sociobiology*, I believe it's called. And now I see the same racist message being preached again in Professor Eisenstadt's writings, and hear it being expressed here today."

For the first time Millie was momentarily speechless. Obviously she had recognized the speaker.

"I think, Gerald," she began slowly, "that you might find it helpful, before you graduate with your Masters degree in Education from North Pacific University, to read up a bit on modern genetics and Darwin's *authentic* theory of evolution. And you would also benefit greatly by *actually* reading *Sociobiology: The New Synthesis* before commenting on it. Or isn't that done in graduate school these days? However, the exaggerated hostility of the current mindless mass reaction to Wilson's book on the part of the academic community indicates that you are not alone in failing to understand biological determinism. In the first place, you may be surprised to learn that it was, like the roots of today's cultural relativism, nurtured by French and German philosophers. *Not* by Darwin. These were the very same philosophers who were committed to the Romantic Idealism with its state of 'Pure Being' which became so popular in the late nineteenth century. Likewise, you are not alone in failing to comprehend the difference between that ugly theory and a necessary recognition of the inevitable role that genes and both sexual and natural selection play in human behavior."

"The very fact that one of our own students should be burdened by this misunderstanding," she was now addressing the audience, "indicates a grievous failure on our part as educators of the teachers of the future."

Devastating! Evelyn thought. But not so much for poor Gerald Davis as for Millie's future prospects as a tenured member of the faculty of North Pacific University. Didn't the woman have any common sense at all?

Now it was Tony Kohut's turn. How had these young men got here anyway? Although there had been no funds for Millie's trip, theirs would have had to have been financed by the Department. Evelyn hadn't heard a word about a plan to take the students away from their classes for a two-day foray down to Oregon in the midst of a busy term. Obviously, she now noted, their contributions were well-orchestrated.

"Professor Eisenstadt," Tony seemed not in the least intimidated by Millie's previous comments. Had he taken them in at all? "I've just been reading Thomas Kuhn's book about scientific revolutions. He explains how scientific paradigms such as your obviously 'scientistic' one, and that of cultural relativism and psychoanalysis, don't depend on what is 'out there' in nature as we used to think, but instead originate in the mind of man. He maintains they're simply a matter of consensus and they either rise or fall solely on the basis of political power. And he says that scientific 'truth' is always changing, depending on whose version of reality is politically dominant at the time. Doesn't that show we need a new relativistic philosophy of science? Maybe one built on the 'Sociology of Knowledge'?"

"I'm happy to hear that you're reading Kuhn," Millie sighed as she began her response. "But I think that when you examine his original writings more thoroughly you'll discover that he's not actually saying any of those things." Then, glancing at the chairman who was making exaggerated motions toward his watch, she continued. "I just don't have the time right now to explain Kuhn's revolutionary ideas but perhaps you and I can continue with this some other day, back home at North Pacific University. I *would* like to emphasize, however, that when Thomas Kuhn talks about paradigms he does not mean the models currently held by social scientists. He considers our field to be *proto-scientific*. By that he means it's not yet a true science. The process of paradigm change, in his terms, applies only to a field of study that's already scientific in its methodology and content. He's talking about *authentically* scientific problem areas where one theory has gradually won out over all other contenders. And it has won, *not* because of the political power of its proponents, but because of its power in generating testable and ultimately compellingly confirmed hypotheses. In fact, Kuhn maintains that the achievement of such a consensus on one overarching conceptual framework is the defining characteristic of a paradigm. Furthermore, according to him, it is this very consensus, along with agreement on a common language to describe the phenomena under study, and a common methodology for testing the conjectures generated by the defining theory, that determines whether or not a discipline is indeed a *science*."

As the chairman rose to his feet, Evelyn heard Gus Rasmussen's voice from behind her. *He must have come in after me*, she thought, *and couldn't find a seat.*

"I can't help but wonder about our speaker's qualifications for discussing these highly sophisticated philosophical matters," he said. "Ms. Eisenstadt's background, like mine, is in sociology. I would certainly object if philosophers and historians began to intrude on *my* field of expertise. I shouldn't wonder if philosophers, in their turn, feel somewhat resentful about witnessing this sort of gross oversimplification of their discipline, in a public forum, by a rank outsider who may be ill-equipped to understand the complexities of the ideas under discussion. I would like to suggest that . . ."

The chairman interrupted abruptly at this point, hurriedly thanking the speaker and bringing the session to a close. The extended applause that followed was a surprise to Evelyn but, for Millie's sake, she was relieved to hear it. She was similarly astonished some time later to see the long line-up of people, each with Millie's book in hand, waiting to get it signed by the author.

On the way home the following day Millie appeared immersed in her own thoughts. Evelyn, too, was silent as she considered the damage Millie had wantonly done to her chances for survival at North Pacific University—indeed, in the field of sociology in general. "I can't help but think that much of what you said, and your attack on Margaret Mead in particular, was not only unwarranted but could do long-lasting harm to your future prospects in academia", she finally ventured. "Why did you do it, Millie?"

"I'm not surprised you don't agree with me. As to why I did it, well I had already said all those things in published form, as you must know if you've read my work. I imagine that was why I was asked to speak. I realize my ideas are controversial in our field of studies. But does that mean they shouldn't be expressed? Especially when I believe firmly that they happen to be right? Sure, I'm fighting against an overwhelming current, and sometimes it gets bloody lonely out here. I guess I just have to say, here I stand and, given what my research and logic and common sense have shown me, I can do no other."

"But did you have to question the very veracity of Margaret Mead of all people? And Franz Boas?"

"I merely raised questions about Boas' objectivity and Mead's research. It boggles the mind to believe that she actually found what she claims to have found in Samoa. It's too damn close to what Boas and other opinion molders in anthropology had conditioned her *to expect* to find. Rousseau's archaic myth of a primitive Utopia! It's the sheer unadulterated romanticism of the cultural relativists that raises my hackles. Do you remember Voltaire's comment after reading some of Rousseau's fantasies about the superiority of the 'state of nature'? 'I feel obliged to walk on all fours,' he said."

"You are absolutely hopeless!" In spite of herself Evelyn relaxed into laughter. Her anger at Millie was subsiding, but she couldn't quite drop the subject. "Sometimes I feel that you're still living in the past, Millie," she ventured. "You seem to be so much a part of the old paternalistic masculine mind set, all cold logic and no room for emotion or intuition."

"You mean I 'think like a man'," Millie laughed. "I've been told that before. That my kind of feminism, based on the notion of females being every bit as capable of reasoning as males, and of succeeding in all the subjects formerly considered the sole domain of men, as long as they have equal opportunity, is out of date. And people like me with it. In fact I've even been accused by some of being a lesbian of the type who insists on assuming the male role not only in bed but in every other aspect of life."

Evelyn was momentarily silenced by a rush of guilty embarrassment. She herself had often toyed with precisely that explanation of Millie's success in science and her obvious proficiency in philosophical discourse.

"You must know that I would respect your sexual orientation whatever it is," she hurried to assure her friend. "I think of these matters purely in terms of gender . . . not sex. Just because some of us believe that certain ways of thinking are connected with the fact of being of the male gender, and have been played up disproportionately by our male-dominated culture, doesn't mean that they have anything to do with sexual orientation. The two are very different things."

To Evelyn's disappointment, Millie chose to drop the discussion at that point. For once they had seemed close to the open exchange on sexual preferences that, but for Millie's typical reticence concerning personal subjects, Evelyn would have managed to engineer long before. She was decidedly curious about this aspect of Millie's life. In fact, she would like to have had Millie's lesbianism confirmed, if only so that she would have no cause to worry about the obvious closeness of her relationship with Abdul. They drove the rest of the way home in an uneasy silence in which Evelyn's half-buried resentment of Millie gradually resurfaced.

It remained in the days to follow, as they settled back into the routine of teaching. For she felt her very self to have come under attack in some deep-seated, emotional sense. In fact, it now seemed that the mere presence of Millie was beginning to arouse in her remnants of this feeling of affront and damaged pride in her own accomplishments— a sensation of her very identity as an intellectual having been criticized and found wanting. If this was happening to her, an old and committed friend, how were the opinions of other faculty members likely to have been affected by Millie's reckless behavior?

She began to experience a growing empathy with the leaders of the Women's Cultural Revolution who were now recognizing Millie not as one of them, but as a potential enemy. It seemed, from what Evelyn could gather, that things were going from bad to worse in Millie's B. Ed. After Degree class—or 'BEAD Group' as it was now commonly called. She had overheard numerous conversations about jokes being played on the sociology prof who, in spite of being female, appeared to have acquired a reputation as a sexist. Evelyn was saddened by this, even as she had no doubt at all that Millie was the unknowing instigator of most of her own troubles with that particular class. Interestingly, the problem was indeed confined to the BEAD people. For Evelyn had been informed from numerous sources that Millie's standard undergraduate classes were extremely well-attended and much lauded by the regular Education students.

Evelyn was also aware that part of the problem was the fact that Meredith Walker happened to be in the special 'After Degree' class. *Could it be*, she wondered, *that Millie simply can't cope with another equally strong-minded and assertive female?* But it was not only the feminist contingent in the class whose enmity Millie had gained. As Evelyn understood the story from Meredith, most of the male students had turned against her as well. Meredith had reported with some degree of pride in her newfound organizational skills, that the group was now on the point of progressing from a state of subtle insubordination to one of active rebellion. The entire affair was becoming so puzzling and worrying that Evelyn decided to broach the subject to Abdul at the first opportunity. He was obviously on friendly terms with Millie, in spite of the fact that they were so far apart in world views. Abdul could usually be counted on for a relatively objective assessment of what was going on in the Faculty as a whole. Furthermore, as a non-member but close affiliate of the Foundations Department, he was in a position to view the matter from a less biased perspective than her own. That evening, during one of his nocturnal calls, her chance came when he agreed to remain later than usual, and to share one of her midnight snacks.

"Abdul," she began, after they had finished off the leftover chicken legs, and were reaching for the apples and cookies. "I'm worried about Millie."

"Why?" Searchingly, the expressive dark eyes met hers.

"You must have heard that the conference talk didn't go at all well, at least from the perspective of our philosophers. Millie attacked almost everything the rest of us stand for, and I don't think that Willard Grange and his group will soon forget some of the things she implied about their ideas . . . and, in fact, their life's work!"

"And what do they regularly imply about hers?"

"That isn't really the point, is it? She's the one without the power; without tenure or even a clear role here. I think her official status is merely that of Visiting Lecturer or some such thing."

"As is mine," Abdul reminded her.

"But, unlike you, she just doesn't seem to know how to win friends and influence people. There's no way that *you* won't be offered a permanent position here next year, Abdul. I happen to know Harvey thinks you're great and would like to have you with us, if you don't get a better tenure-track offer from the Methods Department."

"You may be right, Certainly Harvey has been making encouraging overtures to me lately. But I really don't think Millie has anything to worry about. Unlike most of us here, her reputation is country-wide. She will be in demand in other universities because of her textbook, if for no other reason. The Dean would never let her go and, if necessary, he will communicate that to Harvey. Many of us in the other Departments admire and enjoy her greatly. She is like a breath of fresh air in this place, to tell the truth. In fact, I feel much more confident of her prospects than of mine."

Abdul left soon after, and Evelyn was surprised and pleased at how reassured he had made her feel in the space of so little time. She was aware of her propensity to worry to the point of exaggerating relatively minor problems and incidents, and decided to thrust Millie's affairs aside. Her friend would no doubt prosper in this Faculty more successfully than she, herself, appeared to have managed to do thus far. Perhaps, as Abdul had suggested concerning the temporary nature of *his* situation, it was time to worry more about her own prospects. However, the more she thought about it the more convinced she became that it would not be Millie's ideas—and those of her latest hero, Edward O. Wilson—that would form the wave of the future. Reckless as always, Millie seemed bent on fighting a losing battle against the tide of history. Whereas Evelyn, instead, was determined to be riding its very crest!

CHAPTER 5

DECEMBER, 1976

With the approach of the Christmas break, things were both speeding up and quietening down in the classrooms and around the faculty common areas. Most of the professors and lecturers were busy supervising exams and marking them, or with planning their courses for the following term. Students were, for the most part, making themselves scarce.

Not the members of the 'B. Ed. After Degree' class, however. Something was obviously afoot. For several days now, Evelyn, busily immersed in end-of-term requirements, had been half-registering the fact that those particular students appeared to be spending an undue amount of time either standing about the environs of the main Education building or gathering at the door of the Head's office. Now, with the prospect of a hurried early bag-lunch in mind, she crossed the lawn to walk from her office to the box-like construction housing the faculty lounge. Suddenly she was intercepted by a line of waving placards beneath which she recognized the familiar figure of Meredith Walker, accompanied by some twenty classmates. The signs, swinging obtrusively into her line of vision, registered various complaints about a certain required class. The most noticeable message was emblazoned in giant letters on a lengthy banner waving above the others and being wielded by three carriers. "SOCIOLOGY PROF UNFAIR TO WOMEN!" it read. A second, particularly eye-catching sign was edged in black and carried the ominous words, "NO MORE CYNTHIAS!"

Hoping to avoid an occasion for direct communication with the disgruntled protesters, Evelyn veered from her course and took a roundabout path leading to the back door of the building. As she entered she encountered Millie, evidently employing the same tactic. It was not the usual lively Millie, however. Her friend was moving slowly as if, for once, the heavy body presented an unsustainable burden. Her shoulders slumped dispiritedly below a face at once haggard and purplish red in color. She looked at Evelyn in obvious embarrassment rather than pleasure.

"I suppose you've seen them." Direct as always, Millie flung out the comment as she preceded Evelyn down the hall.

"What in the world brought this on? What have you been doing or saying to them, Millie?"

"It's all bloody puzzling. In fact, I'm not all that sure myself about what's actually happening, much less what caused it. Let's find a quiet spot in the faculty lounge and I'll try to tell you about it."

Fortunately it was late for morning coffee, and the lunchtime gathering—if, in fact, there would be one in this end-of-term period—had yet to materialize. As they helped themselves to a hot drink the two found they were virtually alone in the large lounge. Settling into a relatively isolated corner of the room, a dejected and withdrawn Millie took a long sip from her cup and gazed into the distance. She was clearly reluctant to engage in this conversation. Evelyn opened her lunch bag and considered the pair of rather unappetizing tuna and tomato sandwiches that she had thrown together that morning. They compared somewhat unsatisfactorily with the two monstrous, steaming hot dogs that Millie's problems had obviously not prevented her from picking up at the cafeteria.

"Why haven't you told the rest of the faculty about the extent of your problems with the BEAD people Millie? Some of us might have been able to help you before things came to this pass."

"What *could* I have said, any more than I'd already told you about the situation, Evelyn? From the very beginning, the majority (but not all of the class, mind you) has simply refused to accept me as an instructor worthy of any kind of respect. I really think it all comes down to that."

"I know you've mentioned your discomfort concerning that class. But none of the other members of the teaching team seem to be having any trouble with them. What, exactly, have they been doing?"

"It's not all that easy to describe." Millie sighed, seemed to consider for a while, then decide to continue. "Since the middle of September, there's been this strangely hostile attitude toward me on the part of most of them. In no time it got so bad that, on the mornings when I was to meet them, I began to feel an overwhelming reluctance even to climb out of the car and begin the walk from the parking lot to that little semi-detached building where the BEAD class is held. You know how much I've always loved teaching. It's totally new to me to experience such a sensation of outright dread at the thought of facing a class. As the weeks wore on I was forced to repeat like a mantra to myself the words, 'I won't let them get me down. I won't! I just won't!'. Actually, the only thing keeping me going was the fact that my other two classes, of Education undergraduates, were such a pleasure to teach. But this one just got more and more difficult and . . . well . . . even acutely unpleasant in a personal sense. For example, I'd often notice a cluster of the young women from the BEAD group sitting on one of the benches in the lawn or standing in the hall as I approached the classroom. They'd never simply go in and prepare for the lecture. I'd determinedly toss off a cheery greeting, but the response was invariably silence and a cold stare from those standing close by . . . followed by a wave of scornful laughter rising behind me. I soon learned that these particular individuals were part of the leadership of the Women's Cultural Revolution. When the time came for me to begin the lecture or discussion or whatever, there would still be only a handful of people in the room . . . the three pleasant and earnest nuns, and usually just one of the men, a bright young immigrant from Korea. This very early became the pattern. I always knew that the others would drift in, by threes and fours, noisily disrupting my introductory comments over an increasingly prolonged period. And this has been happening ever since the beginning of the session."

"But something must have started it, Millie! I know you mentioned some time ago that you thought it might be related to the fact that you weren't able to attend the group-building sessions at the retreat up the coast. Do you still think that's the root of it, or is it something about the way you're teaching the course. Something you can alter? Is it possible that you've been treating them too much like high-school students?"

"I suppose my approach may be different from what they're used to. I do believe in structuring my content and presenting it in a logical way, before the class proceeds to open discussion. But the attacks have been of such a personal nature! You know my teaching style. I've never been accused of being boring! But these students almost seem to delight in belittling me and in playing childish games in class. For example, I think I told you that near the beginning of the term a bunch of them pretended not to know the simplest things, such as how to use the library. I foolishly took them at their word and arranged a class excursion to the library, with an action lesson on the basic tools of research. They had the entire group snickering at my expense and asking the most simplistic questions about how to locate books, etc. And, as I said, they never enter the classroom until after I begin to teach; then they come in so as to create the maximum disturbance in arranging their desks and books. They deliberately hand in assignments a week or so late, knowing that I take off marks for that. And then they all get together and challenge me on their grades."

"Was there any warning at all of their plan to complain about you formally and in such a public way?"

"Not really. I *did* feel that things were going steadily from bad to worse, until the final marks for their semester's work were given out this week. I hadn't noticed it, as I don't pay any attention to gender in marking, but it seems that most of the female students found themselves in the bottom half of the class. Although, come to think of it, the *top* rankings all went to females as well. But I guess those don't count."

"What do you mean, 'Those don't count'?"

"Well, just to make things more complicated, as you know, three of the females in the class are nuns. Chiefly because they're interested and working hard, they're consistently at the top of the class where marks are concerned. They haven't joined in any of the organized attempts at disrupting the proceedings. In fact, they came to see me yesterday especially to let me know that they've refused to be a part of any of the goings-on, which they informed me were exceedingly well-orchestrated and the source of much amusement among the majority group. Interestingly, they were accompanied by the one male student, Jim Chon, who's been a loyal supporter throughout. He also spoke up strongly about what he saw as deliberate and prolonged harassment of a professor. The four of them said they planned to tell the Head exactly what's been happening."

"Have any of the other members of the BEAD teaching group had similar problems with these people?"

"No, not at all. That's what makes the whole thing so damn difficult. I've asked Abdul about his experience with them, and it's as if he's teaching an entirely different class. He says he simply can't understand it. For example, Meredith Walker, who doesn't mind expressing her extreme scorn of me to my face, and does the barest minimum in her assignments for my course, produces excellent work for him. I realize this is something that will certainly argue against me, where their charge of sexism is concerned. If all the other professors in the program are giving these same female students good marks, and they're getting low grades from me, nobody's going to believe that it's because they refuse to do any work in my class. Even the male students in the group who've been playing along with them are at least taking their assignments seriously and completing them on schedule."

"And even if it *is* accepted that these women are not working in your course, I guess Harvey will be asking the obvious question. Why aren't they? Really, none of it makes any sense, Millie."

"That's what I've been thinking. And what's worse, I don't even feel like fighting this, Evelyn. I guess you might say they've attacked me where I'm most vulnerable. I've always taken pride in my abilities as a teacher. The response from my students over the years has consistently validated this. How could I have made such a bloody mess of things with this particular class? Maybe they're right. Maybe I'm just past it somehow."

"But what about your other classes?"

"Oh, that's the only thing that keeps me going! Everything's absolutely great with them. Moving from the BEAD group to my regular Sociology of Education classes is like moving from nightmarish darkness into sparkling daylight. We're having lots of fun and the student participation and output is all that anyone could desire."

"Well then! The problem can't lie entirely with you. Unless it's that you're just not suited to teaching graduate-level students. How about talking this over with some of the rest of the faculty, Millie? Those not involved in the BEAD program. I'm thinking, for instance, of the history group."

"I've thought of it, just as I considered telling *you* more about what was happening. But I guess my pride won't let me go around weeping on people's shoulders. If we had regular Departmental meetings I'd have had the opportunity to raise the issue in a normal way, and to request advice openly. But I realize that's not the way this place is operated. In fact, as things stand now, I'd rather you not mention it to anyone else. Clearly this is seen by the Foundations people as my problem and I'm going to have to solve it, one way or another."

"But now that the members of the class have gone public, people *are* going to be aware of it, Millie. For instance, Harvey's going to want to talk to you about it, surely, if only to hear your side of the story. In fact, I'd like your permission to approach Meredith Walker, before things get completely out of hand. I know her somewhat because of our mutual involvement in the cause of feminism. Maybe we could get you two together somehow and you could work out your differences."

"I think this goes far beyond personal differences between two people, but you're welcome to try. And thanks for listening, Evelyn. This can't have been the most pleasant way for you to spend your break away from marking papers."

A few days later Evelyn got her opportunity when Meredith came to her office one morning to plan an upcoming meeting of the Women's Cultural Revolution. The fledgling feminist organization had been doing surprisingly well, with members being recruited at a great rate from all of the other Faculties. She had gotten to know a Meredith Walker who seemed a totally different person from the troublemaker described by Millie. The young woman who approached her desk this morning and settled confidently into the chair facing her was trimly dressed in a long, shapely, navy-colored skirt with hip-length, fitted jacket over a white, collarless top. Her every move exuded a business-like capability. Evelyn recalled that her previous degree was a BA with a major in economics. She certainly wasn't about to accuse this self-possessed young adult of deliberately attempting to disrupt one of her required BEAD classes! The introduction of the topic of Millie must be carefully executed, to say the least.

"I was wondering," she mused aloud some time later, "how your faculty recruiting plan is coming along. Have you had any luck in interesting any of the other female professors here in Education, for instance?"

"You've got to be joking! Can you imagine Mrs. Korensky taking up the banner of the Women's Cultural

Revolution? She actually thinks it's a *privilege* to make coffee for the male professors and to defer to them on all intellectual-type issues. And the few other women in Teaching Methods are no different. I did approach the two female educational psychologists, however, and they said they'll think about it. They didn't strike me as overly enthusiastic, but they're probably feeling their way, as they're relatively new here."

"What about Dr. Eisenstadt, the only woman besides me in our Foundations Department? She's new this year as well, but she most certainly does not believe in deferring to the men."

Meredith was silent for a few moments, her eyes grown suddenly guarded. "How much do you know about her?" she finally asked.

Evelyn had no intention of revealing their long, friendly relationship. Her comments would have more effect, she thought, if this were not known.

"I can tell you a little story about her," she volunteered. "It was just after she arrived at the beginning of September. There was the social affair to welcome new and returning faculty, organized, as it has been every September since I came here, by the Faculty Wives Association. I received the usual phone call informing me about what food I should bring and letting me know that, as always, I would be expected to serve the lunch and coffee, along with the other women of the university community. They were mostly wives of professors. Ever since my arrival I had accepted this duty tolerantly as some sort of established ritual, even though the assumptions behind it had bothered me considerably from the very first. Well, on this particular day, not long after the call, Dr. Eisenstadt came storming through that very door there. 'Did you ever hear such bullshit?' she asked me. 'I've just been told that I'm expected to serve tea and snacks to the male professors at the party. You can bet Mrs. Harvey Garfinkle got an earful from me! It'll be the last time she ever asks another female professor to play waitress to the men. Don't you dare go along with those sexist expectations, old girl, or I'll disown you as a fellow academic! If you haven't already refused to do that kind of kowtowing, phone her back right this minute and tell her where to put her invitation.'

So you can see," Evelyn finished, "why I would have expected you to view that type of female professor as a very likely candidate for your feminist movement."

"What did you do?" Meredith asked.

"Of course I obeyed Dr. Eisenstadt. Immediately. Feeling like such a fool because I had never taken such a stand myself. Oh, another thing that's just occurred to me! I happen to know that Dr. Eisenstadt is a long-time, active member of the Canadian Council of Women, this country's national branch of the World Council of Women. So she is, in fact, greatly concerned about female equality."

"Naturally I'm with her on the issue of serving food to the men. But, to be frank with you, Dr. Ashton-Brent, there are a lot of Professor Eisenstadt's beliefs and ways of behaving that I and my fellow feminists feel distinctly uncomfortable about. And we don't have much respect for the Council of Women either. We think a much more radical women's association is needed in this country: one that's tax-supported, and thus able to exert more influence. In fact, I'm not surprised to hear that Professor Eisenstadt is with that old, out-of-date group. Her entire approach to feminism reflects theirs. And it's a position we firmly disagree with. For example, you call her a feminist, but she actually opposes most of the key planks in our program."

"Such as what, exactly?"

"Such as attempts to begin achieving parity by instituting preferential hiring for female professors and quotas for the intake of graduate students, based on gender. She calls it reverse discrimination, if you can imagine! And that's not all, by any means. It's not easy to explain, but I'll try. We have her figured out as the epitome of an earlier kind of feminism that was okay for its time, but is really terribly out of date and even a serious obstacle to progress today. All the early pioneers of the feminist movement had to learn how to succeed in a man's world. They had no choice. So they imitated men and eventually began to beat them at their own game. Harriet Martineau in England, Susan B. Anthony in the United States and Nellie McClung in Canada are good examples of that sort of feminist. They were imitators of men, *par excellence*. They didn't question the world view of males, or the essential foundations of the prevailing power structures. They merely bought into the system and fought to win a place within it for women. They learned how to acquire the dominant male world view and to climb in the structure as it existed. And they had to become aggressive, male-like people to accomplish it. In fact, most of the members of the Canadian Council of Women whom I've met are of that type."

"Yes, of course you've got a point. But don't forget that things were still very difficult for women even a mere decade in the past. Especially in academia. I remember meeting a former male colleague of Millie's at a conference not long ago. He was reminiscing fondly about how unique she was as an able and confident intellectual in the 'man's field' of social-scientific theory in the early sixties. He described with great amusement an incident at a philosophy symposium, during a particularly boring lecture, when he had whispered some sort of ironic aside to Millie (the only female in attendance) about the talk, and she started to respond, also in a whisper. The speaker stopped suddenly and called out, quite derisively '*Miss*' Eisenstadt! (Not 'Professor' . . . or 'Doctor', mind you, as he was addressing the males in the group.) Pray, are you with us?' Quick as a flash Millie responded 'I'm away *ahead* of you!' Now you would probably say that was an extremely arrogant, male-type of reply. But don't you think it was justified in the circumstance?"

"Well, perhaps, but times have changed, and she doesn't seem to have noticed that. It goes beyond idiosyncrasies such as personal arrogance. It involves the entire rationalistic scientific perspective which she seems to advocate. Dr. Eisenstadt is still mired in an obsolete 'modernism', while we feminists of today have moved away beyond that, to a kind of 'post-modernism'. My generation now realizes that the defining aspect of the male world view rooted in the Enlightenment is the traditional left-brain-dominated science. We reject that view utterly, and especially when its methods are applied to the social studies. Another of these male concepts involves authority. You know, the idea that some people have the right to determine what and how others should learn, for instance. And another is the notion of hierarchy, which is inevitably involved in authority of every kind. We revolutionary feminists want to get away from structure in every form, and to promote bilateral relationships based on holistic unity and equality and mutual respect. All this is anathema to Professor Eisenstadt, as you'd realize if you ever looked in on one of her classes. We just don't think she would fit in with what we envision our group to be. Not at all! Now you, Dr. Ashton-Brent, you strike us as being totally different, and that's why we work so well together."

All this gave Evelyn considerable food for thought, in that she had often engaged in precisely the same arguments with Millie. Still, a difference in emphasis within feminism hardly seemed to be sufficient cause for what was happening to Millie now, at the hands of fellow feminists.

"But precisely what has all this to do with your rather public denunciation of Dr. Eisenstadt's class?" she asked.

"It has everything to do with it! At our retreat last September we students, as a group, arrived at a consensus on how our program should be run, and the faculty members in attendance agreed. All through our university experience, in the course of our undergraduate work, we had heard nothing but negative things about irrelevant and 'Mickey Mouse' Education courses. So we decided that we'd insist on getting out into the schools for half-days as soon as it could be arranged, and from that experience in the afternoons we, *ourselves*, would identify what we needed to know in order to function successfully out there. Then we would, again as a group, let our Education professors know what should be offered in their morning sessions. We were also determined to evaluate our accomplishments ourselves, both in the schools and in our own classes. We would insist on applying previously self-identified objectives and grade ourselves accordingly. And that's precisely what we've been doing in all but Professor Eisenstadt's class . . . ever since October, when the entire system was set in motion by Dr. Garfinkle and Dr. Rasmussen."

"How strange! I never heard anything about the specifics of your plan. The rest of us should have been told about it. Especially the self-evaluation! Am I right in guessing that Dr. Eisenstadt didn't go along with all this?"

"Are you ever! She practically hit the roof when we

informed her of it, and especially when we steadfastly refused to do her assignments and listen to her endless lectures and participate in her boring discussions about things we'd never before heard of. In fact, it was her stubborn stand on this matter that forced our hand this past week."

Evelyn was so thrown by what she had just learned that she was at a loss as to how to respond to Meredith. She cut the interview short and excused herself as soon as it was feasible to do so. For the remainder of the morning she puzzled over the matter. Why had none of her colleagues told her about all this? She had known that the BEAD program was intended to be experimental—but such a radical departure from established ways of doing things surely warranted discussion at the Faculty level. Who had made the decision? Why hadn't Harvey at least called a Departmental meeting so that the Foundations' contribution to the experiment could be thoroughly discussed; and Millie appropriately informed and given some guidance? And Abdul! He was a member of the BEAD teaching team. Why hadn't he told her about it, and why hadn't he helped Millie to define and accept her new role within the total process? Was everyone just flying blind here?

Finally, she decided to do something she knew Abdul didn't particularly appreciate. She would go to his office on the Teaching Methods floor of the building and ask him to have lunch with her in the large university cafeteria, where they could talk in reasonable privacy. As luck would have it, she caught him at his door, apparently on the point of leaving before the noon rush. As usual, he sought to avoid their being seen together by arranging to meet her in fifteen minutes, after cleaning up a bit. She headed on her own over to the cafeteria, where she picked up some food, then found a quiet corner table and settled down to wait.

"What is it, Evelyn?" Abdul, also bearing a tray, had finally arrived. He sat down opposite her, with a sigh that seemed to signal resignation and forbearance. "Is something troubling you? You seem upset."

"I *am* upset. I've just been talking to Meredith Walker. She was telling me about this radical experiment that's being conducted with the BEAD program. Why have you never mentioned the details of it? Especially the fact that Millie refused to go along with it?"

"I was not aware that she had. Millie, I mean. And also I was not under the impression that there had been any overall design for the project decided from on high. However, the new approach does appear to be working well for my Social Studies Methods course. The students go out into the schools in the afternoon, when the teachers can make time for them, and in the mornings they bring us the problems they have encountered in our specific subject area and we attempt to solve these as a group. I have found that the motivation to learn is very strong because they feel that they're self-directed, and have been granted the respect due to students in a graduate-level program."

"But this is not actually a graduate program, Abdul. These students have no grounding whatsoever in the subject they're supposedly studying . . . that is, education. I can see how it might work somewhat differently in your area, where many of them have a prior degree in history or geography, and only need to learn how to simplify and organize the material. But when it comes to the philosophy of education itself, or the psychology or sociology or history concerning it, or to classes on child development and the actual process of encouraging children to learn, how are they to know what kind of knowledge and skills are required for the task?"

"I wonder how many of us know what is needed out there in the classroom? It is a different world from what we find in here, Evelyn."

"That may be. But I do know that Millie is more experienced in that world than are the rest of you 'pure' academic types who are members of that teaching team. I would think that her opinion should count for something."

"As to that, I was simply not aware of the extent to which she was dissenting from the team position. Neither she nor Harvey has mentioned that point to me."

"Don't you, as a teaching team, get together for regular meetings to discuss common approaches and problems . . . and students?"

"Why no. As you are no doubt aware, Harvey was designated by the Faculty to organize and supervise the operation. And you know his opinion on formal meetings. No one has ever even suggested the need for such a thing as meetings of the teaching team. He communicates with each of us privately, and we with him, if we have any problems."

"Abdul, haven't you heard anything at all about what's been happening to Millie with that class?"

"I had no knowledge of anything other than what you mentioned some time ago. That is, until recently when all those banners suddenly erupted around the Education grounds. I have been reluctant to make suggestions about teaching methods to anyone as experienced as Millie. But now that this has happened I do intend to talk to her at once and to offer my help."

"I'm happy to hear that. Maybe she'll listen to you, Abdul. I know she respects you and enjoys discussing ideas with you."

Abdul was gazing hungrily at the attractive lunch of lentil soup and Caesar salad with herb bread now rapidly cooling in front of him. Evelyn began to tackle her own meal, deciding they had run the subject into the ground for now, and it was time to turn to more cheerful topics. She hadn't seen Abdul for several days, and had a lot to share with him. At any rate, her serving of chicken salad was too delicious to ignore. The lunch break passed all too quickly, with Abdul uneasily watching the door throughout and clearly anxious to be off. Evelyn soon found herself sitting alone once more, sipping coffee and gathering her thoughts for the afternoon ahead. Should she try to talk to Millie again, now that she knew more about the causes of the student rebellion? Or should she let it rest for a while, and see what developed? It was really Harvey's responsibility to get across the idea that those teaching in the new program were all part of a team, and what had been decided upon as the direction to take would have to be accepted by all. There was so little she could do, and the last thing Millie would want was sympathy. So she settled on returning to her office and the work awaiting her there.

There was no sign of Millie among the group gathered in the faculty lounge at various times during those last few days before they went their separate ways for the Christmas break. In her absence, the news of the rebellion of her BEAD class was discussed in hushed tones, almost as if it were a death in the faculty. Evelyn realized that what had happened was, in fact, every instructor's nightmare. To have practically an entire class declare openly that they would no longer study under you; that, in their opinion, you were unfit to teach your subject to them! And then for them to advertise the fact to all and sundry by carrying banners that shouted it out, comparing your behavior with that which had caused the death of Cynthia Montague! Surely this kind of affront to a professor could not just be left without any response from the administration. It seemed that she was not the only one who wondered about this, for on the last day before they closed up shop completely, Muthu accosted Harvey as he made one of his comradely swings through the lounge, this time to wish everyone a happy holiday season.

"One moment, Harvey," he said. "We are all wondering about these strange happenings on campus concerning Millie Eisenstadt. Can you enlighten us?"

"Nothing to worry about. It's all settled now. Just a little misunderstanding. The signs are down and the students involved in the marching have gone home for the break. All it took was a willingness to do a bit of compromising, and that's what I'm here for, as Head of the Department. The BEAD students are now quite happy and so are we."

"I am very concerned about the effect of all this on Dr. Eisenstadt's authority as a member of the faculty. Are you doing anything to restore her credibility with the students in general? What about her undergraduate classes? Accusations such as these, if allowed to stand, could destroy the reputation of the best of professors. And, because Dr. Eisenstadt is new here this year, and with no locally established reputation among the students, she is in an especially vulnerable position."

"Authority, Professor Muthu? You must know that I am not one for emphasizing or restoring authority! Too much bureaucracy and legislated authority has been the Achilles Heel of Education Faculties for years. Respect, now that's a different matter. But that's the students' to give. Not the Head's nor the Dean's. And I'm sure you'd agree that we all have to earn it."

With that, Harvey swept out the door of the lounge. Gus Rasmussen, who had entered the room with him, remained behind, grinning almost gleefully behind his wispy beard. He poured himself a cup of coffee, then pulled up a chair and joined the group, next to Abdul. Just at that moment Sam Barnes, who had been sipping cocoa and listening quietly to the conversation up to now, cleared his throat and began to speak in his characteristically blunt manner.

"I don't know about the rest of you, but I'm beginning to feel bloody uncomfortable about all this. It's as if there's so much going on beneath the surface around here, and nothing ever gets discussed honestly and up front. Undercurrents are everywhere, and veiled accusations seem to be the order of the day. Everything being done in the name of democracy and our being 'just one big happy family' and dedicated feminists all. It makes me damn uneasy. Today it's Millie who's under attack, and there doesn't seem to be any way we can do anything for her. I can't help but wonder who's going to be next."

"Now Sam," Gus admonished jokingly. "You're always accusing me of seeing conspiracies behind every bush. Especially in the politics of my American homeland. Surely you're not going to start imagining them here." Gus was obviously enjoying all this. He lounged back, spreading jean-clad legs straight out in front of him.

"We've never, in all the years I've been in Canada, had as much excitement here as there's been this past few weeks! I think we should be thanking the Women's Cultural Revolution for stirring this place up a bit, and spreading a bit of much-needed democracy."

"And what about the reference on the sign to Cynthia Montague? Is that some kind of a wake-up call as well?" Helen Korensky, who had been listening thoughtfully, now broke into the conversation. 'No More Cynthias!' What does it mean?"

"Just what it says, I expect."

"But what is it really saying, Gus? It could be taken to mean that she is being celebrated as unique, and that there will never be another like her," Willard Grange now entered the conversation, speaking in his precise, learned fashion. "Or it may be an injunction that we must never again countenance conditions under which a young girl like Cynthia could become the victim of such a meaningless tragedy. If the latter, we are required to accept the premise that we, as a faculty, had some responsibility for the existence of those conditions."

The ensuing silence went on for so long that Evelyn finally felt driven to break it. "Perhaps that's a premise that we should indeed be taking seriously," she said thoughtfully. "I must admit I've been feeling that we all somehow failed Cynthia. It might be a good thing for us to take that message to heart over the coming holiday season. It wouldn't hurt for all of us to try to do a better job of protecting both the human rights and the actual physical safety of our students, and especially of the females who have for so long had the short end of the stick in academia."

"If you say so, Madame," Muthu responded laughingly.

With that the gathering broke up in the midst of much wishing of the best of the holiday season to one and all. Evelyn walked home along the shore front, thinking that the coming break didn't offer much hope of excitement for her. She wondered if she might possibly persuade Abdul to go someplace with her—just the two of them. She was beginning to worry about what was happening between them. She had read somewhere that intimate relationships never stand still; that they either develop in a deeper and more formally established direction or they begin to disintegrate. It was becoming increasingly clear to her that Abdul had no intention of making any changes; that he wanted nothing more than the almost fleeting sexual encounters in her apartment after dinner on the evenings when they both happened to be free. And, now that she thought about it, she realized that he was no longer hiking companionably at her side along the trail on their weekend outings. The fact that he appeared to be spending much more of his spare time with Gus Rasmussen surprised her a bit, until she recalled that they had actually both arrived at around the same time, and in somewhat similar circumstances, and held very similar views on politics and ideology in general. Still, she and Abdul also agreed on most issues, and shared the love of hiking as well.

They also shared an involvement with the Unitarian Church. Shortly after Evelyn had arrived at NPU she had looked for the nearest community of fellow Unitarians. At a discussion group there one day she had been surprised to encounter Abdul Issa. It was before they had become intimate, and she now recalled that it was also before they had discovered they were neighbors, as well as being merely colleagues at work. In those early days of their acquaintance Abdul had mentioned a number of times how much he felt at home with the Unitarians—among whom were many humanists who held a world view very close to his own.

"I would never have thought it!" he exclaimed with rather uncharacteristic enthusiasm, during a discussion of religion in the faculty lounge one day. "I was extremely lonely when I came here, as I felt very far away from family and friends. So I suppose I was looking for a supportive network. But it was only with great reluctance that I first accompanied Gus to the meeting place of the Unitarians who had helped him come to Canada as a Vietnam War 'draft dodger'. You can imagine my surprise to discover a religious community where the minister does not push

Christian or even theistic doctrines from the pulpit! Where they practise non-superstitious rituals to celebrate life's passages, as well as nature's seminal events such as the passing of the seasons and the Winter Solstice. Where people can concentrate on trying to live ethically, and on making the world a better place for those who come after, in spite of the fact that they may differ on beliefs about the ultimate nature of things. And where we can gather in discussion groups and puzzle away at building a world view for ourselves that makes sense in terms of both our personal experience and the findings of science. And where we don't all have to agree."

"I sometimes think that the very fact of the openness of Unitarianism could be its fatal weakness." This was ventured by Muthu, who had been listening in silence up to then. "As a historian with a special interest in the evolution of religion, I have thought about this a great deal. I can understand how the respect for scientific inquiry and the humanism that has been defining the denomination for most of the past two centuries would attract you, Abdul. But its very non-orthodoxy and lack of hierarchy and coherent doctrine makes this movement dangerously vulnerable to 'take-over' from within, by fringe groups already on the rise within the larger society."

"Such as?" asked Evelyn.

"Such as throw-backs to nineteenth century spiritualism. Or momentarily popular fads such as 'New Age' mysticism. Or a revival of Ralph Waldo Emerson's Transcendentalism with its insistence on private intuition as the ultimate source of 'truth'."

"Admit it, Muthu. You're just opposed to all religion." This from Sam Barnes, who had been listening on the fringes of the group.

"Yes . . . . Yes, I believe I am. I sometimes wonder if there is any other human institution that has caused so much harm to its creators and to the health and security of the world for which we humans must assume responsibility. For example, consider the Hinduism in which I was raised. The corruption caused by the ugly caste system so deeply rooted in it, and still firmly reinforced by it, has permeated the entire society. However, I admit that not all religions are equally guilty here." Muthu spoke thoughtfully, meticulously filling his pipe as he did so.

"But surely you admit that the *moral* aspect of religion has been absolutely necessary for us deeply fallible humans!" Sam's half-joking comment came out sounding more like a conclusion than a question.

"As to that, I would beg to remind you of Pascal's comment on the matter. 'Men', he said, 'never do evil so completely and cheerfully as when they do it from religious conviction.' In fact, only the vilest of modern criminals would stoop to the depth of evil recommended in certain parts of the holy books of all our world religions. I need only refer you to the directives of the Hindu teacher, *Manusmriti*, on the gross cruelty that should be visited upon the *Shudras* (or Untouchables). Or to the Biblical record of the Lord's command for Joshua to oversee the slaughter of the inhabitants of Jericho and other conquered cities. Or to the precise words of Mohammed in his call to 'Become a Muslim if you want to be safe . . . . If you refuse you will be bearing the sins of the Christian people." Muthu's reply had been instant, with each statement accompanied by a wave of his pipe for emphasis.

When Sam chose not to respond, Evelyn broke the rather uncomfortable silence by admitting to her own Unitarian background. She then grasped the chance to explain in some depth the historical roots of the movement in the humanism of Renaissance times. As a sociologist, she also decided it might be helpful to go into the human need for ritual—something Unitarianism had long provided, she claimed, without the spiritualistic and mythological trappings common to most religions. Abdul was clearly interested in all this. He appeared not to have been turned off unduly by Muthu's critical remarks for, from that time on, one of the places where she could almost always count on seeing him on weekends was at the Unitarian center. With so much in common, she thought now, surely theirs was a relationship worth saving! She resolved then and there to go ahead and plan a holiday trip back to Boston, in the hope that he might be persuaded to travel with her.

Another resolution was to find out all she could about the Harvard biologist, Edward O. Wilson, while she was in Boston. She was disturbed about what she had heard so far about the man's dangerous ideas, and wanted to come back armed with sufficient information to warn Millie not to be singing his praises in public or referring to his work in her classes. From what she had read, it appeared as if the entire field of respectable sociology was opposed to what he was doing and saying. Millie—in spite of her supposed grasp of scientific theory—was such a babe in arms when it came to that sort of thing! She was an enthusiastic supporter of Robin Fox and Lionel Tiger as well, in what Evelyn considered to be their misbegotten efforts to portray human behavior as merely one with that of animals.

The day after she had completed the last of her marking and returned all the student papers, Evelyn decided that she deserved a little treat. She called Abdul but got no answer, even though she had slipped a note suggesting such an outing under his door the night before. So she resigned herself to phoning a few friends and acquaintances in the forlorn hope that she would find someone available at short notice. When this ploy also failed she determined to go out for lunch on her own.

The restaurant to which she headed was located immediately west of the main north-south highway to the east of Richmond. It was in a little out-of the-way location that was a favorite of Abdul's: one of the few places to which they ever went as a twosome. After the first visit she had realized why. The booths were curtained on two of the unwalled sides. In fact, the front of each was only partially open for the convenience of the waiter or waitress, who had to pull back the folds so as to ask for, and deliver, the orders. This layout made it a great place for a slightly self-conscious single diner. Evelyn felt she didn't really need to be spotted by any of her students eating all alone on a day that called for celebrating. Privacy was what was offered here, and privacy was what she needed. It was thus with deep dismay that, upon slipping into her seat and managing to catch the waiter's eye at the same moment, she heard a familiar voice exclaiming from within the booth next door.

"I know you warned me of your varied tastes, old boy, but damn it all, this is ridiculous! From a stringy old maid to a Playboy seductress to the circus fat lady! I figured it was high time I got you out of here for a bit of a holiday, and Australia's Gold Coast sounded like it would just about fit the bill. What you need is a good dose of the sight of all those luscious bodies riding the waves on surf boards."

"But Gus, I can't let you pay for my ticket all the way to Queensland, Australia!" Abdul's voice—clear as a bell. A pause, then, almost as an afterthought, "And please, Gus, why must you accuse me of having an affair with every casual friend in the Faculty who happens to be female?"

"I just don't think you're aware of the power of your sex appeal. You'd have to be blind not to see how those dames respond, Abdul. But don't worry, pal, we'll soon be out of here. And as for you paying, I got the round-trip tickets cheap. You can share the living expenses once we get there."

Evelyn sat, frozen in place, the implications of 'stringy old maid' striking like a blow in the solar plexus. Along with it came the realization that the waiter would appear at any moment, and she would have to speak and be identified by the two next door. She couldn't let them know she had overheard. Giving herself no time for second thoughts, she sidled quietly out the far side of the booth. She then turned and approached noisily, ostentatiously appearing to spot Abdul and Gus for the first time as she did so.

"Well, look who's here!" she forced herself to exclaim cheerfully. "Mind if I join you two? I was heading out to do my Christmas shopping before I leave next week for Boston, and decided I'd better snatch a bite first."

Evelyn noted that her own extreme discomfort was reflected doubly in the appearance and behavior of the other two. Gus glared with scarcely veiled hostility. Abdul spent the brief time before they hurriedly excused themselves in attempting to show interest in her impending trip, and in asking for her advice and information concerning general Faculty affairs. He studiously avoided any mention of Millie's problems, however, or of the still-simmering tragedy of Cynthia. Gus, clearly disgruntled at the unwanted interruption, seemed to get a degree of satisfaction from going into great detail about arrangements for the Australian adventure on which he and Abdul were embarking the following week. When the waiter approached, the two men refused coffee and dessert and asked, instead, for their bill, which Gus insisted on paying on their hurried way out.

Evelyn was very soon left on her own, ruefully examining the large serving of holiday food ordered in a desperate effort to rescue some pretence of celebration from the debacle. What a way to begin the Christmas season! She sighed despondently as she struggled to come to terms with the now-confirmed fact of her holiday trip home alone to Boston. She hadn't actually realized until this moment what close friends those two had become. And why did it seem to her that there was something a bit incongruous about the friendship? At that moment another devastating realization struck. Abdul had made no objection whatsoever to Gus' characterization of her as a 'stringy old maid'!

CHAPTER 6

JANUARY, 1977

Evelyn was sitting at her desk, brooding about her boring holiday break in Boston, when a sudden eruption in the neighboring office startled her out of her late-afternoon's drowsiness. The loudest voice was clearly female, and Evelyn guessed it belonged to the young woman who had passed her open door about ten minutes earlier. She had grown so accustomed to the low murmur of conversation in Sam Barnes' office that she automatically tuned out, as she hoped he did when it was she who was interviewing students. But this was different—in both tone and volume quite impossible to ignore.

"But you *can't* give me only a 'C' for my term's work! It'll ruin my average!" Clearly this was an agonized cry from the very heart. Although Evelyn couldn't quite suppress a smile at the all-too-familiar refrain, she felt a twinge of sympathy as well—for both participants in the altercation going on at the other side of the partial wall separating the two offices. She could not quite make out Sam's responses, but she recognized his 'patient' and 'reasoning' stance in the intonation and spacing of the sentences.

"Don't think you're going to get away with this, you patriarchal Mormon jerk!" The words resounded over the partition in an explosion of anger.

"I think you'd better leave." Sam's utterance, suddenly loud and distinct, was followed by a scuffling sound near the door which suddenly burst open, then closed noisily as the student emerged with a rush of feet and a stumble. A book and several papers tumbled to the floor and scattered in front of Evelyn's door. She got a quick look at the face that turned back to glare behind her before its owner bent to rescue her belongings. It was a singularly beautiful, olive-skinned face, with a pair of dark-brown eyes, now fiery with rage, peering through the long sheaf of shiny black hair which flowed unrestrained almost to the floor beside the crouching figure.

The colorful long blouse and the slightly flared, floor-length skirt below contributed to the girl's exotic appearance as she rose to her feet and fled rapidly down the hall. Evelyn's first, incongruous thought was that she looked like an Indian princess. Almost immediately, Sam's burly figure was at Evelyn's door. He was shaking his head, his grin even more even rueful than usual.

"Come on in, Sam, and explain yourself. Tell me what you've been doing to that poor aboriginal girl. Haven't you learned yet that you're not supposed to give anyone a low mark in an Education course? And especially not one of the students from the Rain Forest College? And, by the way, how is it that she's taking a course in our Department anyway?"

"My God, isn't that the limit, though!" Sam tumbled into a chair near Evelyn's desk and ran all ten fingers through his close-cut thatch of hair. "Did you hear what she called me? 'A patriarchal Mormon jerk', no less!" He was now mopping his forehead with a large white handkerchief. "I just hope she doesn't come back to class tomorrow. Somehow I don't think that our Miss Charles is cut out to be a teacher, and the sooner she learns it the better for all concerned. And, as to your last question, yes, their students do sometimes have to pick up particular courses in the Education Faculty, just as they do in Arts and Sciences, depending on their program."

Another voice intruded from the hallway. "I'm a bit surprised at her reference to you as a *Mormon* patriarchal jerk, Sam. A jerk maybe, and patriarchal at times too, I've noticed, but students nowadays don't usually consider it quite kosher to slur one's religion or ethnicity. I shudder at what would happen if you referred to her as the female equivalent of a 'native Indian jerk'! And, by the way, she's the first female student I've seen from the Rain Forest College. I thought they were all male." It was Millie, smiling broadly from the hallway, and looking almost like her old sarcastic self as she proceeded into the office and seated herself in the remaining chair.

"Yes, there are a few women. But very few. Usually they just happen to be daughters of chiefs, as is our Miss Charles, by the way."

"To get back to the Mormon thing," Sam mused, after the three of them had exchanged news of their respective holiday doings. "I do find my family religion to be bit of a handicap in teaching here. Especially where modern females are concerned. I guess it would be a different story in Utah, or even in the area around Cardston, Alberta where my grandparents came as pioneers. But in British Columbia we seem to have a mighty poor reputation. It's probably due to what's been happening at Bountiful. You know, that little Mormon settlement near Creston in the East Kootenays? A bunch of our more fundamentalist brethren began to congregate there over twenty years ago, and I guess they've pretty much defined our British Columbian presence for the public. All in all, and especially, I think, here in the Lower Mainland, we appear to strike people as members of some strangely backward foreign tribe."

"So?" Millie smiled mischievously, adding "And what else is new?" before continuing in a more serious vein. "Hasn't your denomination also been known as the Church of Latter Day Saints? I seem to recall something about it being established under that name throughout the southern part of the province of Alberta in the early days of this century."

"Jesus Christ." interposed Evelyn.

"What's eating *you*, Evelyn?" Millie looked at her with a startled expression. Sam merely grinned widely as he stretched his arms in an obvious attempt to relax.

"I just meant that I think 'Jesus Christ' is in their name somewhere," Evelyn explained lamely. "But I'm sorry I interrupted. What were you going to say, Millie?"

"Let's see . . . where was I? Oh yes, I remember my grandmother telling me that the Mormon church (whatever the name) was the only worship community in their entire area when her family first settled on what was then untouched prairie land somewhere southwest of Alsask, not far from the Alberta-Saskatchewan border. That particular area from Kindersley west to Hanna was still unreachable by railway at the time as well, I believe. I think it was around about 1907. (When the rail connection was finally built, it was known as the 'Goose Lake Line'.) A small Jewish pioneering settlement was established there, but most of them moved on before too many years had passed. So, eventually, there were scarcely any Jews at all, for my grandparents to relate to."

"How awful!" exclaimed Evelyn. "And how lonely it must have been for them!"

"Although, come to think of it," this was accompanied

by one of Millie's wry grins, "the Mormons who soon began to populate the area *did* believe that the American Indians were, like themselves, descendants of the 'Lost Ten Tribes' of Israel, even though Mormonism taught that the darker-skinned tribe had, due to the hell-raising habits of its founder, never quite measured up. That claim really incensed my grandmother, by the way. After all, she knew it was *her* tribe who were God's chosen people. Not the Indians and definitely not the Mormons! She also suspected no end of strange goings on among the 'Saints'. Polygamy and so on. And she lived in fear of answering a knock and finding a couple on her doorstep, religious tracts in hand."

"Yes, it's true we Mormons were among the earliest pioneers in Southern Alberta," Sam acknowledged. "Although not many of the settlements were as far north as the Goose Lake Line. My own ancestors were among those who had originally traveled overland from Illinois and Iowa to settle in the Salt Lake valley. Then, around about 1887, groups of them began to leave Utah and come up through the wilds of Montana to the Cardston area of southern Alberta. They drove horse-drawn wagons loaded with all their worldly goods, and herded cattle ahead of them. Ultimately, those Mormon settlers began to work the coal mines and gradually built up flourishing Mormon communities. They were all strictly monogamous by the way. The Canadian government of the time insisted on that."

"I was told that the Mormons had something to do with the development of the Southern Alberta Irrigation System. Was there any truth to that?"

"Yes, Millie, there was. I'd forgotten about that bit of our history. And I shouldn't have, because my grandfather was directly involved. He used to tell us kids about how, in May of 1899, the church leader in his hometown of Dingle, in Utah, ordered a group of men and their families to go to Canada to settle and work on the canal. Those folks had nothing to say about it. They'd apparently been 'called' by God. It seems, the Mormon church had contracted to build a canal for the Alberta Irrigation and Railway Company. The settlers traveled in their old wrecks of wagons and with about five horses per family. The trip took about a month, and it was very rough going through the hills of Montana. Especially getting through the Flathead and Blood Indian Reserves. The Mormon President Card himself was in charge of the canal work and the placing of settlers. Our family was settled in Magrath, which was near Cardston, and about twenty-five miles from the city of Lethbridge. That's where both my father and I were born and grew up."

"I hope you won't mind my saying this, Sam, but ever since I met you I've wondered how someone with as keen a mind as yours could swallow all that stuff Mormonism preaches, even though you *were* brainwashed into it as a kid." As Millie blurted this out, Evelyn almost literally writhed in embarrassment. Whether Sam minded or not was clearly irrelevant where her forthright friend was concerned.

"I do have to admit to feeling a mite embarrassed about the missionary activities and the strange myths that the founder, Joseph Smith, seems to have visualized in his seer stones." Sam appeared unruffled by Millie's question. "In fact, I've questioned and rejected pretty well all of the fundamental theology of my family religion, but not its values. I still think that, like most religions, Mormonism provides necessary moral guidance to us poor, weak humans, and I don't mind admitting that I do my best to live according to its teachings, and to bring up my children to do the same. You see, in my opinion all of the world's great religions have something to offer humanity in these troubled times. I think they share an ethical core which we could *all* support *if only*, in each case, that precious core of universal values were separated out from the jungle of mythology which grew up around it during the course of history. I see that as the major task of advanced theologians and philosophers throughout the world in the centuries to come. If we're going to survive, that is."

"Just so long as you don't include in that precious core all the various 'imaginary friends' and their contradictory tribalistic directives," said Millie.

"And does your core include polygamy?" Evelyn now felt brave enough to interject this tongue-in-cheek comment. If Millie could joke about it, then so could she.

"I have to admit that my own early ancestors were probably obeying the original church edict recommending polygamy. That edict existed, by the way, right up until 1890." Sam had chosen to take her query at face value, the historian in him possibly seeing it as an opportunity to educate her on the topic. "And I've been told that even the Manifesto issued that year, which officially banned polygamy, didn't actually eliminate the practice for some time. Especially among some of the Elders and other elites (who *did* strictly forbid it for their followers, however). And it has apparently survived among a few fundamentalist groups in certain remote places such as Bountiful, here in British Columbia. Although, and in case you two have been wondering if I'm available, I haven't considered 'celestial marriage' in my own case. Frankly, I don't think Mary would approve."

"And here I thought I'd been keeping my feelings hidden!" Millie exclaimed. "But just to get off the subject of our unrequited passion to be members of a 'latter day' harem, Sam, I wanted to say that whenever you start feeling sorry for yourself for being discriminated against on the basis of your Mormon background, just imagine what it was like to grow up as one of the few Jews in rural Alberta! My father was allowed one role, and one role only. It was that of itinerant trader who had to be constantly guarded against for his tendency to make too shrewd a bargain; that is, to `jew` people down."

"The fact is that Mormon communities were so tightly organized and inward-looking and self-contained that I didn't experience anything of the prejudice you must have faced, Millie. And, of course, it helped that we felt superior to the rank and file of our non-Mormon neighbors. As you pointed out, we saw ourselves as spiritual descendants of one of the original 'Lost Tribes' of Israel, another of these being the actual ancestors of the Amerindian natives of North America. And we believed we were the only authentic Christians as well. This made us triply God`s *Chosen People!* So if I`d known you then I would have considered your family mere upstarts, and no doubt joined in the discrimination against you."

"I seem to be getting left out of this conversation," Evelyn found herself complaining. "But I`m really interested in this matter of religious background. Only from a strictly sociological and historical perspective, of course. I hope this won't be viewed as a racist question, but I've always vaguely wondered, Millie, how a Jewish gal like you came to have such red hair and freckled skin. Where did that come from?"

"One of my family`s rather well-kept secrets is that my paternal great-grandfather married a 'wild Irish rose'. She was actually a girl called Rosie Murphy who, not being overly concerned about religion, promptly and obediently converted to Judaism and then proceeded to ignore completely all its beliefs and rules and rituals. I have always been accused of having taken after her. Especially since I declared myself to be an agnostic non-theist."

"Aren't you being a bit redundant there?" asked Sam. "I thought 'agnosticism' and 'atheism' (or non-theism as you called it) were pretty much the same thing."

"Not really. Agnosticism was Thomas Huxley's term to describe a scientific way of being in the world. It means the deriving of one's beliefs empirically, from available, objectively testable evidence, rather than from non-negotiable axioms. And it means holding these beliefs tentatively, subject to the discovery of new evidence that may disconfirm them. Rather than looking for 'proof', the agnostic or scientist actively seeks 'disconfirmation'. Atheism, on the other hand, is simply non-belief in supernatural beings. I always maintain that atheism is a necessary result of being agnostic. That is, you can't be agnostic without very quickly becoming atheistic as well. But agnosticism is not necessary in order to be an atheist. I've known some very dogmatic atheists, in fact. Take Communists, for example. They hold many of their doctrines concerning politics, etc. as unquestionable 'truths'."

"I still don't quite understand. Why, in your opinion, must an agnostic *necessarily* be an atheist as well?"

"Simply because an agnostic thinker refuses to hold *any* belief concerning the supposed existence of beings or events that are, by definition, unknowable to human experience. And, it seems to me, that has to include beliefs in Supreme Beings of all varieties, whether gods or fairies or Santa Claus."

"And, about Mormonism . . .," Evelyn interrupted what was threatening to be a lengthy dissertation on one of Millie's favorite hobby horses. She continued, addressing Sam, "I read the other day that it's on its way to becoming the world's fastest-growing religion. Other than Islam, of course. As a historian, can you offer any ideas as to the reason for this success?"

Millie's eyes gleamed. "How about the coincidence (and continued incidence) of polygamy in both, and the inferior role of women implied and furthered by that practice?" To Evelyn's surprise, Sam appeared to agree.

"I find the most intriguing aspect of all this to be the fact that both Mormonism (chiefly in the past, that is) and Islam today have justified polygamy as being designed chiefly for the 'protection' of their females. The claim was that monogamous cultures expose women to the dangers of prostitution and all manner of abuse. Oh, and I just thought of another interesting commonality." Sam was obviously enjoying this.

"We can only assume that the leaders and official interpreters of the fundamentalist current in both religions believe that males are biologically programmed to *require* a variety of sexual partners, and if these are not guaranteed legally, the voracious creatures will roam around spreading their semen wherever and whenever the urge strikes them. I happen to consider that to be a pretty dim view of men. And as to the female of the species, polygamy is apparently based on the assumption that she's so inherently deficient she requires an overdose of authority and structure in order to function at all. It's always implied, if not actually spelled out, that a female is equal to only one-half a male in the eyes of God. Much of the teaching of fundamentalist Islam today, and of Mormonism in the past, has tended to see women not only as lesser beings, but as founts for the corruption of innocent males. Why else keep those provocative bodies well covered up? And especially so in the case of the Muslims?"

"By the way," mused Millie, nodding in enthusiastic agreement. "have you ever looked carefully into the Islamic version of heaven? It seems that the 'Afterlife', for those who have devoted themselves sufficiently to pursuing 'jihad' in this world, is peopled by hordes of 'pure' virgins. By this they mean female beings who have never, and *will* never, indulge in the 'impure' practice of menstruating. I wonder how many normally functioning Muslim women have ever thought to ask where that leaves *them* after they die? No mention is made, in any of the theological literature that I've read, about an Afterlife for *them*. Now there's an issue you modern feminists could really set your teeth into, Evelyn!"

"It's a good thing Mary isn't here to hear all this. She'd leave me immediately for even participating in such a conversation." Sam's eyes gleamed as he tried for a few moments to suppress the loud guffaw that accompanied his words. "You are positively blasphemous, Millie!"

"Yes, isn't she?" Evelyn joined in the laughter. "I'm afraid it's going to get you into trouble with some important people someday, Millie."

"An even more scary thought has just occurred to me." said Millie. "Consider for a moment all the scarcely masked hatred (or, at least, mistrust) displayed by fundamentalists of such religions for that half of their own tribe on whom they depend for *sexual intercourse*, and for producing their offspring. Now add to this an obsession on *non-intercourse* of any sort whatsoever with the Other, or Infidel. It seems to me this amounts to a potentially lethal mix for those who need simple absolutes in an increasingly complex world. Mind you, I'm not criticizing only the fundamentalist roots of Islam and Mormonism here. None of us is immune to this kind of thinking. I'd guess it's very possible that both these features appeal to the genetic potential for tribalism in all of us. However, the real danger comes when we structure and preserve cultures that *reinforce* our more base urges. And that's what these sorts of religions do."

"I simply cannot accept that all humans have a genetic need to lose themselves in exclusive, tribal types of religion," Evelyn objected. Feeling the recent comments of the other two might be moving the conversation toward the dangerous ground of biological determinism, she decided to add a note of levity. "Take me, for instance. I was raised in a relatively elitist and affluent Unitarian community in Boston. We were always taught to pride ourselves on our tolerance of all the *lesser* breeds of belief and ritual. That's why I put up with you two with your strange backgrounds and skeptical outlooks when thousands wouldn't."

"Oh yes, the Unitarians. I don't really know much about them, other than what you've told us, Evelyn. However, my impression is that, whereas we righteous Mormons enjoy predicting that secular humanist types such as our Millie here will rot in Hades for not believing in anything, we suspect that you Unitarians may well meet the same fate for believing in both *anything* and *everything*!"

"As to that," said Evelyn, "I must tell you a little story about Millie's one visit to the Unitarian church here. It happened to be the September gathering in which we celebrate what we call 'the water ritual'. People who wish to do so come up to the podium with a sample of water from someplace they've visited during the holidays. It's really designed to give the members a chance to explore with all of us any special meaning derived from their travels. But of course Millie couldn't (or wouldn't) accept that! She had to make fun of it."

"I swear I sat politely through the entire, interminable

experience. I merely told you on the way home that I planned to take part in the ritual the following year," Millie interrupted. "I suggested bringing a sample of my pee and explaining that it symbolized an entire summer's exploration of my 'inner being'."

After the laughter had abated, Millie apparently decided it was time to change the subject.

"Evelyn," she said, "tell us some more about how your Boston holiday went. I thought of you several times when we were socked in with rain and fog and even two days of ice here. Did you have the 'White Christmas' that all you Christian types dream of?"

"Now, Millie, you know very well that we Unitarian Universalists don't consider ourselves a Christian denomination, although liberal Christians are welcomed as members. As are Jews. And we might possibly be persuaded to accept the odd *humanist* of Jewish background. Though I'm afraid we would probably have to draw the line at Mormons, even non-orthodox ones." Evelyn wanted to show them she knew very well when she was being teased. "But I admit that many of our congregations *do* join in with many of the Christian celebrations. As for your question, I merely had a good visit with my parents. Just the three of us. And, yes, we did have snow, which I enjoyed. But I'm happy to be back here. I'm increasingly finding that visits home to Boston turn out to be rather quiet affairs. I don't seem to have any close friends there any more." *But it would have been so different*, she thought, *if only Abdul had been with me.*

"I just thought of something relevant to what we've been discussing." Millie offered, after a pause. "Sam, it's apparent that you've come a long way from the strict theological box that you were born into. It says a lot for you that you've managed to develop this distanced and critical, yet still tolerant, stance of yours concerning those beliefs. Not to mention your wonderful sense of irony about it all. I doubt whether I could have come half so far, if I had been born into such circumstances. How about you, Evelyn?"

Evelyn readily concurred. A few minutes later a considerably more relaxed Sam got to his feet.

"Speaking of tolerating others' beliefs, Millie," he turned with his hand on the door knob, "How are you making out with those nuns in that advanced degree class of yours... the one they call BEAD?"

"Just great. They seem to respect me as a person and I, them. Our conflicting world views don't come into it at all, because we find we can agree on the need to develop some kind of universally applicable ethic in children. And we agree, as well, on the primary role of reason and scientific inquiry in resolving our man-made problems. (You notice how we liberated women still like to say '*man*-made' when it comes to problems, Sam!) And it's a damn good thing we *do* get along, because my class is now down to those three and one male student."

"No! Whatever happened?" Evelyn exclaimed, as Sam appeared to find himself for once at a loss for words.

"It seems that Harvey and those who were complaining about me got together and decided to solve the problem by forming a new BEAD Sociology of Education class with Gus Rasmussen at the helm. The four students who stood by me refused to go along with it, so I'm being allowed to continue teaching them. That way, Harvey assures me, he's avoided any formal imputation of my teaching abilities."

"I think it stinks to high heaven! At any point in all this, were you given a chance to defend yourself against their accusations?" Sam's voice was steely with suppressed anger.

"I was only informed of the decision when Harvey called me in for little talk after I returned to resume teaching duties last week. But I guess that's the way things are done around here."

"But it *is* a pretty good solution, isn't it?" Evelyn thought it was time to try to bring a little perspective to the situation. "You're now free of all the stress and unpleasantness associated with teaching people who don't respect or accept you. And those students will no doubt learn a lot more during this second term if they're with someone like Gus, with whom they can feel comfortable. As you're so fond of saying, Millie, sometimes we just have to accept the least worst among a number of unsatisfactory alternatives."

Millie gazed at her steadily for a couple of minutes, her face gone suddenly expressionless.

"Yes, I suppose you're right," she said finally. "I'd better get back to work. After all, at least until I'm informed otherwise, I still appear to have all of two and one-tenth classes to prepare for." Sam quickly took his leave as well and, for Evelyn, the day settled back to the usual routine.

She had seen little of Abdul since the beginning of the new term. Although he was unfailingly polite and friendly whenever they happened to meet in the lounge during coffee breaks, no effort had been made by either of them to resume their nightly encounters in Evelyn's apartment. She struggled mightily with this unsatisfactory state of affairs, finally managing to convince herself that the entire episode with Gus, including the trip to Australia, had not been Abdul's idea. Late on the day of her happy conversation with Millie and Sam, she found her thoughts returning to Abdul. She missed him so terribly. Was he lonely for her as well? Surely they had both suffered enough for what was probably no more than a bit of typical male thoughtlessness on his part! What right had she to be so unforgiving? Her mind was a virtual whirlpool of such musings when she happened to drop in at the lounge for the day's last cup of coffee. Discovering him alone in the room seemed like an omen. She just couldn't resist the temptation to offer him another chance.

"Abdul," she said now, as she approached him, "I've got some left-overs in the fridge from yesterday's dinner. How would you like to share them at my place tonight?" The brief hesitation on his part made her wish, momentarily, she hadn't spoken. Then a warm smile spread across his face, and he agreed to come up at 7:00 p.m. Somehow, at that instant, she felt that all would be right between them after all. And so it seemed, when he knocked at her door and greeted her warmly. During their dinner conversation he responded readily to her questions about the Australian trip and, in exchange, she offered a few wry comments about Boston in winter. It was not until she lay beside an uncustomarily relaxed Abdul sometime following their sexual encounter later that evening that her mind began to dwell once more on the events of the afternoon. Abdul seemed to notice her pre-occupation and inquired about it as the two of them got up to dress. She told him about what had happened to Millie's BEAD class.

"I think I agree with Sam on this one," he spoke thoughtfully, after listening carefully to the story. "I do not like this, Evelyn. It indicates a lack of respect for Millie's rights that the other members of your Department should not readily countenance."

"But what about the rights of the students? I was given the other side of all this by Meredith Walker, and it's clear to me that there was a *conflict* of rights in this case. As much as I'm usually the first to criticize Harvey when he steps out of line, I just don't see how anyone could have arrived at a more practical and mutually acceptable solution. If there's fault anywhere, it probably lies with your BEAD teaching team for not communicating better, and for not putting pressure on Millie earlier to organize her course in accordance with the rules that you had all established for the program. And *especially* for not vetting such a revolutionary approach at the Faculty level before launching it merely at the demand of the students."

"With hindsight, I have to think you might be right. However, my own excuse is that I simply assumed that the project had been thoroughly discussed by your Foundations Department as it had been by ours, and that you were all in agreement with the Methods people on this. And that we would all conduct our individual classes as we saw fit. And of course that, if any one of us felt that our subject could *not* best be taught in the student-centered, non-pedagogical, non-evaluative context, she or he would be free to use a more traditional approach. At no point in our preliminary discussions during that initial retreat was any mention made of coercion, or of fixed rules to be obeyed by all the team members. If that had been the case, then it should have been made clear to the participants, professors and students alike. And it most certainly should have been carefully explained to the one person who was not present at the retreat. To my knowledge, this was never done. Millie had no reason whatsoever not to assume that she could conduct her Sociology of Education class the way she had originally planned it. I had certainly understood that to be the case. We are all at fault in this, and I for one shall try to make amends to Millie."

So a potentially happy and fulfilling interlude in Evelyn's day was transformed—by Millie's self-made problems, she couldn't help but feel—into a less-than-satisfactory prelude to a restless night. Abdul was becoming surprisingly preoccupied with the situation, and any hope that he and Evelyn might have had for an extended quiet time together that evening was shattered by his insistence on worrying away at the problems with the BEAD program.

And indeed, in the days to follow, Abdul appeared to be going all out to make Millie once more feel at ease in the faculty lounge at lunchtime. His recently acquired habit of coming and going chiefly with Gus and Harvey was altered somewhat as he began to appear more frequently in Millie's company—invariably engaged in lively, laughter-punctured conversation. Evelyn suspected that, without Abdul's active encouragement during the weeks that followed, Millie would have remained in lonely solitude in her office. She was still not the exuberantly self-confident character of former days, but the old, somewhat crude, sense of humor was beginning to rebound and she was moving once more as if the heavy body had become less burdensome.

The day Harvey surprised them all by announcing a meeting of the Foundations of Education Department, there was a large contingent of faculty members from all the subject areas eating their lunches in the lounge. Harvey had entered in a harassed, rushing manner with a small newspaper in his hand. He continued to finger this nervously as he informed the Foundations people of the time, late the following afternoon, when they were all invited . . . even urged . . . to gather in the little meeting room alongside his office.

"Something has come up," he said, and could not be persuaded to pursue the matter any further. With a marked absence of his usual *bonhomie*, he turned and made for the door, almost colliding with Gus and Abdul who had paused on the point of entry.

"What's got into Harvey, I wonder?" Gus made the inquiry in a general way to those assembled around the lounge.

"He had this week's student newspaper . . . that *Pacific Tide* thing . . . and kept sneaking looks at it," Helen Korensky got up purposefully as she spoke. "Has anyone got a copy in here? No? Then I'm just going to dash out to get one. There should be a pile of them around somewhere. I don't know about the rest of you, but he's got me mighty curious. Whatever it is, it has to be very serious for you Foundations people, if Dr. Garfinkle is actually calling a meeting over it."

"Has one of us written a column for the student paper, criticizing their university education?" asked Muthu hopefully. "Or, better yet, criticizing our administration in the Foundations Department?"

"Or, even better, the *lack* of administration in our Department?" Stanley Wheeler joined Muthu in the attempt to lighten an atmosphere gone suddenly tense. For a while, the two engaged in a creative contest of trying to outdo one another in proposing imaginative causes of a crisis in the Foundations Department. Evelyn noticed that Millie was not responding to the humorous forays around her. Her body seemed turned to stone. She was breathing quickly and the hands on the arms of her chair were clenching and re-clenching in a sporadic way. The round face was suffused with the deep purplish red color that made Evelyn wonder if her old friend was developing a serious health problem. Hardly surprising, she thought. If only the stubborn woman would try to lose a hundred pounds or so! After some minutes of banter she noticed that the entire group were cooperating in a subtle attempt to direct the conjecturing about the meeting away from Millie. To a person, they were resisting any impulse to glance in her direction, but the outpouring of anxiety and sympathy for her was manifest. The problem must surely be with Millie's BEAD class—any reference to which they had for several weeks been studiously avoiding when she was within earshot. What else could it possibly be?

Helen had not returned by the time lunch break was over, so Evelyn found herself rather reluctantly joining the exodus back to classrooms and offices. She made sure that she found one of the student papers on the way, however. It wasn't long before she realized that she was not going to have to wait until the next day to discover what had upset Harvey. The news blazed at her when, back in her office, she opened the front page.

"EDUCATION PROFESSOR ACCUSED OF FRAUD, SEXISM AND RACISM!" was the headline. Whatever could it mean? Was it those latent lesbian proclivities of her friend that she had always suspected? And 'fraud'? Had Millie not really completed her doctorate at the University of Miami? But she already had one anyway—in chemistry! She was so sure Millie was the target that she had read halfway down the page before recognizing that the problem was something else entirely. A young Rain Forest College student named Valerie Charles was accusing one of the historians in the Foundations of Education Department—mercifully, as yet nameless—of not one, but several serious breaches of professional ethics.

Evelyn quickly scanned the remainder of the news item. The professor in question was said to be known to have a history of female sexual abuse. The student had objected to his threat to give her a low grade for the autumn term's work unless she granted him sexual favours. When she refused to go along with his demands he assigned her a 'C' and suggested that she not return to his class. This, in spite of the fact that she had always before maintained a 'B' average, and had previously been given every reason to expect an 'A' in this particular course. When confronted, the professor attacked her physically, ejecting her from his office so roughly that she was thrown to the floor.

The editors of the newspaper, when given the story by the Women's Cultural Revolution, ran a background check on the "abusive professor" and discovered that he claimed to have obtained his doctorate in history from an institution of which no one had ever heard. In fact, it was presumed to be a mail-order degree of some kind. On further researching their story, the student editors had come up with several other female students who were willing to testify against the man, including one with whom he supposedly had an affair the previous year after intimidating her with the offer of "an A for a lay".

If any of this is true it's positively damning, Evelyn thought. Of course they were talking about Sam Barnes! But it was a Sam Barnes who was totally at odds with the character she had thought she knew. How could all this possibly have been going on while none of them suspected anything? And *where* did it all take place? Certainly not in Sam's office. She could vouch for that. No one in the entire faculty put in longer hours in the office than she did. While there, she could hear practically every word spoken next door and virtually interpret the meaning of every movement, as well as witness the coming and going of every visitor. And a fraudulent doctorate? Simple, honest Sam? How inconceivable it all was!

There was none of the usual easy conversation among the members of the Department as they gathered for the meeting early the following morning. Evelyn had called on Millie, hoping for a chance for an exchange of impressions, but had found her office empty. Now the missing occupant was arriving a few minutes late, eyes smoldering, moving with none of the recently returned lightness of step that had always surprised people who didn't know her well and who expected the lumbering movements characteristic of obesity. A stunned-looking Sam came in later still, after Harvey had actually begun the meeting. He moved a chair to the side and sat down on it, wooden-faced, avoiding all eye-contact, as if already he felt estranged from them all.

"I imagine everyone's read *The Tide* by now," Harvey began, with much throat clearing and shuffling of papers. "So I don't think it will be necessary to repeat the details of the deplorable charges made against one of our members. I'm also sure that, like me, you are all withholding judgment on this entire matter. We're here today to discover what's been going on. Not to assign blame and, in particular, not to indulge in any witch hunt."

"May I take it, then, that this meeting is to give Sam a chance to respond to these outrageous charges?" asked Stan Wheeler.

"And to back him up in any suit he chooses to launch against the student newspaper?" This from Muthu who sat forward tensely, for once without an unlighted pipe in hand.

"All in good time. I've called you together today at the request of Dean Scott who, by the way, will be meeting privately with Dr. Barnes and myself this afternoon. He has asked me to explore the matter in the presence of all of you, so that no one will have any excuse to accuse us of a conspiracy of silence around this. I'm going to assume that, by now, everyone knows the nature of the charges. Would you mind, Professor Barnes, if we ask you at this point to tell us your side of the story? If there is any possible justification for the behavior described in the newspaper account, now is the time for you to lay it all out for us. I'm sure I can speak for the others here in assuring you that we're all willing to lean over backward to give you the benefit of the doubt."

"I hardly know how to begin, the whole thing is so crazy. It's like asking me when did I stop beating my wife when I've never laid a finger on her."

"Are you saying that there is absolutely no basis for any of these accusations?" Harvey's tone was incredulous.

"None whatsoever! I've been wracking my brain all night trying to think of anything I might have said in jest to any female students at any time that could possibly have given them the impression that I was threatening to mark them down if they didn't have sex with me."

"What about Valerie Charles? Her case is the most recent, so you should have no problem with your memory here. Was there no intimidation on your part in this case?"

"Not unless you consider the implied threat wielded by every instructor, by virtue of his role and the authority assigned to him by the university, to give low marks to a student if that student fails to fulfil the course requirements satisfactorily. Miss Charles evidently was in the habit of missing classes and not submitting assignments. I merely did what I hope any of you would do in such a circumstance. I advised her to withdraw from the course if she didn't intend even to attempt to do the required work."

"What happened in your office a couple of weeks ago when Ms. Charles was there alone with you?"

"We had a heated argument, at least on her side. She came in to complain about the grade I had assigned her for the first term's work. When I refused to alter this, after carefully explaining exactly where and in what specific ways her achievement had failed utterly to come up to par, she began to scream epithets at me. I quite calmly showed her to the door, and she rushed out in a rage."

"You claim you didn't strike her and throw her to the floor in the hallway?"

"I most certainly did not. I admit I did hear a bit of a thud and a scramble after she had erupted through the door and banged it in my face. But whatever happened to her at that juncture, I had no part in it."

"As you are no doubt aware, another of the charges against you is by a former student of yours. It involves your having conducted a long-term affair while she was in your class, an affair which you initiated and maintained by the bribe of an 'A' for her final mark. Do you deny this as well?"

Harvey was waxing quite eloquent by this time. *He's actually enjoying this*, Evelyn thought. There was a pause while all those in the room seemed to be holding their breath.

"I wish, for the sake of my marriage, that I could deny the affair with this young woman. The fact is that I can't." The words sounded strangled, and Sam now spoke to the floor. "But I swear it did not begin until after her graduation. She came in to see me to tell me about her good luck in getting on with one of the local schools as a beginning teacher, and then sort of got the habit of coming to me whenever she needed advice. She was extremely attractive and, I realize now, a bit aggressive when it came to getting what she wanted from a man. But I was the senior person, both in age and position, and I take full responsibility for what happened. However, it *was* between two consenting adults, and extremely brief, and with no professor-student relationship involved by the time it began. It is also currently a serious issue between my wife and me, which is bad enough in terms of consequences for my family. But I really don't think it has anything to do with the university, *or* with the Women's Cultural Revolution."

"That remains to be seen, I'm afraid." Harvey managed a tone and manner both authoritative and slightly unctuous. "And now, *Dr.* Barnes, we come to the questions raised about your credentials. The Dean tells me he has checked the copy of your doctoral certificate in the office files and found that it was apparently awarded by a 'Bennet Institute'. However, try as we might, neither of us could recall ever having heard of such an organization. Of course we haven't had time to do any research to check it out. Could you enlighten us on this matter?"

"You mean, could I tell you something about the Bennet Institute? Or do you want some official proof of its existence?"

"Both, I think. You understand, it's not that we're accusing you of getting the job on the basis of false credentials. Not at this point anyway. Nor are we trying to impugn your alma mater. But, even if it *is* legit, you must admit that it is hardly one of America's top ten universities!"

"I'm quite aware of that. However, I've never made any claim to having been educated at one of the top universities. The Bennet Institute is a Mormon college in Utah which, although its standards are, in fact, higher than those of many comparable American institutions, is not fully accredited internationally. This is because of its insistence on hiring only those instructors, and admitting only those students, who share the Mormon faith. I have here all the official information on its status, which I will be happy to share with you."

"Did you inform the Dean of the rather questionable

status of your doctoral degree when you applied here nine years ago?"

"Yes I did. But no graduates or instructors at the Bennet Institute would consider their degrees to be questionable from an *academic* viewpoint. If you recall, at that time Canadian universities (and especially Education Faculties) were expanding at an extremely rapid rate and were most anxious to hire experienced and qualified people. I imagine I was hired on the basis of my publishing and teaching record rather than on the prestige of my doctorate. I should also remind you that many people with only a Master's degree were also being taken on then."

"Now it's your turn," Harvey turned to the tense, listening group. "If any of you can think of something that I've overlooked, now is your chance to ask about it."

"I don't think that faculty members should have to put up with this kind of thing." Millie's voice was ringing with indignation. "It's clear that these so-called charges are nothing but a bloody bunch of bullshit! I'd like to move that we issue some kind of declaration of support for Sam, and that we do it at once so all this hateful gossip will be quashed before it does any more damage to innocent people."

"I really do not think we can do that at this moment in time." Willard Grange spoke quietly and in his usual fussy manner. "Qualified support, yes, pending further inquiries. But for the sake of the reputation of the Department, not to mention the entire Faculty of Education, we must be extremely careful to have all the facts straight before issuing any statement. I do not think it is too much to ask that Professor Barnes provide us with some supporting evidence for his claims, given that there would appear to exist a number of witnesses on the other side."

"But how the hell can one prove a negative?" sighed Leslie Brittan, aiming his remark at the ceiling as he pulled at his beard.

"Sam, you heard what Dr. Grange has just said." Harvey resumed his leadership role in the discussion. "Do you have any witnesses for anything you've just told us? Concerning the charge of abuse of power in your relations with female students, I mean."

"The only thing I can propose is that you interview a random sample of my current and previous students. I can't believe that they're all out to get me! Also, I think that Evelyn overheard something of the altercation with Valerie Charles. Isn't that so?" Sam turned to her with a pleading, hunted look in his eyes. "And Millie must have been coming along the hall, because she joined us in Evelyn's office a few minutes later."

Evelyn felt a surge of panic. She hated being put on the spot this way. She had indeed witnessed the ejection of the student from Sam's office, and had overheard her shouted remarks. But as to what he had done in the moment before she saw Valerie scrambling to collect her books on the hallway floor, she had no real way of knowing. It was true that she invariably heard most of what went on in his office, and was almost certain that no hanky panky of any kind had ever taken place there. *Almost* certain, that is. But what if they had whispered? She *had* been aware of the frequent visits of the former student with whom Sam had just confessed to a relationship, and recalled not having been particularly curious because several of her own recently graduated students had become nuisances at times, in their obvious need for encouragement during that difficult first year of teaching. What troubled her now was the question of what she could possibly say at this early stage in the proceedings that did not commit her to more than she was willing to vouchsafe—especially until she had a chance to talk with Meredith Walker and was given access to the information that the feminist group had gathered.

"I met Ms. Charles as she rushed past me in the hall, eyes flashing murder, but certainly revealing nothing hurt but her pride." Millie now broke the uncomfortable silence. "I wish I could say that I overheard the preceding conversation, but I didn't. Other than a loudly shouted bit of name-calling on her part. However, Sam's shaken manner and the subsequent comments by both Evelyn and him certainly support the events as he has just described them."

When she could no longer ignore the expectant faces turned in her direction, Evelyn began to speak carefully and with considerable reluctance.

"I'm sorry to say that I can't really corroborate anything I didn't actually witness, other than the fact that Ms. Charles did shout something insulting at Dr. Barnes. Then I heard him ask her to leave at once. Almost simultaneously there was a crash and a fall and I saw her on the floor, gathering up herself and her books. That's really all I know from first-hand experience. I wish I could tell you something more definitive, but I'm sure you all wish me to restrict myself to what I actually saw and heard, and to avoid including my interpretations and assumptions."

"Of course, of course, Dr, Ashton-Brent. You're absolutely right." Harvey assured her comfortingly. "Indeed, we all understand that you would have been trying your best *not* to listen to the conversation in the next room. I think," he said now, looking at his watch, "I'm going to have to bring this meeting to a close. From this point on, because of the gravity of the charges, the matter will have to be pursued at higher levels within the university. But I can promise you it will be done as expeditiously and fairly as possible. One more thing. For the time being I will have to ask Professor Barnes to turn his classes over to our other two historians as, from this moment forth, he is on temporary leave of absence. I realize it's a lot to ask of Professors Muthu and Wheeler, but we hope to have things back to normal in a few weeks at most. Meanwhile, the less said about all this the better, especially where the press and student body are concerned. My appreciation to all of you for your cooperation. Including you, Professor Barnes, for suffering our questioning with such patience."

Sam turned without a word and went quickly out the door. But where could he go other than to his own house? And what kind of reception would he find there? Evelyn felt a sharp twinge of sympathy, thinking of his straitlaced wife Mary, brooding at home with her new-found awareness of his unfaithfulness. But then, momentarily, she was conscious of the intrusion of the wickedly mischievous question of why a Mormon wife would really trouble herself so much about that. Brushing this aside guiltily, she continued mulling over the problem. Suddenly she became aware of Millie's rush past her as she, too, hurried out. A few minutes later Evelyn found herself walking down the hall in the company of the philosophers, in almost funereal silence. What could one possibly say after the explosion of such a bombshell other than surmising, on the basis of too little evidence, about the guilt or innocence of those immediately involved, and the suspected complicity and possible motivations of all concerned?

All that she had ever experienced of Sam Barnes, the ever-helpful colleague and enjoyable neighbor, argued against the possibility of his guilt. Certainly, as his virtual office mate, she was in the best position to know what the man had been up to when he was not in class. More times than she could count she had been both interrupted and profoundly bored by what she couldn't help but overhear from his office. She had even gone to the trouble of having ceiling-high book shelves built all along their shared wall. And both had arranged their desks on the far sides of the twin offices. But still, every conversation on either side managed to intrude to some extent into the neighbor's space. Now, try as she might, she could think of no suspicious circumstances whatsoever that might be consistent with the charges cited in the student paper and confirmed by Harvey. But could she be sufficiently certain to bear witness in Sam's favor when he was out of her sight and hearing? After all, she had not recognized the significance of the visits of former student with whom he had admitted to an affair. A certain long-conditioned circumspection where her career was concerned now made her reluctant to put herself into a position from which there could be no retreat if subsequent evidence went against him. She decided that the safest approach would be to introduce the subject at the coming meeting of the board of the Women's Cultural Revolution, and to refrain from discussing it with anyone until then.

Two evenings later, Evelyn arrived at the meeting to find the rest of the board members in a state of high excitement and anger. As one of the few representatives of the professional staff of the university, she couldn't help but feel somewhat intimidated by the clear anti-faculty sentiment being expressed in no uncertain terms by those present. It was all-too evident that Sam had already been tried and found guilty by these young women.

The subject dominated the discussion. Sam's forced relinquishment of teaching duties was announced with approval and loudly applauded. It seemed that there were at least three students, in addition to the graduate claiming a long-term affair, who had now registered a willingness to testify against their former professor. The Women's Cultural Revolution had obviously decided to take an active role in collecting evidence and identifying potential witnesses. Furthermore, their special interest in supporting the plaintiffs had come to the attention of the national press, members of which were arriving tomorrow to cover the story. Meredith Walker was to be interviewed, and was now intent on getting specific information and advice from the membership. Already the project was feeling too much like a crusade for Evelyn's taste. She wondered if she could risk counseling prudence without being considered an out-and-out doubter and possible traitor to the cause of battling sexism.

"I really wonder if we should be giving all this to the press at this time," she ventured hesitatingly. "These are terribly grave charges being leveled against Dr. Barnes. Perhaps, in the interest of justice, we should wait until the matter has been assessed, from all angles, by those with the responsibility for doing just that." Sensing an immediate rise of antagonism in her listeners, she paused. "I just mean I wouldn't want us to be accused of conducting a witch hunt here," she finished lamely.

"But, don't you see, we've been warned about the danger of a cover-up (supposedly to protect the reputation of the university) unless we act quickly to ensure that all this gets known by the general public." This came from an earnest young woman whose name Evelyn had momentarily forgotten. "Some of us have had personal experience of how this type of expedient typically gets managed. We don't want that to happen here. We want to make sure that this man never gets another chance to abuse his power. As a matter of fact, Dr. Rasmussen suggested early on that getting the media involved might be the only way for us to go. Anyway, it's done now."

The following afternoon Evelyn discovered just how thoroughly and devastatingly it had, indeed, been done. The editors of both the local and national newspapers had been unable to resist using a catchy front-page headline, "A PASS FOR SERVICES RENDERED!" A certain Mormon professor had been accused of sexual abuse by several female students, and his temporary leave of absence pending further investigation was duly noted. Also mentioned was the possibility that he did not possess a legitimate doctorate. The charge of racism was repeated.

The Women's Cultural Revolution was given credit for spearheading the investigation, after having received complaints from a large number of students. Meredith Walker was featured as the leader of the new organization for women's rights on campus. She was quoted, as well, on the need for a complete overhaul of university curricula—one which would entail, at the very least, a Women's Studies program and a mandatory sensitivity workshop on sexism and racism for all instructors. Near the end of the piece was an oblique reference to the mysterious death of a young woman on this same campus at the beginning of the term: a death which had never been satisfactorily explained.

The next day the Faculty of Education was buzzing with suppressed excitement and concern. At lunch time the faculty lounge was uncharacteristically crowded, and the conversation waxed at fever pitch. Evelyn came in with Helen Korensky and some of the latter's colleagues in English Methods. However, the two women soon left the others to join the group of Foundations people gathered around their Head, who seemed to be trying to calm everybody down. Harvey had just been interrupted by Stan Wheeler.

"Did they ask *you* for an interview, or the Dean or Associate Dean? Couldn't someone from the administration have explained the unproven nature of the charges so that, at the very least, that reference to Mormonism might have been left out of the report? No one will have any problem in identifying him now. And in condemning him. As it is, no matter what comes out about his case in the future, the poor guy's professional career is finished. The story has been picked up this morning by every newspaper in the country, and he's been judged and found guilty by readers from coast to coast."

"I'm just as concerned about this as you are, Stan. And, no, none of us has spoken to a reporter. We may have been wrong, but we had to decide very quickly on a plan of action. Remember, we've never encountered anything like this before. Our joint decision was to refuse to discuss the situation until the investigation is complete. The report in the paper did, in fact, emphasize that what they were describing was the charge only . . . that nothing had as yet been substantiated."

Muthu, who had been sucking furiously on his unlit pipe, cleared his throat.

"What is most worrying to me," he said thoughtfully, "is that reference, at the very end of the article, to Cynthia Montague's death. The reader is left with the clear implication that there is a connection between these events, that Sam is somehow involved in that tragedy as well. Why else mention it in this particular context? Is it possible that our radical feminist group has been hinting at such a possibility? If that is, in fact, the case, then we are in very murky waters indeed."

"I can't think of anyone less likely to have been romantically involved with Cynthia than Sam Barnes." Millie spoke up firmly. "Surely we're not about to allow people to go around making subtle accusations about something as serious as that? Of all you fellows who used to enjoy indulging in a teasing relationship with her in and out of class, one of the few that I'm sure was never the least disposed in that direction was Sam. You'd be able to vouch for that, as his closest neighbor, wouldn't you Evelyn?"

"I can at least say that I never once heard or saw evidence that would indicate that he felt anything but a strong disapproval of Cynthia's tendency to flirt with her professors. And vice versa."

"I understand," said Helen, "that we have a professional association here at the university now. It's called the Canadian Association of University Teachers, or CAUT, for short. I know I've joined it and, in fact, I think pretty well all of us are automatically members. I hope Sam has been to see them to enlist their help in fighting all this."

"Muthu and I are planning to insist on it," said Stan Wheeler, "But we haven't been able to contact him. His wife just says he's not living there any more and then hangs up the phone."

"The charge of racism against Sam." Ned Smith spoke thoughtfully. "How does that come into the picture?"

"I believe the young woman, this Valerie Charles, is a native Indian belonging to one of the local tribes, and attending the Rain Forest College," volunteered Abdul.

Norah Edgar, one of the young female psychologists who had joined the Faculty that year, had been sitting quietly listening to the conversation.

"As one who doesn't really know any of the people concerned, I've been noticing something a bit strange going on here. I hope you won't mind my mentioning this, but in spite of all this indignant clamor concerning Dr. Barnes's troubles, no one seems to be asking the obvious question. Why would all these students be making such damning accusations if the man's not guilty?"

"I . . . suppose . . .," Millie spoke hesitantly, eyes narrowed. "You'd have to conclude that someone's out to get him."

"But why? And why Dr. Barnes, in particular? None of you has offered any satisfactory explanation of why this should be the case. Not in my hearing, anyway. Or of why at least four women would be willing to come forward and lie about something as intimate and humiliating as this. What could possibly be in it for them, other than a good deal of personal embarrassment? And I guess the other question I'd like to ask is, just how does Dr. Barnes' response to this differ from exactly what one would expect of any one of those sexist male academics that each of us has known at one time or another? I mean the men who were indeed taking advantage of their position of power to intimidate or abuse female students."

"In other words," Helen interrupted, "You're saying, what else would we expect of a guilty person in this situation but a stream of indignant denials?"

"And of an innocent person?" this from Muthu. "What are *his* options?"

Evelyn had been re-living the conversation among the young feminists at the meeting she'd attended two days previously. She had been thinking of the similarity between the two discussions—the members of each group not even considering the possibility that they could be wrong in their judgments. And she had been wanting to say something but not quite daring to. Now that Dr. Edgar had voiced some of her own reservations she decided to take the plunge.

"I've been trying to keep in mind that we . . . all of us . . . should wait for the evidence. Isn't it just remotely possible that Sam is not the person we've all imagined him to be? Although I have to admit that it would have been difficult for him to keep something like this from everybody."

"Especially from you, surely?" Muthu's glance at her was uncustomarily cold. "And where do you suggest he lived this second life? In some hideaway between his office and home, where I happen to know that he is a very involved husband and father? Indeed, my understanding is that he is supposed to have conducted most of his intrigues behind a closed door in his office. And that is the very office in which every word spoken can be heard by you."

"But, Muthu, I'm not saying he conducted any intrigues. I'm merely noting that I wasn't there every minute of the time Sam wasn't in class. Can't you see, that's what's worrying me about being asked to witness to the professionalism of his conduct?"

"Dr. Edgar," Millie broke the uncomfortable pause following this exchange. "I guess my answer to your very legitimate questions is that, in fact, I happen to have had personal experience of the kind of treatment at the hands of a male professor that you've mentioned. That's precisely why I'm confident that Sam is *not* guilty. He doesn't in any way fit the pattern that's all too familiar as far as I'm concerned. What makes me particularly indignant about all this is that it's highly likely the type of abuse of which Sam has been accused is, in fact, going on right here in this Faculty, almost literally before our eyes. But the real perpetrators know how to get away with it. They're very rarely, if ever, authentic moral conservatives like Sam. I'd say they're much more likely to be extreme libertarian types who mouth left-wing doctrines."

Most of the men in the group had remained silent, obviously deferring to the women on this. Now Muthu stirred again and, after a long, vigorous suck on his pipe, spoke slowly and with an unfamiliar gravity.

"I can only beg that we keep in mind two principles.

The first is the presumption of innocence until the evidence indicates otherwise. Surely the colleague who has shown nothing but a strong ethical character in all that we have observed of his actions and articulated ideas is deserving of that? The second principle is related to the first. The very expression 'knowing someone' implies being able to predict what that person would or would not do in specific situations. I submit that, as one who has worked and played closely with Sam for a number of years, I have not only a right but *a duty* to state my conclusion that he is incapable of the kind of activities of which he has been charged. Now you all know where I stand on this matter."

"Your loyalty is admirable, Professor Muthu. Let's hope it's not misplaced." Gus Rasmussen rose from his seat and moved toward the exit, delivering a parting shot as he glanced back over his shoulder. "However, I'm damn sure that some of us, and certainly more than a few of his students, have had very different experiences of Sam Barnes. And time will tell which of us is right."

CHAPTER 7

FEBRUARY, 1977

With the dark, wet weeks of the rain-forest winter gradually giving way to intervals of sunshine, and fresh breezes dancing in from increasingly placid reaches of ocean, Evelyn felt a surge of expectation. Surely, as the crocuses, daffodils and snowdrops began to sprout so, too, would a more hopeful, forward-looking climate in the Faculty of Education. But there were few indications of this. She now saw little of Millie, who no longer joined the group in the lounge for coffee breaks and lunch. She had to admit that the absence of the Faculty's two most colorful characters—Millie Eisenstadt and Sam Barnes—had cast a major pall over the conversation. As it was, nothing seemed to lift her spirits: neither Helen Korensky's gossipy chatter (interspersed as it invariably was with common-sense observations) nor the incomprehensible abstractions passed to and fro by her colleagues in the Philosophy of Education. Nor even Muthu's occasional droll interjections.

For one thing, there was Abdul's worrisome behavior of late. He had stopped coming up to her room at night. She was not quite sure of the timing on this, but try as she would, she was unable to recall a single visit since an argument between them on an evening a week or so after the news of the Sam Barnes debacle. To add to the problem,

Abdul was another former regular who now appeared to be absenting himself from the informal gatherings in the faculty lounge as well. She had only fleeting glimpses of him in hallways, usually either alone or with Gus Rasmussen. And at least twice in the past week she had seen Abdul and Millie walking toward the latter's office with their heads together as if in earnest conversation.

Evelyn felt not only grievously wounded by Abdul's cavalier treatment, but resentful of the fact that he appeared to recognize no necessity for an explanation of his sudden change of heart—if that was, indeed, what had happened. Surely she deserved at least some kind of declaration of his intent, if not an apology. But, then, she was forced to face up to the uncomfortable fact that she had allowed him to begin the liaison and to carry it on with an equal lack of discussion. Where there had been no courtship, and then no public acknowledgement of the relationship, it was possible that he felt a corresponding lack of need to inform her of its ending. She reminded herself somewhat wryly of the soundness of a common sociological analysis of just such situations. Why had she, of all people, failed to realize that, if something is not in any way confirmed by one's peers or by the community at large, it might almost never have existed?

She tried to reassure herself with the idea that, once the Dean's formal interview and decision on the Sam Barnes case was over, the situation would get back to normal. The meeting was slated for the last week in the month. Apparently Sam had finally phoned the officials and informed them of his whereabouts. However, as far as Evelyn could tell, he was avoiding all contact with the members of the Faculty. All in all, the case had caused her a great deal of concern and embarrassment, not to mention the struggle with her conscience over the role that she, herself, should play in the proceedings. For it seemed that someone had reminded the Dean of the proximity of the two offices, and of the fact that Evelyn would be the one witness who could either make or break the case brought by the Women's Cultural Revolution against Dr. Barnes. And, for a while, she had really believed that she should and would fulfil that role. But the more she thought about it, the more problems she began to see with that course. She recalled that Abdul had noticed her gradual change of heart during the last few evenings they had spent together. At the time it had seemed gratifying that he was finally discussing a serious topic with her, and at great length.

"Why are you agonizing over this?" he had asked her one night. "Surely you must do what duty demands in such a case. You are, in fact, the only person who can testify that it is extremely unlikely, if not impossible, for Sam to have been carrying on the office liaisons of which he stands accused. As you people are so fond of saying, what is the big deal here?"

"But merely because I never heard anything remotely suspicious does not mean that he wasn't doing what the young women are accusing him of. There are other places where he might have taken them, knowing that I'd be present in the office. And by no means was I there during *all* of his free hours. How can I possibly *guarantee* that he isn't guilty as charged?"

"That is not your task, nor your responsibility. All that is being asked of you is to stand up at that hearing and tell the university officials about the circumstances of your office situation, and recount what you did and did not witness, where Sam is concerned. Is that really too much to be expected to do for a friend and colleague? And in the service of justice?"

"But Abdul, that's not how the Women's Cultural

Revolution will interpret it. For them, the very act of my giving evidence which might serve to exonerate Sam will mean that I've succumbed to pressure from the male establishment. That I'm willing to allow myself to be used in the service of *injustice* . . . not of justice! Any influence I may have been able to build up with them will be destroyed. I've been talking the situation over with Harvey, by the way, and he made precisely that point."

"I beg your pardon! I had not realized that Harvey Garfinkle was now your chief mentor." Abdul's tone had become coldly ironic.

The fact was that Harvey had been extraordinarily attentive to her of late, demonstrating a side to his personality for which she had heretofore not given him credit. More than anyone else, he appeared to be aware of the seriousness of the moral dilemma facing her, and to sympathize and agree with the legitimacy of her concerns about probable consequences of available alternatives. Why, she wondered, couldn't Abdul similarly understand that, merely by appearing as a witness in Sam's defense, she would be aligning herself in an irrevocable way with the male patriarchy that she and her fellow Women's Cultural Revolutionaries were battling? And to what end?

Even Abdul admitted that, after all the adverse publicity, Sam would never be able to continue a career in Education anywhere in North America anyway, regardless of what the Dean's committee decided about his culpability in this particular instance. Harvey had helped her understand that her own future career couldn't help but be tainted as well by the slightest hint of association with Sam's cause. And she didn't need that, not now. Not when there was every sign that this was to be the year of her long-awaited promotion to Associate Professor.

There was also the question of who else would be testifying before the Dean's committee, on both sides of the issue. That would inevitably be important in the determination of her own decision as well. Her curiosity concerning this drove her to seek out the company of Helen one day at lunchtime. To her relief, a little tentative probing loosed a veritable flood of information from that quarter. It appeared that Helen, as usual, had unerringly found a way to keep abreast of the latest developments.

"I'm going to be rather involved in the process myself," she declared proudly. "The Canadian Association of University Teachers (CAUT) was looking for disinterested parties from other Departments who might attend the proceedings as impartial observers. You know, to represent the general professional interests of all of us. They would take part in some of the 'in-house' discussions afterward with the official committee, to contribute to the appropriate assessment of evidence. So I volunteered. I hear that Abdul will be there in that capacity as well, along with one of the Ed. Psych. people."

"Has the Dean informed you about which of the members of the Foundations Department will be called to testify?" Evelyn asked.

"I don't think it's official yet. Although I hear by the grapevine that Muthu, Stan Wheeler and Millie Eisenstadt have offered to be character witnesses in support of Sam. Apparently Leslie Brittan wants to appear as well . . . I think to question the appropriateness of the procedure as a whole. He seems concerned chiefly about the precedent that will be set by this entire affair. On the other side, I hear that we have a rapidly growing number of young members of the Women's Cultural Revolution clamoring to have their voices heard."

Evelyn revealed nothing, but she felt a surge of relief to

know that Sam would not be relying solely, nor even largely, upon testimony from her. All three subject areas within the Department—sociology, history and philosophy—would be represented on his defense team. And with Helen and Abdul, as representatives of CAUT, placed in key positions of influence with the Dean's committee for the final summing-up and interpretation of evidence, surely there was no need of her to enter the lineup. She decided to do a little reconnoitring with Meredith Walker's group and see what she could learn there, about the state of their preparations for the coming showdown. However, as she made a few polite noises about the pressures of work, and rose to leave, Helen looked up at her intently and spoke with considerable urgency.

"As an outsider, Evelyn, and strictly off the record, I would like to offer a bit of advice to you about your own possible unique role in the case. If you have another moment to spare."

Reluctantly, Evelyn sat back in her seat. Whatever Helen had to add, she really didn't want to hear it.

"I do think that Sam will be counting on *you* to supply something no one else can. That is, a long term, eye-witness (and, what's even more relevant) *ear-witness* account of his behavior and typical relationship with the students in his classes."

"But can't you see, Helen, that's exactly what's been causing me to have serious reservations about testifying? Precisely because I cannot in all honesty tell them what Sam wants and expects to hear from me . . . that I know with absolute certainty no hanky panky could ever have occurred in his office . . . I'm terrified that whatever I say will end up doing him more harm than good. Whoever is cross-examining me will very easily be able to twist my testimony so as to interpret it merely as a blatant attempt to protect a colleague. If there were anything absolutely definitive that I could offer I wouldn't hesitate for a second. As it is, for now I feel I have to consider it further, along with all the implications for my own future as well as Sam's."

With that, Evelyn hurried off, not wishing to hear any more arguments from Helen who, by her own admission, was supposed to be a neutral observer and not a proponent for Sam's cause.

The following evening, the Women's Cultural Revolution was holding a meeting which Evelyn was anxious to attend. Here, she would surely glean valuable information that would aid in her decision-making. No sooner had the group been called to order than it began to appear that there was indeed a wealth of evidence against Sam. At Melanie's invitation, a total of nine young women rose to speak. What each had to say was utterly shocking to Evelyn. In an almost methodical process, Sam was being presented as a serial sexual abuser whose exploitative activities had been occurring in a remarkably consistent pattern from the time he first arrived at NPU. In each case the story was that, at about half-way through the term, he would select one attractive female student from a class—often one with a good scholastic record—and begin gradually to lower her marks for assignments and exams. When she finally gathered the courage to meet with him in order to query her grades, the proposition would be offered. She would be told, in no uncertain terms to either "come across for him" in a private meeting place of his choosing, or "accept a failing grade for the course". Most claimed that they promptly left the class, without telling anyone the reason why. When asked why they didn't report him then and there, each had a similar response. "No one would have believed me", they said. This sent a shiver through Evelyn of the memory of Millie's experience, carrying with it the ring of authenticity. If it had been true even for someone as self-confident as Millie, why couldn't it be true, as well, for these young girls?

The one exception was Sylvia Cornish, a teacher who told the gathering that she became involved in an affair with Sam that lasted for a year after her graduation. When Evelyn asked why she remained intimate with him long after he would have had any hold over her, she replied that he had threatened to reveal her "method of wringing unearned marks from professors" to her current school principal.

The final witness against Sam being proposed by the Women's Cultural Revolution for the upcoming meeting of the Dean's committee was a distinct surprise to Evelyn. Meredith Walker now approached the podium in the front of the room with her usual purposeful stride. "I have a story to tell", she began, rather hesitantly, "although, unlike the previous ones, it's not a personal testimony. I'm sure that all of you shared my shock and sorrow at the fate that befell our fellow student, Cynthia Montague. And I'm equally sure that you all wish that we could somehow achieve a measure of justice for her, tragically belated as it will have to be. For some months now I've been feeling a personal responsibility here. This is because I received a phone call from a house mate of Cynthia's, who has since left the country, informing me about something that Cynthia had bragged to her a couple of years ago. The claim was that she'd been intimately involved with a member of our faculty. Cynthia had also made a point of saying that, because he was a family man with a responsible position and impeccable reputation, he'd do anything she asked so long as she promised not to reveal the relationship. The friend admitted to being a bit shocked at the glee expressed by Cynthia concerning the power she was thus able to exert over this man, and wrote it off as merely an all-too-typical exaggeration. However, when she read about Cynthia's sudden and unexplained death, she couldn't help but wonder if what the dead girl had told her had any basis in fact. If it did, she realized, it could be very significant. She wondered if she should be informing the RCMP. I talked her out of it. But now I wonder if I should have."

Gus Rasmussen who, although remaining in the background, had appeared to be engineering the program up until then, began to sputter with surprise and some observable dismay.

"But . . . but . . . this is mere hearsay, Meredith. You will only weaken our case by including this sort of unsubstantiated gossip concerning a tragedy that has already been satisfactorily explained!"

"Believe me, I've thought about that ever since I received the information. That's why I've never repeated a word of it until now. But, don't you see, the description fits Dr. Barnes so perfectly! Think of what he had to lose, as a respected member of Canada's Mormon community as well as an established Full Professor here."

"There's something else as well," Evelyn heard herself offering, against her better judgment. "Professor Issa told us that Cynthia was meeting someone outside that night, after the party. Someone who was to drive her home. That's why he says he let her go off on her own, in such a dubious condition. Professor Barnes and his wife were, as usual, not at the party, so he would have been perfectly free to be waiting for her outside, long after Mrs. Barnes had gone to bed."

"Most of the inhabitants of Richmond were not at the party," Gus reminded her coldly. "And most of those who attended had left the building by then. That argument simply doesn't hold water. No, I strongly advise you to refrain from making any specific accusations concerning the Cynthia Montague case. Accusations that could be readily refuted and thus appear to support Sam Barnes' claims of general innocence. Far better to use the technique I've been recommending. Veiled implications of his culpability in the affair . . . that's been working well for us. For God's sake don't spoil it by tipping your hand now. Especially when that hand is damn near empty!"

"I don't quite follow your reasoning, Dr. Rasmussen." Norah Edgar spoke from the back of the room. "At least I hope I'm misreading what your words seem to imply. However, I do agree that any re-introducing of the Cynthia Montague tragedy would only confuse the issue. Certainly the information you've just given us, Meredith, introduces the very real possibility of a sinister connection to the incident on the part of Dr. Barnes. But, on the other hand, it also offers a picture of him not as a perpetrator of abuse, but as the innocent victim of a conniving female. The Dean and others doing the judging might begin to wonder how many more of the incidents provided in the testimony are of this nature. Are you sure you want that?"

The matter of Cynthia Montague was dropped, for the time being, at least. It had given Evelyn food for thought, however. That night, in the privacy of her room, she suddenly realized, without consciously recognizing precisely when it happened, that she had reached her decision. She would keep herself totally separated from the entire ugly dispute. She wanted no part of either side of what was shaping up to be a very destructive battle from which none of the participants were likely to emerge unscathed.

The end of the first half of the final semester was now

approaching. Evelyn found herself so pre-occupied with preparing and marking mid-term assignments and exams, not to mention all the struggling with decisions that would have to be made concerning borderline students, that she had little time to worry about the count-down to Sam's crucial interview with the Dean's committee at the end of the month. In fact, when the day came, she thought it best to absent herself from the university immediately after her morning classes. Fortunately she had no commitments for the afternoon. She decided to devote the rest of the day to a shopping spree in downtown Vancouver, and to try to forget, as much as possible, the events occurring on campus.

However, on the following day she discovered that further avoidance of the topic was impossible. First there was Helen Korensky's visit to her office during a lengthy morning coffee break. Helen seemed obsessed with recounting the entire episode, moment by moment, and obviously felt the need for an interested listener. Later, at lunchtime in the faculty lounge, the room was alive with the subject. Each participant was apparently driven to relive his or her memory of what had occurred, and the remainder of the 'bag-lunch' crew were more than eager to listen. In fact, they did more than listen. Most of those not present at the Dean's hearing did their best to encourage, by avid questioning, ever more revelations of even the most minute details of the occurrence. Evelyn soon found herself almost as fully involved in the story as were those who had witnessed it firsthand. She walked home that night immersed in it, and discovered later that sleep was impossible. Almost as if she had herself been a participant, the events of the meeting pressed themselves upon her. To her dismay she realized that she had indeed been drawn into Sam's devastating experience, regardless of her efforts to remain aloof. Each time she closed her eyes and pulled up the covers, she began to see it all, as if it were happening in her presence at that very moment. In the end, it seemed, there was to be no escape—not for Sam and not for her, his former office partner.

On the morning when Sam's day of judgment finally arrived, the rain was streaming down the windows as the time approached for the Dean's committee to convene. It seemed, to those in attendance, as if the damp gloominess from outside had permeated the indoor areas as well, so dark was the general mood of the participants. At first, the group beginning to gather in the Faculty meeting room was surprisingly quiet. Only the sound of chairs being moved and bodies settling in broke the stillness. Harvey had arrived early and was seated at the table in the front, busily shifting papers and making notes. Two other narrow tables lined the room, one on each side, arranged so as to face one another. The three men who were to testify in Sam's support could be seen hesitating near the entrance, with Muthu waving his unlit pipe in an urgent fashion as he made a point to Les Brittan; while Stan Wheeler nodded vehemently in agreement. They were soon forced to move on into the room by the arrival of Meredith Walker and a contingent of four nervous-looking young women. A further threesome of students followed on their heels and paused, looking about expectantly, before beginning to move toward Muthu, Stan and Les Brittan. In response to a wave from Harvey, the opposing teams settled themselves at the tables facing one another across the small room. Abdul Issa and Helen Kerensky entered and were quickly ushered by Harvey to his table. Then came the Dean of Arts and Associate Dean of Education, who were promptly shown to the chairs on either side of Harvey. As Helen had predicted, these three administrators, along with Dean Scott, were to form the official committee in charge of arriving at the decision regarding Sam's guilt or innocence. Soon Norah Edgar of the Educational Psychology Department joined Abdul and Helen. The second-last empty chair at the head table was taken by the Dean's secretary, armed with the pad and pen required for her short-hand notes.

After what seemed to the others to be an interminable wait, Millie appeared. Looking about in a distraught fashion she moved laboriously toward the side on which sat Muthu, three of the attending students, and the other two Foundations professors. Finally Dean Scott came through the door, pausing to close it carefully after Sam Barnes, who had accompanied him. The Dean settled himself in the remaining chair at the head table, leaving Sam standing awkwardly by the entrance. A motion was then made by Harvey toward a small student desk to the right of the doorway, on the fourth wall of the room, facing the Dean's group. For a moment Sam looked puzzled, then almost stumbled over the desk before lowering his large-boned body into it.

The change in Sam was shocking, especially to those who had worked closely with him. He had lost considerable weight, and the once-jovial eyes were no longer defined by the spark of humor typically flashing from them. Those eyes were now darting about in a dazed fashion, while at the same time their owner failed to acknowledge even the few who attempted an embarrassed greeting. To the almost visible relief of the assembled group, Dean Scott soon broke the awkward silence by clearing his throat and proceeding to get the meeting underway.

"I want everyone here today to understand that this is a strictly informal attempt to get at the truth behind the recent allegations against Professor Samuel Barnes. My role, as I see it, is to question the witnesses for each side and then to take my time considering all of the evidence brought before us. Helping me in this task will be Dean Simpson, Associate Dean MacArthur and Department Head Garfinkle. Professors Edgar, Korensky and Issa are here as neutral observers representing their professional association, CAUT. I want to assure Professor Barnes that, in spite of the profusion of campus gossip, there is absolutely no prior presumption of guilt on the part of any of the four of us who will be weighing the evidence. So, let us get started! I have decided that the best procedure for accomplishing our task will be to begin by hearing one accuser at a time."

"Now," he continued slowly, after a pause during which there was much shuffling of papers and whispering among potential witnesses, for and against. "If we could begin the proceedings with Miss Sheila Radwinsky who, I understand, was a student in Professor Barnes' class on the History of the Family a few years ago."

A tall, thin blonde girl came to her feet hesitantly. After glancing fearfully at the committee members and then at Sam, she began to read rapidly and almost inaudibly from a prepared script. She was interrupted at once by Dean Simpson.

"Could we please hear the complaint in your own words?" he asked.

"I . . . I feel that Dr. Barnes created a . . . well, you know, a climate of sexism in his classes?" she offered falteringly, her voice rising interrogatively at the end of the sentence. Obviously she was finding this opening role a difficult one.

"Would you please outline exactly how that was done?" Dean Scott's tone was brisk, if not a trifle impatient.

"Well, you know, he said things about females that made us all uncomfortable. Of course we all knew about him being a Mormon and so conservative and everything, so we weren't all that surprised when he said about how polygamy must be a good form of marriage because . . . you know . . . women are weak and in need of protection. And he said Mormons and Muslims . . . you know, they both could teach modern society a lesson about how to handle 'uppity' women. Anyway, it was clear to all of us girls that there was simply no way we could ever be treated fairly in his class."

"And *were* you in fact treated unfairly?"

"Well of course. Because we're all 'uppity' women, as far as he's concerned. Or else we wouldn't be in university in the first place. You know . . . we'd be at home, like his wife, where he seemed to think that women belong."

In several follow-up questions it became clear that the Dean was vainly seeking a precise and factual answer, while the witness was plainly becoming less uncomfortable and even increasingly loquacious in the recitation of her general complaints against those who, in her mind, represented the male patriarchy. Finally, in an obvious effort to interrupt the flow, Les Brittan raised his hand.

"Dean Scott, I'm wondering about a few rules of procedure. Would you agree to the idea of my asking a defense witness either to question or to respond to each complainant? And then to giving Dr. Barnes an opportunity to tell his side of the story as well? If so, I would now like to suggest that we offer someone from the defense side a chance to participate." At the Dean's ready agreement, Les turned to the people seated beside him. One of the students, subsequently introduced as Carrie Hayden, stirred uneasily, then leaped to her feet and spoke.

"I simply can't believe this! Professor Barnes was only joking when he said things like that. I always assumed that he realized we were all aware of his Mormon family background, and he felt he could get his message about the evils of polygamy across best through irony. But apparently," she flashed an angry look at Sheila, "he overestimated his class. It's clear that appreciation of irony requires a degree of sophistication which not all of his students possessed."

"I think we should now move on." Dean Scott responded quickly, before Sheila could answer this charge. "But first," he added, "I want to assure you, Dr. Barnes, that you are welcome to intercede at any time, if you feel you would like to offer an explanation of something."

A brief pause followed, with everyone looking expectantly toward Sam, who gazed only at the floor.

"If there are no other comments on Miss Radwinsky's evidence", the Dean then continued, "I will now ask Miss Gloria Carleton to describe *her* experience with Dr. Barnes."

The next speaker appeared to have gained confidence from what had gone before. She was an attractive brunette who, like her fellow witnesses against Sam, was attired in uncustomarily conservative garb. As had the first witness, she glanced uncomfortably around the room, her eyes flitting from the head table to Sam. She took a deep breath and then, unlike Sheila Radwinsky, proceeded to speak firmly, as if she had memorized her contribution.

"I would also like to address the subject of the 'sexist atmosphere' that Professor Barnes tended to establish. I don't agree with Carrie Hayden at all! Someone must have got to her. Why I, myself, had a very threatening sort of thing happen to me where he's concerned. Of course I experienced the same discomfort that Gloria did by his general approach to women. You know, what he revealed in his numerous off-hand comments. But actually something worse happened to me when I took his class last year. I was having problems understanding some of the stuff he was teaching, and was particularly worried about a term paper I was trying to write. He invited me to drop in at his home one evening, when he said he'd have more time to help me. When I arrived I found, to my surprise, that his wife wasn't there. Dr. Barnes had seductive music playing in the background, and insisted I drink a glass of wine 'to relax' he said. I felt that he expected some special sexual services of me, and left as soon as I reasonably could. From then on I made sure I was never forced to be alone with him again. I got a low mark from him on my paper, by the way."

"Let me get this straight. Did Dr. Barnes, in fact, make any explicit sexual advances to you in the course of the visit to his home?" Dean Scott was leaning forward earnestly as he spoke.

"No . . . o, but I had drunk only one glass of wine and made sure that I left as soon as possible. I shudder to think of what he planned to do if I'd responded as he seemed to expect. By the way, I *did* hear what happened to several others who weren't as careful as I was."

"I would like to ask Miss Carleton something." Les Brittan had managed to get the Dean's attention. "First of all, who are these 'several others'? Why are they not here to speak for themselves? I'm sure you are aware, Dean Scott, that we cannot accept this kind of hearsay evidence. There's been far too much of it already in this case!"

At Dean Scott's urging, Gloria Carleton spoke again. This time the words came more hesitantly.

"They were afraid to go public . . . both because of not

wanting their families to know and for fear of what would happen in terms of their careers."

"Isn't it the case," Dr. Brittan continued, "that you and Dr. Barnes were not, in fact, alone in the house at all? That the three Barnes children were there, and that Dr. Barnes had to leave you at least twice when they required attention or help with homework in another room, and at least once to get his youngest settled down in bed? And isn't it also the case that what Dr. Barnes, a known teetotaller, served you was what he always served all his visitors? Wasn't it, in fact, a de-alcoholized wine?"

"Oh I don't think so! He went to his wine cabinet and I could see the bottles lined up there, and the one he poured from. And he did go out of the room from time to time, but that only roused my suspicions about what he was up to all the more."

"Dean Scott, I have here an assurance written and signed by Mrs. Barnes to the effect that, on the night in question, she had been called unexpectedly to attend an urgent church meeting and that the three children were at home with their father all evening." Quickly, the document changed hands.

One of the students who sat next to Stan Wheeler then raised her hand and was acknowledged by the Dean.

"My name is Sara Moynihan', she began. "I only wanted to add that I also have had problems understanding some difficult material in class and Dr. Barnes was always very willing to give me extra help. Sometimes by myself and sometimes with a few others, and either in his office or at home in the evening. Sometimes his wife was there and sometimes she had to leave for a church meeting just after we began. He always brought out the non-alcoholic beverage, and he liked to joke about how we could 'pretend we were drinking wine like regular grown-up people' So, you see, there was nothing exceptional or sinister about Gloria's experience. Except her interpretation of it!"

Dean Scott thanked Sara and appeared to decide that further pursuance of this particular subject was not likely to get them very far. He called on the next witness, who happened to be Valerie Charles. He asked her to describe in detail her problems with Dr. Barnes.

"I think everyone knows about my problems with him," came the indignant response. "How he insulted me in his office and then physically threw me out the door! In my case, Professor Barnes freely revealed his racism as well as his sexism. And that's a truly scary combination for someone with my background to stand up against. For example," she hurried on, anticipating the Dean's likely request for details, "when he discussed the evolution of the family in class, it was always obvious to me that he meant that development 'progressed' from the clan and tribe (representing aboriginal peoples, of course) to the extended family and then the nuclear family of the present-day Bourgeois and Imperialistic white man's world. And is he ever sexist! He always laughed at any suggestions about the traditional role of women being inferior to that of men, saying things like, 'Of course!' And he told us that there is no real archeological or anthropological evidence for any actual long-term dominance of matrilineal societies. Or for the existence of goddesses. Not even the Earth Mother, if you can imagine!"

At this point the Dean asked if Dr. Barnes had anything to say concerning the perspective taken in his teaching on these two key subjects. The response followed a long sigh from Sam.

"I'm afraid I *am* somewhat guilty of failing to cater to

current ideology in my classes," he admitted. "However, because of being aware of the 'hot potato' quality of these particular issues I always tried very carefully to present the evidence on them and to let the students interpret the facts and decide for themselves. It appears that it didn't work."

"Oh but it did!" The remaining student sitting on Sam's defence team burst out enthusiastically. "Oh . . . sorry, my name is Mai Li Cheong. I just can't imagine how anyone could think that Dr. Barnes is either sexist or racist. My experience in his classes has been the total opposite. Frankly he's so totally color-blind . . . and so totally gender-blind . . . that I was amazed. I think that's why these people got so confused. We just never . . . really never . . . encounter a professor who pays no attention at all to ethnic background . . . or to whether you are a male or female. So females have all learned to expect some deference, or at least a little special attention, and even more so if they belong to a minority ethnic group as well. A lot of the girls like to be flirted with in class, and when someone comes along who treats them just like the men they get the feeling they are somehow being put down. Especially when he expects just as much from them as from the men, where ideas and class work is concerned. The same goes for people with different skin color, or from a minority ethnic or religious culture. Many seem to want special attention, or at least for people to recognize that they're different from the majority. Professor Barnes definitely just never noticed things like gender and ethnicity. For me it was a really nice change. I liked it that, whenever I managed to speak up about one of my ideas, it was listened to and taken seriously by Professor Barnes. I knew I wasn't going to be either frowned at or teased about pretending to be as intellectually sophisticated as a Caucasian male. 'This is just *so* great!' I always thought."

This outburst was followed by a hush. Even Dean Scott was, for a moment, silenced by the boundlessness of Mai Li's enthusiasm. Then he cleared his throat and called on the next witness, who was Sylvia Cornish. Suddenly there was an audible intake of breath in the room. Most of those in attendance were aware that this was the young woman with whom Sam had confessed to having had a short-lived affair. Sylvia got to the point in an extremely direct fashion, as she proceeded with her version of the story.

"Sam Barnes seduced me," she declared calmly. "In the hallways after class, in his office in the late afternoons, and in hotel rooms. I don't really think it was the reward of good marks if I cooperated, that finally broke down my resistance. Although he certainly promised that. I have to confess I was really flattered and overwhelmed by his attention. I guess he was hard for me to resist. I suppose I was partly to blame, because once I had given in to him, then I didn't want it to end. We continued seeing each other after I graduated and began teaching. But he got tired of me after a while, so one night he just abruptly told me that it was over."

"Are you telling us that your intimate affair with Dr. Barnes actually began, not after you had graduated, but while you were still a student here? And while you were taking his class in the Foundations of Education? Please be most careful with the facts here. I'm sure you're aware that this is a most critical point." Dean Scott's voice conveyed considerable urgency.

"Of course. I certainly wouldn't have begun the affair once I had left the university. I don't know why you'd think that! There would be no opportunity!"

"Did you not, in fact, come to see Dr. Barnes frequently,

to ask him for advice and help, once you began teaching? And was it not then that your affair began?" Les Brittan was speaking quietly but with extreme seriousness.

"No, not at all. He seduced me while I was his student."

"Do you have anyone who can bear witness to this?"

"No one in particular, but there must be lots of people who saw us together in the halls and saw me going in and out of his office."

During this discussion and, in fact, through the course of the hearing up to that point, a change had been gradually creeping over the demeanor of Sam Barnes. The utter hopelessness so apparent to the observers when he entered the room seemed to be diminishing. By time Sylvia's contribution had ended, the abject, lost look on his face had almost disappeared as well—along with the deadness in his eyes. These had now come alive, and Sam was seen to be observing and listening closely.

Meredith Walker signaled that she would like to speak.

"I can't say that I, or anyone else, actually witnessed Dr. Barnes sexually abusing his female students, but I feel the point must be made that people like him are very practiced in making sure that they are never seen. That's precisely how they get away with it for so long.

And while I'm on my feet I want to take the opportunity to express my gratitude for what you're doing here, Dean Scott, in providing women on this campus with the opportunity for justice at last. I'm confident that you won't let us down in your judgment regarding the future teaching career of this man. I'd also like to remind you at this point in the proceedings that I'm here to offer assurance to you as to the integrity of these poor abused women. And, at the same time, to assure *them* that the Women's Cultural Revolution is behind them all the way."

"Thank you, Miss Walker, I'll no doubt be requiring your help and advice on those very points, if not now, then in the near future." The Dean looked over at Millie, who had raised her hand slightly and was attempting to catch his eye.

"I would now like to call on Dr. Eisenstadt as the first of three character witnesses for Dr. Barnes. She seems to wish to speak to this."

Millie, her face more florid than usual, immediately rose to her feet.

"I've known Sam for less than a year", she began. "But we've shared a lot of problems in that time and have discussed many things very deeply. With Sam, unlike most academics, 'what you see is what you get'. He holds a number of conservative political and social views that may not be popular with today's young people . . . or within academia in general, for that matter. So I can see him getting into a lot of folks' black books on that account. But sexual abuse, or even mildly sexually inappropriate behavior? Never! I feel that I know Sam well enough to say that here is a man who is quite incapable of the kind of actions of which he has been accused in this room today. I'm convinced that he could never even remotely contemplate doing such things."

Stan Wheeler was the next to rise. He paused, eyes carefully taking in the group on the two other sides of the table.

"Unlike most of you here, I've worked closely with Sam Barnes for a number of years. We've taught together and developed the habit of sharing the daily problems of teaching in the most open way possible. I've often visited with him and his wife in their home, and happen to be very familiar with their children and their daily habits. If there was strife between husband and wife it was invariably around the issue of religion. Sam's insistence on de-alcoholized wine was central to this. It had, in fact, become almost a joke between them. I took it to be his assertion of independence from the more fundamentalist aspects of the Mormon religion. However, Sam Barnes has always been very much a family man, in most ways loyal to his wife and extremely close to his children. This is why he has already suffered so grievously from the consequences of the irresponsible and egregiously false accusations brought before you today. I think you should all be aware that it is the very *fact* of these accusations, much more than the revelation of his actual short-lived affair with a former student, which has destroyed his marriage. Even worse, it has lost him his precious children as well, for the Mormon Church has now officially excommunicated him. And the Barnes family, as well as the entire Mormon community, has been ordered to banish and ostracize him completely. His guilt or innocence is not even an issue for them. The admitted affair and the publicity surrounding the sex-abuse accusations alone were sufficient for them to condemn him. I think these young women should be aware of what they've already done to this innocent man."

The extended period of dead silence following Stan's emotional speech was finally broken by the sounds made by Muthu pushing back his chair and rising to his feet, pipe in hand.

"I have only a few words to add to what has already been said in defense of Professor Barnes. I, too, have taught with him for some years. And in all that time I have never seen even a hint of the kind of abusive tendencies of which he stands here accused. I want to add that I have written to his previous university and been assured in no uncertain terms that the *very idea* is inconceivable where this man is concerned. I have here, Dean Scott, numerous letters documenting this. Dr. Sam Barnes is an honorable man. Yet, the mere fact that these accusations have been made and publicized throughout the entire country has destroyed both his family and his career. Regardless of the final outcome of the tragedy being played out here today, I doubt very much that he could continue in his chosen field in any school in North America. This good man's life has been ruined. This is what we will all have to live with. Let us hope, at least, that all who have participated in the event culminating here today will learn a lesson from it, so that we never, ever, allow such a travesty of justice to occur again on any campus in this country!"

"I think it's time for me to bring this hearing to a close," Dean Scott spoke wearily, after a few minutes of silence. "Dr. Barnes, would you like to make a few final comments on anything that has been said here today?"

"Thank you, Dean Scott," Sam hesitated, then rose to his feet. "I want to express my heartfelt appreciation to those who have spoken on my behalf. You will just never know. . . ." His gaze, now restored to much of its former keenness, rested in turn upon Millie, Stan, Muthu and Les. Then his eyes, suddenly shining with tears, met those of the three girls who had spoken up for him, lingering for a moment on each.

"You couldn't possibly understand . . . how much it has meant to me. In fact, your warm support has now given me the courage to fight this thing, when I had all but decided to give up. I wish to thank, as well, those faculty members who are here representing the Canadian Association of University Teachers. I'd like you to know that I now intend to contact our organization officially, once I've heard this committee's final word on the matter. You see," he smiled wanly, "all this really has revived my fighting spirit!"

"I'll be notifying you concerning a private meeting between the two of us sometime near the end of March," the Dean responded quickly. "I want to be sure our committee has had sufficient time to scrutinize and discuss all the evidence with the utmost care, and to meet with CAUT representatives as well. Meanwhile, I trust that you'll try to relax and, as much as possible, put these problems out of your mind. Please keep in touch with me and with all your good friends here. I thank you for your patience and forbearance, Dr. Barnes. Also, I would like to extend that thank you to all who have participated here today. I am particularly grateful for the young ladies who were courageous enough to appear before us, and for Miss Meredith Walker, with whom I will be consulting in the coming days. If our committee requires further information from anyone else we will let you know. I now declare this meeting to be officially adjourned."

That night, Evelyn found herself revisiting the entire scene in her mind, as it had been presented by her colleagues. She recalled a wry comment made by Stan Wheeler during the re-hashing of the event in the faculty lounge. At one point she had noticed that he was grinning absently, and asked what he could possibly find amusing in the entire sorry mess. He explained that it was the fact that Sam might have to rely on their professional association, CAUT, for help and advice. The story that followed was enlightening, and just so . . . so typical of Sam, Evelyn thought. As Stan began to recount it, memory of the entire experience flooded back to her. It was several years before, in the midst of an economic downturn, and just after the Social Credit Party had been returned to power. The government declared that there would be no increase in funding for NPU university at that time. The tenured professors had already successfully bargained for a seven-percent increase in salary. The inevitable consequence of the resulting financial squeeze was that many of the non-tenure-track instructors would have to be laid off. Sam, although himself a tenured Associate Professor and thus well-protected, decided to take up the cudgel for those underlings on the academic ladder, among whom was Evelyn. She recalled that, as a relative newcomer to British Columbia at the time, she was afraid that her temporary position might be at risk.

Typically, Sam brushed off any hint that his motivations were selfless, brusquely declaring that the loss of so many junior members of the staff would add considerably to his own teaching load. He began to make the rounds among all the tenured faculty, asking them to sign a petition to the administration declaring that they would be willing to forego their raises providing the non-tenured people were allowed to retain their jobs. According to Stan, Sam had begun his project full of confidence. It seems that he was at that time leaning toward a left-liberal position where politics and economics were concerned—although always remaining a conservative on *social* issues. In fact, he had worked tirelessly during an election not too many years before, to help bring about the defeat of the long-term Social Credit government led by WAC Bennett. Since that time, however, Sam had become increasingly worried about the pattern of deficit spending established by the New Democrats under the leadership of the new Premier, Dave Barrett, and the resulting burgeoning government debt. It was something previously unheard of in British Columbia. And then his experience with the petition confirmed his change of heart.

According to Stan, what Sam actually found, to his amazement and disappointment, was that, while the majority of the more economically conservative members of the university faculty willingly signed the petition, it was totally rejected by those whom he knew to be left-wing. To a person, their excuse for the self-serving behavior was that the course he suggested would simply be playing into the hands of the corporate elite (represented by the current Social Credit government). He was told that the government was operating, in this instance, through the university administration. And that both institutions were united in the usual capitalist effort to keep taxes low for the rich, while permanently weakening the bargaining power of the union.

"The last straw for Sam," chuckled Stan, "and what turned him into a staunch Conservative in politics, was when he was called up on the carpet by the local branch of CAUT and warned against ever repeating anything like that again. And now, to think that he might have to rely on them for support! I can't help but worry a bit about just how forthcoming that help will be, when push comes to shove."

The reference to Social Credit brought back to Evelyn another happy memory of Sam. Ever the willing teacher of Canadian history, he had been quick to resolve her puzzlement concerning this political party, of which she had never heard before coming to Canada. The movement was indeed peculiar to this country, he told her, except for the curious monetary theories upon which it was based. These had been imported from Britain when the Alberta Progressives had arranged to have Major C. H. Douglas (the originator of the 'social-credit' concept) testify during the review of the Canada Banking Act in 1923. Twelve years later the Alberta election was won overwhelmingly by the new right-wing revolutionaries who had embraced the idea. Their leader, 'Bible Bill' Aberhart, campaigned on Douglas' recipe for the solution to poverty through the printing and distributing of government 'dividends'.

Concerning this particular election, Sam had one of his good first-hand tales. It seemed that the leading Elder of their church had decided to make a stand against the new party. He ordered all the district's Mormons to vote against it. Strangely, however, when the votes for their polling district were counted on election day, every single vote was registered *in favor of* Social Credit. The scolding Elder must himself have been seduced, at the end, by the promise of the monthly dividend of $25.00 per household: a considerable sum in a drought-stricken farming community where the concepts of welfare and universal medicare were yet to be introduced.

Sam also told Evelyn about how, by the time she arrived, the party had become a fixture in Alberta. This success was in spite of the fact that only one of the promised dividends was ever distributed; and that occurred almost three decades after the critical first election. He then added that, in 1952, Social Credit had moved into control in British Columbia as well, under the leadership of W. A. C. Bennett, who remained in power for two decades.

Both Evelyn's nostalgic recollection of Sam's folksy way of introducing her to this humorous example of the strangeness of Canadian politics and the relieved sense of amusement afforded by Stan's tale proved to be short-lived, however. Far more telling were Helen Korenky's comments when the two women were alone; although, in essence, she was merely corroborating what others had previously remarked upon. A couple of things in particular had struck

Helen about the event in the Dean's office. She had gained the distinct impression that all the girls who were giving evidence against Sam were frightened of something and strangely unsure of what was expected of them. They had glanced continually toward the Dean's side of the table, as if seeking direction and/or approval. Helen's second strong impression was of the almost startling change in Sam as the meeting wore on. From the utterly dejected and hopeless human being who entered the room, she said, he had changed markedly. She thought that he had even seemed, toward the end, to regain much of his old self confidence and general upbeat demeanor. What had happened there, Helen wondered, that she must have missed? What had caused the strange behavior of those bearing witness against Sam and, at the same time, Sam's gradual re-emergence of confidence?

CHAPTER 8

MARCH, 1977

Although Evelyn's hiking opportunities were now increasing with the reluctant approach of a Lower Mainland spring season, she felt strangely cut off from the other out-of-class activities among the faculty. It was becoming increasing apparent that Abdul was avoiding her on the hiking trail just as he was at work. She desperately missed those close encounters with him, and with Millie and Sam, that had enlivened the early part of the academic year for her. So it was that, when a chance came for the possibility of a talk with Millie, she grasped it. As usual, it was Helen Korensky who introduced the opportunity. One afternoon, while the remains of their group were gathering for coffee in the faculty lounge, Helen interrupted the stream of complaints about the heavy burden of work now bearing down upon everybody as they began the preparation of final term assignments and exams, by waving a colorful picture book in front of them.

"Okay, I give up," said Les Brittan, pulling at his shaggy beard. "What is it?"

"If you haven't seen it yet, you'll never guess! One of my students brought it to me. It's written and illustrated by our Methods Department, believe it or not, with special mention in the Acknowledgments of Professor Abdul Issa's contribution on economic/historical analysis. *And* with appreciation for the advice and editorial help, as well as for the artistic contributions, from one of your own colleagues, Professor Gus Rasmussen."

Evelyn became increasingly curious as the book was passed from hand to hand in almost total silence. All of a sudden she recalled where and when it had been discussed before. It was in connection with the Canadian history curriculum for the Rain Forest College. But everyone was acting so strange! Why was nobody remarking on the book? And why hadn't Gus or Abdul brought it in to show them all before this?

By the time it reached her she had begun to experience a sense of foreboding. Something must be wrong with it, else why this odd reception? So it was in the form of a cartoon comic book. There was nothing intrinsically wrong with that, surely? Of course, Evelyn had realized long since that her fellow educators in the Foundations of Education were not the most innovative of human beings. She was not surprised that they might lack appreciation for such a radical departure from academic custom. But couldn't someone at least have uttered a congratulatory word?

"Has anyone read it?" she asked, as she began to thumb the pages. Still no response.

The book bore the title of *The Conquest of Canada: How We Got from There to Here.* She wanted very much to peruse it carefully and then to discuss it with Abdul and Gus. And, even better, it would be a great excuse to go to see Millie in her office. Surely it would appeal to her sense of fun! She wondered how closely the two men had been involved in the project. She decided to query the group about it.

"I think Gus suggested the comic-strip format," Norah Edgar offered. "And Abdul supplied the Marxist theory obviously fueling the interpretation throughout. However, it appears to me that what the group, as a whole, lacked was someone with a smattering of knowledge about intellectual development. And about what's appropriate in terms of teaching technique and context for this particular body of students. The authors seem to have been utterly unaware that many native Indian students, although of university age, nonetheless diverge tremendously from the norm in terms of prior preparation and stages of learning. While a comic book might grab all of them initially, they need a whole lot more varied and in-depth study of such a large and complex subject."

"What about a little familiarity with the actual *facts* of Canadian history!" exploded Stan Wheeler. "It looks as if that's lacking as well. And I *have* read through it, by the way. I simply cannot understand how this could have been okayed by your Methods Department, Helen. It was never even discussed at a general Faculty meeting. Why in the world wouldn't they have asked *us* for some advice, as the only historians in Education? As it is, it reflects badly on our Foundations Department as well, seeing that one of our own sociologists was involved in producing it. Once again we're going to be the laughing stock of the people in the other Faculties. Boy oh boy! I shudder to think of what Sam Barnes would say, if he were here, about the harm this kind of shoddy and distorted history can cause. Not just to *our reputation*, mind you, but to the poor aboriginal kids who buy into it and, eventually, to the rest of society as well!"

Evelyn felt herself objecting strongly to discussing the book in this negative way with none of the authors or contributors present.

"Could I borrow it, Helen?" she asked. "I'll read through it this evening and return it sometime tomorrow." At Helen's eager nod, she got up and left the room with the book in her shoulder bag.

Against her wishes, Evelyn had to admit to mixed feelings when she had completed her reading of *The Conquest of Canada* that night. Actually if hadn't taken very long. It struck her as absurdly lacking in content, for something that promised to provide aboriginal students with a solid background in Canadian history. As a relatively recent immigrant from a neighboring country not particularly noted for in-depth knowledge of things Canadian, she was, of course, not conversant in the subject. But she couldn't help but flinch at the obvious superficiality of the coverage and the strong taint of Maoist bias on almost every topic touched upon. Like any sociologist, she was well aware of the injustice and harm inflicted upon the native peoples throughout the Americas by the European settlers. But was it true that, up to the coming of the white man to Canada, the aboriginals had lived an idyllic existence, invariably at peace with their fellows and functioning as concerned and responsible guardians of their environment? Had the North West Trading Company and the Hudson Bay Company really set out systematically to rob the hunters of their furs and deliberately decimate their numbers by spreading infectious diseases among them? Had the Royal Canadian Mounted Police actually carried out what amounted to an organized genocide at the behest of the Canadian government? And as for the claim that those specific tribes in residence at the time of the settlement of the West (the colonial period, as the authors called it) had inhabited every square inch of British Columbia ever since time began—well, she knew enough about recent archeological and anthropological findings to look askance at that one!

The next day, Evelyn decided to take along two bag-lunches and drinks, and to visit Millie in her office. The book would provide the excuse for getting their friendship back on its former easy basis, and she really wanted the benefit of Millie's Canadian background on this matter. At the shouted "Come in!" she entered, then stopped abruptly in embarrassment. All she could see was Abdul lounging across from Millie at the desk, in earnest conversation.

"Evelyn!" both spoke at once. Then, "What a pleasant surprise!" Abdul blurted, after a pause in which each seemed to be waiting for the other to carry the conversational ball. "I must go back to my work," he continued, "so I will leave now and allow you two to have a good visit." Already on his feet, he touched Evelyn's shoulder as he passed her and was out the door before she had collected her thoughts enough to urge him to join them. However, there was to be no time wasted in awkwardness where Millie was concerned.

"That book!" she exclaimed, as Evelyn removed it from her pack before seating herself in the chair vacated by Abdul. "You know, Abdul has been strangely reluctant to show it to me. But I've heard it's out, and that he had some input into the planning of it. I've been dying to see it. Is it as bad as he's been hinting? I do think he's beginning to wonder if he should have involved himself in the project at all. At least without a chance to edit the final product."

The two examined the book together for a few minutes then, deciding to leave it for Millie to peruse in private later, they settled down to lunch and chatter about their daily class work. Evelyn felt a wave of relief at Millie's easy acceptance of her visit. She always felt more relaxed in Millie's office than her own, as it was one of the larger ones, with two comfortable chairs for guests and plenty of room for books. And, most important, in this particular arm of the building the offices were not built in twosomes. She often wondered why she had not been given first choice when this one had become available before Millie's arrival. Maybe they had been keeping it for that Marxist scholar Harvey was angling for. She passed Millie her share of the lunch, hoping that the cabbage rolls would be considered adequate. Before long they were making plans to meet for lunch again the following day, specifically to discuss the book. Millie promised to provide the food and to try to persuade Abdul to join them.

Evelyn was relieved to note that her friend now appeared to be much more like her old self, and apparently once again totally engaged in the day-to-day pleasures and stresses of teaching. She regaled Evelyn with amusing stories of recent experiences with her students, inviting the same sorts of revelations in return. One not-so-amusing anecdote involved a number of Millie's top students in one of her regular Sociology of Education classes, who had recently told her that they were transferring to another Faculty next year because of their disappointment with the lack of intellectual content in many of the Methods courses. Both women discussed this at some length, wondering if, in fact, the best people were actually being selected *out* of Education, at a time when good teachers were so badly needed.

Altogether, it was like old times when the two had met regularly in the evenings in one of their rooms at the women's residence at New Oxford. No mention was made of Abdul's ambiguous relationship with them both; nor even of the continuing tenuousness of Millie's position at NPU. Evelyn grasped the opportunity to tell Millie about what she had learned concerning the new 'sociobiology', during her visit to Harvard over Christmas holidays. She informed her of the criticism the theory was garnering from no less a personage than Stephen Jay Gould. And of the fact that even the Chairman of Wilson's own Biology Department had apparently implied that he considered sociobiology to be a misguided doctrine. After Millie refused to rise to the bait on that topic, the two went on, quite sanguinely, to other matters.

They exchanged only a few words about the possible professional tragedy facing Sam Barnes. It was enough, however, to satisfy Evelyn that Millie was managing to maintain contact with him. It was as if, just this once, both women were resolved to relax and enjoy the resumption of the friendship they had shared for so long. At one point, Evelyn even felt sufficiently easy about their restored relationship to remark that Millie looked as if she were feeling better than she had in recent months. She was glad she had taken the plunge, for Millie responded readily, with the news that she had recently been diagnosed with diabetes and was now on medication which (happily) seemed to be controlling the disease. "Abdul is the only other person who's aware of it," she said. "And he's not going to tell anyone. I don't want any more excuses for our honorable leaders in academia to write me off. It's Type B," she added, humorously. "Wouldn't you know that I couldn't even manage an 'A' in that arena these days! I guess I really am over the hill!"

On the way back to her classes Evelyn felt better than she had for weeks. *Maybe,* she thought, *everything will turn out well after all.* It was while drifting along in this relaxed mood that she almost stumbled against Harvey approaching from the hallway that passed Millie's office. His pleasant smile and obvious surprised pleasure at the encounter buoyed her emotional state even more. This rapport with Harvey Garfinkle was still new enough for her to wonder at it and appreciate it afresh each time they met. Had he changed so drastically, she wondered, or was it simply that recent experience in the Department had altered the way she viewed things in general?

"Great to run into you like this, Evelyn," he was now saying. "The wife's visiting family in Saskatchewan until the end of the month and, as I'm on my own this evening, I thought you and I might share a bite at one of those great restaurants in Vancouver's Chinatown. There are a number of matters I'd like to get your advice on. You know I really do value your objective perspective on our Departmental problems and future plans. How about it?"

Nothing was dearer to Evelyn's heart than being asked for advice by a senior administrator—especially when it must surely mean that prospects for her own promotion were finally secure. After travel arrangements had been made for the evening she rushed on to her waiting class. She thoroughly enjoyed the remainder of the day, thinking of her conversation with Millie and wondering what the evening held in store.

As it turned out, the advice that Harvey was seeking was not of any apparent critical nature. They spent most of the time when they were not enjoying the beef with noodles and broccoli—accompanied, at Harvey's insistence, by a large serving of sweet and sour chicken—on catching each other up on faculty gossip. She decided against mentioning Millie's health problems, however, remembering the latter's reservations and thinking that Harvey definitely did not need any more reasons for withholding the offer of a permanent position. At any rate, he seemed chiefly to want to unwind, and to be re-assured concerning his role in the Sam Barnes affair. In fact, it was Sam who was obviously uppermost in his thoughts throughout the evening.

"I've tried my best to be totally neutral where the issue of his guilt or innocence is concerned," he said earnestly, after they had drunk the last dregs of the Chinese tea and were preparing to leave the restaurant. "I've given the Dean my interpretation of the evidence as presented, and have asked that I not be involved in his final decision. I understand that he'll be meeting with Sam next week. I only wish I had a chance to see the poor sod before that, just to offer a little personal support and to assure him that I'll do everything I can to see that he gets a decent job somewhere for next term. Would you, by any chance, know how to get in touch with him? It seems that he's moved from the rooms he rented immediately following the fiasco."

Evelyn had to confess that she hadn't the slightest idea of Sam Barnes' current whereabouts. She had been further reassured about Harvey's basic decency, however, by the expression of honest concern and the worry in his handsome face.

"I think if he were in touch with anyone here it would be Stan and Muthu . . . or Millie," she offered. "Why don't you ask one of them about him, just in case? Or send a message to him through them?" She paused, as something began to nudge at her memory.

"In fact," it suddenly came to her, "Millie did happen to mention that she picks him up every Thursday night and they go out somewhere to eat. Millie has a motherly streak in her, you know, and I think it's coming to the fore right now where poor Sam is concerned."

The news that someone was looking out for Sam seemed to cheer Harvey considerably.

"Maybe I'll just wait until he's talked to the Dean at the end of next week," he said. "Once he's digested the decision, whatever it is, he may be in a better mood to discuss future prospects and plans. In fact, it might be a good idea if the Department organized a little informal get-together with him at that time, just to let him know he's not on his own in this."

The following day Evelyn found that she did not have to wait until lunchtime for the discussion with Millie. For a change, her friend appeared in the faculty lounge on time for the morning coffee break, armed with the comic-strip book and a glint of amusement in her eye. Abdul had drifted in as well, and was deep in rather agitated conversation with the two historians. Millie charged toward the three men, with Evelyn, not wanting to miss anything, following in her wake.

"Well, Abdul, I've finally had a chance to read the new history text." Millie said cheerfully. "I think I can recognize your influence in the general perspective and analysis. I'd love to discuss the book with you and these other guys." Her inclusive glance made it clear to Evelyn that she was to be considered one of the 'guys'.

"I just happen to have a copy here as well," Muthu gestured with the book rather than the usual pipe in hand. "As an immigrant coming late to the Canadian scene, I have always suspected that this country's history was more comedy than tragedy, Abdul. So I can see how you might want to argue that the cartoon format is appropriate. But did you social studies experts really have to reduce the entire thing to abject farce?"

"What I want to know is, why restrict this masterpiece to the Rain Forest Federated Indian College? Why aren't you teaching the same valuable stuff to all the social studies students in your Methods Department? In fact, why don't we pass it on to the historians in the Faculty of Arts?" This came from a grinning Stan Wheeler.

"Come off it, you guys!" Millie interjected. "Stop giving

Abdul such a bad time and let him have a chance to defend and explain his work."

"I suppose my only defense is that it is not, to any considerable extent, really 'my work'." Abdul, usually so unperturbed, was now looking decidedly embarrassed, and seemingly unable to respond in the joking vein of his critics. "The authors *did* come to me for advice on explaining how European imperialism would have operated in a quite typical fashion within the Canadian colony, and how it probably happened that the aboriginal people became its primary victims. Just as we native Africans did on my continent. Surely you historians, and you sociologists as well, cannot possibly have a problem with that interpretation. I would have thought, Muthu, that as an Untouchable from India, you would have understood all too well the effects of British colonial oppression!"

"It is true that I was born into a grievously oppressed group, or caste." Muthu's face had suddenly become serious, his words even more measured than usual. "I was the first ever, in my family, to have a chance to become literate. But the point is . . . and this is a very important point . . . it was largely due to the influence of Western democratic culture that this became generally possible for Untouchable children when I was growing up. A member of my caste named B. R. Ambedkar had been one of the first wave of such children who was fortunate enough to be educated. He spent his university years in the United States, where he learned about, and came to admire, the principles of justice and democracy on which that system was founded. He went on to study American constitutional law, and upon returning home became one of the chief drafters of the new Indian Constitution created in the period following India's Independence in 1947. A major priority for Ambedkar was always education for what the

British had called 'Depressed Classes' (and the Hindus classed as 'Untouchables'), and this was reflected in the new Constitution."

"Did he think that education would be the solution to the problem of caste in India?" asked Millie.

"Not entirely. He always worked for social and political/economic reforms as well, believing that change had to be introduced at all levels, simply because the institution of caste had poisoned Indian society throughout. I was more fortunate than most of my people, as I was born in Cochin, which happened to be ruled by a very enlightened Maharaja. In 1940 I was selected as one of the growing number of Untouchable children to be given the opportunity for free schooling in whichever of the available religious schools might have room in any particular year. And, later, I was one of the fortunate few members of my caste who were awarded university scholarships. I remember so clearly the day in 1956 when I went to class and heard the news that the princely states of Cochin and Travancore, along with British Malabar, were amalgamating to form the new Kerala, under the Maharaja's jurisdiction. Again, one can trace a Western cultural influence even in our Maharaja's liberalism. There is no doubt in my mind that the Christianity which had been planted back in Roman times in what was then known as Keralam had, because of its continuing connections to Western civilization, created a less insular culture in my region than existed in other parts of the sub-continent. One need not agree with the *content* of the Christian message to grant that."

"But aren't you forgetting that India's problems were caused in the first place mainly by the Brits . . . good Christians all?" Evelyn interjected.

"I would like to remind you that all that the long-existing

cultural pattern which has oppressed my people for so many centuries was *not* a product of British colonialism. Certainly, British rule had many faults, but that was not one of them. India's caste system had a much older historical source. It was a result of the invasion of the Aryan tribes from the north sometime before the second millennium BCE, and the fact that the resulting Hinduism became so firmly entrenched within the entire Indian culture. Just as many of the problems besetting the aboriginal population in this country are no doubt a result of deep-seated problems within their own cultures."

"Oh, I almost forgot!" Muthu added, after a few minutes of silence during which his listeners seemed to be struggling to digest this stream of information. "It may interest you to know that Ambedkar ultimately rejected Hinduism completely and formed a humanist branch of Buddhism, very similar to that taught by the early Buddha."

"That is all so new to me, and it's just so . . . so fascinating," came Millie's enthusiastic voice. "Muthu, you are a virtual mine of information. A real gem!"

"I know," the prompt rejoinder was accompanied by a mischievous grin and a wave of the unlit pipe. "That's what my name means!"

"I understand what you are saying," Abdul began thoughtfully, ignoring the interplay between the other two. "I accept that the Marxist analysis, as put to use in the book, may have been somewhat inadequate. I should have insisted on checking how the group of authors were actually applying it in their interpretation of the history of this region, before the book was published. However, as for the comic-book format, and the selection and presentation of facts, I really cannot accept any responsibility there. At no point in the process did I pretend to any comprehensive knowledge of Canadian history. I merely assumed that those who had accepted the task of writing the book were amply qualified. I now wonder if I was not perhaps mistaken." Abdul, also uncommonly grave, looked off into the distance, as if hoping thereby to avoid the censure of his friends.

"I may have been too ready to assume historical parallels between what I knew about the African situation and what happened here. Perhaps I am biased by my own history," he continued. Then, suddenly, he smiled crookedly, his expression becoming mischievous.

"I recall being told about how the Christian missionaries came to my country of Basutoland intent on doing away with all the devilish practices of the 'primitive' idol worshipers throughout the country. But they failed to find any . . . idols, I mean . . . or even any of the 'evil' worshiping rituals that they had expected. The natives of the area (my mother's ancestors, by the way) happened to be intensely practical people, uninterested in myths and rituals. Nevertheless, the missionaries were utterly obsessed with the need to locate the evil they had traveled so far to eradicate. Finally, in desperation, they fastened on the practice of family cattle exchange. One of our few customs involved marriage. The bride's parents would make a gift of a cow or steer to the groom's family. This dastardly work of the devil, the missionaries declared in the full fire of righteousness, must be rooted out at all costs! I may have assumed, perhaps too readily, that the same sorts of attitudes and behaviors prevailed here in colonial times."

"I love that story, Abdul," said Stan. "You probably know damn well that exactly the same thing happened right here on the West Coast where the potlatch was concerned!"

"Nonsense!" came Millie's amused voice. "Any rational

person would recognize the devil's hand in a barbaric ceremony involving the over-generous and flamboyant entertaining of one's friends and family. Contrast that, for instance, to our own sophisticated, civilized rituals, such as people crouching in rows in a crowded building, pretending to be drinking the blood and eating the flesh of the object of their worship."

"Enough, Millie!" Evelyn remonstrated, smothering her laughter. 'T'aint funny, McGee!" Abdul and Muthu were obviously puzzled by the expression, but joined in the laughter.

"Abdul," Stan was now attempting a return to a more serious vein. "Am I right in thinking that you might be somewhat concerned about the uses to which your ideas and explanations have been put, and are likely to be put in the future?"

"I am not sure I understand exactly what you mean, Stan."

"Muthu and I have discussed this at some length, Abdul. Because of his own personal experience, I think he can express what we both feel better than I."

"I can only try." This from Muthu with a clearing of his throat and a wave of his pipe. "After reading through this . . . this travesty of history . . . my strongest impression is of implied insult and . . . yes, even abuse . . . of the aboriginal students. I find the assumption that they could not possibly understand and, if necessary, challenge the content of Canadian history as it is presented to students in the other colleges to be utterly unwarranted and degrading. That is not to say, however, that the teaching *approach* should not be made appropriate to their background, nor that the important role of their ancestral tribes should not have been included and acknowledged honestly. But this should be done in *all* our history books, not only in *theirs*! Also, I find in the book the dangerous message that these aboriginal peoples must be taught to accept the role of 'victim' in perpetuity. 'You are not to blame for any of the failures we expect from you, for just look at what was done to your forebears! We, all non-aboriginals, are totally at fault. Nothing that goes wrong for you in life can ever be blamed upon you.'

The reason I am emotional about this is that it takes me back to certain incidents in my own early educational experience when some well-meaning teacher attempted to impose the same type of self-crippling load on me. I recall that it happened in a very humane Christian school I attended at one time. Thankfully, it was definitely not the prevalent opinion in the Sikh and Muslim schools that accepted me. They had many faults, but insinuating that I must be protected from having to measure up to the same standards as their own kind was not one of them.

I have to add that I can also share the distress of those aboriginal students who were forced to undergo foreign religious indoctrination in their earlier schooling. I was continuously exposed to a great deal of that. However, to my everlasting gratitude, being shoved about from one school to another (and one religion to another) gave me the best inoculation possible against the doctrines of all of them. I am including here the Hinduism of my own family background, multifaceted and non-militant though it was, that sought to condemn me to an inferior slave-status for life!"

"Of course I sympathize with what you are saying, Muthu, but how does it apply to my role in this project?"

"Don't you see, Abdul," Stan interjected, "that by your Marxist interpretation (which, I realize, was oversimplified by others) you have offered the perfect 'out' for all those unfortunate enough to have been born near the bottom of the current social ladder. You've also provided the inevitable Utopian answer to anything that goes wrong. No mundane, pragmatic problem-solving and long-term, step-by-step solutions necessary. None of the years of hard work and self-sacrifice, for instance, to acquire the skills needed to integrate into modern society: those intellectual and technical tools that got Muthu where he is today. In fact, since 'modern society' is an inherently 'evil' product of the 'white Imperialists', there is actually an imperative *not to integrate*! Nothing but a violent uprising of the oppressed masses... in this case, 'tribes'... will do the trick. Not even equality will ever satisfy the kids brainwashed into this version of history. The descendants of the colonials must be made to pay, and current inhabitants must therefore give up their hard-earned property to make way for its return to the descendants of the original landowners."

"I agree. We're creating irresolvable problems for future generations. Indian kids included. It's our generation's version of 'There'll be pie in the sky by and by!'", said Millie.

"Pie? Who's got the pie?" Gus was joining them, grinning widely. "I gather you're discussing the book. So only the Jews are justified in demanding their ancestral land back, is that it Millie?"

"I'll have you know, Gus," replied Millie, her face flushing, "that my family were among those Jews who, like Hannah Arendt, opposed Zionism way back then. And their main argument was that, in the end, they failed to see how it could possibly work. They were afraid that establishing a religion-based Jewish nation in the heart of the Muslim Arab world would result in nothing but endless violence. I remember clearly my father arguing in favor of some kind of a federal state for all who wanted to be citizens of the new Palestine, regardless of religion, with Britain as overseer for a few years to ensure the operation of the rule of law and an all-inclusive democracy."

"Why yes," interrupted Muthu. "I seem to recall that the original 'Mandate for Palestine', signed by the Allies near the end of the First World War, specifically designated Britain as the 'mandatory in charge of administering that part of the former Ottoman empire known as the territory of Palestine'. It included what is now known as Jordan as well. How unfortunate that they did not complete that undertaking!"

"Yes, that was exactly my parents' position. Like them, I think we should not be committing ourselves to unachievable and unworkable Utopias aimed at correcting all the errors of past history. What we should be aiming for, instead, is 'justice in our time'. I realize that such a goal was hard to envision after the Jewish experience at the hands of the Nazis. Just as it's hard to envision for those Palestinians today who insist on 'the right of return' to the area which has now been the home of Israeli citizens for more than a half-century. But it's obvious that an incursion of such overwhelming numbers of Arabs can't be allowed to happen at this point in history, because it would lead directly to the destruction of the Israeli state . . . and possibly its people too.

I guess what I'm trying to say is that the only way to ensure *justice now*, given the conditions created by history, is not to try vainly to undo that history. What we have to do, instead, is to provide equality of opportunity for every person, from this day on, as an *individual*. Not as a member of a particular group . . . be that group ethnic or religious, or a tribal combination of both. And I'm saying *really* ensure justice! Which means we have to use the schools to compensate for deficiencies in early family socialization, no matter whether the source of those deficiencies is tribal culture or strictures of caste or economic class. And no matter how hard it is to do."

"But what right have *you* to define them as 'deficiencies' rather than equally valuable, alternative ways of responding to experience? For example, what makes you think that our habits of governing and sharing resources are so much better than the ancient rule of the Chiefs?" Gus Rasmussen's voice was loaded with scarcely concealed scorn.

"Who was it who said, 'You can't go home again'?" asked Stan. "It seems to me that just about sums it up, with all of the tragedies and injustices in an imperfect world that the conclusion implies."

"And how about 'Never try to get above your station in life' and 'Mother knows best'?" Gus turned to Abdul, grinning widely, "Abdul, let's leave these characters to their exchange of homilies. There's a little matter I need your opinion on."

"In a moment, Gus. I wanted to ask Stan something about the content of the book that has puzzled me. Is it really true that no treaties were ever signed with the native peoples in British Columbia? That they did not ever agree to renounce ownership of their land in exchange for money, or other privileges?" Abdul was speaking earnestly.

"True as far as most of the province is concerned. Except, I believe, for much of Vancouver Island."

"Well, I would think, then, that a central aspect of achieving 'justice in our time', Millie, would have to be reaching some kind of agreement on as-yet-unsigned treaties. These resolutions would have to be reasonably fair, in terms of native land claims and relative population and what has been previously achieved through the Indian Act, etc."

"But how do we deal with the fact that more than a

hundred percent of the province has been claimed by various tribes, with many of the claims overlapping?" asked Stan.

This was followed by a frustrated silence on the part of everyone. Clearly, native rights was one Canadian problem that was not going to be resolved by a group of academics passing the time of day. Finally, Evelyn decided it was time to attempt a change of direction.

"Gus, I understand that you had the idea of the comic-book format. Did you actually design the characters?" she asked.

"I just gave the committee a start by providing a few of them. Oh yeah, and I actually drew those particular ones as well. You guys didn't know about my artistic talent, did you?" Gus paused for the now-relaxed laughter. "Seriously, the Mountie leader, Colonel Shotgun, was my creation. You know, the bloke who saw his mission as ridding the West of both the Indians and the buffalo, in one fell swoop?"

"Gus, did you do any reading about the role actually played by the Northwest Mounted Police, as they were then called, in the settling of Western Canada? Like what happened in the Cypress Hills, for instance?" Millie was no longer laughing.

"What and where the hell are the Cypress Hills? And what have they to do with the history of the Canadian West?"

"To put it simply, Gus, just about everything! But I think I should defer to our historians for a more thorough explanation here."

"Well . . .," Stan Wheeler cleared his throat and sat for a moment, obviously organizing his thoughts. "I guess I'm the logical one to elaborate a bit on it, as I'm one of the few Canadian-born historians in this place. And, as it happens, I did my Master's thesis on the subject."

"Go ahead, I'm listening, Stan," sighed Gus. "Just as long as you don't insist on giving us the entire thesis verbatim."

"Well, to try my best to make a long story short, Cypress Hills is the name for a strangely Arctic-like, desolate area which escaped most of the glaciers during the ice age. It protrudes high up along the northern boundary of Montana and the southern edge of Canada's flat lands, joining what are now the Canadian prairie provinces of Saskatchewan and Alberta. This area functioned for years as more or less the demarcation line between that part of Canada and the United States to the south. What is relevant to our discussion, however, is the fact that the Cypress Hills marked not only the geographical border between the two countries, but a major cultural boundary as well. It was a boundary separating two very different approaches to the settlement of the West.

The American settlers were chiefly cowboy hunters and 'wolfers' who poisoned buffalo carcasses in order to get rid of wolves. They moved into the region during the latter half of the nineteenth century. These guys made their own rules as they came. And those rules just happened to demand the extermination of any and all Indians encountered. This was because the Indians were bent on stealing the cowboys' most precious possessions . . . their horses. The tribes quite naturally considered a horse as the most coveted of all available booty in any contest between any two competing groups. Just think of the hunting and fighting advantage it gave them! For the American cowboys, on the other hand, the penalty for horse thieves had always been death by hanging. This outcome was, likewise, quite natural to them. And, wherever horse thievery and its inevitable punishment didn't fully accomplish the extermination of the resident Indians, the whisky trading following the influx of the settlers pretty much did."

"But surely the same thing was happening north of the border," interjected Abdul.

"That's just my point! On the Canadian side of the Cypress Hills country it was a vastly different story. This difference was rooted in the lengthy, stable monopoly of the Hudson's Bay Company from at least the 1820's on. The company controlled the enterprise in which the Indians (and especially the Métis) functioned as important and valued middlemen in the fur and pemmican trade throughout the entire region from the far north of Canada all the way south to the American border. This mutually beneficial cooperation tended to further a respectful and peaceful interaction between the two groups. It was a type of relationship not found on the U.S. side.

However, after a particularly brutal massacre of a band of Assiniboine by the American cowboys, wolfers and whisky traders, the Canadian government decided to enter the picture. I think it was sometime in the mid-1870s that they passed a bill creating the Northwest Mounted Police. From then on, the new Force was responsible for establishing and maintaining law and order throughout the entire plains area of what was then known as the Northwest Territories. And, on the whole, it did a damn good job!

There's a lot more to the story, but in the end, what it all meant was this. On the Canadian side of the Cypress Hills and throughout the plains stretching westward, the law came first; and *only then* came settlement. *Peaceful* settlement. On the American side the precise opposite occurred. Seems to me that's worth noting in any *Canadian* history of the West."

"Thanks for the lecture, Stan. But why bother with what happened in one small region called Cypress Hills when we all know what happened generally through the whole of North and South America, whenever the white man's law met non-whites?" said Gus.

"But an interesting fact is that our earliest law-enforcement *wasn't* conducted solely by white men," Millie interposed. "Right here in British Columbia in the 1850's the governor of the colony of Vancouver Island, James Douglas, appointed a number of black constables to his local police force. As I understand it, these were either free African-Americans from California who had come north looking for gold, or escaping slaves. In 1860, one of them, a man called Mifflin Gibbs, actually set up a rifle corps of blacks that became the first officially organized military force in Western Canada. So how's that for a fascinating piece of colonial history that doesn't quite fit your picture, Gus?"

"And I've got another!" exclaimed Stan. "You people didn't even mention the critical role of Fort Walsh. Why it was the key to . . . ."

"Yeah, yeah, Stan. I don't much care at this point if Fort Walsh was the key to the doorway to heaven. What we're talking about right now is *our* new book. Not Millie's fanciful tales nor your thesis!" Clearly, Gus' patience had run out. "And . . . oh yeah, I wanted to tell all of you about my other original character, Jock McTerd, the Scottish fur trader who never met a squaw he wouldn't rape."

A dark expression crossed Millie's face.

"You 'foreigners' won't know this, but that *does* hit a bit close to the bone. And it didn't end with the fur traders, I'm afraid. But, to give them their due, at least a fair number of those Scots, at least, did respect the Indians enough to pair off with a native spouse and raise a family with her. Unlike the English, who tended to take a different woman at every camp. And leave them behind when they returned home.

However, right into my own time, when I was growing up on a farm in South-Eastern Alberta, I remember the Indians from a nearby Reserve would routinely set up camp outside the village at harvest time, because work was plentiful then. And the men of the village, including some of the supposedly most respectable ones, would make visits to the camp at night, making use of the women. We kids never did figure out the details. I mean, whether it was done when they knew the males would be in the beer parlor getting drunk, or whether (as I was told) those same males had made deals with the whites for the use of their families. All I know is the anger I felt, and feel to this very day, for those helpless women."

"Recently I have heard a few extremely ugly rumors about sexual abuse at some of the religious boarding schools which, I understand, Amerindian children were forced to attend. Did you ever encounter any evidence of that sort of thing, Millie?" There was an obvious urgency to Muthu's question.

"Nothing really specific. But, several times when I was evaluating student teachers in such places, I did get uncomfortable feelings. Nothing that I could actually put a finger on. Always I noticed that the nuns and other female teachers in the Catholic and Anglican schools held themselves strangely aloof from the children. (We didn't happen to be working with any schools run by the United Church, so I can't comment on them.) I had a habit of laying a hand on a shoulder and so on, or giving a lost-looking little character a hug as I leaned over to help or explain something. But those religious teachers seemed to treat them as if they were contagious. In analyzing their 'practice teaching' experiences later with my students, I was told that they had experienced the same weird sensation about the almost inhuman coldness exhibited. On the other hand, one day a student hinted about seeing something quite the opposite and even more disturbing, but only in one particular case. He had noticed what he termed 'a lot of fondling of little boys' on the part of a certain priest."

"So you agree that the concept of 'exploitation' might not be so far out of line after all," said Abdul.

"Of course, what appears to have happened in those schools was inexcusable. But the probable connivance of the Indian men in the first incident Millie described is also part and parcel of the point we've been trying to make." Stan rose as he made this remark and headed for the door.

"I came to know several successful teachers of native Indian background during my days out in the field supervising practice teaching in Alberta." Millie continued to ponder. "At that time, by the way, it was common for those fed up with the dead-end of Reserve life to leave their culture behind when they moved to the city. A fellow teacher whose parents had done just that once told me that this was unfortunately necessary because they soon discovered the only way to survive in the new life was to cut themselves off entirely from their extended family. Otherwise, they were absolutely inundated with freeloading relatives in every house they rented, and ultimately dragged down into the welfare culture and the cruel streets of the inner city. Just think what an agonizing choice that must have been!"

"Why yes, now I remember reading a research study on that very subject not long after arriving here!" Evelyn exclaimed. "A sociologist in Calgary discovered a pattern of just such occurrences. The key difference between those natives who had successfully integrated and those who had not was that very phenomenon of having been forced to cut all family ties. What it meant was that, not only were they *integrating* into modern society, but they found themselves, of necessity, being *assimilated* into that society's culture in the process!"

"Talk about Hobson's Choice!" Gus exclaimed with disgust. "You either give up your family culture and buy into ours, or we'll see that you lose out."

"That's not quite right, Gus," said Millie sharply. "It's possible to retain an aesthetic appreciation of the arts and myths of one's ancestors, if you will, (and some of these successful people did just that) without clinging to the archaic way of life *pictured* by those arts and myths. Especially when it's a way of life long-since corrupted and rendered irrelevant and unworkable by irrevocably altered social and physical and environmental conditions. For example, what if all the people spread throughout the world whose ancestors once designed the cave drawings along the coast of Brittany were to insist on living today as those cave-artists did, and in reclaiming the land they once occupied?"

"I take it you're saying that the aboriginals should not be trying to politicize a culture representing a long-ago (possibly largely imaginary) past, in a fruitless effort to apply it to life in the present. And social scientists, of all people, should not be encouraging them to do so," Abdul suggested.

"I'm afraid I don't agree. I consider the rescuing of endangered cultures to be just as important as doing the same for endangered species," Gus said.

"In certain instances," Millie conceded, "you may have a point, Gus. Or you would have if cultures didn't evolve naturally a damn sight faster than species. But yes, thank you, Abdul . . . that's exactly what I *am* saying! History is full of lessons about the disastrous results of just the sort of practice you're recommending, Gus. We should all know by now that confusing art and mythology with politics can have appallingly dangerous consequences."

"Dangerous for the power elites of the day, perhaps," was Gus' rejoinder.

"As this conversation seems to have degenerated into a battle of wits between you two, I think it's time to call it a draw. What was it you wanted to see me about Gus?" Abdul's good-natured interjection effectively brought the conversation to a close, and the others parted company soon after he and Gus left. For some time, however, Evelyn continued to bask in the warmth of the effect of listening in on the spirited conversation. Once again, it had seemed like old times.

The following Thursday, Harvey and Evelyn had lunch together—to 'celebrate', Harvey told her. And there was indeed something to celebrate. It seemed that Harvey's recommendation of Evelyn for promotion had been accepted the previous day by the university's Tenure and Promotions Committee. Soon it would be official. At last she would have the security of the coveted Associate Professorship! Harvey appeared to be as 'wired up' about the occasion as she quickly became. They laughed and talked with a closeness she hadn't felt with him before. In fact, on the way back to class afterwards, she even wondered if she had drunk a little too much of the wine that Harvey had insisted on ordering, and paying for, to accompany their roast lamb and lemon-baked potatoes. She only hoped her students weren't noticing that she was virtually floating into class.

Friday began on the upbeat also, with a few hurried calls to the offices of Millie and others to share her news. She persuaded herself afterwards that she had felt a premonition of some dreadful occurrence, just because things were going so well. But the fact was that nothing of the sort spoiled her enjoyment of that long-awaited experience of real success in her career. The entire day went swimmingly, until she finished her last class and headed for the faculty lounge, to join whoever was there.

It appeared that almost the entire faculty had responded to the same urge to relax and celebrate the approaching end of classes. For most, from now on it would be merely a matter of making sure that assignments were in, and then launching into the preparation of final exams and the seemingly endless task of marking. Evelyn hurriedly scanned the crowded room, then headed for Millie and Helen, who were settled into the far corner. She had begun to re-think her spontaneous morning phone call, realizing that Millie had not responded with any similar news of her own prospects for the coming year. Surely they would be letting her know soon! Evelyn had missed a good chance, when she and Harvey were on the subject, to ask about her friend's future here. He had to know by now. Why hadn't she thought of that, instead of merely celebrating her own good fortune? But it would not have been appropriate, she realized immediately. If the news had been bad, her inquiry would have placed Harvey in an embarrassing position. In fact, he had been breaking the rules letting her know about her own case before the word was officially out, and she should have kept quiet about it.

As it happened, she now overheard Helen inquiring about the very same thing. Millie looked uncomfortable.

"I haven't been told anything," she said. "I really am getting worried about it, although much of the time I succeed in putting it out of my mind. However, it means I simply can't feel comfortable about making any plans for the coming term. My students are beginning to ask what I'll be teaching next year, and other related questions. I feel like such a dummy, having to repeat that I simply haven't been informed yet. I do wish that Baby Blue Eyes would call a meeting of the Department and get everything out in the open."

Evelyn had opened her mouth to object to the label, which she now felt to be quite unsuitable, when a flurry of activity near the doorway interrupted their conversation.

"Speak of the devil!" exclaimed Helen. There was Harvey, with Gus close behind him. He moved in a rushing, harried fashion, then stopped abruptly before a table around which a number of their male colleagues were lounging.

"Look at Harvey's face. Something's up!" exclaimed Millie. Then, "Let's go over," she murmured urgently to Evelyn.

By the time they reached the group Harvey and Gus had rushed on out. It was left to Les Brittan to explain hurriedly that they were to gather as quickly as possible in the Departmental meeting room, where Harvey would join them as soon as he had contacted everybody. Ned Smith asked at once what the trouble was, but no one knew. They all agreed, however, that it must be something extremely serious.

"I've never seen Harvey in such a state!" exclaimed Stan Wheeler. "His hands were shaking and he could scarcely speak. Surely this Department has had all the calamities we can stand for one year! What in the world can have happened now?"

They discovered what it was—all too soon. Harvey and Gus entered the room, with Muthu and Willard Grange. Their little group was now complete, at least as complete as it could ever be with the gaping hole left by the lively personality of Sam Barnes. Why did she suddenly think of Sam? Evelyn wondered. A moment later she decided it must have been another of her premonitions.

"Please . . . please everyone. Sit down." Harvey was struggling for words. "I've got bad news for you. Terrible news! It's Sam Barnes. They found him this morning. He killed himself. Jumped off the Lions Gate Bridge sometime last night, the police think."

Evelyn heard a groan from beside her, and turned to Millie. She was bent over the table in front of her, hands clasped to her head, her body wracked by deep, shuddering breaths. The others were silent for the longest time, it seemed. Silently staring at Harvey who, like Millie, had now collapsed, shoulders moving convulsively, his hands over his face. Then, finally, the questions began to come. But Harvey had no answers, apparently, nor did Gus, who appeared so shaken he could scarcely speak. Nothing was known but those bare facts. Sam had committed suicide by jumping off the Lions Gate bridge.

"Does Mary know?" Willard Grange finally broke the silence.

"I phoned her as soon as the police informed me. They'd contacted her first thing this morning, and she's already been down to identify the body . . . Sam, I mean. She asked me if I would arrange for some kind of a memorial gathering here among his friends. She said she had just got off the phone with one of the Elders of her church. He'd called to assure her that their religious community had forgiven Sam's sins, both as an apostate and as an adulterer and sexual predator who had brought disgrace to his church. And that they were prepared to accept him back into the fold for a Mormon ceremony and burial. But for Mary it appears that the forgiveness has come too late. She began sobbing and muttering to me about never, ever, raising Sam's children in a religion that would force its members to shun a husband and father even before his sins had been proven. At that point I assured her she need not concern herself about a memorial service. We would look after everything as soon as possible, and keep her informed."

"It's a damn pity she didn't feel that way when their tribe drove poor Sam into the wilderness and ordained that he couldn't even see his own kids!" Stan exploded, after the tide of agreement with Harvey's suggestion had ebbed.

"They were no longer really *his* tribe," said Muthu. "It is *we* who are his tribe, and of course we shall act accordingly, now that he is dead."

"How about my arranging our little farewell party for Sunday afternoon?" Harvey asked. "I'm pretty sure I can get the faculty lounge for the purpose." Again, there was quick agreement. Obviously, no previously laid plans would stand in the way of this.

"To think that I was always telling Sam he'd outlive the bunch of us, with all the cocoa and milk he drank while we poisoned our systems with coffee and beer." This came pensively, from Willard Grange, after another awkward silence.

Millie was oblivious to them all, engrossed in what seemed to be an angry—and even strangely fearful—brooding. It was as if some dark specter had appeared before her; something that had trapped her; something that no one else could see. Then Evelyn began speaking, falteringly, for both of them. She and Millie would go to see Mary at once, just in case there was no one to whom she could turn. Willard Grange nervously lit a cigarette, and a number of the others followed, obviously trying to relax. Muthu fumbled for his pipe and began to fondle it. Ned Smith blew his nose loudly. Les Brittan gradually stopped tearing at his grizzly hair and beard with the fingers of both hands, and Gus Rasmussen rose unsteadily from the table and rushed out—speaking to no one. In a few minutes all but Harvey had left, heading off in various directions, to a person appearing shaken and strangely vulnerable.

Mary Barnes seemed pitifully grateful for their visit that evening. Soon after their arrival she ushered the three youngsters upstairs to settle them for the night. They appeared to be unaware of what had happened to their father. In fact, they could be heard demanding to know when Dad was coming home. Millie and Evelyn exchanged glances. When was she planning to share the dreadful news with them?

"Don't the children know?" burst out Millie as soon as Mary returned.

"I haven't felt able to tell them. I don't know how. Or what. Ordinarily I would go to one of the Elders for advice, but now I don't feel that I can do that. Nor do I want to. What do you think I should do?"

"Well, you can't have them discover it at the farewell gathering on Sunday. That would be just too, too cruel. If this hideous tragedy has been so hard for *you* to handle, what do you think it's going to do to them?"

"Mary, why don't you talk to them after breakfast tomorrow morning?" Evelyn suggested softly, feeling that Millie was being a bit too unfeeling here. "That would give them the entire day to assimilate the loss a bit, before they're confronted with the finality of it in public the following day. We'd be happy to help with it, but I really do think that the children would not want strangers around at such a time. Take them to the park, or to any favorite place that they had often shared with their father. And let them cry and talk about him as freely and as long as possible."

"I'll try." Mary's shoulders heaved and she collapsed into

wild sobbing. *The situation doesn't bode too well for Sam's children,* Evelyn thought.

"It's so strange," she said to Millie on their way home later. "Sam's first concern was always for the welfare of those youngsters of his. I realize that the church had talked Mary into going along with ostracizing him completely, but he could have gone to court for access. It seems so out of character that he would do such a thing. I mean, leaving them in such a dreadfully shocking way when they're at such a vulnerable age."

"The entire affair, from start to finish, has been totally out of character for Sam," Millie grunted, glaring angrily through the windshield as she maneuvered the car along Number 2 Road in the gathering dark. But Evelyn could get no more out of her. So she retreated into her own thoughts, returning again and again to the question of how any human being in the prime of health could even consider committing suicide. If Sam could have seen nothing ahead but endless years of manic depression, for example—or chronic, unbearable pain—now that would have made his act comprehensible. But opting for killing oneself in the prime of life, with three cherished children to live for! How could any career failure, or even public disgrace such as he was in the process of suffering—how could that drive a sane, emotionally balanced person like Sam to such a desperate, irreversible act? Especially if he were indeed as blameless as Millie appeared to assume.

Empathizing with the agony of Sam's final hours kept Evelyn awake most of that night. Saturday was spent chiefly in preparing for what was to come the following day, and in persuading herself that the little ceremony and time of companionship, which Harvey and she had hurriedly organized, would help them all—including Sam's family.

Sunday dawned bright and clear. It was one of those perfect spring days so treasured and bragged about by the inhabitants of the Lower Mainland. Evelyn felt reasonably confident that the affair would go well. Promptly at 2:00 p.m. the small group began to gather in the faculty lounge, where the tables had been dispensed with and the chairs arranged in straight lines, facing the front, with an open space between the two sides. Mary had brought what remained of her little family: Adam and Sarah, who were almost teenagers, and eight-year-old Noah. Evelyn noted that a large number of the faculty were present, including Dean Scott. Muthu was seated on the far left of the same row as she and Millie, with Helen Korensky and Abdul Issa on the right, close to the aisle. Most of the Foundations faculty were grouped near the front of the room. Members of the other Education Departments and a few historians from the Faculty of Arts helped to make up the remainder of the gathering.

Harvey wasted no time in getting the program underway. As soon as everyone was settled, he brought the loaded buffet table to their attention, inviting them all to remain for some informal reminiscing at the close of the brief ceremony. He then welcomed Mary and her children and made sure that they were seated at the front. Adam, Sarah and Noah were uncustomarily silent, their dazed-appearing eyes taking in the scene. Mary, now reasonably composed, got them settled. Harvey spoke for a further few minutes, addressing Mary and her family in comforting tones. Then he called on Dean Scott.

"I didn't know Sam Barnes as well as the rest of you did," the Dean began, hesitatingly. "But I want to express my great regret at any negative part I may have played in what I see as three recent major tragedies where he was concerned. First and foremost, of course, is the series of accusations (none very well supported, I might add) which drove him to this act. Second is the fact that, except for the intercessions of a few of his close colleagues, he was left alone to more-or-less blow in the wind during this critical time. Third is the fact that I was just one day too late in meeting with him to inform him of my decisions regarding his position here, and his future job prospects. Indeed I had some rather good news to convey which might well have saved his life. I had intended to tell him that, although there was no way he could continue teaching at this university, I had contacted a friend of mine with the Department of Statistics in Ottawa and had recommended Sam most highly for a position with them. That very morning I was informed that the job was his if he wanted it. Just in time for our planned meeting, I remember thinking. But if only I had not waited for that response! If only I had arranged to meet with him earlier in the week! I just want to say that I shall never forgive myself for having taken so much time in arriving at my decision and in finalizing these arrangements for him."

"I have something to say as well," offered Stan Wheeler, moving forward. "Is it okay if I do it now?" At the nod from Harvey, he continued. "I'd like to mention some of the things about Sam that I particularly valued, over the years of our working together. What I most enjoyed and respected was his self-appointed task of deflating academic bandwagons. He was so very good at attacking idols of every type . . . at revealing the nakedness of our endless circus of academic emperors! We educators tend to be all-too-prone to rather mindless innovation. No matter that something has never been tested and is unlikely to work in practice, if it's new we're for it! If anything is referred to as conservative we automatically trash it. Along with the person who supports it. Sam was one of the few who dared to criticize the essentially meaningless 'in' slogans so dear to the hearts of most of us. 'Student-centered', for example, and 'values clarification'. And, oh yes, we mustn't forget his scorn of our fondness for all those simplistic 'black and white' dichotomies, such as the use of phonics versus 'the whole-language' method of teaching reading; 'humanistic' versus 'competency-based' education; and so on and on. And, in the end, he paid dearly for it."

The next to come forward was Abdul Issa. His diction sounding more stilted even than usual, he began with what at first struck Evelyn as an uncharacteristically personal and even incongruous remark.

"My second name is Mosa. It was given to me by my mother, who was a member of the Basotho tribe in Southern Africa. In her native Sesotho language the word Mosa means 'kindness'. You may not know this, but all African names have meanings. I fear that, many times in my life, I have not lived up to the meaning of my name in the treatment I accorded others. I am feeling especially regretful concerning my relationship with Sam Barnes. I was not always kind to him. Because his beliefs were so different from my own, I too-often merely considered him to be rejoicing in a strange type of deliberate ignorance. I confess that I did not value his opinions as I should have. Nor did I even take them seriously enough to consider them at all. I am sorry, Sam, for not granting you, in life, the human dignity that you deserved. I wish, at this time, to promise, in the hearing of everyone here, that I will do my best to ensure that you are granted that dignity in death."

After several minutes of what appeared to be stunned silence, there followed a number of other brief appreciative comments on Sam's attributes. However, none touched Evelyn as Abdul's had done. She wondered if he was also now re-thinking his selfish—and even cruel—treatment of her. Was it possible that he was subtly trying to send *her* a message as well? Should she approach him about their aborted relationship, or was this perhaps not the time for that? Her thoughts were interrupted by Muthu, who was seated beside her, as he began to sidle over toward the aisle. She moved her chair out of his way, and watched him proceed slowly to the front.

"I am finding it most difficult to speak about Sam," he faltered, "because we were so close. But there are one or two of his most basic characteristics that have not yet been mentioned, and should, I think, be emphasized. I would wish, first of all, to tell you how I enjoyed his sense of humor. He saw the comedy in everything, and the days of all who knew him have been forever brightened by the memory of his smile and his joking ways. And then there was the direct nature of his honesty. You always knew exactly where you stood with Sam. As we are all too well aware, this made him many enemies. Directness can be a crippling attribute in modern academia. Finally, I want to give a message and a re-assurance to all who loved him . . . particularly his wife Mary and his greatly treasured daughter Sarah and sons, Adam and Noah. It's a simple message, but all-important, given the tragic circumstances of the past months. I want to tell you that Sam Barnes was an *honorable* man. Please, don't ever forget that."

Dean Scott gave a few final words of appreciation, then invited everyone to partake of the refreshments at the front of the room. During the general movement and swell of conversation following this, Evelyn noticed that Millie remained as she had been throughout, staring at the floor and seemingly oblivious of what was going on around them. Her face was abnormally and darkly red and her breath was coming in rapid gasps. A spasm seemed to rock her as she rose suddenly and turned toward the door. Evelyn followed, determined to see her safely to her car.

"Millie," she ventured, "I'm worried about you. Have you been taking the medication for your diabetes?"

Millie stumbled against a chair, then staggered in an effort to find her balance as a hand shot forward from behind, grasping her by the arm. "Bugger off, Gus," she barked rudely, snatching her arm away with such force that she almost sent her would-be helper flying backward. Then, "Gawd almighty, Evelyn," came the muffled explosion, as she stormed out the door. "Diabetes is the least of my concerns right now! There's something bloody fishy going on here, and I'm going to get to the bottom of it somehow. I can smell the stench a mile away, and you can be damn sure it's not coming only from Sam's poor drowned body!"

CHAPTER 9

APRIL, 1977

As the end of the tumultuous university year approached, the stunned members of the Foundations of Education Department somehow managed to resume a semblance of normality. For Evelyn, the prospect of carrying on with the usual end-of-term duties had at first seemed utterly daunting. Yet here she was, hard at work at her desk in her now-quiet and neighbor-less office, nearing completion of the final tasks of the spring term. Often, she found herself wondering how people could be so resilient. Was it because the recent deaths, tragic and close-to-home though they undoubtedly were, had struck others—not themselves? Was it some spiritual will for personal survival, or even a secret rejoicing at being sufficiently deserving or fortunate to have remained alive when death had come so close?

    To her surprise she had been able to focus even on the task of marking student papers, always the most onerous aspect of teaching, in her opinion. In fact, she was now totally immersed in the student term paper in front of her. The final assignment for her course on the Sociology of the Classroom was a research paper dealing with the subject of gender equality. This particular essay had been submitted by a male student. She was singularly pleased with its ending.

"Perhaps women will no longer be considered of slightly inferior status," he had concluded, "if the time ever comes that society learns to value those unique attributes that the female of the species has to offer. We can think of her special kind of imaginative emotional response to problems in comparison to the male's cold logic, for example, and her capacity for warmth and empathy in social relationships. We can include what is equally precious and unique to the female, but so seldom ever considered: that mysterious life-creating womb. Once those things are valued over our current emphasis on science and the mere fruits of the intellect, then perhaps it will be the males who will all be feeling discriminated against."

Millie would, of course, not like it, but this was indeed the kind of understanding that Evelyn had been endeavoring to get across in the course. She had been emphasizing the need for teachers to build upon what little girls bring to the learning process, not merely to focus on the task of imposing male patterns of cognition—and white male patterns at that! Relieved that she had found at least one paper she could happily mark with an 'A', she moved on to the next in the pile. It was precisely at that moment that Harvey's distinctive rhythmic tapping sounded on the door.

Harvey's visits had by now become almost routine. Both were obviously enjoying the easy, friendly relationship. Evelyn was aware that Harvey might well have preferred something more intimate, but she liked to think she had learned a few lessons from previous mistakes along her perilous road through the male-dominated academic world. She was now convinced that once a woman in an inferior position succumbed in this respect she soon lost whatever power and status she held in the eyes of the other. Just what her attraction was for Harvey she wasn't yet sure. But she was enjoying their exchanges and, for the first time since arriving at North Pacific University almost eight years before, felt definitely 'inside the loop'—if only in the role of a listening post, as appeared to be the case today. Harvey was now launching into his concerns about the latest explosion of publicity on the Sam Barnes case.

"The news media are having a field day," he said. "Sam's death gives them more fuel for speculation than Sam alive could ever have done. Now that he's not around to sue for libel they feel safe in speculating that he was guilty as charged, else why would he have committed suicide?"

"Of course everyone will think that now! I wonder if it occurred to poor Sam that it would look like an admission, or if he was just too confused and desperately ashamed of how he had hurt his family to even think of consequences. Isn't there anything that can be done, by the Faculty, to rescue his reputation?"

"I feel just terrible about it, but there isn't an awful lot that I, or any of us, can do. And it isn't helping the reputation of the Faculty of Education either. At this point, nobody wants to hear what any of Sam's colleagues have to say. It looks like the only authority the journalists are listening to these days is Meredith Walker. The whole thing has become a *cause célèbre* for the Women's Cultural Revolution."

"Which can't be all bad, I guess, if it brings attention to the issue of sexual abuse in the academic world. But, Harvey, it has occurred to me that nobody has said anything about how the police have handled this. Have they spoken to you? Has there been an autopsy? Something Millie said made me wonder if they're completely satisfied that there's no evidence of foul play."

"Constable Gortini of the Vancouver Police interviewed

me right after they found the body. Judging by his attitude, I'd say they're quite satisfied that it was a clear case of suicide. The coroner's verdict has now confirmed this. No evidence of any cause of death but drowning, and someone reported passing Sam wandering alone on the Lions Gate late that night. I wasn't aware of it, but apparently he'd recently rented a small apartment just across the bridge, in North Vancouver. But, hey, I didn't come here today only to keep worrying away at that tragedy and the mess Sam left behind," Harvey's expression brightened.

"I intended to tell you that I'm calling a meeting of the Department for 2:00 p.m. tomorrow. Spread the word to anyone you happen to see. I'll be announcing your promotion, and I've got a few other surprises as well. In fact, everything's set in terms of our team for next year. And it looks really promising."

Evelyn wanted to ask about Millie's situation but didn't dare, just in case the news wasn't good. She had found that, whenever her friend's name was mentioned, Harvey's face assumed a stony look. Maybe he'd heard the Baby Blue Eyes label. *As usual, that poor woman is her own worst enemy!* she thought. Why did she always seem compelled to antagonize the very people who were in a position to wield the most power over her career?

As soon as Harvey left, Evelyn set off for Millie's office, carrying with her the student paper to which she had assigned the top grade. She intended to convey the news about the Departmental meeting and also show off the essay. Millie was at her desk, apparently deep in the same task that had been keeping Evelyn busy. A paper with the red letter 'A' was on the surface of the desk closest to the visitor's chair, so Evelyn promptly picked it up.

"Here," she said, "we'll have a reading exchange. You

have a look at my prize term paper and I'll read this one of yours. Oh, I see it's written by a BEAD student. One of the nuns, I take it?"

"Yes, do read it. I've actually had a lot of pleasure teaching that tiny remnant of my former class. Makes a change from the regular undergraduate courses, where the room's filled to overflowing."

There were some minutes of silence while the papers were being read. Then came one of Millie's explosive laughs.

"Evelyn, I'm fascinated by this paper. The writer is obviously a seriously sophisticated guy. You can tell by his style and organization. But listen, if you promise me you won't change his mark, I'd love to give you my impression. Okay, then. I think he's got to be either parroting your ideas back at you (to perfection, in fact) like an all-too-typical 'A' student who's learned to a fare-thee-well how to make it in the kind of academic world we've been busily creating, *or*..."

"Or... what?"

"Or he's produced a hell of a good job of a classic ironic 'take-off' on radical feminism. 'Mysterious life-creating womb', for example. Give us a break!"

"That's not fair, Millie. Just because you and your kind can't accept the modern approach to female equality, it doesn't mean that the new generation has any trouble with it. Face it, my girl, you're just a little out of date! By the way, I've been enjoying this paper of your nun's for a different reason. She's produced a really great analysis and criticism of the position on moral education presented in your textbook. She implies that the book's stance actually comes dangerously close to outright moral relativism, even though you don't ever admit that. She's referring to the idea developed near the beginning of the book on how human values and ideals, although rooted in biology, have been given form throughout history by the sociocultural environment. She obviously doesn't buy your argument about replacing religious *absolutism* in morality with *universally applicable* values. You know, the way you're always going on about how values, when tested in terms of their consequences over time, can acquire an objectivity somewhat equivalent to well-confirmed knowledge?"

'You got that right. And so did she. It's my position exactly."

"And, look here. This is clever! She uses your own theories and information on cognitive development and turns it all back on you. Her conclusion seems to be that most of humanity is not in a sufficiently advanced stage of development, intellectually and emotionally, to behave morally in the absence of belief in an absolute Good beyond nature. She's referring to a Supreme Being capable of doling out punishment and reward after death. In other words, most of us cannot now, and likely never will be able to 'be good without God'. Her argument is very well presented. I can certainly see why you gave her an 'A' grade."

"Yes, and she managed, as well, to throw in Pascal's Wager, and the ontological and cosmological so-called 'proofs' of God's existence! But I suppose what really lifted it above the other submissions, for me, was that she sort of broke ranks near the end of the paper. She actually went so far as to raise the issue of the possible negative effects of her precious supernatural imperative on the overall intellectual development of human beings. I think my use of Isaac Asimov's idea of the need to develop a 'built-in doubter' in children got to her . . . a little, at least. See . . . right here she notes something important about the downside of the theistic religious position. She admits it requires children to be socialized into non-debatable beliefs from an early age, and to remain uncritically in these closed systems throughout adulthood. And that it's all too likely to affect their approach to life in other areas, such as politics. She even acknowledges Hannah Arendt's famous comment on the issue. You know, about how it's not the *nature* of the banister that counts, once people have been taught to rely on one. Any absolutist dogma will do, if it's sold by a charismatic leader and reinforced by the masses. (Remember how Arendt noted that it proved all-too-easy for German Christians to adopt the Nazi banister?) All in all, quite a feat for a nun!"

"And now," Millie resumed a minute or so later, as she dropped her red marker and paper with a flourish. "How about forgetting our marking duties for a while and going over to the lounge for a cup of coffee? I need a break."

"Oh, I almost forgot. I wanted to talk to you in private about something. A Departmental meeting has been called for tomorrow afternoon at 2:00. I hear that the full slate of instructors for next year will be announced, as well as some promotions. Have you heard anything yet about your position having been confirmed?"

"No, I'm afraid it hasn't been, nor is it likely to be. Dean Scott called me in to see him a couple of days ago, and we had a frank talk about the situation. He more or less told me that Harvey isn't planning to give me a contract. Nor even to provide a place for me on a temporary basis."

"God, Millie! What a time to find that out! And, you mean to say Harvey has still not faced you with the news? I'm disappointed in him. That's rather dirty pool."

"I gather that the Dean agrees. He tried his best to soften the blow, tactfully assuring me that he knew I wouldn't wish to stay on where I wasn't appreciated or even wanted. He realizes it's now far too late for me to apply for any other university positions. In fact, he told me he'd gone ahead and put out feelers to the people in Science Methods and to the sociologists in the Faculty of Social Science. If those possibilities don't work out, he says he's sure he can arrange something for me with the school board for the coming year. As he put it, failing a positive offer from the university, the school board position will give me a chance to get established, hopefully in happier circumstances, for the following year."

"You're taking it a lot better than I could. Will you be giving tomorrow's meeting a miss, then?"

"Why, no!" Millie seemed surprised at the idea. "I'll get a hell of a kick out of seeing how Harvey whitewashes the news for the consumption of the others. And, of course, I'm dead curious about how the rest of the gang will take it."

"You have to admire Harvey's timing," she added, apparently as an afterthought. "I didn't even get a chance to inform my classes that I wouldn't be staying on next year. But something happened this morning that restored my faith in humanity. I've told you about Jim Chon, the only male student from my little BEAD group. Well, he came in to see me, all upset about a rumor that I was being fired. I don't know where he heard it. He wanted to organize a student rally in my cause, and said he'd already talked to a number of students from my undergraduate classes who are anxious to take part in it. I thanked him for the support, but refused the offer. I told him that I'd always criticized professors who 'used' their students in this way for personal or political purposes. But it did warm my heart!"

It made Evelyn feel better as well, and reminded her that she had something else to talk to Millie about, in the privacy of her office. She was aware that Millie was not satisfied with what appeared to her to be the undue readiness of the local police and coroner to agree on a verdict of suicide in the case of Sam's death. She asked now if anything of interest had turned up as a result of Millie's own rather mysterious inquiries.

"I do have a few very worrying bits of information that Sam gave me the last time I ever saw him, and I've been trying to follow them up . . . with some success, I think. But there's no way I'm going to talk about them before my meeting with the Vancouver police. That's scheduled for next week."

Millie then changed the subject abruptly, announcing that it must surely now be time for lunch and, seeing that they had missed their coffee break, they'd better not miss that as well. With the mention of Sam her demeanor seemed to have altered drastically. She was now distant and brooding, the relatively upbeat mood of the past hour or so suddenly gone. Evelyn couldn't help but contrast Millie's placid acceptance of what would certainly be interpreted by the academic community as a serious failure and stumbling block to her own professional future, with her attitude concerning what had happened to Sam. It was all extremely puzzling, to say the least.

As the hour for the meeting approached the next afternoon, Evelyn found herself unconsciously employing various delaying strategies, in her dread of what was to come. She had made a point of not revealing to Millie the news that her own promotion had been confirmed, sensing that it would be too cruel. The room was full when she got there. Even Millie had arrived ahead of her.

Harvey opened the meeting with his usual show of informality and *bonhomie*. After greeting those assembled—all, with the exception of Millie, by name—he reviewed briefly the highs and lows of the year now ending. Ned Smith was congratulated on a new book, just published.

Gus Rasmussen's contribution to the textbook for the Rain Forest Federated Indian College created by the Social Studies Methods group was deemed worthy of note. Stan Wheeler and Muthu were warmly thanked for their heroic job of taking over Sam Barnes' classes. Evelyn was congratulated for an article in a prestigious international journal, and her promotion was announced with great fanfare. Then came a sketchy overview of what would be happening in the Department in September. Everyone was expecting the announcement of a replacement for Sam in the History of Education area, so when Harvey's secretary entered the room at that point in the proceedings with Abdul Issa close behind, he was greeted with a wave of applause. Obviously, this had been expected.

"Abdul has agreed to join us. Not merely on a temporary visiting basis for the coming year, but in the tenure-track position of Assistant Professor. And we'll be welcoming another new member to our Department as well. I'm sure you'll agree that this is a real coup! I've finally managed to persuade Professor Werner von Schmidt to move to Canada. Some of you will know of him as a leading specialist in Marxist theory at Berkeley. I've been communicating with him for some time, hoping to get him here on a permanent basis. However, I was never able to persuade him to leave the U.S. until now."

This news was received with an outpouring of obviously rehearsed congratulations from Gus Rasmussen, and expressions of considerable surprise and puzzlement from others.

"But I understood we already had a full contingent in Philosophy of Ed. We'd been told we'd reached our limit of instructors for the present, at least." Ned Smith's unenthusiastic words obviously reflected the opinions of most of those present.

Harvey ignored the comment, turning instead to questions that were coming thick and fast concerning plans for the coming term. Evelyn realized with dismay that he was not going to mention Millie at all. And the interesting thing was that no one had even enquired about the matter. The most positive way of interpreting this was that they were all assuming there would be no change of personnel in the Sociology of Education. Why didn't someone think to ask for definite reassurance about Millie's future status? Evelyn felt an urge to do it, which she immediately stifled, realizing that her friendship and sponsorship of Millie in the past would render suspect anything she said now.

After a few more minutes of general conversation involved with plans for the coming year, there was a sudden stir. Millie, who had been silent throughout, was struggling up from her seated position. Without a word, and glancing at no one at all, she lumbered toward the exit, her graceful, light step now seemingly a thing of the past. Evelyn, watching her departing form, felt a wave of concern. Why hadn't she noticed before how much additional weight the poor woman had gained in the past month? Had she quit taking her medication? Millie was now moving slowly out the door, from behind looking like nothing so much as an exhausted, decidedly obese old woman.

When the meeting broke up some time later, Evelyn found herself leaving the room just behind the philosophy group. Willard Grange turned toward the others and paused, holding up the procession momentarily.

"I'm puzzled," he said. "Isn't Werner von Schmidt the Berkeley scholar who has written so much on the Marxist version of the function of the family in the ideal Communist society? And on the role of capitalist economies throughout the world in the exploitation of women? I don't see how that fits into what we're doing in Philosophy of Education. Jesus! I wish our honorable leader would consult with us before he makes such a major decision as hiring a Full Professor to teach in our field!"

The next morning Evelyn's phone rang just as she entered the office. It was Harvey, informing her that he was planning on meeting with the sociology group in an hour, if that was okay with her. So he was now beginning the process of consultation—a bit after-the-fact, it would seem, but that was evidently Harvey's way of administering a Department. However, anything to take her away from marking term papers and constructing exams was, in fact, okay with her these days. But not for long, she reminded herself. The students were slated to begin their finals the following week, so she'd better be ready for all the time the invigilating and marking of exams would require! Almost an hour later, at the point of dropping in to pick up Millie, she suddenly realized that her friend would, of course, not be included in Harvey's plans. Turning abruptly, she headed for the main Departmental office, just off Harvey's own.

As she had expected, Gus was there, and the two men were already deep in excited conversation. So this shouldn't take much time, she thought, with only the three of them now involved in decisions. But, just as she was beginning to consider an appropriate opening gambit, the door opened and Abdul entered. He paused at the threshold, taking in the scene.

"Am I too early?" he asked.

"Why no," said Harvey. "You are, in fact, the last member of our 1977-78 Sociology of Education teaching team to arrive. Congratulations to you and to us, on your having joined our group for the coming year."

"But I thought..." Abdul turned and looked searchingly behind him. Then came the change of expression as recognition dawned. "Are you saying you have hired me to take Millie's place in sociology? That you are letting her go? That I'm not going to be teaching with the historians as we had all been led to expect? But my expertise is not in sociology! I am an economist, with a strong background in world history."

"I thought you understood where you were being placed, Abdul. Surely you were aware that Millie was here on a temporary basis only. That her permanent appointment was subject to approval by the administration. We decided some time ago she just didn't meld well with the rest of our faculty. Now you, with your Marxist approach to economics, will provide a perspective that was missing not only from our sociology area, but from the entire Department."

"Well," Evelyn just couldn't restrain herself at this point, "I have to agree on that, at least. Millie would be the first to admit that she's an expert neither in economics nor Marxism!"

She knew she should say more. This was her opening to argue that they surely did not need more Marxism in the sociology courses now available for students at NPU; that Millie's perspective of Deweyan Pragmatism offered a much-needed balance in this ideology-ridden field of study. But she simply could not bring herself to utter the words. Harvey would interpret it as an overt attack upon his personal integrity and capability as an administrator. And what would be the results of such a well-meaning, but reckless, interjection anyway? It was far too late to save Millie's current position and career prospects. How would it help anyone concerned if she were to jeopardize her own as well?

Abdul appeared to be examining and weighing similar concerns. His eyes had become fixed on the distance somewhere beyond all four of them, the normally mobile face now gone strangely dead. Then, gradually, an expression of extreme distaste moved across his features, and he wiped his hand across the shining brown forehead as if to clear it of something repulsive.

"I am sorry," he said abruptly. "I need to think about all this. If you will excuse me, I feel I must go for a walk along the seawall." With that he rose to his feet, looking about distractedly as if he still expected to see Millie coming through the door. Then he turned to go.

"What the hell is this all about, Abdul?" Gus exploded. "You've just signed a contract most people in your position would give their eye teeth for. What's eating you anyway? Is it the possibility that your big fat Mama won't be around to suckle you next year?"

"You knew!" Abdul looked at him coldly. Then, incredulously, as his black eyes flashed around the group, "You all knew! Yet nobody deigned to inform the two people who were most concerned!" He turned and moved quickly out the door, closing it firmly behind him.

Evelyn sat, immobilized by the speed at which the situation had unfolded. She knew she should have interceded, should somehow have prevented Abdul from leaving the room. Harvey's barely concealed anger was sufficient to tell her that. This was definitely not the way to make a good impression on one's first day in the Department. But she had been so taken aback by Gus' angry comment that Abdul was gone before she fully realized what had happened. She was all-too-familiar with the strangely perverse way that Gus seemed to view people and events. But this obsession with imagining some kind of romantic liaison between Abdul and Millie? Millie as a 'big fat Mama' . . . well maybe, but suckling Abdul . . . or anybody? The vision was just too, too weird for even Gus to contemplate, she would have thought. She could scarcely wait to share the laugh with Millie. The news of Abdul's joining the sociology group in her place would require some careful explaining and justifying, however. She had a strong feeling that Millie would find it extremely hurtful, perhaps even as a kind of betrayal on his part.

It was only later, when she was on her way to their planned restaurant luncheon, that Evelyn realized that she could not regale Millie with the 'suckling Mama' story without revealing the entire situation concerning Abdul's appointment to her position in the Sociology of Education. So she decided that Millie should first have the chance to enjoy her meal. The previous day's Departmental meeting must have been unsettling enough, she thought. She knew Millie sufficiently well to be aware that this news about the identity of the person replacing her would be much, much worse.

As it happened, however, this was not to be. They had scarcely opened their menus when a friendly voice sounded from across the room. Stan Wheeler approached their table, with Muthu close behind him.

"Mind if we join you two?" Stan asked, as he pulled out the remaining two chairs. Both men were seated before the women had a chance to reply.

"Have we ever got news!" Stan burst out. "We've just now come from a meeting with Harvey. Believe it or not, the fabled Werner von Schmidt is to join *us*. Not the philosophy group as we were all assuming yesterday. He'll be taking Sam Barnes' position as Full Professor. Of course we would have appreciated a little say in the matter, wouldn't we Muthu? But I guess we don't rate that, not being world-acclaimed Marxist theorists."

"Whatever is that going to mean for Abdul then?" asked Millie. "Surely Harvey's not just been leading him to expect the appointment, and then reneging and handing it over to someone else at the last moment!"

Muthu was silent, looking at Millie with a concerned expression on his face. Suddenly Stan seemed to think again.

"I . . . I'm not sure I should be . . ."

"Abdul has been given your position, Millie." Muthu spoke quietly, reaching across the table to put his hand over hers as he did so. Millie frowned then, suddenly looking dazed, glanced inquiringly at Evelyn.

"I was going to break the news after we had eaten, Millie. I'm sorry."

"We're the ones who should be apologizing, Evelyn . . . and Millie. It was most thoughtless of us to join the two of you at this time, and then for me to reveal this news so precipitously," said Stan.

"Nonsense!" Millie found her voice, although it came out with a strangled sound. "I had to hear about it, and the sooner the better. Evelyn, tell me everything you know about the matter. How and when did you find out what was being planned?"

At that point they were interrupted by the waitress arriving to take their orders—not any too soon from Evelyn's point of view. At her suggestion they decided to order their lunch and try to relax somewhat before dealing with what was, to all of them, a totally unexpected and painful matter. They immediately agreed on the idea of making this as gala an affair as possible, given the circumstances, and the very real possibility that it would be their last chance for a visit together. The little group chose fresh wild salmon all around, with the exception of Millie who asked for her usual rare Alberta steak with onion and mushroom sauce. In addition, Evelyn insisted on a bottle of Okanagan Valley wine to accompany the large seafood platter and hot, herb bread which were to serve as appetizers.

It was not until the food was placed before them, and they had been eating quietly for some time, that Evelyn felt it was safe to return to Millie's question. First, however, Muthu decided there was one much more important thing to do.

"I should have thought of this sooner," he said, raising his glass of wine. "Let's mark this little celebration of our year together by drinking to Sam". In silence, they followed his example. "I'm confident that the honest, fun-loving self that was Sam Barnes is here, in the memories of all of us now, and will be in the future, for as long as we live to possess those memories."

Millie gazed at the others thoughtfully, and with obvious affection. She had become much more relaxed. Evelyn was happy to note her reaction and glad they were having this little interlude. The days ahead would be a test of her strength and buoyancy, to say the least. At her age, and with the current state of her health and appearance, it would not be easy to relocate. As they ate their food Evelyn reflected, as she often found herself doing lately, on how women in modern society become generally invisible as persons of interest, once they have passed the age of forty. She had heard her older friends discussing it, and lately had begun to experience a preliminary taste of the phenomenon herself. It seemed that almost overnight, people (especially men of all ages) began to look past you in a crowd, eyes searching out others, as if you did not even exist.

Apparently her friend, at least when she was exhibiting her normal intellectual effervescence, had managed to avoid the experience to some extent. But that situation would no doubt soon be altering drastically, given the recent changes in Millie herself. Evelyn felt herself shuddering mentally to think of what was ahead for her in her search for an appointment for the coming year, given her age, appearance, and recent career record. And, especially, in the absence of favorable recommendations from her latest place of employment. For Evelyn, much as she had come to appreciate Harvey Garfinkle and enjoy his company, was quite convinced that any contribution from him to Millie's coming job search would be entirely negative.

"I want to say something else about Sam," Millie's voice interrupted her meandering thoughts. "There is reason to believe that I will soon have information to share with all three of you which will help with the reinstatement of his reputation, at least. I don't know if I told you, but when we heard the ghastly news that day I promised myself I wouldn't rest until justice had been achieved for him. That has been my main focus ever since. To hell with my job for next year! This comes first for me. Next week I'll give you all a call and let you know if I have what I expect to find. Maybe I'll wait until after I've met with the police and discussed the new evidence with them, and what it's all leading to. At that point I may need some help from you guys."

No amount of questioning would squeeze anything more from her. Millie said she didn't have the confirmation she needed yet. But it was coming in a few days, of that she was sure. For the present, they should just continue to enjoy their special luncheon together.

"If only Abdul were here with us," she added. "Then it would be a perfect little farewell occasion for me."

"You don't bear him any ill will then?" Stan asked. "I would have thought you might, given what has happened."

"Not at all. I'm still waiting for the full story on it, Evelyn, but I'm sure there's an explanation for Adbul's role in the whole affair."

"Yes there is, Millie. You're right in thinking that he had no part in anything underhanded. He was as surprised and dismayed, when he heard the news this morning, as you were a little while ago." She left the subject now until after they had finished their dessert. As usual, she had foregone this herself, anticipating sufficient vicarious satisfaction from the sight of the men sharing an apple crumble, and Millie avidly tackling her pecan pie and ice cream. Finally, Evelyn judged it was time to describe in detail what had occurred in the meeting, in spite of Harvey's longstanding rule against just such practice. When she finished there was silence for a moment, then Stan burst out.

"Would you believe that Gus character! You know, I can't for the life of me understand the close friendship between Abdul and him. The only thing they seem to have in common is their ideology."

"I guess that's enough," Millie said thoughtfully. "Especially when they're both interested in ideas and get excited about, and are committed to, the same ones. They look at the world through the same window. That means a lot. And, of course, they did arrive here around the same time, I understand, and Adbul has told me how helpful Gus was then."

All too soon the luncheon was over, and the four colleagues had to return to their offices. Just as she was leaving the group, however, Evelyn remembered something.

"Millie," she said, 'I drove to work today for a change. I noticed your car wasn't parked in its usual spot. Would you like a ride home tonight? It won't be very early, as I want to get a lot of work done this afternoon. How about six o'clock, or maybe a bit later? I'll call around at your office when I'm ready, if it's okay with you."

"Yes, I'd really appreciate that. My car's in the garage for servicing. I was going to have to phone for a taxi, which is a hell of a nuisance as they never seem to be able to find the right building out here." Millie grinned with obvious relief as she waved them off.

The rest of the day passed slowly for Evelyn, as she worked her way through the final term projects and papers stacked on her desk. She scarcely paused until Harvey, fresh from his meeting with the philosophy group, dropped in with afternoon coffee for them both. When he quizzed her about how Millie had taken the news, she couldn't help but let him know that her friend was not completely defeated by it.

"It seems to me," she said, "that Millie's far more concerned . . . excited even . . . about the evidence she's beginning to accumulate involving Sam's death. She refuses to discuss it with me but, in fact, she plans to notify the police about it very soon. Interesting, that."

Harvey had little time to spare, and Evelyn was soon once again free to bury herself in her work. It was almost seven before she came to the end of the task she had set herself. Grabbing her purse and jacket, she quickly locked up and rushed out. When she turned down into the hall leading to Millie's office, however, she stopped in her tracks. Abdul was only a few yards ahead of her. She watched as he knocked at the office door. She didn't want to interrupt the meeting between these two—important as it was bound to be. As she turned to retrace her steps, she heard the door open behind her. A short distance back along the way she had come, a sudden sound brought her once more to a halt. It was a strangled scream, in a voice scarcely recognizable as a man's. More screams of "No!" . . . "No!" then a torrent of strange words and the name "Millie! . . . Millie!' shouted over and over. She raced back to the office door and into the room—then stopped in horror at the sight before her.

Abdul was on his knees moaning in his native tongue and grasping at what looked, at first glance, like a large mound of flesh on the floor midway between the desk and the door. Millie was a crumpled, motionless heap sprawled in a twisted position on her back; her face—what could be seen of it around the gaping hole created by the wide-open mouth in the center—a greyish blue color, eyes open and bulging, like glazed marbles on the point of popping out. The grimacing, foaming mouth and distorted, convulsed facial features overwhelmed the entire scene for Evelyn, in what they revealed about the agony of that final, frantic, agonized gasping for air. An ugly dark mound of mucous-like substance covered the nose and chin and seemed still to be in the process of pouring down the motionless chest. The room whirled and the floor seemed to tilt as Evelyn caught the side of the desk for support.

"Call the ambulance!" Abdul's insistent, almost hysterical voice finally began to penetrate her stunned consciousness. She stumbled around Millie to the phone on the desk and, after two failed attempts to dial, finally got through and managed to give their location and the necessary description and directions. Meanwhile, Abdul was wiping away the vomit and trying to administer artificial respiration. But it was soon obvious to them both that Millie had been dead for some time.

Much later, at the hospital, as the attending Emergency Room doctor gave them his diagnosis, Evelyn listened in stunned silence, vaguely aware that she was taking very little in. A classic case of diabetic shock, he seemed to be saying, no doubt caused by an overdose of insulin, taken under the pressures of work or stress from other causes. Too much insulin in such a situation causes the blood glucose level to drop dangerously low. There was clear evidence that Professor Eisenstadt had given herself an injection in her office sometime that afternoon. In fact it appeared as if she had finished whatever amount she had brought with her, as the ambulance attendants had found only the used needle and insulin container on the floor. "Obese patients suffering from diabetes are particularly vulnerable to such accidents," he added.

Harvey, who had insisted on rushing over to the hospital morgue as soon as he was informed, had been sitting for some time with his head in his hands, shoulders shuddering. At this point he looked up and agreed, regretfully, that Millie had indeed experienced an extremely difficult year. In fact, he offered, she had only this week been informed that she was to lose her position at NPU. When Evelyn demurred, remarking that—although all this was indeed true—Millie had appeared to be handling things rather well, Harvey again spoke up, his voice heavy with regret.

"It's all my fault. I'll never forgive myself. If only I had known about her diabetes! I could have managed somehow to arrange for her to stay on here, for another year at least."

"It is I who must bear the blame." Abdul spoke for the very first time during the long period of waiting in the hospital. "It is I who was usurping her position. And it is I who went walking all afternoon rather than face her with the news of my betrayal of our friendship. I should have thought of the effect of this news on her health, for I was one of the very few whom she had told about her illness. I could have prevented this, if I had gone to her sooner. I am convinced of that!"

"For heaven's sake, you two! Don't do this to yourselves! Millie would have been the last person to have wanted it."

Evelyn found herself trying to comfort both men, although she believed that there was indeed a grain of truth in what each had said. And although she felt badly in need of comforting herself. She had known Millie far longer than had either of them, and been much, much closer to her, she believed. Why did neither one think about how this was affecting *her*? Suddenly she felt an overwhelming need to escape their company, and the hospital environment as well. There was nothing of Millie in this place. That agonized, grimacing face and lifeless mound of flesh, now marked so eternally in her consciousness, was not the Millie she wanted to remember. She had to get out of here.

She rose, asking the physician in charge if he would inform her if any subsequent information came to light, or if he had any further need of her. He reminded her that he would have to get in touch with Millie's family doctor as soon as possible, preferably before the death warrant was signed. Evelyn had already attempted to obtain this information but, because of Millie's mother's advanced senile dementia, had gotten nowhere when she phoned for it. The home helper in attendance had no knowledge of Millie's ever going to see a doctor, nor of the recent diabetes diagnosis. *How like her just to have dropped into a walk-in clinic!*

The attending physician now assured them that he could

see no reason for them not to leave. Abdul rose with her. She paused momentarily as Harvey inquired about how soon the body would be available for burial. He informed the doctor that the university would look after everything, as Millie was survived only by an elderly, ailing mother. He would now proceed to her home to see what he could do for the mother, he said and, if possible, to locate—and arrange the necessary communication with—her family doctor. The others were to leave it all to him. Feeling somewhat guilty, but realizing that she had never even met Millie's mother, Evelyn was quite satisfied to do just that. Good old Harvey! Too often they all tended to underrate him. And how ironic that he should come through like this, in the end, for Millie, who would have hated being in any kind of debt to Baby Blue Eyes!

The final weeks of April went by for Evelyn in a blur of marking exams and issuing final grades, combined with the task of combing through Millie's address books in order to inform her far-flung friends and numerous professional connections about her tragic death. In the course of all this she was being constantly interrupted for advice concerning memorial arrangements. In the end, the planning and organizing of Millie's farewell celebration (she would have hated a religious service of any kind) had been taken over by Mrs. Garfinkle and the Faculty Wives' Association. Evelyn and the other females in the Faculty of Education had been asked to arrange for the serving of the food. (Another irony for poor Millie—this one, in fact, almost at the level of tragic comedy!)

Even the members of the philosophy group had been visibly affected by Millie's shocking end. On the last day of the official term, just after the memorial get-together, the three of them rather tentatively approached Evelyn in the faculty lounge, fitting themselves gingerly into the chairs beside her.

"I hope I never, ever, live through another year like the past one!" This came from Willard Grange sometime into the ensuing conversation, which had been rather forced and desultory until then. The exclamation was accompanied by a high, squawking moan which, along with the nose that looked sharper than ever, and the blueish chin that seemed to have almost disappeared into the folds at his neck, made Evelyn think momentarily of a wounded blue heron.

"You can say that again!" Ned Smith echoed him in a loud sigh. "The loss of our beautiful Cynthia was bad enough, but we could all understand that sometimes these horrific accidents do happen with students far away from home. And then the loss of Sam, although all-too-ghastly and untimely, could be dealt with as one of life's tragic coincidences. But now Millie . . . !"

"I see what you mean, Ned. I hate to sound flippant, but how does that corny old saw go? Two losses we can just possibly account for. But losing three people in one year is beginning to look a hell of a lot like carelessness on somebody's part, wouldn't you say?" Les Brittan's words, accompanied as they were by his familiar wry chuckle, seemed to return them all to a semblance of normalcy. Evelyn was grateful to him. Clearly, the three were attempting to make amends for their previous, often openly scornful, treatment of Millie. In fact, the next comment, offered hesitatingly by Les, confirmed her hunch.

"Seriously, Evelyn, there *is* something I've been wanting to say to somebody, and I guess you're the logical person to say it to. I wish we could undo some of our behavior toward poor Millie. It was no way to treat a newcomer to our midst. It was just that the woman was so damn arrogant and seemed to think she had been appointed Professor Emeritus of 'Everything'! It really got to us, I'm afraid."

"And that wasn't the worst of it." Ned Smith was now speaking. "I think what set us all against her from the very start was the way she wangled her position here. I don't know if you were aware of it, Evelyn, but we were informed on very good authority that she was hired *only* because of her connections with the upper administration at the university."

"That's true." Willard Grange piped up. "Word was that the order came down from above, and our Department had nothing whatsoever to say about it. However, I realize now that having her thrust upon us in that way was no excuse for the way we treated her."

Evelyn made an effort to restore the previous lightness to the discussion by assuring the group that Millie's shoulders (not to mention the rest of her) had been sufficiently broad to carry the burden of their combined negativity. However, she couldn't help but wonder privately if they would have behaved in a similarly hostile fashion toward a male scholar who had displayed the equivalent of Millie's obvious breadth and depth of knowledge in so many related fields, even if he *had* been chosen by the Dean.

Although her term's work was finally completed, Evelyn had a sense of something yet to be done. Then she realized, almost reluctantly, that it had to do with Abdul. She couldn't leave Vancouver for the summer without a talk with him. No doubt she would be seeing a lot more of him in September, but there was so much that was now unfinished between them. And there was so much of the living Millie that they had both experienced during the past year. She very much needed a sharing of memories and mutual recognition of the still-incomprehensible fact of their friend's death. So, for the first time since she had known him, she went downstairs one night to his apartment. She did it only most reluctantly, as he had always discouraged any hint from her about how he lived and worked in his own abode.

Abdul opened the door promptly, then greeted her with an astonished, even dismayed, look. After hesitating a moment he asked her in, ushering her, rather formally, to a comfortable chair. As if any chair in that strange little place appeared even to approach the level of comfort! What she could see of the apartment surprised her. Knowing Abdul, she had not been expecting anything grand in either size or decoration, but the boxlike, Spartan effect of the surroundings was a shock. It was obviously a 'one-room-with bath' set-up, the tiny kitchenette attached to a living room complete with pull-out couch. No coverings or pictures on any surface. Nothing whatsoever that in any way spoke personally of Abdul. No wonder he had never asked her to visit him. What in the world did he spend his money on?

"I'm sorry, Abdul, for bursting in on you like this. But I'm leaving for an international sociology conference in Amsterdam in a couple of days, and don't plan on being here for much of the summer. And there's a lot I wanted to talk to you about." A tremor of what looked like pain flickered in his eyes. "Nothing personal concerning us, of course," she added hastily.

"It is quite all right, Evelyn. I should have contacted you before this. I, too, wish for us to have a conversation. About many things. In the first place, I owe you an apology for what must have seemed like extremely rude and unfeeling treatment a few months ago, when we stopped seeing each other. There were many reasons why I felt that it would be best for us to be no more than friends and colleagues. I wish I could explain them without giving hurt to you and others, but please believe me when I say it was for the best for all concerned."

"That's okay. Well . . . it's really not okay, but let's just say it's all in the past. What I would like to discuss with you is Millie and her sudden terrible death. I just absolutely can't accept that she's dead, Abdul. No one so full of life one minute could be gone the next! Especially not in that ghastly way. If only I had quit work an hour earlier! She choked to death on her own vomit, Abdul. You saw it! So did I. How could it have happened so suddenly, without her even being able to call for help? And she was so full of plans, for reinstating Sam's reputation mostly. In fact, she was so involved with her 'detective' project when I talked to her that very day, that she really wasn't all that heartbroken about your having been given her job, Abdul. I realize it'll be hard for you to believe, but she didn't hold anything against you. She knew it was just Harvey's way of administering the Department."

Abdul had been listening intently, head bent and sorrowful, black eyes focused on his twisting hands. Something in her rush of words suddenly alerted him.

"What was that you said a moment ago . . . about Sam?"

"I happen to know she was following up some leads about those accusations against Sam. She wouldn't tell me anything more, unfortunately. I think she was almost afraid it might possibly amount to nothing solid, and she wanted to be sure that she really had some hard evidence in case it did, before revealing her hand. You know how practical and critically minded our Millie always was about things like that."

Abruptly, Abdul came to his feet, and Evelyn felt somehow called upon to do the same. *I guess he wants to get rid of me*, she thought. *Nothing's changed between us, that's for sure.* Almost immediately came the realization that there had really never been any 'us'. She had only kidded herself that such an entity had ever existed. Suddenly, in the midst of all this self-recrimination, she noticed that Abdul had something serious to say to her. Clearly, it was something that, for him, at least, was better spoken from a standing position.

"Evelyn, I want you to know that I am not accepting the position that Harvey offered. I do not intend to become an Assistant Professor in your Department. And I fully realize that, by breaking my contract here at this late date, I will never make it to that level in any Department at this university, nor any other Canadian university. Harvey made that rather clear when I told him about my decision."

"But . . . but Abdul, what do you intend to do? Where will you go?"

"I am leaving Canada tomorrow, heading first for London where my father is now on a sabbatical from his university in Lesotho. Further than that I have no plans as yet. I know only that I have one brief life to live, and I think I can put that life to better use in some place other than the ethically polluted, back-stabbing atmosphere I sense around me in this university. I will concentrate on my novel, and possibly try to teach illiterate children in my own country. There is a school in Roma to which I have been sending my excess money. It is on Catholic Church property and is operated by the church, so that is something of a problem for me. But, as of now, it is all there is for the needy children in my home district. And the sisters have promised not to use my financial help for proselytizing purposes. Or, just possibly, I might be able to get involved once more with the African National Congress, working with supporters of Nelson Mandela from a relatively close but much safer location than one would find across the border in South Africa."

Abdul had been moving about the room as he talked, distractedly fingering one piece of furniture after another. He was now approaching the curtainless window. Evelyn rose to join him. She searched for comforting words: words that would convince him to remain at North Pacific University for the coming year. But none came to her. So she stood in silence, looking out the window with him.

Evelyn noted with something of a shock that there was no view of the ocean such as she had access to from her own apartment. Abdul's modest living quarters faced only a cluster of other buildings, meandering off in unplanned disharmony into the flatness of the surrounding delta, and to the clusters of bush-land climbing the ridges on the far horizon. She remembered fleetingly, how, as a newcomer to the area, she had been astounded to discover the hundreds of miles of Fraser River valley beyond this view. It was a fertile valley extending all the way to the towering Coast Range of mountains separating the Lower Mainland from the breathtakingly beautiful Okanagan valley beyond. Suddenly, her musings were interrupted by Abdul as he turned to her again, speaking urgently.

"You know, Evelyn, how I have always believed that Marx's original theory held the answers to humanity's problems. In fact, I now realize that I was fully as dogmatically committed to those beliefs as the fundamentalist is to his religious doctrines. But the way Millie was treated here, and the way she died, has made me see things differently. I have come to sense that Marx may have been overly optimistic about human beings. A short time ago Millie and I were arguing over precisely that point. She suggested that Marx had failed to take sufficient account of the human hunger for power, and of our universal tendency to abuse such power unless somehow constrained from without. She also said that he had not understood bureaucracy, and how it inevitably takes over and operates within large organizations, *whether public or private,* to encourage the substitution of self-aggrandizement and mindless rule-following for the original objectives."

"Yes," said Evelyn. "I think it was on that very point that she pretty well managed to make me rethink Marxism too."

"You are probably aware of what else she had to say about Marx, then. She convinced me that he was in error in defining the problem as being the *nature of the ownership* of the means of production. Rather, it is in the way people tend to behave within the huge monopolies so often deemed necessary to *control* such production. Whether the organizations involved are governmental or privately owned is not the issue, according to her. It is the bureaucratization and abuse of power that tends to take over whenever an operation exceeds a certain size and has a monopoly on a given service or product."

"Absolute power corrupts absolutely, no matter what the source of that power, was how she put it," offered Evelyn.

"Yes. She was of the opinion that the problem has seldom been the 'enemy without'. Rather, she said, it was these all-too human foibles on the part of the participants that condemned Marxism to failure wherever it was tried. Failure similar to the small-scale type we see here, in this little university Department. She thought that it was Marxism's fatal separation of Utopian visions from the predictable consequences of power-seeking behavior in the real world (along with the bureaucratic mind-set nurtured by large-scale organization) that allows people to preach the theory while utterly failing to practice its original humanist ethic."

"Now that she is gone," he finished ruefully, after another lengthy pause. "I can recognize the value of what she was saying. I do not expect you to understand, Evelyn, but I feel I can no longer be a part of this hypocritical game. Academic elites should be ethical leaders. Not merely successful manipulators of power and of bureaucratic rules. The immediate losers in all this are the students, but the longer-term loser is society as a whole. And the culture each individual action helps to forge."

"I can only repeat, Abdul. Millie would not have wanted you to leave. She knew you had nothing to do with what happened to her here. Please stay, and try to make things better for the next Millie . . . or Sam . . . or Cynthia, or whoever happens to get on the wrong side of the system."

"You say 'the system'. But one of the lessons I learned from the life and death of our friend, Millie, is that a corrupt system depends for its success on the acquiescence of the people within it . . . *all of us.* Each person must take a stand, Evelyn, no matter what the system signals or threatens, even though it may mean that one is all alone. Refusing Harvey's offer of reward for my silent complicity in what was being done to Millie is my stand. What is the saying from your culture that Millie liked to quote? 'Here I stand. I can do no other'."

Upon returning to her own apartment following their awkward farewells Evelyn found herself drawn to her open window. She leaned out, drinking in the sight of the placid ocean below, re-thinking the (not-unusual) one-sided conversation during what was probably her final encounter with Abdul. So much about Millie, she thought, and so little about her, Evelyn, his former lover. And his attitude toward Harvey Garfinkle! How that had suddenly changed, in spite of the fact that he and Harvey and Gus had become such a close threesome during the past few months. He seemed now to have bought Millie's negative assessment of their Head—hook, line and sinker. Most unfair, she decided. Why hadn't she thought to remind him of the generosity of the job offer he had so thoughtlessly spurned, and about how Harvey had come through for all of them in this ordeal? And of how thoughtful and helpful Harvey had been to her during the past few months? That might even have changed his mind and persuaded him to stay. But, in her heart, she knew it was too late now for second thoughts. In embarrassing Harvey Garfinkle in such a public way, Abdul already had, knowingly and recklessly, burned his bridges.

Suddenly she seemed to hear, once more, "the strange wild sound" of honking in the distance. *What nonsense!* she told herself. *Why romanticize a flock of flying geese?* It couldn't possibly be her beloved Siberian Snow Geese. They had long since flown north for the summer. But the cry continued, carried on the barely perceptible ocean breeze. Once again the words, *something lost,* came fleetingly to mind.

CHAPTER 10

JUNE, 2004

As the sunlight streaming in her bedroom window finally signaled the end of the long and sleepless night, Evelyn struggled gratefully from her bed. Surely, whatever faced her on this day could not be worse than the agony of the hours just passed. She had arranged for Ms. Montague to interview her at her home in Toronto's Rosedale district at 10:30 a.m., thinking that might be less disruptive of her own previously laid plans. Also, she had wanted to get it all behind her as soon as possible. Maybe this would at last provide 'closure', whatever that overworked term was supposed to mean. While waiting, she decided to make a list of questions she would like to ask about what the reporter had discovered thus far. That should prove enlightening, and much more interesting than merely being on the receiving end of an inquisition.

At precisely 10:30 the doorbell rang. *A good sign that the young journalist is competent*, she thought. There was something about the clothes worn by the young woman at the door that jolted her backward in time. So similar to the styles of the seventies. Was it some kind of an omen? She ushered her guest into the living room and asked her to wait there for a moment while she turned on the coffee. The friendly voice at her back, addressing her as Dr. Ashton-

Brent and remarking on the attractiveness of the room, made her realize that she had been followed into the kitchen.

"I'm afraid I don't remember your first name," she apologized, turning around abruptly. "And you can call me Evelyn."

"It's Anthea. My father wanted to name me after his dead sister, I believe, but couldn't quite bring himself to. So he settled on something that sounded similar to Cynthia. I think I prefer it that way too. Oh, before I forget, I want to apologize for my rude interruption of your celebration last night. I had only just arrived on a flight from Vancouver, and scarcely had time to drop my luggage at the hotel and rush over. But I did want to catch you before it started. And it's a good thing I spoke to you when I did, as I was most anxious to locate Dr. Garfinkle as well. It was a stroke of luck for me that he was there too."

"Vancouver! I suppose you were down in Richmond looking up people there who might be able to help with information about Cynthia? And who did you find? I'd love to hear about them as I've become totally out of touch with North Pacific University over the years."

"I'm afraid not many of those who knew Cynthia as a student are still there. In fact, that's the type of information I had hoped to get from you. My partner is remaining in the Lower Mainland area for a few days, so if you can give me any leads he will follow them up. For example, could you tell me which of your colleagues at that time would have known Cynthia? And any fellow students with whom she may have traveled as well? Oh, and before I forget it, were there any others at your party last night who were at North Pacific University the year of Cynthia's death? If there were, I would like to talk to them as soon as possible."

"The only one I can think of is Meredith Walker, who

led in the pioneering of a feminist organization that year. Actually, it was probably Cynthia's death that helped to motivate the female students and, in a way, to instigate the entire thing. And I have no doubt that it also helped me get a university-wide Women's Studies program established the following year. I'm sure Meredith would be pleased to meet with you, as she was always most concerned about that tragic event, and the way it was more or less swept under the rug." Evelyn promptly gave the reporter details on how to contact Meredith, feeling quite certain that there would be no one more happy to be involved in this particular project. She then poured the coffee and got them both settled in comfortable chairs, with a small coffee table between them.

"Now," she continued, "if you don't mind, Anthea, I'd like to ask *you* a few questions about who you *did* manage to find at NPU. What about Gus Rasmussen, the only educational sociologist there in my time other than Harvey Garfinkle, Millie Eisenstadt and myself? I've often wondered what happened to him, as I've never encountered a thing he's published in all these years. Nor have I met him at any sociology or education conferences. Is he still around?"

"No," Anthea replied tersely.

"Then there were the two educational historians. One was Stan Wheeler and the other was Muthu Swami. At least, Swami was the surname Muthu used when one was officially required in Canada but he told me once that, as a former Untouchable from India, he had actually been raised with only the one name. There were three philosophers in the Foundations of Education as well. They were Leslie Brittan, Ned (or Edward) Smith and Willard Grange. And that's it. The entire teaching faculty of our little Department."

"One of the historians you mentioned, Professor

Muthu, is in his final year of teaching there. He sent you his congratulations, by the way. Professor Wheeler retired a few years ago, but we found him through Professor Muthu, and he was most cooperative. And there was also an elderly lady named Helen Korensky. She has been retired for a long time, she told me. She was formerly a Professor of English in the 'Teaching Methods Department', I think they called it. Actually it was *she* who made a point of getting in touch with *us*. I think one of the historians told her about the reopening of the case. Professor Korensky was most anxious to help. In fact, she informed us rather vehemently that she has never been satisfied that Cynthia died accidentally. Or even committed suicide."

"What about the educational philosophers who were my colleagues in the seventies?"

"Dr. Brittan died quite a few years back, we were told, from complications due to emphysema. But Professor Smith is still teaching there. And so is Willard Grange, although he's not very well, and is retiring this year."

"Did you discover any members of Cynthia's cohort who might have been friendly with her? For example, I know she was living in an old house just off the campus grounds with a number of graduate students from other Faculties."

"We've been trying to follow them up, but it hasn't been easy. So far we've found no fellow lodgers who admit to having seen or heard anything that night. We did manage to locate the only other two people who were graduate students in your Department at that time (according to all of our informants there). You may remember them. Their names are . . . let me see . . . Tony Kohut and Gerald Davis. Davis is now a top administrator in the British Columbia Department of Education, and Kohut is a high-school principal. Can you think of any graduate students from other areas of study who may have been her friends? We were disappointed that those we interviewed, who had been living in the same house, didn't appear to have known her all that well." Anthea was checking her notes carefully as she responded.

"Actually, you already seem to have identified the people who were probably closest to Cynthia. Except for a man called Abdul Issa, by the way. Although he actually taught Social Studies Methods, he often attended our Departmental affairs, and I know she took a class from him once. She may also have been good friends with grad students in other Departments, besides than the ones in that group lodging. But I wouldn't have been aware of that. You know, I'm afraid I'm not going to be of much help to you. I'm really curious, though, about whether any of the people you and your partner have already talked to were able to shed new light on the matter."

"I hope you won't mind if we don't discuss that until after our interview. What I need from you at this stage is exactly what I was looking for from them. Your particular perspective on what happened."

At this point, Anthea suddenly assumed the persona of the practiced investigative journalist. First, she pulled out a small machine and, after asking for permission to tape their conversation, turned it on. After a few searching questions, she sat back and asked Evelyn to try her best to tell the story of that dreadful university year in her own words, including every detail she could recall having to do with the deaths not only of Cynthia, but of Sam and Millie as well. This unexpected expansion of the investigation intrigued Evelyn, and she promised to help as much as possible. During the two hours that followed, she found herself being ruefully grateful for her unintended mental rehearsal during the previous sleepless night. Nevertheless, she was exhausted and feeling incredibly stressed by the time Anthea finally stopped the tape.

"I managed to contact Dr. Garfinkle, and have been trying to persuade him to meet with me tomorrow," said Anthea as she packed her belongings into a bulging shoulder bag. "I hope to gather the same type of personal reminiscences from him. I haven't yet pinned him down, however. And after the interview with him, I'd like to meet with you again, if you don't mind. Could you possibly keep the afternoon, three days from now, open for me? In the meantime, I hope to discuss the entire affair with Meredith Walker as well. My intention is to present you at that time with a list of specific questions which I've put together after listening to the tapes of your story as well as those of the other two. And in the context of all the tapes we made in British Columbia. The person working on the story with me is also planning to be here by then, hopefully with more tapes."

Evelyn readily agreed, as she was now most anxious to go into greater depth on the circumstances surrounding the three deaths; and to receive the promised feedback from Anthea on what had been learned thus far. Clearly the young journalist was not prepared to share information at this stage. Perhaps something would be learned from Harvey that Evelyn did not yet know. She realized that the two of them had avoided the subject totally whenever their paths had happened to cross or intertwine over the intervening years. Harvey had a way of sensibly concentrating on looking forward, she thought wistfully, rather than wasting his emotional energies regretting past tragedies.

That evening he phoned to inquire about her experience with Anthea Montague. Evidently he was still in his hotel in downtown Toronto. He suggested they meet the following evening for dinner, to discuss what he referred to, rather disparagingly, as "the English girl's ill-conceived project". At that point in their conversation he became rather insistent in advising her not to reveal anything more than she felt she absolutely had to.

"She obviously hasn't considered the harm that dredging all this up might well do to Cynthia's reputation," he said.

Evelyn thought it best not to argue about this. Clearly Harvey had not carried the weight of conscience over the fate of Cynthia that she herself had suffered all these years. After suggesting an eight-o-clock dinner, and a restaurant near enough to her home so that she could comfortably walk, she inquired about the date and time of his interview with Anthea.

"There isn't going to be any interview," he replied firmly. "I let her know in no uncertain terms what I think about the re-hashing of that unfortunate series of accidental deaths in an international newspaper. In my opinion, it can do nobody any good. Good Lord, it might even cause a resurgence of gossip and ugly innuendo about North Pacific University . . . and possibly even about the rather questionable backgrounds of the victims. One of whom was her own aunt."

"What was her response?" Evelyn was curious. Even with her scanty experience of Anthea, she felt it was highly unlikely that the pair of obviously committed journalists would drop their project at this stage. Harvey admitted that his argument had been unsuccessful, but added that at least "that girl" was now aware that she would get no help from him. Evelyn decided that it would probably be best to avoid the subject of Harvey's refusal to cooperate when she met with Anthea later in the week. After all, she was as curious about what the young journalist might reveal through her choice of specific questions as the latter no doubt was concerning what might be learned from the answers to them. In Evelyn's opinion, Harvey had been so much on the fringe of the entire affair that he would have had very little of importance to add anyway. If Anthea raised the subject she would assure her of this.

That evening Evelyn went to the restaurant, looking forward to the dinner with Harvey and hoping for news that he had changed his mind and had met with Anthea after all, so that they could share impressions. After almost a half hour had passed and he hadn't arrived, she tried phoning his hotel room. There was no answer to any of her several calls over the next half hour. Harvey had come to Toronto on his own, as his wife had died more than two decades ago. It had been a car accident, caused by her brakes having failed on one of the steep hills along the narrow 'Sea to Sky' highway between Squamish and Whistler. Evelyn recalled how devastated the poor man had been that he had given in to the strong-willed Mrs Garfinkle and allowed her to travel alone that night, not long before they were slated to move to his new position in Montreal. However, her spontaneous surge of sympathy, which had been aroused by the memory, now cooled somewhat as the realization began to dawn that he definitely was not coming. He must have forgotten their date and gone somewhere else. Like many single women of her age, she was all-too-familiar with the experience of being 'stood up'. But it was so very much out of character for Harvey that she felt a twinge of worry. The next morning, when her phone calls continued to go unanswered, she dialed the hotel desk. The clerk informed her that Dr. Garfinkle had been called back to Montreal, to deal with some crisis. After phoning both his home and university office there she gave up. She decided at that point to try to forget this decidedly untypical behavior, and to concentrate on the upcoming meeting with Anthea.

When the day and the moment finally arrived, however, she found herself unprepared for the shock of the discovery that this time it was indeed going to be very different. Anthea began by asking if Harvey had been in touch with her. Evidently, after repeating his adamant refusal to cooperate with her, he had been invited to an interrogation by a policeman who had just arrived from British Columbia. In response to Evelyn's startled exclamation she said that, yes, the police were now involved. Apparently, a regional murder squad was currently in place in the Lower Mainland of B.C. It incorporated not only the twelve municipalities previously using RCMP detachments as their local police forces, but also the five cities of Vancouver, West Vancouver, Port Moody, New Westminster and Delta which, historically, had been responsible for their own policing. This new squad was officially looking into the recently re-opened cases of the series of deaths at North Pacific University in 1976-7. There was even more, Anthea told her excitedly. Harvey, like herself and Meredith Walker, was considered by the police to be a 'witness of interest'. However, when they called on him the previous evening, he had disappeared. Evelyn found all this deeply shocking. And, in the case of Harvey's disappearance, extraordinarily puzzling as well. To think that she had considered his merely not showing up at the restaurant or returning her calls as uncharacteristic! She was suddenly aware that the investigation had become something much more serious than simply a story by a couple of British journalists. The sharp stab of pain in Evelyn's spine told her that her stress level had risen. She tried her old remedy—this time, imagining a mountain hike and a particularly beautiful view of the Vancouver coastal area from high up in Cypress Park on the North Shore mountains. But Anthea's presence was not something to be ignored for long. She was now continuing, obviously choosing her words carefully.

"In fact, a member of the squad is meeting with Meredith this very moment, and will soon be talking to you as well. By the way, they have asked me to request that you not leave the city until you have their official permission. It's merely a formality, of course. But before your interview with them, I want to go over my list of questions with you, and get all your information on tape. I will begin by asking about the conference you mentioned, at which Cynthia was your roommate. I need to know the identity of every person from your university who attended."

"All four of our sociology group were present, as well as Sam Barnes, representing our historians. I'm pretty sure that two of our philosophers were also there. Yes, now I remember. Les Brittan and Ned Smith shared Dr. Garfinkle's car, along with me. And our three grad students traveled together, in another car. I'm sorry, but I don't really know about graduate students from the Arts and Sciences who may have attended. Oh yes, there was one instructor from another Department within the Faculty of Education, who was presenting a paper as well. It was Abdul Issa from Social Studies Methods."

"Now tell me more about your conversation with the two students in the hotel room next door. Try to remember every detail of their response to your inquiry about Cynthia's whereabouts."

"All I can say is that it was very clear she had not been with either one. But they did seem to know something about what she was up to that night. It was something questionable or suspicious, and amusing to them. Something that they certainly were not going to share with me."

From that point Anthea guided her back through a series of specific incidents: what she had witnessed first-hand of Cynthia's demeanor and behavior on the night of her death; Meredith Walker's disclosure of the letter from the former student concerning Cynthia's previous year's experience with, and alleged threats toward, a professor fitting the profile of Sam Barnes; Sam's comments about Cynthia as a student; Sam's teasing attitude toward Harvey, with his oblique references to his own reliability where discretion was concerned; every detail about the precise nature of Millie's diabetes and with whom (to her knowledge) it had been discussed; Millie's hints about important evidence that Sam had been pursuing; her own overhearing of the conversation between Gus Rasmussen and Abdul Issa in which Cynthia, Millie, and she, herself, had been lumped together by Gus in some weird category of omnivorous man-hunters; the strangely questioning, almost fearful way the three young female witnesses against Sam were said to have been glancing, throughout their testimony, toward the group at the head of the table in the Dean's conference room . . . and so on and on until she was unutterably weary of it all. But the worst was yet to come!

"Now I have something to tell you." Anthea spoke slowly, sounding as if she were exhausted as well. "You had best prepare yourself for a shock. You have never asked me about the identity of my fellow journalist. The person who has been working on the case in the Vancouver area."

"I didn't think . . ." began Evelyn. But Anthea's politely decisive voice overrode her.

"His name is Abdul Issa. He has been a free-lance journalist in London for a number of years. He's the one who contacted me about doing the story in the first place. Then I persuaded my bosses of its potential. I think what finally sold them on it was my own personal family interest, and Abdul's direct involvement."

"But . . . but I understood that, when Abdul left NPU so suddenly twenty-seven years ago, he was intending to return to Southern Africa. He told me he wanted to devote himself to the cause of the African National Congress. And he mentioned possibly doing some teaching of illiterate young people as well."

"Evidently he did that, for a while working against apartheid by operating an underground cell from neighboring Lesotho. I think he had been enraged and feeling terribly guilty about not being with his 'brothers' when the Soweto massacre occurred two years previously, while he was safely ensconced in Canada.

No doubt you already know all this, but he described how, in fact, it had been the 1960 Sharpeville massacre of Congress supporters that had radicalized him in the first place, as a boy of eighteen. He says it was on that day that he became a committed Communist. However, after Nelson Mandela's imprisonment in 1964, I suspect that Abdul lost hope in the possibility of change. He completed a Master's degree in economics at the University of South Africa in 1968, and applied for and received the appointment to North Pacific University in Canada where, as you are aware, he remained until the summer of 1977.

Then, by 1981, after a further four years in Southern Africa following his return, Abdul became discouraged once more. Mandela was still languishing in prison, and the struggle for their cause appeared increasingly hopeless. To make matters worse, he had some disillusioning experiences with the group around Winnie Mandela. In 1980, his father had retired from what is now known as the National University of Lesotho. The plan was to spend about six months of every year in London, and he somehow managed to have both of his wives and families accompany him. So, the following year, Abdul decided to emigrate to Britain to be near them all and resume the writing career that he had always wanted. His novel was published in the mid-eighties, and he became rather successful in free-lance journalism after that.

Now, however, everything has once more changed for him. He tells me that his one overwhelming goal for the remainder of his life is to contribute whatever he can to shedding light on this unresolved murder case. You wouldn't believe how heavily it has been weighing on him all these years!"

It occurred to Evelyn, as she listened in a state of shock to these revelations about the man she had once loved, that he had never really discussed any of this early political experience with her. Had he been so scornful of her privileged and protected background that he thought her incapable of understanding, or even of interest in such matters?

"Why hasn't he come with you today and told me all this himself?" she managed to ask.

"Because there's a great deal more to Abdul's story. Much of it he admits he simply could not bear to face you with. He asks you to forgive him for taking the easy way out, but thinks it better that you know everything before you meet again."

So it was that what Evelyn thought of ever after as 'Abdul's Story' began. As she listened she thought that there was probably no one better equipped to tell it than this sensible, forthright young woman: this person who apparently had all of her Aunt Cynthia's attractive qualities and none of her weaknesses. According to Anthea it all began during the year of Abdul's arrival as a youthful landed immigrant and new instructor at North Pacific University.

Not long after being warmly welcomed by the Faculty of Education and its Teaching Methods Department, he met Gus Rasmussen. The two soon found that they had a great deal in common. Gus had also only recently arrived and was applying for landed-immigrant status. Unlike Abdul, however, Gus, as an American Vietnam-War objector and draft-dodger, had a ready-made group of local friends. He was surrounded, immediately upon arriving, by a supportive community of anti-war protesters. The local Unitarian church had even gone so far as to take a personal interest in locating both the teaching position for him and a home in Richmond near the university. The two men shared a strong commitment to Marxism and to Maoist Communism, and Abdul benefitted greatly from Gus' connections in the Unitarian community.

It wasn't long before they discovered that they shared something else as well. Abdul had been raised, and subsequently university-educated, in a culture that viewed sexual activity only in the context of heterosexuality—and, then, only as an aspect of lifetime mating (for the female, at least). In his father's world, daughters were carefully and constantly watched, so as not to be 'spoiled' for the marriage bed. It was true that, in the context of his mother's tribal community, female virgins even as young as thirteen were commonly considered much-sought-after 'fair game' for most young males, and polygamy had been the cultural norm prior to the coming of Christianity. However, Abdul would have none of that kind of exploitation of innocents. Consequently, he was still a virgin when he had the opportunity (as a relatively privileged son of an Islamic Indian academic) to attend the University of South Africa. Homosexuality was totally unknown to him, until his father warned him about it the night before he left home. A "decadent, filthy practice" was how he described it: a practice known to occur only among the "mad animals" of the European colonial classes. During Abdul's years of graduate study he thought no more of the subject, but did experience several mutually enjoyable affairs with female fellow students.

During these maturing years, homosexuality had remained in the darkest recesses of his imagination as something dangerous and ugly—something to be avoided at all costs. Then, one evening soon after his arrival in Vancouver, when he and Gus returned to the latter's home after a night out on the town, the inconceivable occurred. Gus invited him to sleep at his place, as they were both in a state of half-drunkenness. Sometime during the night he was awakened by a body slipping into bed beside him. He was still half asleep when the fondling started, and ever after he was to blame himself for not reacting immediately in order to prevent what followed; to prevent it before it became so all-enticing and potentially fulfilling that he could not force himself to pull away. From that night on he was deeply disturbed about what had happened between the two of them. However, it was impossible to convince Gus (or even himself, for that matter) that the experience had not been mutually enjoyable and intrinsically worthy of almost routine repetition. Abdul began slowly to recognize and justify himself as a member of what was to him the previously incomprehensible category of 'bisexual'.

Gus had problems with this, however. He maintained that bisexuals simply "wanted to have their cake and eat it too". He was convinced that Abdul's previous sexual experience had been of a heterosexual nature *only* because his native culture disapproved so acutely of homosexuals. As time passed, and Abdul became more closely acquainted with his new colleagues (including those who were female) Gus grew increasingly possessive. Whenever Abdul objected to this tendency to jealousy he would be assured that it was merely an attempt to protect him from conniving females: all of whom, according to Gus, were hungry for sex with a handsome black man. Several times in the months and years that followed, Abdul tried to break off the relationship, worried about what seemed to be turning into an obsession on the part of his lover. But Gus would never allow the issue even to be discussed. They were made for each other, he always claimed, and it was only a certain few of their female colleagues who were trying to break them apart.

This was why Abdul was so insistent upon secrecy when he and Evelyn began to see each other. He had acted on impulse when he went up to her apartment that first evening, and regretted it almost immediately. For some time he honestly believed that he could keep the relationship hidden from Gus, and went to great lengths to do just that during the entire course of their affair. He was relieved, therefore, when Gus eventually became occupied with jealous concern about another female who, he imagined, had Abdul in her sights. It was Cynthia Montague.

Cynthia had enrolled in Abdul's class on Social Studies Methods in the autumn of 1974. She began to come to his office rather regularly after that, ostensibly for help and general advice with her program. He did his best to discourage her, always assuming a distinctly formal approach and cutting her visits as short as possible. It was a difficult juggling act, as he was her instructor and she was nothing if not persistent when she had her sights on an attractive prospect. However, he felt that he had been reasonably successful. By the time almost a year had passed with little further personal contact between them he was fairly confident that he had been able to soothe Gus' concerns, while maintaining an easy, yet professional, relationship with Cynthia. Gus even appeared to have begun to enjoy an openly friendly interaction with the attractive student himself.

Abdul was therefore not unduly surprised when he glimpsed Gus waiting at Cynthia's car as he began to escort her out on the night of the party. Cynthia immediately confirmed that "Dr. Rasmussen" was the reliable friend who had promised to see her home.

"He's safe, you see." she assured Abdul. "I happen to know he's gay. But I thought he would have given up on me tonight!"

She was obviously relieved to find her escort still waiting. Abdul said goodnight and turned back abruptly at that point, hoping to avoid Gus seeing them together, and confident that his lover was to be depended upon where young, inebriated girls were concerned. So it was that, next morning when the news came of Cynthia's death and the manner in which it had occurred, Abdul was horrified and shaken to the core with guilt over his own role in the tragic event. He could see no other likelihood than that Gus was, in some way, responsible. At the very least he must have been negligent in failing to see Cynthia safely to her door.

But Abdul was tortured by even worse possibilities. The entire setup was frighteningly consistent with what he had only recently come to suspect about the deviousness of Gus and the almost manic quality of his jealous obsessions. Nevertheless, Abdul could not bring himself to act upon his suspicions, hoping against hope that he was wrong.

From then on he lived in a welter of fear and guilt. For awhile, he felt utterly trapped in the relationship with Gus. Then, Meredith Walker's radical new feminist movement entered the picture. Gus' subsequent involvement in the Women's Cultural Revolution came as a great relief, as it took his attention away somewhat from Abdul's activities. Not long after this, Abdul began to feel that helping Millie through her difficult year had to be his primary concern. The two had established a strong intellectual bond almost from their first encounter. It was a friendship totally untouched by sexual feelings. In fact, both were the kind of people whose closest relationships in life had always been intellectual in nature—something the majority of observers (even academics) find difficult to fathom. Therefore it was profoundly shocking for him to hear Gus group Evelyn, Cynthia, and Millie in his veiled, but revealing, references to Abdul's 'womanizing tendencies' that day in the restaurant. From that moment on he began to fear for the safety of Millie as well as Evelyn. He was glad that he had, only a few days previously, reluctantly agreed to Gus' plan for a Christmas holiday in Queensland.

Then came the accusations against Sam Barnes. Abdul threw himself happily into Sam's defense, possibly sensing that he might make amends for his cowardice regarding Cynthia's death by helping to correct a wrong this time. What he viewed as his personal connivance in the former case no doubt contributed to his disappointment in Evelyn for her unwillingness to take a stand for Sam. However (at least according to his rethinking of the situation years later) it was chiefly for her own protection that he abruptly stopped seeing her. From the time of Cynthia's death he had become deeply worried about what Gus might be capable of doing.

When Sam's body was found, Abdul, like almost everyone else, readily accepted the verdict of suicide. It was only as he was preparing to leave the country after Millie's devastating death that an inadvertent comment from Evelyn changed everything for him. What aroused his suspicions was her reference to the fact that Sam had revealed something to Millie—something about his being in the process of gathering evidence which would shed surprising new light on the case. This brought back to him, with a sudden jolt, the change in Sam's bearing which had occurred near the end of the Dean's meeting. Belatedly, he realized that it had not been a thoroughly despondent, suicidal man who left the meeting that day, although that may have been an apt description of the Sam Barnes who had arrived.

As he was closing the door behind Evelyn when she left his apartment on the night of her first and only visit there, he suddenly remembered Millie having once given him a copy of the key to her office. He immediately began looking frantically for the key; then found it and rushed out. A hurried examination of Millie's office revealed the fact that, fortunately, no one had yet thought to clear it of her belongings. Except for the signs of a desultory cleaning, it appeared that nothing had been disturbed or packed away. After a thorough search of the files, he found a large one identified as 'BS'. On the point of passing it by, he suddenly recognized the label as a reversal of Sam's initials. With his awareness of Millie's probably justifiable urge to be secretive, coupled with her sense of humor, he felt immediately that this had to be it. In the file Abdul discovered a number of intriguing items of information. At first glance they seemed merely a combination of some rather strange occurrences— minor events that somehow didn't quite fit what he had taken to be the existing order of things. But he slowly began to note that each led, in one way or another, to Gus!

At that agonizing moment of realization Abdul recalled, for the first time, the specifics of what Millie had told him concerning her diabetes. She had assured him that only he and Evelyn knew about it. It soon became evident that all three shared the conviction that it should not become public knowledge, because of the possible effect on her career. Then, with a jolt, he recalled the day of Sam's memorial service, when Millie had abruptly departed. Gus had obviously overheard the subject being mentioned in the hurried conversation between Millie and Evelyn. Gus was immediately behind Millie as the two women left the room, while Abdul had followed him.

'Type B' was how she had referred to it earlier when she had discussed it with Abdul. For the first time he wondered exactly what the diagnosis meant, and he proceeded at once to look it up. It didn't require much research for him to discover what most lay people are unaware of concerning that particular form of the disease. It tends to strike middle-aged, overweight people, and the treatment is *not the injection of insulin*, but merely a hypoglycemic agent taken by mouth. So whoever had arranged Millie's murder—and *murder* he was now convinced it was—had known the *fact* of her diabetes, but none of the details concerning it! Although what he obtained from Millie's office consisted only of the one bulky file of class lists and notes, that file was actually a mine of information. In it there was also a series of Sam's scribbled reminders, each fastened with a paper clip to something either in Millie's writing, or an affidavit signed by a third party confirming one of Sam's leads. Most interesting was a collection having to do with a certain room in a downtown Vancouver hotel. It appeared to have been rented on a fairly regular basis in the name of Dr. Gus Rasmussen. Several witnesses who worked in the hotel declared that there had been a series of young girls brought to the room on various nights over a period of at least two years by a man who apparently fitted Gus' description.

Abdul found all this utterly baffling. What in the world, he wondered, would Gus be doing with young girls? He had always seemed to be totally turned off by them where sex was concerned. And who *were* the girls? Apparently Millie had asked this as well, and had thought of an intriguing and distasteful possibility, for there was an attached note from her with a reminder to show pictures of all the female students in the NPU yearbook to the night clerk. He wondered if she had managed to do it, but found no other reference to the matter.

Another of Sam's notes had to do with his own encounter with Harvey Garfinkle in a restaurant, also in Vancouver. Harvey was having dinner with Cynthia Montague, and the two were behaving in a decidedly intimate fashion. Attached to this was an affidavit signed by the waiter who served them, declaring that the persons in the pictures he had been shown (and which he had also signed) were indeed a couple who came regularly to the restaurant for a period of about four months during 1975.

Interesting, Abdul thought. But scarcely incriminating. Was that what was behind Sam's half-joking references to

Harvey about his own discretion? So the Head of the Foundations Department had conducted a short-lived affair with Cynthia! Still, how many other members of the Faculty had also been there? This was the kind of thing that Millie had suspected all along. But there was nothing further attached to the item, other than a brief note in her handwriting, commenting on how, if Gus were aware of the affair, it might explain the confidence he would have felt that Harvey would pose no threat to his own activities.

Ultimately, however, it took only one agonizing night for Abdul to come to the conclusion that there was actually nothing in the material he had found, when considered piece by piece, that could be considered decisively incriminating. Sam, and subsequently Millie, had obviously been in the relatively early stages of their search. The RCMP would not even begin to take any of it seriously, he thought, except for the information on the diabetes. This he immediately sent by mail to the Emergency-room doctor, suggesting that he contact the police. A second night of tossing and turning convinced him that his only recourse was to disappear at once, so that Gus would never find him. At least, he thought, that poisonous relationship (for which he had to admit joint responsibility) would no longer be the source of harm to innocent people. The decision to leave the country had been made, at any rate, for he had already forever spoiled his chances at Canadian universities.

So Abdul went home to Southern Africa, where he remained for four years. After settling in London in the summer of 1981, his life in general went well, although he could never entirely put the ghastly experiences in Canada behind him. Eventually, when considerable time had passed, he became involved in a stable relationship with a fellow male reporter. Throughout the 1980s and 1990s there were a few minor successes in his writing and journalistic career and, altogether, he was happier than he had ever been. Until, one evening in the autumn of 1999 when he answered the doorbell, and found what seemed to be a caricature of the Gus he had known—standing there with a diffident, albeit hopefully expectant, grin.

Abdul's first reaction was to slam the door in the haggard face. But Gus looked so pitiful and frail that he simply could not bring himself to do it. Against his better judgment (and even descending to a profanity that was unnatural to him) he ushered in the unwelcome guest. During the process he found himself shouting questions at Gus about where the hell he had come from, how the hell he had discovered where he (Abdul) lived, and what in hell was wrong with him. Gus answered the last question first, telling him that he had been diagnosed with inoperable cancer of the colon. The remainder of his tale concerning what had happened to him in the years since they knew one another was, sadly, all too predictable. Things began going badly in his classes during the years after Abdul left, so Harvey came to his rescue. In 1980 (coincidentally, soon after Evelyn left for greener pastures) a position was found for him in a small college in Manitoba. He remained there until his teaching career was finally brought to a rather ugly end in 1993.

Reading between the lines of Gus' description of what had occurred, Abdul surmised that the termination had been due to his former lover's growing addiction to drugs, and to indoctrinating students in Maoist politics. That ideology was, by then, no longer popular in academic circles. Another contributing factor, Abdul guessed, would have been his increasingly non-traditional teaching methods. Alone, unable to find employment and with few resources, Gus then began to search for Abdul; "my only true love and loyal friend". It was not until almost five years later, however, that he happened upon a column by Abdul Issa in the *London Daily News*. After that it was not too difficult to locate him in London through his journalistic connections.

Abdul decided to challenge Gus at once with his suspicions about the series of murders that had formed the stuff of his nightmares for all too many years. They talked long into the night. What Gus had to say altered entirely Abdul's long-held picture of the situation. It filled him with an anger which crippled him emotionally for days. And every previously planned professional project was driven from his mind for months by the resulting all-consuming need to devise a means of seeing that the case was solved once and for all; that the cold glare of publicity would ultimately engulf it; and that justice would finally be done. Also, and most important for Gus, it made it possible for him to invite his old lover to move in with him.

The upshot of it all was that Abdul found himself being responsible for Gus in what he did not at first realize was to be the final year of the poor creature's life. The sudden arrival of such a questionable visitor, and the all-too-apparent permanent nature of his stay, had the effect of almost immediately destroying Abdul's long-term relationship. In a weak moment soon after the break-up which was, indeed, heartbreaking for Abdul, he made his second irrevocable mistake where Gus was concerned. It was about a month from the day his surprise guest had settled in when Abdul allowed himself to get carried away by grief and loneliness for the recently lost lover, combined with newfound pity for Gus (or for the man he had once believed him to be). He found himself drawn, against his better judgment, into having sex with him. This was before he was aware of the true nature of Gus' illness. Unprotected sex in such a situation was, of course, utter madness, but Abdul admitted that his tendency toward precipitous action had always been a major character flaw. In a few months, Gus' illness was diagnosed as an advanced case of AIDS. And by the time his old friend died, Abdul discovered that he, too, had contracted HIV.

"No! Stop! What are you trying to tell me? That Abdul is dying? That he's too ill to see me?" For a moment, Evelyn felt she simply could not stand to hear one more word of the grim story. "But if he's so ill, how can he be doing all this investigative work?"

"He's not showing many symptoms of AIDS yet. Just increasing exhaustion and bruising, and he's lost a lot of weight. But, I must admit, this trip has taken a lot out of him. I was shocked by the change in him in so brief a period." Anthea fell silent and, for the moment Evelyn, too, felt utterly unable to continue the conversation.

"I have an idea," Anthea suggested after a time. "I think I should let Abdul finish the story with you. You two need to talk."

There followed what seemed like an endless series of days, during which Evelyn's fear of seeing Abdul, in what must be his considerably diminished state, gradually gave way to a growing curiosity about what he may have discovered concerning the case. Overwhelming all else, however, and adding considerably to her confusion, was the agony of betrayal and victimization. Somehow, the revelation of Abdul's long-established homosexual tendencies struck her where she was most vulnerable. Perhaps it was because she had always somehow suspected that those sexual encounters, which had formed the highlight of her life for so long, had been less than satisfying for him.

Finally, she received the long-awaited phone call. He wanted to meet her in a neutral setting, so they arranged for lunch together in a nearby restaurant. Evelyn deliberately arrived a bit late, and she found him waiting in a corner of the comfortably crowded room. However, the man who rose unsteadily from the table to greet her was scarcely recognizable, in spite of the fact that she had been prepared by Anthea. He was shockingly emaciated, his body shrunken and wasted, with the brown skin that had been like velvet now bruised and rough-looking. His once fiercely expressive black eyes were dull and almost hidden by the swollen pouches surrounding them. But, most of all, it was his utter fragility that shook her.

"Evelyn!" he grasped both her hands in his thin, elongated fingers. "Forgive me."

"For what?" she asked, disingenuously, but the icy quality of her own voice surprised and betrayed her.

"For everything."

At the enigmatic answer, she found herself engulfed in anger. It was a long-buried rage never quite acknowledged by her conscious mind; and now abruptly inflamed by the smouldering fuse of her emotional reaction to Anthea's revelations.

"How could you, Abdul?" she tried to word the almost-screamed accusation as crudely as possible, in an effort to hurt him. "How could you come to my bed directly after poking that filthy, vile creature? Or go to him from me? That user of prostitutes! He was probably peddling drugs to them too. All those years, when I thought you loved me, you were screwing him whenever he wanted it!"

A grimace of pain flashed across Abdul's face.

"I know," he said, in the familiar, carefully enunciated way he had with words. "It is inexplicable. Totally stupid and unforgivable. I now realize that I was gay all along; that my father's attitude toward it had made me view sexual activity solely in the context of females. Also, my Marxist ideology allowed no possibility for homosexual tendencies being genetically endowed. Remember, *all* behavior, sexual included, was explained by Communists as entirely environmentally determined. According to the prevailing theories of cultural relativism as well. So I assumed my original sexual encounter with Gus was merely an accident, signifying nothing. And that all I needed to do to correct the error was to become involved, as soon as possible, in a heterosexual relationship."

And I just happened to be all-too-readily available, Evelyn thought. Her bitter musings were interrupted at that point by the approach of a waiter. She and Abdul both blindly ordered the special soup of the day, along with coffee and a green salad. They ate in silence, oblivious to the cheerful conversations around them. Evelyn found herself deep in uncomfortable thoughts which she felt no urge to share with this person who now seemed no more than a stranger from the past.

For Abdul's remarks had touched a nerve where she was concerned. They thrust into sharp relief a contradiction which had long been seething away within her, just below the level of conscious thought. She had always considered herself utterly unprejudiced against homosexuality. Since her days at NPU, in fact, most of her best friends had been gay men. They tended toward gently supportive friendliness, and seemed less scornfully uninterested in older women than were the majority of her heterosexual male acquaintances. No gay friend treated her in the way other men often did, as if she were merely an object well past its expiry date. But, at the same time, as a dedicated cultural relativist who accepted the total environmental origin of all human attributes, she had absolutely refused to buy into any biological or even sociobiological explanations of how homosexuality could possibly have genetic *as well* as cultural origins.

The sociobiologists—whose position of genetic-cultural evolution now appeared (to Evelyn's chagrin) to be becoming increasingly accepted within the academic community—were claiming that even something as apparently learned as sexual orientation could well be largely genetic in origin. (Whenever Evelyn heard this argument she was always driven by a desire to counter it with reminders of the effect of English boys' boarding schools; and of training for the Catholic priesthood. Then she would immediately be forced to brush such thoughts aside as an unacceptable slur on homosexuals.) But it seemed that there was now a satisfactory scientific explanation for the *biological survival* of a propensity to homosexuality, in spite of the obvious fact (as Helen Korensky had been fond of pointing out) that such people do not usually have children to inherit and pass along their genetic characteristics.

According to Edward O. Wilson and others, homosexuals may well have contributed to the survival of the genes for human altruism and, *thereby*, to the survival of the species. This was because—although they may not, themselves, have reproduced—their siblings' children would have carried their genes into the future. A willingness on their part to sacrifice themselves, if need be, for the protection of those siblings during their critical child-bearing years could well have ensured that the altruistic, self-sacrificing genes driving their behavior were nurtured and maintained within the human race. And, of course, the tendency toward homosexuality along with them.

Evelyn had never held with any of these biologically based theories. But she was now finding herself being forced to admit that her long-held exclusive emphasis on the shaping effect of culture and social relationships offered no similarly satisfactory, *non-judgmental* explanation for the phenomenon. If socialization were indeed all-determinant, the occurrence of homosexuality in any society where heterosexuality was the prevailing pattern had to be the result of some 'abnormal' influence. There had to have been either child abuse by a same-sex adult, or some other form of early conditioning contrary to the norm, such as homosexual overtures from 'significant others' in the family or school; or powerful pressures from within a divergent social group. Or else same-gender sex had to be in some way more immediately advantageous than the heterosexual variety to the individual concerned. This meant that, if she were to be completely honest with herself, her intellectual position on the issue actually *justified* the largely unacknowledged antipathy to homosexuality that her social conscience had always forced her to deny. No wonder she had been torn by the issue all her life!

"If you should happen to be wondering, Evelyn, I no longer feel guilty about my homosexuality." Abdul's voice intruded as if he had been reading her mind. "I have been reading this modern sociobiology which I realize you abhor. However, that theory, along with recent findings in molecular biology, resolves the entire problem for me. Furthermore, these genetic-environmental explanations, as applied to homosexuality, make sense in terms of history as well as biology and social science. In Hellenistic Greece, for example, it was the cultural norm for a man to have a wife to manage the household and produce his children, and to have several young male lovers as well. In that instance, it was not the genetic makeup of humans but the *cultural climate* that had changed by the time of Augustus, when same-gender sex was universally condemned. It now appears probable that a predisposition toward homosexuality is inherited by many people. Nonetheless, that particular genetic drive (like any other) can either be reinforced or totally inhibited from birth by the social and cultural surroundings.

I was no doubt still in the stage where I could have gone either way, during that critical period in 1968-71 when I became involved first with Gus and then, somewhat later, with you. I do not mean that it was a matter of *choice*. Sexual orientation has nothing to do with conscious choice . . . even for a bisexual, as I was then. In fact, I suspect that I was on the point of committing to you, Evelyn, during the autumn of 1976. But then . . ." He stopped talking abruptly, and gazed sadly into the distance beyond her.

At that moment it came home to Evelyn that she, who was one of the most vociferous supporters of Gay Pride marches, now found herself in the untenable position of having to recognize that her seething anger against Abdul was, more than anything else, due to *the fact of his homosexuality*. At the same time, she was being forced to face up to a suspicion about her own sexual deficiencies that she had tried to bury for years. If, as her sociological theories had always led her to believe, it was impossible for him to be genetically programmed in that direction, then how *could* he have enjoyed sex with Gus more than he ever had with her? How *could* he have chosen Gus over her?

"I have so many regrets about it all. At times I feel very guilty about my treatment of you. But then I allow myself to wonder how much worse was my behavior at that time than your own." Abdul's voice registered once again through the confusion of emotion that obsessed her. In response to her obvious puzzlement he added, "I am referring to your very close connection to Harvey Garfinkle, both at that time and in the many years since."

Evelyn suddenly realized that Abdul was assuming she and Harvey were involved in a long-term intimate relationship. She decided, somewhat triumphantly, to let him think it.

"Whatever has that to do with anything?" she asked him. "And I don't see how you can even begin to compare Harvey with Gus. Harvey is not a murderer and exploiter of women!"

"Now I understand." Abdul gazed beyond her, into the distance, as he weighed his words carefully. "Anthea did not complete the story. She did say something about leaving the ending for me. That it was proving too difficult for her. And too unfair and hurtful for you."

"What is there that she didn't tell me?" She was struck by a feeling of foreboding, along with the familiar sensation of having made a fool of herself.

"Gus was a lot of things. A procurer of females for sexual purposes, yes indeed; and a co-conspirator in the sexual abuse of several innocent young women. But they were not for himself. He rented the hotel room for Dr. Harvey Garfinkle, the Department Chairman upon whose good favor he depended for his university position. And the girls who frequented that room were not prostitutes. They were his very own students. Students who were flattered by Harvey's attention, and eager to take advantage of it. Some even became members of the Women's Cultural Revolution. Specifically, those who were later persuaded to testify against Sam at the Dean's hearing. They were all merely insecure young people (like Gus himself, actually) who thought they had to do certain morally repugnant things in order to succeed in that place at that particular time. But Gus was never a murderer."

"I don't understand what you're saying. It just doesn't make any sense. Why would Harvey Garfinkle, of all people, want or need to do such things? And what, for instance, did Cynthia's death have to do with all this?"

"Cynthia Montague was also persuaded to help with Harvey's project, distasteful as it was to her, and for the same reason the others were, eventually. She had begun by imagining *she* was seducing *him*, in order to ensure high marks in her program. Some time later she discovered that, for once, she was not the one with the power. Gradually, step by reckless step, our sophisticated Cynthia had been drawn into helping Harvey with his sick games. One day, she must have realized that she was no longer in control. That she was caught in a hideous trap from which there would have seemed no escape. I think the full recognition of what she had done came home to her that night at the Banff Conference. Harvey warned her then that he would destroy her reputation, and any prospects for a Master's degree, if she ever told anyone what she knew about him. Frantic with fear and worry, she tried to turn to you for help, but you brushed her aside."

"Then what exactly *did* happen the night of the party? Anthea told me that you, yourself, admitted that it was *Gus* who was waiting for her . . . not Harvey. And I know for a fact that the Garfinkles were seen leaving for home much earlier." These revelations were almost more than Evelyn could bear, but she knew she could not stop now.

"Yes, they left early enough for Harvey to double back after dropping off his wife. He had arranged for Gus to see that Cynthia got home with no other man in tow. Then he went over to her place to await their arrival, and the predictably rapid departure of Gus, in the darkness of the large attached garage. I finally managed to track down one of the group of Cynthia's house mates (from another Faculty) who is willing to testify that she saw Dr. Harvey Garfinkle hovering around the premises that night as Gus was leaving. At the time the student did not know who he was and thought nothing of it, as people came and went rapidly there. And a number of the male lodgers who owned cars were unknown to her. Also, we must remember, Cynthia's death was not then judged to be suspicious."

"Are you actually saying that it was Harvey who murdered Cynthia? But why? And how?"

"We can only assume that, in spite of Harvey's previous warning, Cynthia had again declared she wanted out, and had foolishly let him know that she intended to go to the Dean if he continued to threaten her. Harvey probably had taken along a supply of LSD, and persuaded Cynthia (by one means or another) to sit and talk with him for a while in the car and share a goodnight dose of the drug. For Cynthia it proved to be a fatal overdose, as the coroner who conducted the inquest at the time has recently informed me. He also admitted they had agreed to keep this particular finding quiet after being persuaded that it would only harm the university's reputation to reveal an addiction that Dr. Garfinkle assured them had already been recognized (and was being dealt with) by the faculty. With Cynthia unconscious, there would have been no problem for Harvey in arranging to leave her in her car with the engine running. And, of course, Gus would be the obvious culprit, if anyone came to suspect that the death was anything other than an accident or suicide. Harvey appears always to have been using Gus to further his plans, while making sure that it was Gus who would invariably be placed in a compromising position if things went wrong. However, fortunately for Gus, but unfortunately for Cynthia, Sam and Millie, Harvey's plans did not often go wrong."

"Are you implying that Harvey killed Sam as well? That he planned from the start to get rid of him?"

"Only some time after the accidental encounter with Sam in the restaurant where he and Cynthia were dining together. Sadly for Sam, his tendency for harmless teasing was interpreted by Harvey as a veiled threat of blackmail. Harvey began to lay the plans for discrediting Sam as a professional, in order to have a strong excuse to fire him. By the time the Dean held his hearing, Harvey must have been convinced (as we all were) that Sam was a completely broken man. But then something occurred during that hearing which apparently altered the situation for Sam, and he indicated, as he was leaving, that he intended to fight back. Harvey no doubt sensed that some vital connection had been made which could only pose a threat to him. He would have had too much respect for Sam's shrewd mind not to fear mightily that his own days of power and prestige within the university were numbered, if he didn't move fast."

"But I happen to remember that, at the time, Harvey didn't even know Sam's whereabouts." This was all getting too much for Evelyn to swallow.

"Unfortunately, he *did* manage to discover where Sam was living, possibly through some indiscretion on your part. You may recall that he had become very friendly with you just then. He arranged to have Gus follow Millie for a few days, and it was not long before she led him to Sam's lodgings on the North Shore. Gus was then ordered to track

Sam carefully, supposedly to make sure that he didn't leave town in order to escape the Dean's official censure. Gus told me he had no problem learning that Sam had developed the habit of taking a regular late-evening walk along the seawall in Stanley Park, then re-crossing the Lions Gate Bridge to his rooms on the north side. This was included in his report to Harvey."

"How dare you insinuate that Harvey got his information from me! That he would have had no interest in cultivating our relationship other than to make use of me! It doesn't say much for me, as a person, does it? Or for you, as my former lover!" Evelyn could scarcely get the words out. She could feel her self concept, so happily reinforced a brief two weeks ago, crumbling rapidly around her.

"Again, I am sorry, Evelyn. I am only trying to explain the kind of man he was . . . and is. I hope that you do not take any of this as a reflection on yourself. I realized from the beginning that this would be difficult for you, given your long-term relationship with him. I think that is why Anthea decided she did not want to continue. Do you not wish to hear any more?"

"No . . . I mean, yes . . . go ahead. But don't expect me to accept your reading of all those events on faith. I'll come to my own decision on the trustworthiness of your evidence."

"Fine. Now, where was I? Oh yes, now we come to Millie, the treasured friend of both of us. I think you must hear this. Shall I go on?"

"Of course I want to know anything you have discovered about what happened to her. How could you possibly think otherwise?"

"Then I shall continue. I believe that Harvey was fiercely jealous of Millie from the very moment of her arrival that autumn. She had done all the publishing that he had always wanted to do but never managed to accomplish. She was widely acknowledged and respected in Canadian sociology whereas he was never mentioned in any national listings of scholars in their field. I think he did everything he could to undermine her from the very start."

"Abdul, are you sure that you haven't allowed that creative imagination of yours to get the better of your reason?" Evelyn found herself breaking in again, in spite of her previous decision to listen silently.

"All this sounds like the worst kind of wild conjecture to me. No one is going to believe these dreadful charges against an internationally known and widely respected figure such as Harvey Garfinkle is these days. You may not be aware of it, Abdul, but he's come a long way from what and where he was when all those awful things happened at NPU. I just can't accept that there's an ounce of truth in what you've been telling me. I hate to say this, but I hope you haven't been talking about all this to the police. Harvey will have the best of grounds to sue you for libel. And I would have to agree with him. What in the world has got into you? You seem to have bought into a lot of self-serving hogwash from Gus."

"I fear there is much about Harvey Garfinkle that you will have difficulty believing. For example, when I was interviewing Ned Smith recently he told me something he said he had never revealed before, not to anyone. He said he happened to know that Harvey was a collector of extremely violent pornography and was already, in those relative innocent days in the early 1970's, the owner of a large collection of the stuff which he stored in his office and showed to Ned one evening. Ned said it made him ill, and he avoided late-night meetings with Harvey from that time on."

Abdul paused at this point, but when Evelyn found herself unable to respond to this bombshell, he resumed, somewhat hesitantly.

"Millie was your friend, Evelyn. Were you not, at any time, suspicious concerning Harvey's role in what was happening to her at NPU? Do you really not wish to hear more about it? For there *is* more."

"Go ahead, Abdul. But please, give me something other than merely wild guesses about what was going on in Harvey's mind."

"I think we need to understand what drove him to do what he did. There is more than his morbid fascination with violence and pornography. He was against Millie's being hired from the time it was first suggested. And he convinced the philosophy group that she was an ignorant upstart who had to resort to some sort of connection with the Dean in order to get hired. None of this is conjecture on my part. Ned told me everything about how the philosophers were subtly encouraged to belittle her, and it was only after her death that they began to experience shame about their part in the whole episode. They recognized, too late, that Harvey had been pulling their strings.

Dean Scott also told me a great deal about the circumstances of Millie's hiring. After reading her application and resume, he had insisted on her being offered the then-newly available position of Associate Professor in the Foundations Department. Because of Millie's qualifications, he went so far as to go over Harvey's head to the higher administration of NPU. As you know, that sort of thing is rarely done. So the order to hire Millie actually did come down from above. Harvey had previously made up his mind to angle for Werner von Schmidt, so he was enraged when informed he would have to take Millie on instead. He solved his problem by pretending to her that the official position would not be available until the following year. That enabled him to hire her on a temporary basis . . . merely as a Visiting Lecturer. She was such an honest person herself that it never occurred to her to check with the Dean about it."

"That much I knew already. I was worried when Millie told me she had forfeited good prospects in Miami for nothing more definite than a temporary 'visiting' position, when I was aware that the Associate Professorship was already available and waiting to be filled. But Millie was always naive about people's motives, and overly trusting. Okay, Abdul, let's get on with your story. What puzzles me is, if Millie wasn't going to be around much longer anyway, how could Harvey possibly benefit from seeing her dead?"

"I can only suppose that, when it became obvious that our notoriously stubborn Millie was suspicious about Sam's death, and that she was hot on the trail of evidence that he had left behind, Harvey must have decided that she had to be stopped. However, it was only after Millie's body was found that Gus began to get seriously worried. He remembered gossiping to Harvey about the diabetes, and then he started making other connections. But he was terrified of his Head by then, for he was becoming increasingly suspicious about the circumstances of Sam's death as well, and aghast at his possible role in that. And he was concerned about the security of his job. Nevertheless, as I mentioned earlier, soon after you left the university, Harvey did, in fact, get rid of Gus. He had encouraged him to get so deeply addicted to drugs by then that no one would have listened to him anyway. And Harvey probably assumed that Gus would not last long at his new posting."

"This is all so unbelievable! It certainly isn't the Harvey

I've known for well over three decades. If what you say is true it means that he was taking advantage of me as well. I guess he just never showed his true face to me, and by supporting my career in so many ways all this time, he made me unquestioningly grateful. How could I have been so gullible!"

"Harvey had a way of ensuring that we were all implicated in his nefarious undertakings in one way or another. You were not the only one who was fooled by him. Or used by him."

"Do the police think they have sufficient evidence to indict him? I still have a problem with the circumstantial nature of it all." Abdul suddenly appeared to find something to smile at in Evelyn's worried remark. "What on earth is funny about that?" she asked.

"I have just remembered a comment of Sam's when I once attacked some position he was taking for that very reason. He referred me to someone who had said, 'Each bit of circumstantial evidence is the merest thread, on its own, worth very little. But an accumulation of such bits, when woven in together, can form a rope with which to hang a man!'

In fact, the member of the Force's new 'murder squad' who called me this morning considers that they now have a fairly strong case. They are even beginning to revisit the supposedly accidental death of Mrs. Garfinkle. Apparently there was reason, at the time, to be curious about the condition of the car's brakes; but Harvey's position and reputation deterred them from the launch of any detailed investigation. It is possible that his wife had begun to get suspicious, and to pose a potential threat.

Be that as it may, however, I did manage to ensure that Gus signed a legally sworn affidavit before his death. Also, apparently another witness has been found in Vancouver who recalls seeing Harvey's car crossing and re-crossing the bridge several times that night. And it now appears that the evidence at the inquest did, in fact, suggest a blow on the head by a blunt instrument. At the time, unfortunately, it was interpreted simply as his having struck a part of the bridge as he fell. Or, alternatively, that his body had encountered something on entering the water.

However, in the case of Millie's murder, there is not much to go on. I understand that, also unfortunately, no one even bothered to look for fingerprints on the insulin syringe before it was destroyed. On the other hand, it did not require much persuading to convince the students who frequented that infamous hotel room, and subsequently accused Sam of sexual abuse, to reveal their entire story. And Gerald Davis and Tony Kohut have confirmed that they overheard Harvey speaking to Cynthia in a strangely menacing way that night at Banff. So it does look somewhat hopeful."

"Something you still haven't mentioned, however, is exactly what it was that caused the change in Sam during the Dean's hearing. I would think that might be of critical significance."

"It was. And information on it was a long time coming. Largely because I had failed to recognize an important item in Millie's things. There was a note in Sam's writing fastened to a large file of his class materials for three years back. A few words only. "Those three girls. Connection?" I had packed the files in a large box along with everything else retrieved from Millie's office, and the box traveled with my belongings all the way back to Africa and, later, to Britain. It was only after Gus arrived with his revelations that the two of us went through everything in it, with a fine-tooth comb, as it were. We discovered Sam had applied a yellow marker to three names only, from the hundreds on all the class lists. Those names were Sheila Radwinsky, Gloria Carleton, and Valerie Charles. Beside each name was a picture from the class year book. And beside all three pictures were the scribbled words: "went to the Head to challenge grade from me" . . . and the date of the formal complaint. (By the way he had also affixed a note mentioning that Cynthia had probably done the same, after he had told her not to return to his class.)

Gus confirmed that these three were among the young females whom he had taken to the hotel room to meet with Harvey on a somewhat regular basis and that, in each case, the original visit followed soon after the date which marked the interview concerning a complaint against Sam. Valerie, of course, had just been introduced to the procedure immediately prior to her signing up for the Dean's hearing. Obviously, it was the recognition, during the hearing, of this singular connection among the witnesses that had clarified the entire situation for Sam, and given him hope that he could launch a successful defense."

"You mean that Harvey promised them help with their grade-average problem in exchange for sexual services? How revolting! And then, when the opportunity arose, he was confident that they would be willing to cooperate in getting back at Sam. But that doesn't explain *Gus'* enthusiastic support of Sam's accusers."

"Gus admitted that he had allowed his long-held dislike of, and ideologically based prejudice against, Sam to blind him to everything else. Also, in the beginning, there were so many young women offering to give evidence against him that Gus couldn't imagine anything other than that the charges must be true. Especially where a notoriously conservative Mormon was concerned. But he later realized that what he had witnessed, and even actively encouraged, was the 'Salem witchcraft effect'. In fact, all of you in the Women's Cultural Revolution were probably affected by it."

At that moment Abdul's cell phone rang. He listened intently for a few moments before uttering a sigh and quickly making arrangements for meeting the caller in a half hour. Then he hung up and, after frowning at the floor for several minutes, turned to Evelyn.

"That was Anthea," he said. "Members of the Lower Mainland murder squad have informed her that they have just finished interviewing Harvey. They tracked him down at his cottage northeast of Montreal. That is the good news." Abdul paused, sighed once more, then continued wryly.

"The bad news is that, in the opinion of the police as of now, there does not appear to be a sufficiently strong case for them to arrest Harvey for murder. Apparently Meredith Walker has not been cooperative. She is insisting that there were many additional young female students who reported abusive behavior on the part of Sam Barnes, as soon as the news of the Valerie Charles incident got out. These were students who, she maintains, had no conceivable connection to Harvey Garfinkle. But, apparently, she cannot recall their names.

And there is the added complication of two separate police organizations having been involved in the various events at the time. The RCMP were (as they are today) responsible for the general policing of Richmond and the Squamish-Whistler area, while the Vancouver City Police Force was in charge of investigating the death of Sam. Communication between them was apparently not very satisfactory in those days, and the opportunity for loss of crucial evidence seems all-too-apparent. Of course we were always aware that, because accidental death was the obvious conclusion in each case, all of the possible sources of evidence were either destroyed at the time or simply overlooked. For example, the needle and insulin container left in Millie's office disappeared when the office was routinely cleaned the following day. Cynthia's car was never dusted for fingerprints and, of course, DNA forensic technology was not available at that time. Mary Barnes had her husband's body cremated immediately before the little memorial service in the faculty lounge, simply because Harvey suggested that Sam would have preferred it that way. The brakes on Mrs. Garfinkle's car were never really examined with care to see what had caused them to fail. The word and reputation of Dr. Harvey Garfinkle were all-powerful in those days. As is apparently the case today, only more so, in the academic world throughout Canada.

Furthermore, the police say the fact that there has been no history of mysterious female disappearances or deaths at his current university during his tenure there makes it more difficult for them to present Harvey as a serial killer so many years ago. Given all this, I have to admit you were correct in noting that our laboriously collected evidence was unlikely to be sufficiently compelling for the courts."

"Does that mean the police won't be interviewing me?"

"No. It seems they still intend to question you within the next few days in the hope that you can provide some fruitful leads. Then they will be returning to the Vancouver area and will attempt to trace all the additional former members of the women's organization who supposedly expressed a willingness to testify against Sam. However, Anthea says that the officer who contacted her a few minutes ago told her that, unless further concrete evidence is uncovered within the next week or so, they might be forced to close the case."

As Abdul paused again, Evelyn felt herself flinch

emotionally from the unwelcome sense of responsibility that these words aroused. A contradictory surge of disappointment and relief began seething within her at the thought that nothing she had to add could possibly contribute the definitive proof required at this point in the investigation. Her own testimony, as previously presented to Anthea, would not provide what the police were looking for. Then, like a bolt from the blue, two unwelcome memories flashed across her consciousness. As if it had happened only yesterday, she could almost hear her voice reassuring Harvey that Sam was being looked after by Millie, who made a point of picking him up every Thursday for dinner. And, although it had occurred a month or so later, that voice of naivety could be heard again, once more reassuring Harvey. This time it was about Millie being much more concerned about following certain leads having to do with Sam's suspicious death than for her own professional future. And then, another bolt struck; and a third memory surfaced. Suddenly, she was reliving that long-ago trip home from Banff. The two philosophers attending the conference with their little group had left by train for Eastern Canada, and she had found herself returning to the coast alone with Harvey. What suddenly came back to her was that she had spent much of the time during that lengthy drive complaining in great detail about her problems with their graduate student as a conference room-mate, even quoting the girl's agonized cry.

"I'm really frightened of him!" Cynthia had moaned. "But I've got to tell someone about what's going on. It's just too . . . too awful. I can't be part of it any more."

Evelyn felt herself recoil at the memory. Why hadn't she remembered those particular words before? And the fact that she had repeated them to Harvey? Was it because she had interrupted Cynthia at that precise point, telling her that she simply could not listen to any more of what she privately considered mere dramatizations; that she had to get some sleep or she wouldn't be able to present her paper in the morning?

Three memories. Three threads. Woven together, and intertwined with those already gathered, they might well provide a rope to hang a man! But *she* could not be the one to tie the knot! Not around any person's neck. And especially not the neck of Harvey Garfinkle! . . . Not the person who had been her mentor and supporter all these years! And certainly not in the public way that would be required of her. She would not . . . could not . . . allow herself to be placed in that position. There was simply no way that she could risk her hard-won reputation by revealing any of this to the police, at this late date—especially her own unwitting connivance. Because of the well-known close association between herself and Harvey in all the years since, her role in that hideous affair would inevitably be questioned—by the public if not the police—and her entire life's work could well be rendered meaningless. Then the comforting thought came to her that, if it were meant to be, she would surely have recalled these vital connections long before. Since she had not, it must mean they were intended to be forever relegated to her unconscious. With an almost physical effort, she forced the memories back.

Finally, Abdul must have registered her discomfort. He continued, as if to offer a measure of reassurance.

"The other item of bad news . . . but only for Anthea and me . . . is that we will not be allowed to publish our report until the authorities make the decision one way or another. If the case *does* go to trial, then we will have to wait until the verdict is in. But, regardless of what the police and courts accomplish, we will ensure that the evidence concerning what occurred at NPU so long ago is accurately and completely documented and that, sooner or later, it is widely distributed. Harvey Garfinkle may not wither in prison, but this story will travel with him for the rest of his life. Perhaps, for him, that will be the most appropriate punishment of all."

Then his expression turned grave. "I may not be living by the time our series is published, but Anthea assures me she will see that it gets a good deal of exposure in Canada as well as Britain."

The comment brought Evelyn back to the present with a jolt. She had been vaguely aware, since experiencing the shock of seeing him seated at the table as she entered the room, of Abdul's fragile physical state. But that he should be contemplating death at such an early date, and just when she had found him again? Surely he was exaggerating the brevity of his future prospects.

"Nonsense, Abdul!" she said firmly. "You'll be fine once you get back home and have a good rest. The time in the B.C.'s Lower Mainland must have been very grueling for you. How long are you and Anthea proposing to stay in Canada, by the way?" She was uncomfortably conscious of the fact that he might be hoping to remain with her, here in Toronto, at least until the case was decided one way or another. She thought it best to rid his mind of that possibility at once. There was simply no way that she could face caring for him during this, his final illness. And he was not even remotely justified in expecting it of her. After his treatment of her, she owed him nothing.

"Do not worry yourself, Evelyn." Abdul was looking at her with a hint of amusement in his eyes. "We are returning to London very soon. But I think you should be aware that, when you and I part in a few minutes now, it is likely to be our last goodbye. I have been thinking of what I might wish to say to you. Have you any final message for me?"

"Why no... Abdul, you... you mustn't talk that way. The drugs they have today work very well I hear. Even if you *have* developed a full-blown case of AIDS by now, you may be in remission for years. I simply refuse to say goodbye at this time. Now that we've encountered one another again, there'll be lots more visits. You'll see. I'll likely travel to England fairly often now that I'm retired."

All the while she was speaking Abdul sat looking at her, steadily and with a quizzical expression. Then he shook his head, with a bleak, albeit rather fond, smile. Finally, he stood up. Once more he held both her hands for a moment, then prepared to leave. A feeling of panic swept through her and she found herself clutching at his sleeve, striving for something meaningful to say in farewell.

"Please don't worry about death, Abdul. I'm sure it won't happen for a long time yet. You'd be wise to put it completely out of your mind! I assure you that I intend to."

"Evelyn," he had turned to her once more. "I can face the idea of dying. I view it as the Buddha did, merely a 'going out' of the knowing, feeling 'self,' as happens with the extinguished flame of a candle. And, like the crumbling, melting remains of the candle's wax, the organism's cells are returned to that nature from whence they came. What is there to fear in that?"

"Are you actually telling me that you don't expect anything of yourself to survive on some other, spiritual, plane of existence? And, if that's what you really do believe, doesn't the finality of death worry you at all?"

"The *fact* of 'going out' is no cause for worry. Except to

the personal ego. But I admit that the *process* of one's death can be a source of fear. I now realize that there are many kinds of death. Some of these are acceptable to me. Some are not. However, I think I am as prepared as one can possibly be for what lies ahead."

"What in the world do you mean, Abdul? I simply can't understand how your mind works!"

"Evelyn, there are many kinds of death. There is the death of a successful and gratifying career which, to Millie and Sam, must have been almost as bad as the loss of life itself. There is the reluctant, living death of unfortunates such as Gus, who are filled with horror and denial at the thought of its relentless approach, and have made no plans to foil its final, devastating clutches. There is the lingering death of the human spirit that can devour all the days of the lives of those who allow the fear of failure to prevent the difficult choices required for a gratifying and productive lifetime. And there is the death with dignity that is arranged for when one's major task on earth has been completed, and meaningful life without unbearable suffering is no longer possible. Think of that when next you hear of me. There are many kinds of death!"

With those words, he turned away once more. With a shock Evelyn registered the unsteadiness of his movements. As he edged along the now-empty space toward the restaurant exit one leg dragged a little, and a foot appeared to be either sore or slightly crippled. Evelyn felt that she should be going to his aid, but she found herself remaining in place, as if glued to her chair. Then, as he neared the exit, she glimpsed a taxi at the curb, and Anthea approaching from the sidewalk. A strong, young arm went around Abdul's shoulders, and the two moved, in a comradely fashion, toward the open door of the waiting vehicle.

Evelyn sat for a long time after the taxi drove away—frozen into immobility as she stared at the hands Abdul had pressed in farewell. Lunchtime was long past, the surrounding tables all deserted. *How foolish of me*, she thought finally. *To imagine that I am hearing now, in the rustle and laughter from the workers in the kitchen, that far-off, plaintive cry of geese in flight.*

BVG